Fall
from
Trace

Fall from Trace

Rebecca Connolly

Phase Publishing, LLC
Seattle

Phase Publishing, LLC first paperback edition
February 2020

ISBN 978-1-952103-00-1
Library of Congress Control Number 2020900531
Cataloging-in-Publication Data on file.

Acknowledgements

To Han Solo, who is the first scoundrel I've ever loved, the perfect combination of charm and sarcasm, and the inspiration for so many of my action heroes. There's a little bit of you in every man I write, because you are, at heart, a romantic. I won't tell.

And for my uncle Rick, who has been telling me for years that there needs to be more action and explosions in my books. This action adventure (romance) story is for you.

Want to hear about future releases and upcoming events for Rebecca Connolly?

Sign up for the monthly Wit and Whimsy at:

www.rebeccaconnolly.com

Chapter One
Wales, 1825

"*Torchon! Torchon!*"

A swift kick to already tender ribs made Alexander Sommerville wake with a grunt, though the sound was weak and pitiful.

"What?" he coughed, his eyes scrunching up even though the evening light was fading.

"Don't you talk back!" Another kick came at him, and he tensed, moaning at the impact.

It was incomprehensible, but the one kicking him was not even one of his captors. Most of his beaters weren't, but beating Alex had become something of a game to the crew of the *Amelie Claire*, and the officers approved heartily. Had he been his old self, Alex would have taken on the lot of them and done enough damage to be considered the victor.

Fists had always been his specialty.

But he was not his old self. He was not even a shell of his old self. Whatever was less than that might be able to describe him as he existed now.

He couldn't even muster indignity at being kicked and ordered about by a fellow prisoner at this moment. Trussed as he always was when they were in port, he only let his head fall back and tried to find the emptiness in his mind that made his life bearable.

"*Torchon,*" the one he only knew as Souris said again, and it struck Alex as odd that a Londoner was addressing him in French, particularly when it was obvious the man knew nothing of the language.

But that was what he had been called almost from the very first day he'd been captured, and it was all he answered to.

Alex rolled his head towards the voice, though it pained him too greatly to open his eyes.

"You plan on sleeping all the way to Liverpool?" Souris asked with no small amount of derision. "Your first time off the boat since I've known you, and you're too pathetic to enjoy it. Breathe in the Welsh air, *Torchon*. You'll be in a Spanish frigate afore too long."

Off the... what?

A sudden jolt bounced them both, causing grunts of pain as they landed once more, and Alex felt his breath begin to race as his weakened senses began to tune into his surroundings.

He was in a wagon, not in his cramped hold. His wrists and legs were bound with rope, not chains, and they were not bound together, only to leads. The air about him was fresh and brisk, not the stale and salty stench of mildew and aged wood.

Welsh, had he said?

That meant they'd landed at Fishguard after his last beating, which had been more substantial than any in recent memory, and he'd been unconscious for quite some time if he'd been unloaded from the ship and dumped in this wagon. Fishguard was their only Welsh port, unless they'd made some unexpected alterations to their route. He'd seen glimpses of it through the small bullet hole in the berth in his tiny corner, and now, if Souris was correct, he was in it.

Physically in it.

Off the boat, and in Wales.

No wonder he felt queasy and lightheaded, though he'd chalked that up to too many blows to the head during the recent bout. His feet hadn't touched land in so long he'd forgotten what it felt like.

The rumbling of the wagon wheels was music to his ears, and the jostling of the wagon itself soothed him in a way he hadn't known in years.

Four and a half, to be precise.

One thousand, six hundred and fifty-eight days.

He'd counted every single one.

When they were in port, he'd spent every night and day in the hold of the ship. When they were at sea, he'd spent daylight hours either on deck or down below. They'd forced him into back breaking and menial labor. He'd had his arms strung up on a hook while he was lashed, stabbed, burned, or pummeled with whatever the officers had on hand. It was all he had known.

He'd been starved when it suited them, but his wounds had been meticulously tended, with special attention to any signs of fever or illness. It wouldn't do for their prized captive to die in their care, so they prevented that extreme with all due consideration.

He would be of no use to them if he were dead.

Everyone else in the world thought he already was.

At least, he assumed that was the case. His lack of rescue had led him to that assumption. Given that he had fully intended to sacrifice himself that night on the London docks, it was an easy conjecture to make.

He'd wished for death. Expected death. Prayed for death even, although he was not nearly as religious as he had once been.

But death had been as elusive as a woman for him and twice as fickle. Every time he had been on the brink of that blessed relief, his tormentors brought him back to life. It was more brutal than his first year onboard, where every night, he would be woken and tortured just as he had reached the most fulfilling part of sleep.

He hadn't slept with any respite after that and could only vaguely recall the sensation of feeling rested.

Or whole.

Why they hadn't killed him after this long was still a mystery. He hadn't given them any useful information, and by now, he was beyond the point of being current and relevant in what he could have told them.

But question him they did, and torture him they did, and imprison him they did.

All to no avail.

Which earned him more beatings and torture and questions.

It all blurred together in his mind, but if nothing else, he could say with certainty that he was no coward, and he was no traitor.

He'd come damned close, though.

But his brothers in the London League would have nothing to fear from his capture, nor would any currently active operatives in any of the branches of government.

Past ones, on the other hand…

It had given him a fiendish delight to occasionally spout details of old missions from decades gone by, which were already known about in certain diplomatic circles, and whose operatives and instigators were all retired, reassigned, or dead.

Studying old missions and reports in his training and recruitment days had proven more useful than he'd thought it would.

That life was far, far behind him now. His instincts were dull and rusted from disuse, even if his training remained. He barely recalled the one known as Trace, though his captors had called him that and *Le Trace* frequently enough to remind him. He was strong from the labor he'd had to endure, but not in the ways he'd once been. He'd not lost his recollection of languages, though speaking them himself was a thing of the past.

He'd spent ages memorizing details he had learned in listening, as the smugglers interacted with various others of many nationalities. Despite most of the crew of the *Amelie Claire* being English, their officers were French, Spanish, and Dutch, in various shades. None of them claimed a particular nationality, and their loyalties lay with the greatest profit.

Despite somehow being a vital prisoner to Captain Battier and the rest, they had never quite managed to mind their tongues around him. Of course, there had been no reason to, in their eyes. He would never leave their ship.

Until now.

"Souris," Alex moaned, rolling a bit to face him, cracking his eyes open just a little. "Why Liverpool?"

Souris snorted loudly, his beard collecting the spit from doing so. "Battier tired of your stench. 'E says you're to be questioned by sommat else and then transferred, as such, to a ship for Australia."

Alex nodded, the worn wood scratching his head. "And you?"

"Dock work, I fink. Work off me debt to Battier at long last."

Alex stared at him for a long moment. "Remind me what your crime was."

"Mutiny, *Torchon*." He grinned, showing all of seven full teeth and two broken ones. "No' of Battier, but of Acosta and Janssen

4

when we're down Bay o' Biscay."

Ah, yes, now he recollected. Three days in the hold without reprieve, and his muscles had cramped beyond belief without food or fresh water to alleviate them.

Souris continued to talk, but Alex tuned him out, just as he had planned on doing.

His mind churned on various details, a strategy beginning to form.

Two drivers, probably minimally armed, carting two prisoners to a distant port. Souris was fairly worthless as a prisoner, but Alex was quite valuable. Force could be used on them, but nothing extreme. He couldn't hear anything resembling hustle and bustle, so they had to be out of the city, probably by some miles. It would be some time before they crossed into England, depending on which road they took to Liverpool, but there wouldn't be much by way of villages or population along the way.

As far as he had been able to decipher over the years, no one knew his real identity. They knew he was Trace, of course, but his real name, his real title, his real life...

That was still secret.

Which meant no one would expect him to speak Welsh, the language of his mother, and no one would know for certain which way he would go.

He wasn't sure how far he'd be able to get, let alone how fast he'd get there ,considering his depleted strength, limited energy, and painfully fresh wounds, but if he could survive getting away, he knew his course.

England. And once in England, Cheshire. And once in Cheshire, Moulton. And then...

A sudden tremor of longing coursed through his battered frame, and he felt himself grow surprisingly emotional at the thought.

Poppy.

The only reason he had for escape, the only thing he could possibly live for now.

He didn't even know if she were in Moulton anymore, let alone Cheshire, but it was the only place he could look.

Provided he could make it there.

"How long have we been in the cart?" Alex coughed, forcing himself to sound weaker than he was, now that excitement began to thrum through him.

Souris gave him a wry look. "Why? You have somewhere to be?"

Alex just continued to stare at him, hoping it still had the same effect it once had.

While Souris didn't look in any way perturbed by the glare, he sighed and spat over the side of the cart. "Three hours, a' least. Maybe four. You were out for a long time."

Technically, Alex had been in and out of consciousness, enough to register the rumble of voices and that his body was being moved, but specifics had been completely lost. And once he'd realized he was not about to be beaten again, he'd just let himself sleep.

He closed his eyes and sighed heavily as he ran through the information.

Three to four hours in a light cart with two horses pulling. They weren't galloping, but the pace was fairly steady and quick. There was no way for him to know exactly how many miles they had gone, nor where exactly they were, but he could make a rough estimate, and he calculated the range of answers quickly.

Apparently, he still remembered that from his training as well.

They'd have to change horses soon, and the drivers would change. Night was coming on quickly, and it would be almost impossible to see him on the dark road with only their small lantern. If they avoided largely populated areas, as he suspected they would, given they had two injured and indentured men in their cart, the new horses would come from less than reputable places with less than ideal lighting.

But he couldn't do anything while they were stopped.

So for now, he would just lay here and wait, moan for effect on occasion, and bide his time.

"Did you fall asleep again, *Torchon?*" Souris asked, scoffing to himself. "Pathetic."

Alex fought the urge to smile, which was a feeling he'd almost forgotten. Pathetic, was it? Souris would see just how pathetic he was in a very short time. As soon as it was dark enough. As soon as they were far enough away. As soon as the drivers and horses hit their stride.

The wagon suddenly jostled again, and they slowed to a stop, one of the drivers whistling loudly.

Alex lay there in silence, eyes closed, envisioning the movements around him.

The driver cocked a gun, which was no doubt held on himself and Souris should they have opted to try something, now that they had stopped. The other hopped down and began the process of unhitching the horses.

Two, perhaps three others from the inn's mews came to help, bringing fresh horses for their cart, and from the smell of things, they also had brought food, bread at least, and it remained to be seen if the drivers would let the prisoners partake in whatever sustenance had been provided.

Alex kept his eyes closed for the whole exchange, keeping his countenance blank and appearing for all intents and purposes to be a very wounded man resting.

Which, after all, he was.

His head pounded with too much thinking already, and his right shoulder throbbed in a numb, tingling sort of way. He felt certain he had dislocated it yesterday.

Or had it been this morning?

Time had had little meaning to him in recent days, and it was hard to keep track of when various injuries were sustained.

The cuts on his back were two days old, that much he knew.

He could remember those.

Couldn't feel them as his back tended to go numb for some time after those sessions, but he remembered them.

He heard the rattle of harnesses and the snuffle of horses as they were led away. Then, he heard the drivers taking their places on the rickety seat again. That was followed by the wagon jolting forward, sending Alex skidding just briefly on the flat wagon bed, scraping his not-so-numb back against the grain.

He winced and groaned audibly, his breath catching at the pain. He exhaled in short bursts through his nose, praying for the numbness to return.

"You're still bleeding, *Torchon*," Souris reminded him

unnecessarily. "I can see it on your tunic."

Alex grunted once in response, fully aware that he was bleeding from his back, and from his feet, and probably from his chin, as well.

Impossibly, he still bled from his injuries. Unfortunate how that didn't stop with frequent beatings.

"Here," one of the drivers grunted from the seat.

Something soft hit Alex's left arm, but he kept his eyes shut.

"What, no cheese?" Souris asked, picking up the item and tearing it, the sound registering to Alex as a loaf of bread.

A thudding noise indicated Souris being thumped in the head, probably with a rifle butt.

Alex would have loved to see that.

Souris grumbled and set half of the bread on Alex's chest. "Here, *Torchon*. First warm bread you've had in years, right?"

It was, yes, but Alex wasn't going to eat it at the moment.

"Apple, *Torchon*." An apple was suddenly placed in Alex's limp hand at his side.

Alex dipped his chin in a nod but still lay there.

Just a bit further... Just a bit...

He cracked one eye open, and could not see the lights of the inn, nor any other but the lantern on the cart. The horses had taken on a steady pace, and the night sky was growing darker and darker by the minute.

There was no way to know for certain what the ground would be like without taking a better look, but he couldn't spare the energy to prop himself up. It would be difficult enough to manage making his way from somewhere in Wales all the way to Moulton, and he honestly might die trying to do that.

Dying while escaping to get to the woman he loved was a right sight better than dying as a captive in the hold of a ship.

Come on, Trace. Center your mind, breathe your focus, let yourself go...

The voice of his mentor in his mind shook him, and he wondered what had brought it on. He'd gone at least two full years without hearing it outside of his dreams, and this moment, though certainly the first adventure since those days, was completely unrelated.

He was no longer the agent called Trace. This was not a task for

Trace. This was the last act of resistance from *Torchon*, and the rebirth of Alex Sommerville.

The only traces he cared about anymore were his own.

Alex counted twenty of his slow, steady breaths, close to dozing off except for the sudden hum he felt coursing through his limbs. Though he was weak, though his mind was cloudy, though he could not and did not recognize himself, he felt alive for the first time in four and a half years.

Action. Danger. Freedom.

Freedom…

Poppy's face swam into focus in his mind, smiling and young as she had been when he'd left her, her copper hair dancing almost wildly on the breeze as she grinned up at him, her fair eyes filled with the laughter she'd always lived with.

Slowly, he exhaled, waiting for the vision of her to dissipate, somehow unable to move while she was there, even in memory.

Moments later, she was gone.

But not for long.

Alex bent his knees with a groan, placing both feet flat against the worn wood beneath him, gripping the side of the cart with one hand.

"Oh, don't be sick, *Torchon*," Souris groaned with disgust.

Alex grabbed the half loaf on his chest and shoved it into his tunic as he clutched his stomach, moaning again, pressing himself up and curving towards the edge of the cart.

Then he jumped over the edge, rolling as he hit the ground, ignoring the pain that slammed into his good shoulder as he protected the bad.

Souris and the drivers shouted, but their words were lost on Alex as the cart continued to move and as he got his bearings on the damp grass around him. He rolled to his hands and knees and pushed himself up to a crouch. Moving as fast as he could, he kept his tread as light and easy as possible. His lungs began to burn already, his body not used to moving quickly without pain as its motivation, and his legs felt sluggish with the pace. But he could push all that aside, could endure anything that lay ahead, now that he had such a glorious prospect at the end.

He'd always said he would die for Poppy, that he would go to the ends of the earth to be with her, and now he'd actually be proving it.

A shot cracked the night air, and Alex ran for it, giving up all pretense of sneaking or crouching. For now, he only needed to be away. He needed distance, direction, and to somehow form a plan.

The area was sparse in population, filled with fields of crops not yet harvested, but the moon was not raised yet, so there was no light for his pursuers to see by. He had the advantage now, and he planned to use every moment of it.

His injured shoulder seemed to scream at the indignity of being expected to move at this rate, but there wasn't anything he could do about that now. No time to set it, no doctor or ally to help, and nothing to immobilize it with. He couldn't ask for help this far from anywhere, and the sight of him in a dirty, tattered tunic and shredded trousers would hardly gain him any respectable allies.

To speak plainly, he was an impoverished prospect traversing at least a hundred miles without proper food, water, or transport. In addition to his lack of supplies, he had multiple injuries, some of which were severe, and, at this moment, he had very little idea about where he was.

Except he was in Wales.

And he was free.

He felt his lips curve into a smile as he ran, exhaling with relief. He allowed himself to breathe in the Welsh air just as Souris had recommended.

He couldn't hear pursuit, nor could he hear the wagon, so he let himself slow and crouch once more. Quickly, but silently, he moved towards a barn in the distance. There were no lights within and nothing to indicate anyone inhabited it, and while he was exhausted, he could not risk taking refuge within the building to rest.

Short of losing consciousness from exhaustion or exertion, there would be no resting until he had reached Moulton. Even then, he would press on as best he could.

The barn was still and quiet, and his eyes adjusted to the darkness easily, now that the surrounding light matched it. Empty, it seemed, but there was an old coat and hat on a peg. He grabbed them and donned both. He was not able to button the coat, but it would suffice. It occurred to him that had this been years ago, he would not have even been able to get the fabric to span his shoulders and arms.

He was much smaller now, and it fit nearly perfectly in both areas.

A bag of oats sat on a table, and he grabbed a fistful, shoving it into his mouth and crunching down on the grainy food quickly. He cast his eyes around to search for shoes to replace his well-worn boots, but there were none. Still, he had endured worse, and his boots would have to suffice for now.

He looked around quickly once more, desperate for anything to make his journey easier.

The snort of a horse brought him up, and he peered into the far corner of the barn where a dark horse stood obediently within its stall.

Alex exhaled silently, grinning now. "Well, now… Shall we go for a midnight ride?"

The horse snorted again, shaking its head.

"I'll take that as a yes," Alex grunted, striding forward. "Good lad."

Moments later, they tore out of the barn at a mad gallop, and Alex clutched at the mane with aching fingers. He'd ridden without a saddle dozens of times in his youth, but that had been a lifetime ago, and he'd nearly forgotten the sensation. Still, the animal was powerful, magnificent, and clearly well trained, one that hardly needed direction from him.

It was a blessed relief, though the increase in speed and the sensation of the wind across his skin and hair was disorienting. Alex leaned down as close to the horse as he could, his body weary already with still much more to go.

Preserve your strength. Stay in your head. Think beyond the pain.

Why was he hearing Eagle's voice now? After years of torture, why now?

He shook his head quickly, desperate to be rid of that past, and he fixed his mind on Poppy and home.

If anything remained of it.

"Poppy," he whispered to the night, "I'm coming. After all this time, I'm coming."

Chapter Two

"What do you mean, you only got four and a quarter? It's worth at least five!"

"Madam, they would not take more, and I was fortunate to get that."

"Stanton, that's absurd!"

"I know, madam, but it is what it is, and we will make the best of it."

Poppy Edgewood groaned and put a hand to her brow. "That is what I say, Stanton, and you're supposed to tell me 'We make what we sow, and we've sown a bunch of...' "

"Don't say it, madam," Stanton interrupted with a barking laugh. "It will sound so much fouler from your mouth."

She sighed heavily and dropped herself into the worn and rickety chair by the table.

"As if anything is beyond me now, Stanton." She ran her hands over her bound but unruly hair, sighing. "It will be all right. We're not destitute, not even close."

"True, madam." Stanton pulled another chair out from the table and sat, though he was almost too big for it. "It's actually a good harvest, so the funds will suffice, once we've completed it."

Poppy nodded to herself, adjusting the rough woolen shawl around her shoulders. "We've saved enough since Mrs. Follows went to stay with her sister, so there is enough to see to winter provisions even without the harvest."

Stanton moaned pitifully and folded his arms across his broad chest. "Even so, madam, I miss Mrs. Follows and her cooking very much."

Poppy grabbed a nearby rag and tossed it at her farmhand and manservant, frowning playfully. "I do just fine for us, do I not?"

He caught the rag easily and grunted. "If 'just fine' means we survive, then yes."

Unfortunately, he was right, and there was no denying it. For all the accomplishment she had once possessed and been trained up in, not one of them had ever been the proper construction of a stew, or roasting a chicken, or even making a hearty porridge. She could once play a waltz, a jig, and a concerto on the pianoforte all in a row without tiring, but one must own an instrument to be able to do such things, and she did not.

She owned a small cottage with two bedrooms, a large kitchen, and one very cramped parlor, as well as the farm on which it was situated, though she owed taxes and fees to Lord Cartwright, the landowner and her patron. But it was a small enough tax and fee that it was hardly felt, and he let her have complete independence.

She'd only met him a few times, as he was almost never in Cheshire and at Branbury Park, so she had no worries of anybody taking her farm away, especially since his agent, Mr. Howard, tended to linger when he came to collect the money every quarter.

She'd be lying if she said she wasn't tempted a time or two to encourage him, but she couldn't.

She just couldn't.

Her life would have been so much easier if she did, if she let him pay call properly, treat her as more than a tenant of his master. Then, she might not be counting every ounce of wheat they harvest or holding her breath for a new litter of piglets.

But her life was not her own, not anymore.

It was Alex's.

Her heart clenched even at the thought of his name, as it always did, but she was quite used to that pain.

Alexander Sommerville was her one great love, the reason for her existence, and the surest reason for her circumstances now. Or his death, rather, had been the reason.

Her mourning of his death, and refusal to truly accept it, had only added to the situation. Rumors, suspicion, and gossip had circulated among all her former friends about her reasoning for going into complete mourning, for remaining close to Moulton, of refusing to give up hope that someday, despite her mourning, Alex would come back. Then those rumors and gossip had spread into her family, and the questions began.

Had they been married in secret? Was Poppy going to have his child? Had there been promises given that could not be taken back? On and on the questions had gone, until she had been cut off without a penny and they'd removed to Derbyshire.

But Poppy was still here.

Poppy couldn't leave.

Because impossibly, unbearably, she still had hope.

"I know that look," Stanton sighed as he pushed to his feet. "And I'll leave you to your thoughts of him."

Poppy looked at her servant, her friend, who had been by her side at almost every moment since she'd taken up the farm and changed her life. He'd been resolutely silent about his life before he'd come into her service, and he held no judgement of her choice in life now. He had been like an uncle to her, with all the cynicism and humor she needed to keep her from gloom and all the loyalty she would have hoped for in family.

Had her family been loyal to her.

But that mattered little now.

"Don't go," Poppy said with a laugh. "I was just thinking of my life as it once was and as it should have been."

Stanton put his hands on his hips and glowered. "Why? What good does that do?"

Poppy clasped her hands before her and smiled ruefully. "Not very much, as it turns out. But thoughts do wander."

"Mine don't."

She scowled at him. "No, of course they don't. Your thoughts are always precisely where they are supposed to be, aren't they?"

"Usually." Stanton shrugged and smiled back just a little. Then, he sobered and snapped his fingers. "I nearly forgot with all we've been getting on with today. There's a letter for you. I put it on your desk."

Poppy frowned a little. "From whom?"

"I didn't check," he said simply, shoving his hands into his trouser pockets.

That earned him a look as she rose to fetch it. "You've been with me for nearly five years, Stanton, and you can't tell who sends me letters? It's not as though it's a great number."

"Perhaps not, madam," he returned bluntly. "But quite frankly, I don't care."

Poppy laughed at that and picked up the letter on her desk, her smile fading as she saw the handwriting. "It's from Violet."

"Your sister?" Stanton hissed as if in pain. "Could be anything."

"I know."

Poppy stared at the letter as she reentered the kitchen. Violet was the only member of her family who kept in touch with any sort of regularity, and the only one who was sincere about it. The others wrote when they had news to share, and never said anything beyond the particular news. Only last month she'd had a letter from Rosemary about her new son, and the entirety of the letter was this one sentence: *I had a son last week, and we've named him John.*

Violet was different. She was six years younger than Poppy, which was just enough space for them to be friends as well as sisters and to bestow honesty without criticism. She kept Poppy informed of almost everything she would ever wish to know about the family, and about her own life.

Each letter was a bittersweet experience for her, and she was convinced this one would be no different.

But how bitter would it be? And how sweet?

"It helps to open the letter," Stanton prodded.

Poppy rolled her eyes and made a face, sitting down in her chair once more. "Thank you, Stanton."

"Always, madam." He bowed a little, which was always an amusing sight, and left the house with a cheery, "I'll just get the horses settled, and then I'll be back with more wood."

Poppy smiled after him, grateful yet again that she had him in her life. He was the only one of the farmhands that lived on site, and the only one who also acted as a servant, though it seemed a poor description of what he actually did.

He was the face of the farm, as it were, though everyone knew that Poppy was the one at the helm. Stanton worked as much and as hard as two men, if not three, and scarcely complained about any of it. He was respectful and trustworthy, and far too intelligent a man to be reduced to laborer, but he didn't seem to think it in any way beneath him.

Truly, she would never have come this far without him.

She looked down at the letter in her hand, sighing to herself. "All right, Violet. What am I missing now?"

She broke the seal and scanned the lines, smiling at Violet's penmanship, which was rather reflective of her personality; light, untidy, and wandering. For an inexplicable reason, just the sight of it brought tears to Poppy's eyes.

Blinking them quickly away, she focused on the content, rather than the sentiment.

" 'Mama is recovering well from her fall, according to the doctor'…" she read aloud, frowning. "What fall? Violet, what fall? When did Mama fall?"

But there was no indication of the actual injury, and Poppy growled in frustration, returning back to the lines.

" 'We anticipate her being in bed another week at least…' Bed? She's bedridden? Violet!" Poppy screeched. " 'And we anticipate that soon she will have energy enough to start complaining, thus returning to normal.' "

She put the letter down, crumpling the paper slightly in her hand.

She hadn't been on good terms with her mother for years, but the image of her vibrant and effusive mother lying in a bed and unable to complain about being in that bed was a haunting one. Whatever injury her mother had suffered had been significant, and the fact that Violet had neglected to inform her of it was infuriating.

But also understandable.

Poppy wasn't there. She wasn't part of their lives, and as such, was difficult to remember. She wouldn't know how her mother was coping from day to day or hear about the little progress that was being made. She wouldn't know how her father spent his days now that his wife wasn't directing him in all things. She wouldn't know how quiet the house would be with her mother bedridden and weak.

She'd miss all of that, just as she missed everything else.

16

Eight christenings, two weddings, three near-fatal events, her brother's ordination, and the loss of the family dog, and still she hurt being away. She hurt over being left out and forgotten. It didn't even matter anymore that they had left her and not the other way around, she would gladly spend an afternoon with any one of them, if only to be reminded of all the things that annoyed her.

Violet went on to describe her suitors, all five of them, and spent the rest of the letter describing each in great detail and weighing the merits of each one.

Poppy surprised herself by reading each and every word, grateful her sister was so long winded and descriptive at times. She would have loved nothing more than to witness Violet enduring courtship and suitors, managing her way through a London Season, and finding men who just might suit her tastes.

They could have spent evenings talking late into the night in each other's rooms, giggling like children. They could have discussed Rosemary's boring, perfect life in the sort of confidence that only sisters create. They could have played duets and sung badly, practiced dancing in the drawing room, borrowed each other's gowns for balls and parties…

She had four nieces and five nephews now, and she'd only met the first. She'd never seen the rest, never held them, never played with them until their giggles filled the air. She'd never met two of her sisters-in-law and had no idea what they thought of her.

Or what they'd been told.

Most days Poppy was too busy to consider any of this, and she was grateful for those days. They kept her from worrying, from thinking, and most especially, from remembering. She never thought about that day her parents had told her to give up Alex or be cut off, or the day the family had left her to close up Whitesdown and then find a place for herself.

She couldn't think about any of it.

She couldn't bear to think about the last day she had seen Alex, how handsome he had been and how reluctant to leave her he'd been. His kisses had had a hard, passionate edge to them that day, something that almost frightened her for its meaning. He'd promised to ask her a most particular question upon his return, and he hoped she would answer favorably.

And then the day that word had been delivered to her of Alex's death...

Poppy pushed up out of her chair quickly, moving to gather the dishes from supper and beginning to clean them. She needed her hands to be occupied, a task to fulfill, or it would all come rushing back to her. She scrubbed the plates with more determination than they needed, wishing she could scrub out the sight in her mind's eye.

She could replay every moment of that terrible day as though she were watching a play on a stage, a witness to her own grief and horror. She could see the tears slowly roll down her cheeks, the distant look that had stayed with her for days, the slow and painful way she'd moved. There'd been no funeral, no body, and no grave she could visit. Lost at sea, they'd said, and buried there.

How convenient.

His uncle, Lord Parkerton, had died just the year before, and he had no other family that she knew of. There was no one to mourn him but her. And oh, how she mourned him! She could still feel the burn of shame in her cheeks when she'd donned black and her friends had whispered about it.

Her friends were all married now, and none of them had spoken with Poppy since her family had left. In fact, just the other day, two of them had come out of the milliner's shop when Poppy had been passing by, and they had both turned their backs and pretended not to see. It was not the first time one or more of her former friends had done something like that.

None of Poppy's neighbors shunned her or minded her addresses. They tended to welcome her with open arms, and often with a friendly basket. Some knew her story and situation, and some had heard the gossip, but not a one of them cared.

For all the airs of the upper class, they had none of the warmth of their inferiors in station.

Poppy was glad to have traded one for the other in that regard.

Yet neighbors did not equate to friendship, and they each worked as hard and struggled as much as she, so there was no real time for outings or teatime conversations. They did not meet often, nor regularly, but they could be called upon in cases of emergency and had done for each other.

Poppy had yet to experience such generosity and selflessness herself, but she had been part of it on behalf of others.

It was a fine way of living, to be sure, and quite rewarding.

But loneliness is a creeping creature, and its pangs were deep and ravaging. In the evenings, when work was completed and she had so much to tell, there was no one to listen. When she missed her sister or her brothers, her parents, or her life, there was no one to commiserate with. When she cried in the night because Alex was gone and no one cared but her, there was no relief. When she felt more alone than anyone ought to feel, there was no one to take away the darkness.

No one to share her burdens with.

The only person she had in her life with any sort of regularity was Stanton, and he would not take kindly at all to her sharing such personal and emotional thoughts with him. It would have made him uncomfortable and gruff, and he probably would have told her to focus on her work and the farm and forget everything else. He had once told her emotions were a nuisance, after all, and that the past was only good for lessons.

Not for visiting and staying for a time.

Poppy was only too prone to spend an extended period of time in her past these days, though she knew it wouldn't do her any good.

The trouble was that it was too easy.

She scrubbed at the pot harder, her brow furrowing with the effort, and when she stopped, she looked at her hands. Once these hands had been delicate and soft, protected by gloves more often than not, fair and without blemish but for the occasional pricking of an embroidery needle. Her nails had been clean and manicured, the perfect embodiment of a fine lady. Every now and again, there might be a scratch on the skin from getting into mischief with Alex by climbing a tree or racing across their properties, but her hands had been fairly perfect.

Now, they were rough and worn, weathered by hard work and aggressive labor. She had callouses on her palm, on every fingertip, and along the edges of each finger. Her knuckles were often inflamed, and her skin cracked and peeled regularly. Lines and scars and dry patches dotted every surface of her hands, and her nails were almost brutally short, uneven, and usually had something under them, be it dirt or food or feed for the animals.

These hands were not those of a young lady.

Then again, Poppy could hardly be considered young anymore. Twenty-seven was not particularly old, but in those twenty-seven years, she had lived a lifetime, and she was decades older than anyone of her age. Her life did not even remotely resemble what she had thought out for herself, what she had planned, or anything like it once had.

She closed her eyes and set the pot aside, knowing it was far cleaner now than it had ever been with her excessive scrubbing.

This was what her life amounted to now. Scrubbing the pots and plates from her own meals, feeding the chickens and pigs, currying the horses, farming with whatever help she could afford to pay, even grinding her own flour to make her own bread, at times.

Oh, how far she had fallen.

Lonely and cast out, working for every morsel of bread, sweating her days away in the sun, and mourning a man who had never promised her anything.

Poppy's hands curled into fists and hot tears filled her eyes. It was wrong to resent a dead man, she knew, but resent him she did. If he hadn't have died, if that was what had truly happened, she would not be in this situation. He could have just broken off their impending engagement, and she would have been with her family now. She should have been wiser, not giving her heart so freely without the official connection between them.

Never mind that they had been in love since she was fourteen and he sixteen. Never mind that they had been planning to marry for years. Never mind that she was so utterly and completely his that she hadn't been whole in almost five years.

She should have been wiser.

And it was his fault she was so destitute, despairing, and dismal.

It was his fault she had grown so attached.

It was his fault she still felt the ache within her at the thought of him.

It was his fault that when she looked out of her kitchen window and could see the shadows of Parkerton Lodge in the distance, she still looked for a light in any window.

As she did now.

But there were no lights within, and no lights without, and the crumbling estate looked as foreboding and desolate as it had the day the servants had departed it.

Poppy exhaled slowly, wiping her hands on dry toweling. She couldn't do this anymore. Couldn't watch for him, wait for him, ache for him. He wasn't coming back, and this was the life she had chosen for herself. This was her future, and looking back would not make it any brighter.

She was done.

She had to be.

A knock on her door brought her head around, and she waited for Stanton to enter. When he didn't, and the knock came again, more firmly, she rolled her eyes as she moved to the door.

"Honestly, Stanton," she moaned loudly. "It's not so cold that you had to fill your arms to the brim with wood."

She reached for the door handle and pulled the door open, fixing her expression into one of mocking amusement.

The man who stood there stared at her with his dark, sunken eyes, leaning both forearms against the doorframe, his chest heaving wildly, and her amusement faded at once.

She knew that face. She knew the line of that jaw, the dark eyes that were endless in their depths, the nose with a slight crook in the bridge from where her brother had walloped him with a tree branch ten years ago. He was thinner, terrifyingly so, and his face was hollow and gaunt, sickly in color despite being tanned, and covered with a sheen of perspiration. His dark hair was cut brutally short, but it, and the scruff on the lower half of his face, were as dark as his eyes, if not darker still.

All changes aside, she knew that man better than any person on this earth.

"Alex…" she breathed, her voice catching on his name.

His corded throat worked on a swallow. "Poppy."

Her hand lashed out and struck him hard across the face, a weak yet harsh cry ripping from her throat. He stumbled sideways, surprising her with his unsteadiness, and a tremor ran across his once broad shoulders and down to his legs. Slowly, he looked back at her, pressing his left arm against the doorframe again and almost sagging against the wood.

"Please," he whispered, his voice fading with shocking rapidity as his eyes widened.

Then they rolled back, and he collapsed to the ground at her feet.

Chapter Three

"What did you do?"

Poppy barely glanced at the large man who spoke as he ambled up from the barn, her eyes fixed on the back of the man lying face down. Her lungs seemed to be shaking in her chest, but she was nowhere near tears. Her fingers had full sensation, her knees were stable, and she was thinking clearly.

Slowly, but clearly.

"I hit him," she informed Stanton, who came to stand on the other side of Alex. "Across the face."

"And that took him down?" Stanton asked, eyeing Alex's frame. "He's got at least two stone on you, if not three, and he's tall. How'd you take him down?"

"I hit him hard," she retorted without any sort of sting.

Stanton snorted softly. "You could hit a man like this with a brick wall, and he'd still smile and thank you for it."

Poppy didn't even smile at the joke, staring down at Alex as her heart began to race and slow at alternating intervals.

How could it be him? *How* could it be him?

Nearly five years after being told he was dead, and now he was here at her door. He wore a dark coat that did not fit, shredded and stained trousers, worn boots, and a strange, pale tunic that was more stained than anything else, though she hadn't looked at it long enough to consider the stains. She could only remember seeing him there, staring at her as though she were a specter of some sort.

He was so changed, she'd have passed him on the street without a second look, but when his eyes were on hers, she knew. Her stomach had shifted sharply, and her knees had nearly buckled, and her fingers tingled with a familiar anticipation.

Even now, they rubbed together anxiously at her side.

"What should we do with him?" Stanton asked, sounding as though he did not care one way or the other.

Unfortunately, Poppy did.

And she resented herself for it.

Exhaling a sort of growl, she gestured at Alex. "I can't abandon someone in his condition and live with myself. Lift him up and carry him into the spare room. I'll make up the bed for him until he comes to, and we'll figure the rest out later."

"Madam?" Stanton raised a suspicious brow of warning. "A strange man in your house with you alone?"

Poppy smiled very faintly. "He's no stranger. Well, I know who he is, at any rate. Rather, who he was." She stared at Alex's back for another long moment, then shook her head slowly. "Perhaps you could stay in the house as well, Stanton. Just to be safe."

Stanton gave her a quick half bow. "Of course, madam. Gladly." He looked down at Alex with some distaste. "Now for this worthless bag of..." He trailed off the moment he rolled Alex to his back, staring at him with a mixture of horror and shock.

"Stanton?" Poppy prodded, looking from him down to Alex and back again.

The larger man was silent for so long it was unnerving, then he swallowed once and scooped Alex into his arms as easily as one might have a sleeping child.

"I think he's wounded, Miss Edgewood."

She frowned at that. "Clearly. He fell unconscious when I slapped him."

Stanton shook his head once as he strode for the darkened spare room. "I think he's *badly* wounded, Miss Edgewood. Come, light some candles, then help me take this coat off."

Frowning still, she did so, wondering what Stanton had seen that she hadn't, and why he had looked so stunned upon seeing Alex.

Had Stanton known him before? Had he worked the Parkerton estate? Lived in the village? There was no way to know, and no time to ask.

Once the candles were lit, she came to Alex, still limp and almost cradled in Stanton's arms. The thick but worn coat was clearly not his, as he would have to be even thinner for it to do so, and she wasn't sure he could get thinner. Peeling the fabric off was too easy, his slender arms sliding from the sleeves too smoothly. The tunic underneath was long in the sleeves, though riddled with holes and loose from wear.

And through each and every hole, she saw cuts and scars, some still red and raw.

Her lower lip trembled wildly, and she wasn't entirely sure why. But as she finally removed the coat completely, she stared at Alex's chest in dismay.

Long stripes of deep red crossed the fabric covering his chest, some the faded brown of age while others were almost vibrant. They wrapped around the side of the tunic, and Poppy knew instinctively that his back would have more of the same. Through the deep vee of the tunic's neckline, she could see a hint of his too-lean chest, and some suspiciously taut and pinked skin that spoke of healing scars.

She covered her mouth with the coat, gripping it tightly in her hands, muffling a startled whimper.

Oh, Alex...

"He's feverish, Miss Edgewood," Stanton murmured, his eyes steady on her now. "Very much so."

Somehow, that broke through her sudden haze, and she dropped the coat to the ground with a firm nod. "Right. Lay him down here, Stanton, then go out to the well and draw up as much water as you can. I have some in my bedchamber still, but we'll need more."

Stanton lay Alex down on the bed, adjusting the pillows behind his head with surprising gentleness. He stared at Alex for another long moment, his expression unreadable, then strode from the room at a fast clip.

Poppy laid a hand on Alex's brow, wondering how she'd missed the startling heat from it when she'd hit him moments ago. But she hadn't exactly been in a mindset of concern at that moment, she only wanted to strike the man before her, whether he was real or imagined, in an effort to rid her mind and heart of him. The stinging across her palm had informed her that, yes, he was real, and she'd felt better for lashing out.

Then he'd collapsed, and her satisfaction had diminished.

She had never been able to strike Alex to the ground before. She'd tried in play fighting and never managed to do more than make him laugh at her efforts, as he'd always been a strong and imposing figure of a man.

Not this.

He was still taller than she was, but now their frames were more similar than they should ever have been.

She watched as his chest moved with each breath, hitching and wheezing nearly every time, and rasping in his throat. His skin gleamed with perspiration, even through the dirt and grime that covered him. She ran her gaze all along his long, lanky body, and for some reason, the sight of his tattered boots brought tears to her eyes. Holes in the toes, filthy and scuffed, and a ring around the ankles where something had chaffed the leather to the point of fraying the layers below.

A perfect ring around the ankles. She didn't want to think about what had made that ring.

"Oh, Alex," she whispered as she brought her eyes back to his sharp, angular face. "What happened to you?"

He did not respond, nor did she expect him to.

Her thumb stroked the skin of his brow gently, and the sensation of his skin against hers triggered a ripple down her spine. She jerked her hand away and sprang back as if shocked. Moving to her own bedroom quickly, her arms stiffly swinging by her side.

There was no time for sentimentality here. The man was quite feverish, wounded, and in need of her care. It made no difference if it were her former intended or the blacksmith's son; she had a duty to see to.

The fact that he was supposed to be dead and was not must not factor into anything now.

Later, however...

She pulled her water pitcher and bowl from the windowsill and grabbed some toweling and linen from the closet, thinking quickly. Bringing the fever down would be important, but if he had fresh wounds, as she suspected, they would need to be tended and dressed.

There was no way to prepare for the extent of what they might find there, and there wasn't a doctor in Moulton. They could send for the one in Northwich, if need be.

That is, if she could spare Stanton for the ride or find a neighbor willing to fetch a doctor at this time of night.

But for now, she was on her own.

She set the bowl and pitcher down on the nightstand and moved to the kitchen quickly for her apron, forcing herself to breathe steadily in and out.

She could tend the man she had loved to an almost frantic degree, so that he would not die in her home tonight. It did not matter that he had apparently died some years ago and broken her heart in the process.

She could.

Walking back into the room, however, seeing Alex, of all people, lying there on the bed, Poppy bit her lip in a moment of hesitation.

Could she?

Suddenly, he moaned, the sound weak and one of pure agony, and she was by his side in a moment, taking his hand and squeezing. "Easy," she murmured gently. "Easy. It's all right."

He moaned again, writhing at her touch, then wincing as his body moved.

Poppy couldn't see what might have injured him, but she shook her head quickly. "Easy, Alex. It's all right, you're safe. Just rest."

He turned towards the sound of her voice, his eyes still closed, and inhaled deeply, his head bobbing in a feverish motion. His lips moved soundlessly, but his fingers returned her hold with the faintest pressure.

She smiled at the sensation. "I've got you. Just rest."

Alex's chin dipped, and his head lay back fully against the pillows, exhaling as though the weight of the world were upon him. His breathing deepened again, and she knew that he was once more unconscious or asleep, though she doubted there would be much difference between the two at this state.

Poppy turned to the pitcher and bowl, pouring the cool water into it and soaking a rag. She glanced at Alex with a wry smile. "I'm not sure if I should cool you or bathe you at the moment. You're a filthy mess, and it's going to take quite some time to change that."

She placed a cool rag on his brow, then soaked another and ran it down his neck and chest. "Honestly, I'm not even sure where to begin here. Your fever is high, you're pale as death, your breathing isn't quite steady… And then there are the wounds…"

Wringing out a third rag, she shook her head at her foolishness. Talking to an unconscious man in light tones as though it would make her feel better. It felt so forced and false, so stupid, considering all she had been through. He had clearly been through a great deal as well, though she couldn't know for how long or why.

She had to find a way. She had to pretend that Alex was someone else, any other man who had stumbled across her path, sick, wounded, and in need of help. That man would need comfort, goodness, and warmth, and as much as she would like to be distant and cold with Alex until she had some answers, seeing him like this would force her to save that for a less precarious time.

This wasn't about her.

It had to be about Alex.

Alex…

A memory flashed across her mind as she set the third rag against his overheated skin.

Alex had just returned from spending two months in London, and she had raced to Parkerton to see him on foot, which had appalled her mother and Rosemary for its indecency. Poppy hadn't cared, nor had Alex. He'd been crossing the grounds to see her as well, forgoing the formality of cravat, coat, or gloves, and when she'd crossed over onto Parkerton grounds and seen him coming towards Whitesdown, she'd run at him full tilt, and he'd done the same, his grin as brilliant as the sun itself.

He'd picked her up and swung her around and around until she was almost dizzy, then taken her face in his hands and kissed her until she was more than dizzy, and she'd swayed into him in her mad delirium for him. Then they'd stood there together, arms tight around each other, murmuring softly, inhaling the scent of each other, reveling in being in their favorite place on earth.

In each other's arms.

"I love you more every time I leave," Alex had whispered with a kiss just above her ear.

"Then may you leave me every day until you cannot love me more," she'd replied, as she'd run her hand up his neck and into his hair. "I'm already there."

He'd kissed her so sweetly, so passionately then, and when they finally parted, they'd walked the Parkerton grounds together at a slow, leisurely pace, fingers entwined.

He'd died four months later.

Except he hadn't.

He was here.

Poppy stared at him again, half expecting him to disappear when she blinked.

What cruel twist of fate was this?

"Water, Miss Edgewood," Stanton called from the kitchen, stirring her from her reverie.

"Good," she managed to reply, turning to the linens she'd brought. "I'm going to start tearing strips to tend his wounds."

She heard the buckets of water hit the floor of the kitchen, and Stanton's heavy footfalls in her direction. "Excellent thought. Some of those are fresh, I'd wager, and need tending." He rounded the other side of the bed and took a closer look at Alex, rolling up his sleeves. "Think he'd take to some barley water, Miss Edgewood? Might bring down the fever."

"I don't know," Poppy murmured as she tore the linen into strips. "I'm not sure how coherent he is at the moment. He barely stirred as I tried to cool him."

Stanton made a soft noise and felt for a pulse on Alex's neck, making a face. "Strong enough, but not good." His brow furrowed and he straightened. "Wounds need tending, but he's not clean enough. Best be about washing him before we think about that."

Poppy balked and her face flamed, her focus on the linen strips intensifying.

"I'll fetch him some of my things for him to wear once we've done that," Stanton said brusquely. "What he's wearing needs to be burned."

She nodded by way of answer.

A loud ripping sound split the air and she turned on the bed to look at Stanton in surprise. He didn't even glance in her direction as he continued to tear the tattered tunic from Alex's body, opening the fabric to expose his chest fully, and swearing softly when he'd done so.

Poppy's vision seemed to blur as she stared at the open expanse of chest and abdomen. While it was just as taut and muscular as ever, she had not expected to see each of his ribs on display. Nor the expanse of marks crisscrossing the skin. Long, angry, faded scars, and fresh, bright ones, some that still bled though not with any intensity.

"Lashes," Stanton stated without emotion. "Among other things, and likely worse on the back."

"What's worse?" she whispered, though she didn't want to know.

He swallowed as he stared at Alex. "Flaying."

Poppy swallowed, a lump forming in her throat. These were brutal marks, and she could not imagine enduring them time and time again. She reached out to touch a short, raised line that ran vertically on his lower abdomen, unlike the rest that seemed to have been haphazardly strewn about.

"And this?" she whispered as she touched it.

Stanton glanced at it. "Stabbing." He pointed to the shoulder nearest him. "Here, too." He shook his head and lifted Alex's arm to pull the sleeve from it. "I have no doubt we'll find more." He looked up at Poppy then. "Can you stomach this, madam? I can manage alone if I must, but it would be easier to have you assist."

"I'm fine," she assured him, though her shaky voice betrayed her. "I've just never seen anyone look like this."

"Nor should you have," he returned with a nod. "This is not the sort of thing any genteel young lady should witness."

Poppy smiled at that. "Then it's a good thing I am neither genteel nor a young lady anymore, isn't it?"

Stanton smiled crookedly at her. "Indeed it is. Let's get this off him, shall we? Then I'll get some vinegar and water to dress the wounds."

She nodded and rose, taking Alex's other arm and peeling the tattered fabric off him. She frowned at the awkward way the arm moved and stared at it once it was bare.

"Stanton…" she said slowly. "Something's not right with his arm."

He came around the bed and examined it for a moment, then hissed something incoherent under his breath. "Dislocated. Not completely, it seems as though he tried to put it back in himself."

Bile rose within Poppy's throat, and she looked up at Stanton with a frown. "Is that even possible?"

"Possible, yes." He lifted the arm again, twisting it slightly. "Successful, not often." He nudged his head at her. "Come over here and hold him, will you? He may not like this."

Poppy came around Stanton and lifted Alex slightly, his head lolling back onto her shoulder as she settled him against her. She bit her lip and looked heavenward, praying for the strength to endure being so close to him, with his head against her and her arms around him.

"Ready?" Stanton asked, taking Alex's arm and holding it away from the body, his grip like one he might have had on a rope.

Poppy nodded and tightened her hold, squeezing her eyes shut.

She felt the pressure when Stanton pulled Alex's arm, a slow and steady pressure that seemed to build, and then…

Clunk.

She opened her eyes and looked at the arm, normal but for the marks upon and around it. "Did you get it?"

"Think so." Stanton bent the elbow and laid Alex's arm across his stomach. "We'll sling that once we're done with the rest. He must be worse off than we thought, Miss Edgewood. He didn't even stir."

Poppy felt a weak sigh course through her, and her arms tightened around Alex once more briefly.

"I was afraid of that."

Stanton took the weight of Alex's body from her and she scooted back out, looking down at her skirts and apron, now smeared with numerous bright streaks of blood. "Stanton…"

He saw it and looked at Alex's back, hissing at once and looking away as he gingerly lowered him back to the bed. "Dammit. Flaying. We'll deal with that later, Miss Edgewood. There's much else to see to."

That was undoubtedly true, but somehow having Alex's blood

31

on her clothes brought all of this to a new level, and a frightening reality settled on her.

Alex was here. Alex was really and truly here, and he was alive. But he was bleeding, feverish, and weak, and if she did not do something, he could die all over again. Only this time, she would be to blame, and the guilt and shame would be of her own making.

Whatever reason had brought him back into her life, had brought him back from the dead, she couldn't resent him while he was like this, nor could she be just a patient, considerate observer.

This was Alexander Sommerville, Lord Parkerton. The only man she had ever loved.

And this time, she would fight to keep him alive.

Poppy exhaled shortly and squared her shoulders. "I'll wipe the dirt and grime from him, you bandage."

"Let's make that the other way around, shall we?" Stanton chuckled. "You've a gentler hand than me, and he might not appreciate a woman washing him in this state."

Her cheeks flamed, but she nodded in agreement.

Silently, they worked in tandem, Stanton wiping the skin down with the cool, wet rags while Poppy soaked strip after strip of linen in the vinegar water, laying it upon the marks on his chest and stomach. She paused only briefly to boil some water and barley for him, then returned once that was done.

Through it all, Alex never so much as stirred, though his breathing was almost steady now. Stanton, for all his size and his words on the subject, had a light touch, gentle in his ministrations and careful to a precise degree.

Poppy watched as Stanton pulled Alex's boots off, though she winced and looked away when the battered and bruised feet appeared. She bit down on her lips hard and focused on dipping more linen into the vinegar and water mixture.

"Might as well keep your eyes averted, Miss Edgewood," Stanton warned. "I need to remove the trousers now. I'll be quick about it and cover him."

She nodded and kept her eyes down at the rags, her fingers absently working at them and wringing them.

"Bloody *hell*, Trace," she heard Stanton whisper, though she had no idea if he was speaking to Alex or just speaking aloud. Not that it mattered in any way, but it was curious.

She had no doubt now that he knew Alex somehow, but it was not the time to ask about it. Nor, she supposed, to ask how he knew the manner of wound and illness care that he was demonstrating that night. It was all part of his past, and they had an unspoken agreement not to discuss that.

Just as he did not know many of the particulars of hers.

"All right, madam," he said at last. "He's covered enough. I'll keep with the washing down here on his legs."

Poppy raised her head and wrung out the linens again. "Anything that needs tending on his legs or feet?"

There was a long moment of hesitation, and then Stanton rumbled, "Not anymore."

Oh, she couldn't bear this. Couldn't stand to see anyone who had been treated this way, let alone someone she had once known so well and so dearly. She knew Alex would never have shown any of this to her, and probably not to anyone, and to see him this way seemed a violation of his confidence somehow. For his own good, certainly, but guilt still flickered within her.

"Right," she replied after a long moment, keeping her tone formal and businesslike. "In a moment, I shall require your assistance to sit him up or turn him so I might see to his back."

"Yes, Miss Edgewood," he said in a matching tone.

It seemed they both needed to feel detached about this, and that comforted her.

Poppy laid another strip of soaked linen across Alex's abdomen when suddenly he moaned loudly, jerking her attention up to his face. "Alex?"

He moaned again, his legs shifting restlessly, his hands clenching at his sides.

Poppy scrambled up to him. "Alex, shh…"

Alex's frame suddenly went rigid and his back arched off the bed as he released a pained cry like the screeching howl of an animal and his arms shook with the force of it.

"Stanton!" Poppy shrieked, taking Alex's face in her hands and trying to soothe him with her touch.

Stanton moved quickly to the center of the bed, placing his hands and forearms along the sides of Alex's body.

"Steady, lad. Steady now."

Alex bared his clenched teeth, his breath hissing past them frantically as he groaned in agony.

"Oh, Alex," Poppy whispered, smoothing her hand across his cheek. "Shh… It's all right."

She rubbed his jaw and throat gently, feeling the tightened muscles there and attempting in vain to help them relax.

"Barley water," Stanton ground out as he forced Alex's body back to the bed. "Or laudanum, if you can get it down."

"We don't have laudanum just sitting around the house," Poppy snapped, throwing a glare at him.

Stanton returned her look with exasperation. "Then get the damned barley water and get his fever down." He smiled a little. "I'll keep him here, go."

She heaved a frustrated sigh and dashed to the kitchen, pulling the water completely away from the fire and pouring a cup of the mixture, her hands shaking as she did so. Then she was taking cup and saucer back to the room and sitting back beside Alex, practically on top of him as she cupped the back of his head with one hand and brought the cup to his lips with the other.

"Here, love," she murmured, stroking his hair as best she could. "Drink a little. Drink."

His neck tensed for a long moment, and his lips pressed together until they were white.

"Please, Alex," Poppy whispered. "Please."

He moaned again, then his face and neck softened on an exhale.

Poppy gently poured the warm liquid into his mouth, some of it dribbling down the front of him. "Don't be a baby," she hissed, finding a way to smile. "Drink it like a man. Swallow it."

Amazingly, he did so, though not much of it before he began to shake and tremble all over.

"Stanton?" Poppy asked with some alarm.

"More cool rags," he ordered, removing himself from Alex and coming to her. "Talk to him, Poppy. Say anything. Just talk to him."

She could count on one hand the number of times Stanton had

used her Christian name, but she knew he had never done so with such gentleness.

Tears burned at the corners of her eyes, and she took the rags from Alex's skin, dipping them in cool water again.

"Violet has suitors now, Alex," Poppy told him as she laid another cloth to his brow. "Can you imagine that? Five of them, if her letter is to be believed."

She continued to chatter aimlessly as though they were old friends who needed catching up as she and Stanton set more cool compresses and rags on his skin until his shaking ceased. Then, they returned to wiping the dirt and binding his wounds, but Poppy continued to talk to him, telling him about the farm, about their financial situation, about the workers she wanted to hire for the rest of the harvest.

Stanton pulled Alex to a sitting position so Poppy could lay strips on the raw flesh of his back, and she forced herself not to stare or think about what had caused such savage marks, or the scars beneath them. Layers upon layers of scars and marks, so his back no longer resembled anything of the sort. She kept up a steady stream of one-sided conversation, which seemed to keep Alex from roaring with pain again, though he did moan occasionally.

They carefully secured the strips with bands of linen, and then Stanton picked Alex up completely while Poppy changed the bed linens.

Once Alex was settled again and sleeping peacefully, Poppy sank into a chair she'd pulled to the edge of the bed and rested her head against the counterpane, her throat raw.

"Go to bed, Miss Edgewood," Stanton urged. "I'll watch him."

She shook her head against the bed. "I'll stay here. But if you could bring in the tub and fill it with water, that would be helpful."

"Planning a bath?"

She laughed softly and looked up at him. "If we can't get his fever down, we might have to set him in there to cool."

Stanton blinked at that. "And ruin everything we've just done for his wounds."

Poppy nodded, the idea exhausting her.

He glared at Alex's sleeping form. "If we have to redo that in a few hours, I will kill him in earnest this time."

It wasn't funny, not in the least, but she found herself chuckling at that. "Thank you, Stanton."

He looked at her with a soft smile. "Of course, madam. Get some rest while you can. It may be a long night." He nodded and turned from the room.

Poppy turned back to Alex, the arm closest to her finally secured to him with linen as well.

"Don't die again, Alex," she whispered harshly. "I've not healed from the first time yet."

Alex said nothing, but his chest moved unsteadily on yet another wheeze.

"Please," Poppy added in a low voice, folding her arms on the bed and laying her head on them. "Please, don't die."

Chapter Four

$\mathcal{H}$e was comfortable.

Such a realization shouldn't have terrified him, but Alex hadn't been comfortable in four and a half years.

Why was he comfortable now?

He forced his left hand to move, but that made the fabric over his right ribs move, which seemed fairly odd for a left hand. His right hand moved, and he gripped at some fabric, then pressed the hand down.

A mattress? Why was he on a mattress?

He tried to lift his head, but that only made it pound harder than it already was, and he felt faintly nauseated at the sensation. Having his head remain still allowed him time to realize that his head was on a pillow, if not two.

Pillows and a mattress? Either Battier was growing soft, or...

Images suddenly poured into his mind, and his breath caught at them. Barreling through the night on borrowed horses, riding as inconspicuously as he could through the day, nearly collapsing onto the third horse's back as they rode on, only faintly aware of the direction they were going, in and out of consciousness the entire time...

And then...

He forced his eyes to open, then moaned when they did so and squeezed them shut again, the room being entirely too bright for his eyes and head to tolerate.

"Sorry, is it too bright in here? I didn't expect you to wake in the middle of the day, or I'd have closed them."

Though his chest did not feel as tight as it had only days ago, it suddenly was as though a crushing weight were upon him, compressing both lungs and his heart, making thought, breath, and anything else impossible.

Poppy.

Vaguely he recalled stumbling along the grounds of Parkerton, hardly glancing at his own property and moving straight on towards Whitesdown only to find the house completely dark and without any sign of life.

Then he'd seen the farmhouse, unoccupied for the entire time he'd lived at the lodge, but now alight and gleaming in the distance. He and Poppy had always joked that they would live there if worse came to worst, and something drove him to that light, that memory.

Part of him hadn't expected her to open the door when he'd banged on it, and yet she had.

Or at least, he thought she had.

Barely conscious when he'd arrived, and clearly less than that since then, things were a bit hazy now.

He heard a motion off to his left, and he forced his eyes opened again. "Wha... Where...?"

"Shh," Poppy said as she suddenly came into view, her hair just as gloriously vibrant as it had ever been, a small smile on her lips. "You're still feverish. Don't strain yourself."

Alex stared at her for a long moment, taking in everything he was sure he had seen when he'd arrived but perhaps not fully appreciated at the time.

Poppy was still as beautiful as she had been when he'd left, as lovely as in his memories. Her eyes were just as blue, an almost startling shade of it, though there were a few lines from the corners now. Her hair was simply braided and pinned, and at the moment seemed somewhat disheveled. Her clothing was not as fine, and in fact, looked rather worn.

Almost everything about her was different from the Poppy Edgewood he had known.

Almost.

So many questions swirled in his mind. Why was she here on the farm? What had happened to her since he'd been gone? How long had he been here? How long had *she* been here? What had she thought when he'd suddenly appeared?

Was she married?

He'd never considered the possibility before, but seeing her here suddenly brought that question to his mind.

Lord above, had he stumbled upon her family's home in this state?

Poppy stared back at him, raising a brow as she clasped her hands before her. "Staring, Alex?"

He shook his head, then winced at the motion and groaned.

"Sorry about that," he murmured, his voice more of a croak and his words slurring. He scrunched his eyes up hard, then opened them again to look around the room. "Sorry to be here."

"It is rather a trial having a guest who doesn't offer to help with chores, that's true," Poppy was saying, though he wasn't paying her much attention.

The bedchamber was small, but neat and tidy, a window off to his left gave him a perfect view of the barn. The door to the bedchamber was open, leaving him a view of the rest of the cottage, and it was equally neat and tidy, but small and cramped. It was everything he had ever anticipated the cottage to look like, and the thought had never bothered him before.

Now that he saw Poppy within its walls, he hated every square inch of it.

He'd brought her to this, he knew. Somehow, in some way, this was his fault. He was to blame. How could he think to come here after all this time? He was dead to her, and dead to the world, and he ought to have stayed dead.

He ought to have actually been dead.

"I shouldn't have come," he muttered, shifting restlessly and gripping the bedcovers, ready to fling them off.

"I wouldn't attempt to get up just now," Poppy said in a wry tone he once knew too well. "You'll find you're indecent."

He froze, his hands gripping the bedcovers, and slowly turned to look at Poppy, who had folded her arms and looked the slightest bit amused.

"I beg your pardon?"

Now she smiled in earnest. "Oh, there's his coherent speech. I was wondering if you were worse than I thought."

Alex growled in irritation. "Poppy…"

"Alex," she retorted, just as she always had done.

He glared at her as darkly as he could manage, though his head pained with it, and waited.

Poppy withstood for only a moment, and then rolled her eyes. "For pity's sake, Alex. You showed up on my threshold after all this time, and then dropped as though you were dead…"

"After you hit me," he remembered, his eyes widening and his right hand going to his face.

"Oh, please," Poppy protested with a snort. "I hit you all the time and you never so much as felt it."

He smiled a little. "Yes, I did."

Her eyes went wide, and she gaped a little.

"You what?"

Now he managed to laugh, though it made his chest ache with deep, racking pains.

"I always felt it when you hit me. You hit hard. It's just that I was very good at playacting, and you believed me."

Poppy seemed to sway a little where she stood, blinking awkwardly. Then she shook herself and put on a polite smile once more.

"Well, regardless, I didn't hit you so hard as to render you unconscious. Since I am not an unfeeling woman or hostess, my servant and I took you in and tended to you."

"You tended…" Alex tried to sit up and groaned loudly with the effort, everything in his body suddenly roaring with indignation. "It was not your duty to…" he panted, his breath hissing through his teeth.

"Stop trying to do things," Poppy insisted, coming to his side, placing her hand on his brow. "You will spike your fever, if it isn't already on its way up."

Alex grabbed at her hand, flinging it away, though he suddenly seemed to feel the heat billowing up within him. "Then… why not… render me more decent… afterwards?"

Poppy smiled and replaced her hand on his brow. "Security

measures, to be sure. Keeps you abed where you need be, as well as more convenience in seeing to your wounds."

"How can you...?" Alex tried, hesitating amidst the mixture of delight and pain her touch gave him. "How can you bear to touch me? To be kind to me? I should be..."

"Dead," Poppy quipped, her lips curving a little. "Yes. Quite a surprise."

"Then let me go..." he trailed off, coughing roughly. "You... deserve..."

Poppy shook her head at him and picked up a wet rag, somehow still smiling. "Well, I can't very well rage at a man so ill, no matter how much he deserves it." She pressed the cool rag to his throat, and he sighed at the contact. "Don't worry, I'll rage at you in all fury when you're not in danger of dying again." Her smile trembled just a touch, and her eyes met his. "I thought we'd lost you last night, let alone the night before when you arrived."

"Two days?" Alex cried, jerking away from her. "I've been laid up in this bed for two bloody days?"

"Hush!" she scolded, pressing him back into position. "You're slurring again, Alexander Sommerville, and it doesn't suit. And if you upset those bandages just when we've gotten you to stop bleeding, I will give you such a scolding..."

He could barely think straight, couldn't make sense of her words. They'd... bandaged him? He stretched a little, testing the matter, and found linen tightly binding his chest and abdomen.

"Poppy," he slurred, his eyes closing, drowsy with his fever, his shoulder aching in time with his head. "My... wounds..."

"Oh, yes," she said in a too-light tone. "I've seen them. Well, most of them, I'd wager. Stanton took care of the indecent aspect."

Alex frowned, groaning again. "Good of him... to protect you..."

He felt Poppy's hand curve around the back of his head, lifting him up a little. "Come on, Alex. Before you drift off, let's have you take a sip of this."

"What is it?" he asked, his words nearly lost in the jumble.

But Poppy understood, it seemed, for her response came. "Willow bark tea. For the pain, and to get something in you so you won't waste away. If you drink it all, I'll give you broth the next time you're awake."

That hardly seemed much of an inducement, but he supposed it was designed to be one. He felt himself nod and drank the tea, the warm liquid relaxing him considerably.

"Excellent," Poppy praised, her voice doing far more for his ease and comfort than the tea could have.

He let himself sink into the mattress and pillows, sighing heavily.

Poppy worked in silence, pressing cool compresses against his skin over and over again, wiping his brow and face and throat with them. Each touch seemed to sizzle as though his body were on fire, and only the brush of the cool cloth could dampen the heat.

But rather than comfort him, it was a painful experience.

In more ways than one.

Had he even a small amount of strength left, he would have been up from this bed, indecent or not, and doing something. Anything, really, at this point. The moment he'd been free, he'd known he would go to Poppy. He would go home, or whatever remained of it, but he could honestly say that he hadn't thought too far beyond those grand ideals.

Now he was here, and he could see what a fool's errand it was.

Oh, he should have done so, to be sure, but to just drop himself on her doorstep after all this time, and in the condition he was in?

Not that Alex had had any say in the condition that he'd been in, and he didn't exactly have anywhere else to go that wouldn't have some significant implications on a rather grand scale, but it was worth stating.

He'd been through hell and back again, and he would have given anything to keep his wounds and his scars a secret from Poppy, and from anyone else. No one needed to know what he'd endured, and there was no explaining it.

There were not even words for it.

A shudder ran through him as dark memories assailed his mind and conscience. Moments he had cried out in sheer agony though no wound had been inflicted, moments he had kept silent when the pain was too great, and moment after moment where his will had been tested to its fullest extent, and still it did not break. The moments where the haunting laughter ringing in his ears was all he could hear as his skin was scorched, stabbed, or beaten, and sometimes all three at once. The hours of hanging suspended in his hold, his arms numb but for faint throbbing where they attached to his body, every breath more difficult to take in.

"Easy, Alex," Poppy murmured, her voice breaking through the fog of his memories.

He turned towards the sound, eyes still closed, breath hitching yet again.

How often had her voice come to him in those dark moments? How many times had she saved him from crying out? Or her face been all that his eyes saw when the truth could not be borne?

"Fever's up again, is it?" a somehow familiar male voice interjected.

"So it seems," Poppy replied with a sigh that told Alex her light manner with him was not as she truly felt. "He did wake, though. And talk."

"That's good. Now if only he'd be awake long enough to take real sustenance. He seems to be wasting away in that bed."

Alex rather felt as though he was wasting away, actually, and having experienced it before, he was quite familiar with the feeling.

"He's not wasting away," Poppy scolded in a tone that Alex was all-too familiar with. "He's only weak, and he is getting better."

"Is he, indeed?" came the dubious response. "I see no great difference."

Poppy sputtered loudly and wrung out a fresh rag of cool water on Alex's head, sending the droplets streaming down his face and neck. "That is because you have not sat beside him all day and all night, Stanton. If you had, you would see a very great change."

"All day," Stanton repeated, his tone disbelieving. "Have you really, madam? I don't think that was necessary."

Alex felt the same way, wondering why in the world she thought he needed to be tended at all hours, and why she thought she ought to be the one to do it.

"It was necessary, or I would not have done it," Poppy snapped.

Back down, man, Alex thought through the vague feeling of listlessness he currently endured. *That tone is dangerous.*

"Of course, Miss Edgewood."

Good man.

"I think I may have to give him a shave in the next day or two."

If Alex could have sprung from his bed, he would have done so to protest that.

"For God's sake, Poppy, do not get near him with a blade at any time. I will shave him, if he needs to be shaved, but I'd rather get scratches like his myself before I'd allow you to wield a razor."

"I beg your pardon!" Poppy protested with a laugh, and Alex would have breathed a sigh of relief if he could have managed it.

There was silence once more, and then Poppy set a cold compress on his brow.

"Did you see to the harvest?" Poppy asked of Stanton, her voice lower still, though she undoubtedly thought he was unconscious or asleep.

Harvest? Yes, he supposed it was that time of year, but the idea of Poppy having to concern herself with a harvest was bewildering.

Boards creaked as though a heavy weight had shifted. "I secured four men to come harvest with us, yes. They will come in three days, and we should be able to take in a great deal with that help. Possibly the entire lower field in two days."

"And how much is that help going to cost?"

Alex did not like how tight her voice was, how strained she sounded. Were they in dire financial straits? Was the farm not profitable? Were things worse than they appeared?

"No more than any other year," Stanton assured her. "And you said it yourself, we have more than expected this year."

Poppy sighed heavily. "Remind me, Stanton, why I decided to settle on a farm."

"Because you were abandoned by your family, and you refused to leave Cheshire and Moulton."

She was… what?

Alex cursed the fever that was rampant within him for it muddled his thoughts and made his head rage further still.

Poppy had been abandoned here? That wasn't too far-fetched, actually. Her family had always disapproved of him, and if she had shown any particular devotion to Alex after his death, they would have been upset by it.

But the second part... She had refused to leave Cheshire and Moulton? He was afraid to consider the implications of that, or the reasons for it. What reason could she possibly have had to stay if her family were gone? He was dead to her, and surely, she would...

Surely, she would...

"Shall we check his wounds again?" Stanton asked, coming over to Alex's other side. "If his fever has come again, the wounds might need attention."

"I suppose we should. He's not sensible at the moment, so he won't mind."

Well, he was not quite insensible, just a trifle ill and weak from being so. He tried to tell them both that, but it seemed words were beyond him.

Not that he would have any say in the matter, as it appeared, as the bandages around his chest and stomach suddenly became loose.

No, he tried to protest. *No, don't...*

Poppy couldn't see his scars. She couldn't be witness to what he had endured.

Stanton could, or any other objective person, he didn't care.

But not Poppy.

Not her.

The wrapping came away completely, and Alex felt as raw and exposed as he ever had aboard the *Amelie Claire*, though not quite so in danger.

But vulnerability was a danger for him, no matter at whose hand. There was far too much to protect, and far too much to hide.

Layer by layer, the bandages on his front were removed, and he could hear Stanton and Poppy talking over him about what was being revealed, though the details were now lost on him. He was finally too far gone to hear them, though he could still feel every brush of cloth against his skin. He could feel the new bandages being placed, the agonizing sting of alcohol against the wounds, apparently still somehow open enough to pain him.

Rough hands sat him up, and Alex groaned at the movement, his head weak and heavier than it ought to have been.

He knew this state, and he knew it well.

Soon, he wouldn't feel anything at all, let alone the burning that was now on his back.

And when the fever broke once more, and he regained some strength, he would still be in this bed, not in his hold. He would be tended by people who cared about and for him, not by his tormenters.

Unless Poppy were to become his torment.

He rather feared she already was.

Knowing she was tending his wounds, knowing how he still burned for her in the most secret corners of his heart, and knowing that it was not possible for him to have her...

Torment beyond torment, and nothing that he endured at the hands of Battier and his men could match it.

He was laid back against the pillows, and the linens around him were tightened once more.

"Shh, Alex," Poppy soothed, her voice suddenly clear again, though he couldn't recall crying out in any way or making any sound at all.

Then, her hands were on his face, and a fresh, cool compress was pressed to his brow.

"It's all right," Poppy's voice came again. "I have you."

Alex felt his teeth grind, his jaw tense, and his mind swirl further still.

She had him, she said.

Couldn't she see that she always had?

Chapter Five

"Surely, we are beyond indecency now."

"I don't know, are you done trying to get out of bed?"

"Well, I don't know, because I am starting to feel better, and in feeling better, I wish to get out of my sickbed, and I cannot get out of my sickbed while being so completely indecent in front of you."

Poppy pretended to consider that. "Well, you *could*, but it doesn't follow that you *should*."

Alex glared at that and tucked his bed sheet over his chest, folding his arms across it, no doubt trying to hide his wounds. However, in doing so, he happened to enhance his lean, muscular frame.

Not that she was complaining, but it actually added to his argument.

And for her own sake, she really ought to concede.

She rolled her eyes and moved out into the kitchen where, only that morning, Stanton had brought clothing for Alex to wear. It would be far too large for him, but at least he would be covered.

And if his wounds continued to improve, she would not need to bind them much longer.

Which would be a great mercy. The more she looked at them, the more they pained her to see. Her revulsion and nausea had never fully abated when she saw them, but she had been able to set it aside to tend to him appropriately.

Poppy picked up the clothes and turned back into the room, forcing yet another smile on her face.

Lord, but she was so tired of smiling.

"Here, Your Grace," she said with a playful curtsey.

Alex raised a thick, dubious brow. "What have I become duke of in the last five minutes?"

Poppy tilted her head at him. "Why, the Duke of Surly, Your Grace. And the Earl of Bedridden."

"Don't forget Viscount Indecent," he muttered, holding out his unbandaged arm for the clothing.

She shook her head firmly, keeping them close to her chest. "That title, I'm afraid, is being revoked and returned to the Crown. Perhaps you will settle for Baron Invalid?"

He scowled and crooked his fingers for them. "The Crown has a sense of humor, I see."

Poppy propped the clothing on her hip. "Well, if you're not feeling particularly grateful…"

"It is most generous of the Crown to bestow such honors to one so humble and undeserving as I," Alex immediately added, adopting a penitent expression.

She didn't have to work quite so hard to smile at that. She'd forgotten how playful Alex could be, how quick-witted and engaging. He had always been able to make her smile and laugh and knew just the way to say it to get the most of both.

And he made it so easy to play along.

Poppy handed over the clothing, shaking her head at him. "Fine, you stubborn fool. But don't think for one moment that this frees you to do as you please. Your fever is gone, and your wounds no longer bleed, but you are weak."

"Am I?" Alex replied as he shook out the linen shirt. "Well, that's good to know. I thought I was feeling quite hale."

"I'm sure you are mistaken there," Poppy said with a sigh, turning her back. "You're pale, not hale."

"Don't be poetic."

"Don't be pathetic."

"I'm confined to a bed by a most determined jailer, how much more pathetic do you think I could get?"

Poppy smiled a little. "I am sure you would find a way."

She heard him groan and whirled to face him. "Alex? What is it? Are you in pain?"

He looked up at her from where he sat on the bed, now decently covered, a little pale and giving her a tight smile. "Fine, Poppy. I'm fine."

She snorted once and came over to him. "Aside from the bandages that are covering what seem to be several lash marks on your front and back, among your other numerous injuries."

Alex's face seemed to change shade and aspect together, his eyes turning to ice. There was no hint of the teasing man from before, and only a haunted look of one condemned. His jaw tensed and his throat worked on two swallows before he shuddered and looked away.

"Yes," he muttered. "Numerous. But at the moment, only one pains me."

Poppy stared at him without shame, though she wasn't entirely certain she saw him at all. Alex should never have cause to look so hollow, so pained and vulnerable. Yes, she knew full well that he was weak and injured, that there was darkness in his recent past, but what she had just witnessed was beyond anything she could have anticipated.

Alex wasn't supposed to know horrors.

"One?" she managed, hating how her voice shook, pushing past his injuries and choosing to ignore his reaction. After all, he was doing the same.

And she could not press him in this.

Alex nodded once, still keeping his eyes averted. "My ribs. On the right side. Broken, I think. Better than they were, but I haven't moved in four days."

"Well," Poppy said in a stronger voice. "Aren't you glad that you were kept abed for that time?"

He snorted softly. "Yes, rather. And even more grateful to be clothed once more. Odd, but it may be the best I have felt in days."

"What, being clothed?" she replied with a laugh. "Don't be ridiculous."

"If you knew how long I have been without proper clothing, you would not think so." He felt the material of the linen shirt, his expression blank. "Quite a luxury, this."

Poppy watched his fingers move gently over the linen, transfixed by the minute motions. Over and over, his fingers ran the fabric between them, an absent grazing of skin against linen. Poppy's own fingers tingled as though she were doing the same, and she rubbed them together at her side to alleviate the sensation.

"It doesn't fit," she whispered unnecessarily.

Alex shook his head slowly. "Doesn't have to. And once, it might have."

"Not now, though."

"No. Not now."

A long moment of silence stretched between them. The only sound was that of the birds outside, and even they seemed to be very faint for now.

"There is no adequate way to repay your kindness, Poppy," Alex finally told her, looking up at her, no hint of a smile or warmth in his features. It was a raw openness that unnerved her, sent a chill through her, and stiffened her knees.

Poppy shook her head at Alex, giving him a warning look. "We'll get a physician in here to examine you properly. If your ribs are broken, as you say, further tending may be necessary."

"You don't have money for a physician," he reminded her, his mouth curving just enough to be considered a smile. "And I have no need of one."

"That is not up to you," she snapped. "While you are in my house and under my care, I will decide what is…"

"You don't have to," he interrupted with that maddening gentleness. "I relieve you of responsibility for me."

Poppy turned and moved to the toweling on the floor from when they had cleaned Alex this morning. "It's laundry day," she said brusquely. "And we have a great deal to do, so I've got to get to it."

"Poppy…"

She gripped the fabric tightly, her nails biting into it. "Don't do that, Alex."

"Do what?" he asked gently, an odd solemnity in his tone. "Thank you? I am indebted, and you have to accept that I will be grateful."

"Don't!" Poppy forced out through grinding teeth. "Don't you dare. If you start to be serious, I will have to be serious, and if I am serious, I will rage at you, and I cannot do that while you are lying in bed so weak and in need of care."

Alex's eyes suddenly held an almost pitying look. "Rage at me, Poppy. You deserve it."

Poppy shook her head, balling up the toweling and linen more tightly. "You think I could forgive myself for doing so while you are unwell, and I am to tend you?"

"Cast me out," Alex urged, still gentle in his tone. "This is not your responsibility. I should never have come."

"But you did, Alex!" Poppy cried, turning to him and not bothering to hide the pain searing her as she stopped pretending at last. "You came to my home and collapsed on the doorstep. How could I not treat your wounds and see to your care? While you are unwell, I must tend you. For my sake if not for yours. I have no choice."

"I'm not that unwell, I promise you." He smiled a little. "Go ahead."

Poppy swallowed and shook her head again. "Not while you're in bed, Alex, I cannot yell at you like this."

He stared at her, blinking for a long moment, then swung his legs to the side of the bed. He kept his eyes on her as he pressed his one free hand down on the mattress, pushing himself up awkwardly to a standing position, his left arm tucked against him. It took a deal of effort for him to straighten up fully, but he kept his expression free of the pain it must have caused him to do so, and he stared at her still.

He should have been a masterful sight, something stirring and speaking of strength and nobility, but he was shaking where he stood. Trembling like a leaf on the breeze. His face was devoid of any and all color, and a mist of perspiration dotted his brow.

He looked weak and frail, and in need of tending, even standing as he was.

Poppy folded her arms over the toweling in her hands and lifted her quivering chin.

"Now," she managed in a small, shaky voice, "if only you could manage to do so without going completely ashen and trembling where you stand."

His brow furrowed at that, and she turned from the room, unable to see him like this for one minute more. He was always so vibrant and virile in her mind and in her memories, so strong and impenetrable.

Not this.

Never this.

Tears filled her eyes and she stormed out of the cottage entirely, out to see to the laundry, as she had claimed, though it had only been an excuse. Now it would be an excuse and a distraction, a task she needed to complete and something to occupy her as well.

She needed Alex gone, but she couldn't bear to have him do so.

She wanted him here, but she wanted her life back as she had known it.

She wished…

"Damn you, Alex," she hissed as more tears rose, and she dunked her hands and linen into the wash barrel with more force than she'd ever done in her life, desperate to scrub away everything for a while.

Alex stared through the doorway of his borrowed bedchamber for a long moment after Poppy had stormed out of it.

He'd sensed that she was putting on a cheerful front with him in tending to him, and that she had been kind during his care, which had only done him good. He knew that she had much that she would wish to say to him, if she were only given the chance. Her slapping him when he'd first arrived had proven that. He wished she would just say it, whatever it was, and stop treating him with a kindness that he did not deserve.

But this?

There was pain in her eyes, in her expression, in the way she looked at him. He'd expected pain, but the reality of it was far worse than anything he'd imagined.

He thought she would be his torment?

He feared now that he might have been hers.

And that was unforgiveable.

He sank down onto the bed, reaching for the bedpost with his good arm to steady himself. They no longer bound his left arm, but it still ached and grew stiff often, and it was weaker than the rest of him.

And he really was very weak.

Alex exhaled slowly, grateful that his head was no longer swimming when he held still and that his fever was gone, but he could not be laid up in this bed or this room for much longer.

He heard loud footsteps coming towards this room and turned towards the sound, letting his features and manner relax into his usual manner. "Stanton."

The large, hulking man appeared in the doorway and leaned against the frame. "Trace."

Alex sighed, turning back to face the window. "I haven't been Trace in a long time."

"I doubt that very much."

That made him chuckle. "Perhaps you're right. Are we ever free of it?"

"Free, sir?"

"Don't call me sir," he scolded roughly.

Stanton pushed into the room and came over to stand beside him. "You outrank me, sir. I know my place."

Alex shook his head slowly. "I outrank no one. Not anymore."

Stanton didn't say anything, which was probably for the best, as Alex would only have refuted or argued.

Alex looked down at his feet, his toes curling against the rug beneath them. "You've written them, haven't you?"

"I did, Trace," Stanton replied with a nod. "And I told them you were here."

He sighed slowly, nodding in thought. "Then they'll be here any day."

"I expect so, sir."

Of course, they would. Having believed him dead, most likely, word of his arrival in Moulton would spur them to come quickly.

For some reason, that did not satisfy him. He wasn't sure he wanted to see them. They would expect the man he once was, and the man he was now was far, far less than that. They would want him back in London, seeing to the details of the London League, renewing his former position among them.

The idea of going back into the horrors he had just fled was something he was not prepared to contemplate.

Not yet.

Perhaps not ever.

"Stanton," Alex said slowly, his fingers drumming against the wood bedpost.

"Trace?"

Alex looked over at the large man that he had known for far longer than Poppy would ever know. "I need your help."

Stanton smiled at him in an almost devious way. "I can count on one hand the number of times you've said that to me. I'm afraid to ask."

That made Alex laugh, and he struggled to rise once more. Stanton reached out an arm and steadied him, and Alex couldn't manage pride enough to care that he required assistance.

"Help me dress," he gasped as his ribs ached again. "I'm sure it was the sight of these scrawny legs that sent Poppy running from the room."

"More than likely," Stanton agreed. He let Alex go for a moment, then moved to the bed to pick up the rest of the clothing. "And your feet look like something scraped out of a barn."

"Smell like it, too, I'd wager." Alex gripped the bedpost again as Stanton helped him with clothing, lifting his leg like a child and unable to do anything for himself.

"I can vouch for that, Trace, as I washed and tended them."

Alex winced playfully. "I don't envy you that. And I dare say you've had the sight of me burned into your mind more than you'd like."

Stanton coughed a laugh and rose, putting his hands on his hips. "Well, I won't pretend that I didn't wish to be blind a time or two. And I won't say it was a pleasure to tend you, especially given what I found."

The man trailed off with clear opening for Alex to elaborate on the subject.

"I can imagine not," Alex murmured, looking out of the window again, where Poppy could now be seen hanging toweling and linen on a line. "You haven't told her, have you? About the extent of it?"

"Of course not, Trace," Stanton said at once. "Though I couldn't keep her from seeing your feet, your chest, and your back."

"You explained what she was seeing?" Alex pressed. "Satisfactorily?"

Stanton hesitated, making a face. "I answered her questions, as best as I could. She asks a fair few, you know."

Alex smiled at that. "Yes, I know. She always did."

"But I did divert her from further questions, if that's what you're asking. She does not know… everything." Stanton shrugged his wide shoulders.

Alex nodded at that. "Thank you, Stanton. It's bad enough to see the wounds herself. Having her fully comprehend the cause of them would be worse."

Infinitely worse, but there was no need to elaborate on that point.

Poppy had always had a very clear and thorough imagination, so he doubted that she was as ignorant as he would like.

Still, there was no way for her to know the full extent.

"I've never seen the amount of marks and scars on an abdomen and thighs like yours, Trace," Stanton murmured in a low tone. "Every other mark on you, I could almost make sense of. But those…"

Alex shuddered, dark memories rolling out in his head. "Yes?"

Stanton moved closer, folding his arms. "I don't understand. What good would such havoc there do them?"

"It was a game," Alex muttered as though through an icy fog. "Nothing to understand. They'd make it clear what they could do, taunt me, run a cold blade along my skin, or even a red hot blade. Then, instead of doing what I most feared, they'd cut elsewhere, as the scars tell you. Always when I was my most terrified. Eventually, I understood the game, didn't fear it as much, so they moved to other areas."

"Why leave you able to still sire children, though?"

Alex glanced at him without emotion. "That's a nonissue for a broken shell of a man, even if it is possible. Perhaps that was a crueler outcome of the game than the scars themselves."

The silence that fell was heavier than most, and the confession left Alex nearly swaying with fatigue.

"Back to bed with you, Trace?" Stanton asked, gesturing for the bed behind him.

Alex snorted and shook his head. "No, if I have any say in the matter. Four days in there, and I'm likely to be raving mad if there's a fifth."

"I always thought you were a little mad as it was, sir," Stanton offered helpfully. "Not sure it'd be much of a stretch."

"Thank you, Stanton," Alex muttered with a snort.

He sighed and looked around the room, sick to death of its pale walls and sparse furniture, everything down to the sprigged quilt and counterpane he'd tried to kick off at least a dozen times in the last few days.

He'd never done well in confined spaces, and his time in the hold of the *Amelie Claire* proved that. This was an improvement, to be sure, but he still felt trapped in a cage.

"Get me out of this room, Stanton," Alex told him, leaning against the bedpost wearily. "Out of this bed, out of this room, and away from anything that indicates I'm a weak, pathetic invalid who can't put on his own trousers."

"He says to the man who's just put on his trousers for him," Stanton grumbled with a smile.

Alex looked at him wryly, then burst out laughing, which hurt a great deal, but he didn't care.

He hadn't really laughed in such a long time.

"Help me to move and get stronger," Alex told Stanton, still smiling. "I need to do something more than lie there and heal. Trust me, I am used to laboring under less than ideal circumstances physically."

"I can see that, sir," Stanton chuckled. "We've the harvest in a few days, you can help with that, if you have the strength. For now, how would you feel about a walk around the house and some real food?"

Alex groaned in appreciation. "It sounds like the south of France in the spring with a bounteous feast."

Stanton winced and waved him on, clearly going to follow behind. "It's nothing of the sort, Trace. Cheshire countryside in a small cottage and some week-old bread and jam. Maybe some cold ham, if I can find some."

"It will suffice, and I will be exceedingly grateful," Alex told him as he made his way from the room. His smile faded and his brow furrowed. "I cannot be more of a burden to Poppy than I already am. She deserves better."

"Aye, Trace," Stanton murmured with real feeling. "Aye, she does. Come on, now, don't make me carry you."

Chapter Six

"*H*e's doing too much."

"He is not, and if you tell him so, he is going to be furious."

"Hardly furious. Cranky, perhaps."

"Oh, and a cranky man is a better sight, you think?"

"Probably. He won't hit anything if he's only cranky."

Stanton snorted once. "He can't hit much anyway with one arm still limited."

Poppy grinned outright and folded her arms, watching Alex lead one of her horses around the paddock by the barn. "It's not stopping him from doing this."

"Doesn't take much at all to do this. He's just walking."

She looked up at the larger man beside her, his expression blank as he stared at Alex, too. "And this morning? He was just feeding the animals. And at luncheon? He was just sharpening the scythes for tomorrow. And yesterday…"

"Make your point, madam," Stanton interrupted, "if you please."

Poppy sighed and adjusted a lock of her hair that had come loose. "He's not fully recovered, Stanton. He's still very weak and shouldn't aggravate that shoulder, let alone the other injuries."

"He's got to recover sometime," Stanton reminded her. "He can't get stronger without doing things."

"I know that," Poppy murmured, looking back at Alex. "But I'd rather he take things slowly than suffer a setback that could be quite detrimental."

Stanton turned on the fence to look down at her, his brow furrowing. "This is slow for him. He was champing at the bit to be out of that bed and that room yesterday, and despite looking pale as death, he walked three laps around the cottage before we ate supper. He may be weak by the end of the day, but I've always considered such exhaustion to indicate a proper use of one's time and energy in the gift of the day. Don't you?"

There was no fair way to answer that question, and he knew it. Of course, she agreed with him, but she couldn't say so when it would mean that Alex would exert himself more and more just to keep himself out of the bed she'd confined him to.

He was still too frail for her liking, and now that he was on the mend, he would be able to eat more hearty foods, which would help matters a great deal. But while his strength was in doubt, she felt this need to tend him, to protect him, and to ensure that his suffering would be minimal.

As she watched him now, she felt strangely mesmerized. No one watching him would think he had any injuries at all, unless they studied his left arm closely, as it was rarely being used. Even if they did, they might still doubt any injury was involved. Alex moved with a sort of grace and ease that any creature alive would envy. Though she could see where he was frail, she knew what he had once been. Ignorant eyes would only see a lean man of angles and sinews and find nothing about him to fault.

He did look healthier for being out of the bed, and being out on the farm certainly lessened the gravity of his situation, but still, she worried.

"He's doing fine, Miss Edgewood," Stanton assured her in a low voice, "and he's no longer restless. Being active will do more for his healing than our tending him will, I can promise you that."

"Perhaps," she replied, still watching Alex.

He smiled at the horses when one of them pushed against his arm with its nose, and Poppy found herself smiling in response. Whatever evils had been in his past, whatever he had suffered, and no matter how changed he appeared, his smile erased any and all evidence of it. There was nothing like his smile, even now, and something fluttered and warmed in her chest at its sight.

It was odd, but now that he was up and moving about, wearing decent clothes, though they did not fit perfectly, made his being here more real. He didn't appear to be a man in need of care and tending any longer, though he still was. Instead, he looked like a man of strength and fortitude.

Alex, as she had known him, had rarely dressed as simply as he was now, only in a linen shirt and trousers, but she found the simplicity suited him very well. He hadn't come from money, though he had inherited a great deal with the title passed to him, and he'd never pretended any differently.

Alex had always been nothing more or less than himself at any given time.

And she had loved that about him.

"What do you think happened to him?" Poppy asked softly, smiling as Alex rubbed the nose of the horse that had nudged him and was now murmuring to it.

"Don't know," Stanton answered in a very gruff tone. "Don't want to know."

Poppy nodded slowly, biting the inside of her lip. "I do. I want to know."

"No, I suspect you don't," came the still gruff reply. "If you knew, I think you'd wish you didn't."

"I'm going to ask him," she told her friend. "Later."

"Don't," Stanton said bluntly. "For his sake, if not yours, don't ask."

"Why?"

Stanton's large hand fell on her arm and squeezed tightly. "There are some things in this world, Miss Edgewood, that only grow darker when brought to light."

A shiver of apprehension raced across Poppy's skin, and she craned her neck at the sensation. She nodded again only once, then cleared her throat.

"Come on, Alex, you can't tell one horse secrets and not the other," she called over to the paddock.

"No?" Alex looked up at her with a crooked smile. "Perhaps I told different secrets to each of them."

"An even greater indignity!" Poppy protested as she leaned on the fence. "You'll pit them against each other."

"I don't hear them complaining." He turned back to the horse and cupped its face, looking at it squarely. "Are you offended, Minnie? Jealous of what I may have told Bessie?"

The horse nickered a little, and Alex nodded seriously as though the response was intelligible.

"What did she say, then?" Poppy asked with a tilt of her head.

Alex threw her a superior look. "If you didn't understand it, you don't need to know it."

Stanton chortled beside her and slapped the fence rail.

"I'll go see to the feed for when the Horse Secret Keeper is done with today's session." He shook his head and turned away from them.

"You're jealous, too!" Alex called after him, which only made Stanton laugh. Alex turned to look at Poppy and smiled gently.

"What is it?" Poppy asked, smiling in return, as helpless in her response as she always had been to him.

He shook his head once. "I'd never have thought it before, but you are perfectly situated here. It is fitting to see you dressed as you are and leaning on the worn fence of a horse paddock."

Poppy's smile turned more amused. "Is it? How so? I was raised to be a fine lady."

"And you never quite managed it," Alex reminded her, grinning now.

"I did so!" she protested playfully. "I was a perfect lady, and I could give you at least five references to such things."

Alex scoffed loudly and turned back to the horses, both of whom were waiting for their walk to continue. He scratched both noses and shook his head.

"She wasn't a perfect lady. Not at all. She pretended well enough, but the reality…"

"I beg your pardon!" Poppy laughed, stepping up on the bottom rail of the fence and clasping her hands together.

"You know you weren't," he retorted with a knowing look. "You know it, I know it, and your mother knew it."

Poppy tossed her head back and laughed harder. "Oh, my mother… She really despaired of me."

"Well, you weren't Rosemary, so…"

She hissed, still giggling, and tried to scowl at him.

"That is too true, and a little unkind to be reminded of. Rosemary was the perfect child, though somehow not as well-liked as I was."

Alex cocked his head. "Unfathomable. She held such promise."

Poppy dropped her head, snorting softly. "She did, didn't she?" She looked back up at him, smiling easily as a breeze swept past them both. "Mother never had a reason to criticize my behavior, but she always seemed to know that I was pretending at it."

"That's because she knew you were with me," he said as he shrugged and began to walk the horses again. "Everybody knew that 'that boy' was going to bring you down." He shuddered in revulsion. "Every mother's worst fear."

"I don't know about that," Poppy answered, keeping her voice coy.

Alex stopped and gave her a very apprehensive look. "Why?"

She grinned mischievously. "Anne Hansen's mother was particularly keen on you, was she not? And for a while there, it was widely rumored that you fancied Anne."

As she suspected, Alex groaned and rolled his eyes, tugging the horses into motion again. "Just because I do not neglect a girl whose fortune comes from trade the way every other local man did does not mean that I ever had any interest in her."

"Oh," Poppy moaned with a pout, "but Mrs. Hansen was so looking forward to having you in their family."

"With the quality of people that fall within that description, I can see why," he muttered.

Poppy snickered into her hands and sighed. "Anne Hansen… I haven't thought of her in ages."

"Undoubtedly for the best," Alex replied, clicking his tongue at the horses. "What happened to her?"

"She married her father's assistant," she recalled with a smile. "They opened up a new location of her father's business in Bristol."

Alex shook his head, smirking to himself. "Well, Bristol will be better for having them, I have no doubt. Her mother might have been opportunistic and tyrannical…"

"That's one way to put it," Poppy interjected wryly.

"…but Anne was a pleasant girl," Alex continued without marking her. "A fine girl."

"She was, yes," Poppy allowed, eyeing Alex curiously. "A bit flighty, though."

He shook his head slowly. "No more than any other girl of her age. She was innocent and bright, nothing of artifice or designs in her, just genuine and good. Is her husband a good man? Is he fond of her?"

That surprised Poppy and her brow furrowed, though her smile remained. Anne had never been particularly close with her, and certainly not with Alex, though they had mingled in the same circles regularly. Poppy hadn't given Anne a moment's thought since she had left with her husband, and she highly doubted Anne had thought of her.

What possible reason could Alex have for wanting to be assured of her presently?

"I believe so, yes," she told him slowly. "He is well thought of and seemed attached to her. Anne was happy with the match."

Alex nodded once. "Good. She deserves to be pleased, not just well suited, and to have fair prospects for her future. I wish her well."

Poppy stared at him while he walked the horses around the paddock again, her smile fading. By his own words, he'd had no interest in her, and yet he had been concerned with her life and security, not to mention her happiness.

"As do I," she murmured, almost wary now. "Alex, why should you have so much concern for Anne and her marriage? I doubt she's given a second thought to you in the last five years."

He raised his eyes to hers, his mouth curving in a hint of a smile. "I've developed a concern for everyone I used to know. Every girl I skipped stones with, every boy I once got into mischief with... I've thought of my past with more frequency in the last five years than I ever did in the many before them. It was all as bright and shiny in my mind as it was when I lived it, and the names and faces came to memory easier than they had in my life. I can remember all of them. Every single one."

There was something eerie about his admission, something sad and mournful, and it made her shiver to hear it. She couldn't let him be lost to the darkness that he seemed so familiar with, not while he was healing and not while she had power and energy to change it.

She swallowed harshly. "Even Peter Taylor?"

Alex stopped and looked over at her, his eyes widening a little. "The blacksmith's son?"

Poppy laughed with real amusement. "Oh, you have got to be kidding me! How did you remember him?"

"Because he was the first boy to kiss you, and I wanted to thrash him for it," Alex admitted, laughing himself. "But you wouldn't have known that."

No, she wouldn't, and she didn't. She had no idea that her first kiss had been something Alex had known about, given that it had occurred when she was five, but the idea that he had resented Peter for it...

It was amusing and touching and confusing all at once.

But she couldn't afford to discuss it now.

"Who else?" Alex pressed, completely oblivious to her state. "Try me."

Poppy forced a warm smile on her lips and thought hard. "Umm... Lucy Norris."

"Red hair and freckles, tried to convince us all she was Irish, but her false accent was Scottish. Also, she was in love with your brother George, which was the strangest idea."

Poppy covered her face and laughed hysterically. "I'd forgotten she was in love with George!"

Alex hooted a laugh. "How could you forget that? She tried to trap him into a marriage officiated by Thomas Clarke, the curate's son!"

"And I had to be a bridesmaid!"

"You were miserable..."

"So would you be, if you were forced into one of her overdone pinafores."

Alex grinned. "Yes, well, the last person who tried to force me into a pinafore earned a pair of black eyes, so..." He waited for her laughter to subside, then nodded in encouragement. "Try again. I know you know more."

Alex sighed as he and Poppy walked side by side through the tall grass on the outskirts of her farm, Poppy running her hands over the top of the grass. They'd been wandering the land for hours, and his legs were close to shaking with the exertion for so long, but he refused to give the slightest indication of that. Poppy would blame herself if she knew, and then she would treat him like an invalid, and he would be stuck in that blasted bed again. He had known freedom too short a time to give it up now, particularly on account of a weakness he had never been at liberty to indulge before.

It was strange how familiar he could be with a place and yet feel so distant from it. These were lands he had roamed and dashed about in without any care or concern for himself or anyone else. Here he had been free and easy, as innocent as he was capable of being, and the only home he could recall.

But home was an unfamiliar sensation now, and a place he knew not. Walking these grounds now felt foreign, like a dream he could not wake from, and there was no ease about it.

Nothing had changed, as far as he could see, apart from trees growing taller and fuller, and yet it seemed that all had changed.

He knew the truth of the matter; only he had changed.

The grounds were the same, the buildings were the same, the very sky was the same, but he was not.

He would never be the same.

Nor would Poppy, for that matter. The last four and a half years had taken their toll on her, as well, and while his shadows would undoubtedly be darker than anything she could imagine, he could not deny that she bore shadows, as well. He could see the strain of the years when she thought he wasn't looking, and there was no hiding the lines on her face nor the callouses on her hands.

Yet, he found nothing lacking in her from any angle or respect, shadows or no. Walking about with her like this was the closest to the sentiment of home he was going to get, and the most comfortable he had been in years.

He had forgotten what this feeling was.

How it felt.

How he'd craved it.

Never mind how he'd loved her, it was this friendship, this

companionable silence, this comfort in her warmth that had always filled him to the brim and kept him from darkness.

And they'd laughed today. So much and without restraint, and he felt whispers of his old soul rising within him, a renewal of the man he'd been. The shadows would return that night once he was alone, as they always did, but for now, he would revel in the rarity of light.

"Do you often walk the old paths, Poppy?" Alex asked, glancing over at her.

Poppy's lips curved up in a bemused smile. "No, actually. Never. Couldn't you tell by the lack of wearing on them?"

He looked down at his feet and smiled a little, seeing that there was almost no path at all before them, though they both knew the exact way of it. "So it is. But it's such a charming walk, and so many memories to accompany you!"

"Hmm, that is true," she allowed, tilting her head for effect. "But I don't have the time or the leisure to take the walks or engage in the memories of them when there is a farm to see to and work to be done. Some of us," she added with a scolding glare at him, "have an occupation to see to and responsibilities to maintain."

Alex raised his hands in mock surrender. "Apologies, Miss Edgewood. I shall find occupation forthwith."

Poppy chuckled and plucked a blade of the long grass, threading it through her fingers as they walked. "And what would you do, Mr. Sommerville? Or my Lord Parkerton, rather."

The sound of his title nearly made Alex gag, his throat clenching in response. "Sommerville will suffice," he managed eventually. "And I thought I might become a steward for whoever currently inhabits Whitesdown. I know it well enough, and better than they do, I daresay."

"Undoubtedly," she admitted, smiling further still. "They're never in residence, so I doubt they know it at all." She gave him a mock frown, then shook her head. "No, a steward won't do for you, though you'd have free reign here. Find a new occupation."

Alex pretended to think on it, then said, "A blacksmith. Mr. Taylor is aging, and unless I am mistaken, Peter is still floundering hopelessly in the army."

"That he is," Poppy agreed, her smile returning in full force. "But I had no idea you had such interest in metalworking, let alone the skills to work in it."

"I don't," he said with a shrug. "I could shoe a horse, but as far as anything else…"

"Then why would you suggest that as an occupation?" Poppy laughed.

Alex grinned sheepishly. "Hot fire, pounding metal with a hammer, exerting myself and working in a dangerous environment… It's a dream come true."

She rolled her eyes with an accompanying groan. "You are behaving like a nine-year-old!"

"A bit older, I think. Probably more like eleven."

"Oh, because eleven is so much better than nine?" Poppy shot back, a familiar mischievous light in her eyes.

"Actually, it is," he replied with a sniff. "It is two full years of additional experience and maturity, which is more than enough time to develop a better sense of self. Ask any young lad in this world, and they will tell you that eleven is far and away better than nine."

Poppy stared at him for a long moment, her mouth gaping, though she still smiled in a way. "Well, nine, eleven, or seventeen, you still don't have the skills required to become a blacksmith, so unless you plan on spending the appropriate amount of time as an apprentice to learn the trade properly, you still need to find an occupation."

Alex heaved a dramatic sigh. "I didn't know this had to be so realistic."

"You're the one who said he would get an occupation forthwith," Poppy reminded him with all the tone and scolding of an older sister. "I just presumed that meant you were currently capable of something."

He winced and looked up at the sky. "Then I suppose I shall become a spy."

Poppy's laughter rang through the countryside around them, dancing off the tall grass and the trees, and possibly reaching even to the scattered clouds above them in the sky of dusk. He smiled at her, delighted in the irony that she would never know, and loving how she laughed with her entire body and without reservation.

Her brilliant hair caught the lingering rays of sun and glinted temptingly as it danced against her shoulders, nearly coming loose from its sensible plait. Her cheeks, not to be outdone, seemed to steal some of the sky's brilliance for their rosy shade, broken only by the edges of her lips as she laughed over and over. Between the glorious sight and the musical tones of her laughter, Alex felt himself more drained of strength and sensation than he had been yet in this venture of his.

Lord, how he'd missed her.

"And what," he managed to ask through a clogged throat, "is so amusing about that?"

Poppy looked over at him, a tear of mirth escaping one fair eye. "Oh, Alex, that is absolutely ridiculous. A spy? I thought we were going for realistic."

He sputtered in protest. "Spies are real," he assured her. "I met one once."

"Did you now?" she inquired, clearly humoring him. "Where, pray tell, was that?"

"London," he said simply.

Poppy nodded rather sagely. "Of course, you did. And I'm sure he was very upfront with you about his being a spy."

Alex gave her a smug smile and clasped his hands behind his back. "I'll have you know *she* was rather direct and upfront about it, and there was nothing that terrified me more."

That made Poppy laugh again, this time a hard bark of a laugh. "Now that, I believe wholeheartedly." She sighed and looked towards the darkened edifice of Whitesdown and seemed to stiffen slightly. "Shall we go back? Stanton will be moaning for his dinner."

"I'm sure Stanton would survive if he had to prepare his own dinner," Alex muttered good naturedly, "but by all means, let us go back."

They turned and walked back the way they had come, Poppy still absently fiddling with the strand of grass in her hands.

"What about you?" Alex asked, not willing to lose this opportunity to silence.

"What about me what?" she returned, lifting a brow. "Am I a

spy?"

He chuckled and shook his head. "I don't want to know if you are, though I suspect you would be quite good at that."

She nodded primly, tucking a stray strand of copper hair behind her ear. "Too right, I would be."

"I know." He smiled at her, though she had turned to look out across the expanse of fields and did not see it. "I meant your occupation, though. If you weren't farming, if you had a real choice, what would you choose?"

Poppy looked over at him again, this time incredulous. "I thought we were being realistic."

Alex shrugged almost easily, his shoulder twinging slightly with the motion. "Why should that not be realistic?"

"Because realistically," she replied with some bite to her tone, "I wouldn't have an occupation if I had a real choice, let alone farming."

Various curses in various languages with varying vehemence raced across Alex's mind, and it was now his turn to look away, pain searing him with acute efficacy. He didn't need to be reminded of her situation, and while he had no proof, he was convinced he was to blame for it. But she wasn't going into details of the time he was gone, and he wasn't asking. Just as she wasn't asking about his details.

Still, they both wondered, and they knew it well.

"I could have been a governess, I suppose," Poppy mused, ignorant to Alex's suffering. "Not for older girls, but young ones. I had patience once and a fondness for children before the girls became silly and frivolous."

"You were never silly or frivolous," Alex recalled with a faint smile.

Poppy shook her head slowly, looking up at him again. "No, I wasn't, was I?"

Perhaps it was the golden hue of the world around them, perhaps it was the soft tone of her voice, perhaps it was the time they had spent reveling in their fonder past, but when Poppy's eyes met his, something shifted on its axis. Things slid into place, things slid out of place, and he wasn't quite sure if everything were suddenly perfectly right or perfectly wrong.

But it was perfect in some way, that much he knew.

"Poppy," he murmured, his voice suddenly hoarse.

Her eyes turned wary, but she said nothing in response.

A thundering of several hooves in the distance met their ears, and they turned towards the sound, Alex's stomach dropping to his toes. He couldn't see who or how many, but it was enough to grab Poppy's arm. "To the house," he ordered. "Now."

She didn't argue, and they both ran for the cottage, Stanton appearing in the doorway as they reached it.

"What is it?" he demanded, brow furrowing.

"Riders," Alex replied, practically shoving Poppy into the house.

Stanton gave him a derisive look. "Get inside, man, you're half dead."

"Am not," he retorted, though his knees now shook in a more tremulous manner.

"What?" Poppy half-screeched from inside. "You should have told me!"

"It's been a long day," Alex retorted hotly. "I'm not dying!"

Stanton suddenly pushed him within. "Regardless, get in, and save your legs, just in case." He shut the door firmly behind him, an emphatic note in the click of the latch.

There was no arguing with that, and Alex moodily moved across the kitchen, ignoring Poppy's glare. He wasn't used to inaction, but now that he had been forced into a retreating, protected position, he was grateful to have it. He wouldn't have been able to run much further than the boundaries of the land, let alone a proper escape. And he would never have been able to properly protect Poppy, no matter how he would have wished to.

He wasn't entirely sure he remembered how to do any of the fighting he'd been endlessly trained on anyway. He hadn't used a weapon in years. His mind was sluggish and clouded most of the time, and instincts were slow, if they were there at all.

He was better served as bait than anything else.

"Trace…" Stanton's bemused voice called, an odd sort of warning as the riders could now be easily heard.

That could only mean one thing.

Alex turned to Poppy with pain in his eyes as his stomach suddenly clenched in anticipation. "I am so sorry," he whispered as he dropped into a chair.

"For what?" she asked, clearly bewildered.

He shook his head slowly, and stared at the door, waiting.

They were here.

Chapter Seven

The door burst open without any trouble.

Clearly, Stanton had stepped aside, as there had been no sounds of struggle at all.

Oddly enough, Alex remained in his seat, looking somehow resigned and miserable while his right foot bounced anxiously, the elbow resting on that knee shaking into his shoulder, his clenched hands almost still with the motion.

Poppy wrenched her gaze from him as the door opened, and her hands balled into fists, unsure what her reaction ought to have been.

First through the door was a very tall man with dark hair and dark eyes, though his complexion was fair, and he was roughly pushed aside by an only slightly shorter man with angular features and bright blue eyes. They stepped into the room, staring at Alex with wide eyes, and Alex stared back, expression carefully composed.

Three more men entered the house after them, though the first, a slender man with almost green eyes, didn't seem as stunned as the rest. The remaining two men, one with a tanned complexion and dark coloring, the other with dark curls and fair eyes, moved slowly, their eyes fixed on Alex as though he were a ghost that would soon disappear from their presence.

It was the one with curls that drew Alex's attention fully, and he slowly rose from his chair, fixed on him with all intensity.

Poppy watched them, the silence of the room almost eerie after the thundering of the horses outside.

Stanton came into the house, and shut the door softly behind him, leaning his back against it as he, too, took in the sight.

"Alex," the man with curls breathed, his pale eyes impossibly wide.

Alex swallowed hard. "Gabe."

Suddenly, the men were embracing hard, arms clenched around each other, the material of shirts being gripped tightly in hand.

Poppy didn't understand the intensity of emotion she was witnessing, nor why the other men suddenly smiled a little, and several throats seemed to swallow hard as they watched the scene.

Eventually, Alex clapped Gabe on the back and shook his head as he pulled back to look at him. "You've gotten old."

Gabe grinned, the corners of his eyes crinkling as he did so. "You, on the other hand, are a sight for sore eyes, cousin."

Poppy jerked in her seat and looked over at Stanton in shock. *Cousin?* Alex didn't have any cousins that she knew of, he'd never mentioned family at all other than Lord Parkerton in all the time they had known each other, and yet…

Gabe pounded Alex on the shoulder, grinning and shaking his head. "Damn, it's good to see you, Alex."

Alex smiled, though it was far less than the joy his cousin displayed. "You too, Gabe." He looked beyond his cousin to the rest. "All of you, actually."

"Probably not me, right, Trace?" the dark one quipped stepping forward to shake Alex's hand.

"Gent," Alex greeted, pulling him in for a quick hug. "Even you."

He shook hands with the tallest two, both of whom seemed somehow superiors of the rest, and they were surprisingly quiet in their conversations and greetings with Alex.

"And who's this?" Alex asked, as he turned to the last man.

"Rook," he replied, stepping forward with an easy, crooked smile, hand outstretched.

Alex's brows shot up. "Rook, who used to work with the Foreign Office?"

Rook nodded once, still smiling. "The same. And it's an honor to meet you at last, Trace."

Poppy frowned as she watched, wondering who these people were. One or two of their faces seemed somehow familiar, but the names were strange, and none of them seemed to acknowledge the fact that this was her home. She'd heard Stanton call Alex "Trace", but she hadn't yet worked up the courage to ask about it.

If these men were calling him Trace, as well, then what did that mean?

Alex looked at the one called Rook carefully, then pointed to his left eye, which Poppy could now see was discolored. "What happened to the eye?"

Rook touched the bruises around his eye carefully, looking a little sheepish. "Oh, that was a belated wedding present from Rogue."

"What?" Alex reared back and looked at Gabe, then back to Rook. "Why?"

Rook shrugged. "He didn't like that I was investigating you and your cases without telling them, which led to you being discovered as not dead, and he felt left out."

"Good lord, Gabe…" Alex coughed, smiling more genuinely at last.

Gabe scowled and shifted his weight uneasily. "I did apologize."

"You did?" Rook asked, eyes wide. "When? Did I miss it?"

Poppy ignored the laughter of the group and looked around at them all, her brow furrowing as her stomach clenched. They all thought he had been dead, too? That would explain the intensity of emotion between Alex and his cousin, she supposed, and certainly their appearance here. But who were they? What had brought them here?

Was anyone going to notice that she was here?

She sat up straighter in her chair, resting her hand on the table, and started drumming her fingers there.

The tallest one instantly noticed, and he smiled at the sight. "Trace, would you care to introduce us?"

Alex frowned at him, then looked over at Poppy, his expression clearing.

"Oh…" He glanced over to the tallest one and the man next to him, both of whom nodded once.

Poppy may have imagined it, but she thought the other men suddenly stiffened at the nod.

Stanton seemed to be the only one completely unperturbed by

any of this.

Curious.

"Poppy Edgewood," Alex began in a vacant tone, "these are… they are…" He exhaled shortly, shaking his head. "I'm not sure if they are brothers or friends or comrades, or something far less complimentary."

"I beg your pardon," Gent grunted, smirking a little.

Alex rolled his eyes, and turned to them, pointing at each without politeness. "Rook, whom I have just met but am already inclined to like better than anyone else."

Rook bowed, grinning proudly.

"Rogue, who also bears the unfortunate curse of being my cousin, Gabe."

Rogue nodded, far less inclined to smile now than before, and suddenly seeming quite dangerous.

"Gent."

"Charmed, Miss Edgewood," Gent replied, also bowing and smiling warmly at her.

"Cap," Alex continued, now indicating the tall one with fair hair and eyes.

"Miss Edgewood," Cap replied, somehow doing a combination of a bow and nod.

"And Weaver," Alex continued, gesturing to the tallest one.

Weaver smiled and nodded respectfully. "Apologies for barging in on you like this, Miss Edgewood. We are usually much better behaved. I'm sure arriving *en masse* like this must be particularly overwhelming for you."

Poppy managed a smile. "Trust me, I'm growing accustomed to being overwhelmed of late."

Alex winced at that, but Poppy wasn't about to apologize or feel the slightest bit of guilt for finally saying it.

"I presume you all thought he was dead, too?" she added, not bothering to keep the bite out of her tone.

Cap looked at the others, then stepped forward. "Yes, Miss Edgewood, we did. We only received word a few days ago that he was alive, and had been preparing to mount a rescue…"

"You were?" Alex asked, looking at him in awe.

Weaver raised a brow at Alex's query. "Did you think we wouldn't?"

"I didn't know what to think," Alex murmured, "or what to expect."

"And then we found out he was here," Cap went on, ignoring the others and keeping his gaze on Poppy. "So, we rode up without delay to see for ourselves."

Poppy nodded in understanding, biting the inside of her lip, and then tilted her head. "And you all are...?"

Everyone seemed to look at Alex, though he stared at Poppy with the sort of trepidation one reserved for wild animals.

"Spies, Poppy," he finally said, lifting his chin, "for the Crown."

Spies. Their earlier conversation returned to her mind, and she swallowed at the pain of it. She'd thought it all a joke, some farfetched occupation he'd pulled out of thin air to amuse her.

Never did she think it was true.

"Even you?" she asked, somehow managing to keep her voice steady.

Alex kept her gaze and nodded. "Even me."

Poppy exhaled once. "Of course, you are," she muttered, any semblance of warm feelings from earlier fading entirely.

One of the men hissed softly, but Poppy didn't care enough to look. She didn't care about any of them.

She just stared at Alex, waiting.

"Gent, Rogue, Cap, and I were all part of the same group," Alex told her. "Weaver is our superior."

"And Rook took Trace's... excuse me, Alex's position," Cap added, gesturing to Rook. "When we thought..."

"Yes, when you thought Alex was dead," Poppy finished for him, drumming her fingers again. "We've all had to make arrangements, it seems. Tell me, Cap, how is it that you all knew to come here to find Alex?"

Cap kept her gaze, though he seemed hesitant. "Stanton sent word."

Slowly, Poppy turned to look at her servant and friend, who stared at her with the first sign of shame. "He did, did he?"

"I knew my duty," Stanton grunted.

"How long is it that you have been with me, Stanton?" she asked, knowing the answer but needing to hear it out loud.

"Nearly five years," he replied. "Came on shortly after your family left."

Poppy nodded carefully. "And you were in Moulton before then?"

Stanton scratched at the back of his head and looked at the others.

She threw her hands up. "Oh, for heaven's sake, it's a simple question. I always thought it was too fortuitous that you appeared when you did in my hour of need. Were you supposed to help me survive? Help me farm? What?"

He cleared his throat and pushed away from the door, straightening fully. "Whatever was necessary, madam."

Poppy stared at him for a long moment, then shot to her feet, glaring at Alex. "You had Stanton come over here to protect me? To keep an eye on me? What business was it of yours how I fared when you were gone?"

"Umm, Miss Edgewood?" Gent broke in, looking almost pale despite his tanned skin. "Stanton was one of our placements."

Poppy rolled her eyes and waved a dismissive hand. "Yes, we've established that, gentlemen."

Gent cleared his throat. "No... Not Alex's. Ours." He gestured to the group. "Ours." He indicated Alex briefly. "He had nothing to do with it."

It was as if the wind had suddenly left whatever sails her little ship had had. "Oh..."

"We felt responsible," Cap explained, his expression softening as he smiled gently, "and we couldn't bear to see you suffer. So, we had our friend and colleague Stanton keep watch and act as he saw fit for however long he saw fit."

No doubt, this was meant to comfort and console her, but Poppy felt neither. She felt hollow and cold, confused and completely lost.

"With your permission, Miss Edgewood," Weaver said kindly, "I think we should all sit down, and perhaps Alex will explain how he came to be here."

She nodded numbly, and they all took seats, though she

remained standing.

If they were spies and had so much they couldn't say, such as their true identities, she might not be able to hear. Might not *want* to hear.

Considering the expressions on the faces of Gent, Rogue, and Rook, they felt the same way.

"Miss Edgewood," Rogue suggested reluctantly.

She started to move out of the room without a fight when Alex shook his head. "No."

Everyone looked at him in surprise.

Alex shook his head one more time. "No," he said again. "Of all of us, she deserves to hear it."

Poppy looked at him for a long moment, and his eyes held nothing but regret and respect.

That would have to be enough. For now.

"For the last four and a half years," Alex began as Poppy sat, "for one thousand, six hundred and fifty-eight days, to be precise, I have been held prisoner in one ship or another. One vessel in those first few days while I healed from my injuries, and then aboard another for the remainder. I worked as a crewmember, only less of one, and did not touch land until a few days ago."

Poppy watched as Alex spoke, frowning as he glazed over so much. Held on a ship? Why? By whom? What had happened? Each of the questions were on her lips, though she couldn't manage to ask even one of them for fear she would miss something more.

"When I realized," he went on, "that I was on land, and in Wales, no less, I escaped. I knew I needed to get back here, I owed that to Poppy…"

She swallowed once, clearing her throat. "But you were so injured when you arrived…"

He nodded but did not look in her direction. "I was very injured when I escaped. I stole a horse from a barn maybe thirty miles outside of Fishguard and rode as far as the horse could take me, then turned it loose. Took another horse, along with some shoes and hat, some food, and kept going, this time without the same haste. I couldn't draw attention to myself, especially not in those circumstances."

"Probably helped that you can speak Welsh," Rogue murmured

with a very faint smile.

"Can you?" Rook asked, sounding impressed.

"Rogue and I had Welsh mothers," Alex explained, though it only brought a flicker of humor to his face. "I am much better at it than he is, though it's still not my strongest language. I sound intoxicated most of the time, which tends to suit for the purposes."

The others chuckled, but Poppy didn't. She stared at Alex still, in a sort of wonder and awe.

He spoke Welsh? He spoke other languages? It was as though she'd never truly known him, and nothing she remembered had been real.

"I don't know how I managed it," Alex went on, shaking his head. "I was hurt and feverish, barely aware of my surroundings, but somehow cognizant of what I needed to do and where to go to reach my destination. I didn't pause to sleep even once, afraid of being discovered or not waking up at all should I…" He paused and swallowed with some difficulty. "But the horses I stole were all well trained and carried me where I needed to go. Once I reached familiar areas, I released the last one and went the rest of the way on foot. Collapsed on the doorstep here."

"Then he was in bed for three, almost four days," Stanton broke in. "But for Miss Edgewood here, we might have lost him."

Poppy's cheeks flushed at the mention of her name, and she looked down at her rough nails. "It wasn't so dire as all that."

"I suspect it was," Weaver contradicted, his voice low. "And for that, you have the gratitude of every man in this room, and quite a few in powerful places elsewhere."

Poppy glanced up at him, wondering if he knew just how little she cared about the gratitude of other people in this situation. At this moment, she wondered if she shouldn't have hit Alex harder when he'd appeared. A great deal of trouble could have been spared if she had.

"Trace," Cap murmured, eyeing him with suspicion, "there is much to be explained in what you've just said, and what you've left out."

Alex nodded slowly, rubbing his hands together in an absent fashion. "Some things, Cap, I can't talk about."

"Understood," Cap replied, "but you also should understand that there are things we need you to talk about."

Again, Alex nodded, and this time, he looked at Poppy.

She returned his look, then glowered. "Now I need to leave?"

He closed his eyes and looked away.

She slapped her knees and rose, keeping her eyes on him. "Will my bedchamber be sufficient? Or do I need to go out into the barn and wait to be summoned back in?"

"Not the barn," he whispered, keeping his eyes averted.

Poppy nodded and looked at the others. "You may all stay here this evening, if you can find the space."

"We have lodgings, Miss Edgewood, but thank you," Weaver said, rising from his chair. "Lord Cartwright is loaning us Branbury Park until we resolve things."

Poppy's hands curled into fists at her side. "Lord Cartwright. Of course, he is also one of yours. Why am I not surprised?" She looked back at Alex, shaking her head. "I wonder if anything in my life is truly mine, or if it is all due to you and this damned interference." She marched past all of them out of the kitchen and into her bedchamber and slammed the door as though she were a moody adolescent girl once more.

She didn't care.

Everything in her life was unraveling, and she was too exhausted, too frazzled, and too hurt to attempt the control she ought to have had. Because she had no control, emotionally or otherwise, and as she lay down in her bed, still fully clothed, all she could do was cry until she could manage to sleep.

"I didn't mean to make things difficult," Cap murmured as they all stared after Poppy.

Alex sighed and rubbed his hands over his face, then hissed as his injured shoulder protested. "I think that was already brewing, Cap. No worries."

"Miss Edgewood has been under a great deal of strain," Stanton informed them, taking the seat Poppy had vacated. "Even before you showed up, Trace. The farm is always struggling, despite the help she receives from the reserves London sends. Trace showing up threw a kink into things, and then to have all of this…"

"I shouldn't have come here," Alex groaned. "I should never have come."

"Alex," Gabe murmured, leaning forward in his chair. "Where else could you have gone? London would have been too far in the state you were in, and too treacherous. You had no way of knowing if any other alternative would be safe."

Alex shook his head, swallowing hard. It was too much, and it was too hard. For him, yes, but especially for Poppy. She deserved better than this. Better than him.

He should have died on the way to her. He would have known he was free, would have escaped, and yet he never would have brought such trouble to her life. Death was infinitely preferable to the torment he was feeling. Even what he endured on the *Amelie Claire* hadn't hurt the way this did.

"Alex."

He looked up at Cap, who was looking at him with all the warmth a father or older brother would have. "What?"

Cap smiled gently. "It's really good to see you. I never expected to."

Alex reluctantly returned the smile. "I didn't think I'd see any of you again. Or anyone."

"You don't have to talk about this tonight, Alex," Weaver insisted. "I know we just sent Miss Edgewood away, but… we have time."

That was highly unlikely, and Alex gave him the sort of look that ought to have told him so. "I doubt that, Weaver. There's never time."

"Tonight, there's time," Weaver said again. "We're staying at Branbury, and the official debrief can happen tomorrow, or the next day."

Alex looked over at the fire and sighed heavily. "I may need a strong drink or two to loosen my tongue and unlock my memory. Most of it I've stored away, though I'm sure it will all come back to me if I let myself remember. My scars tell the story well enough."

"As bad as that?" Gent half-whispered, eyes wide.

"Worse," Stanton grunted, folding his arms.

Everyone stared at the large man, even Alex.

"I've seen the scars on Trace," Stanton told them all. "Protected Miss Edgewood from the things no decent woman should have to see, though she might not comprehend what pain he had to endure to gain those marks. I can recollect each mark in perfect detail, gentlemen. If Trace can't bear to tell you, I can give you a fair enough assessment, so he doesn't have to endure it again."

Alex's heart swelled in his chest, and he couldn't have spoken if he wished to at the moment. He'd known Stanton before he'd left and never returned, but not particularly well, and only in the last few days had he come to know him much better. Never would he have expected to have earned such loyalty from him in so short a time, nor would he have expected the man to have recalled his injuries in such a way.

He would never be able to express what that meant.

He cleared his throat quickly and tried for a smile. "If I don't have to report tonight, will someone at least catch me up on what I've missed?"

Rook raised a brow, treating him with more familiarity than he'd expect from a man he'd just met. "Official or personal?"

"Personal," Alex said quickly. "I'm not sure I can handle official right now. Not with…" He shuddered briefly and craned his neck as a chill ran down his spine.

"Bad news first," Weaver said quickly, clearly having caught Alex's reaction. "Cap's wife Caroline passed about two years after we thought you did."

A flash of anguish cinched Alex's heart and his breath caught. Caroline had always been warm and wonderful, though he'd not seen her much socially, but he knew how devoted Cap had been to her. He'd always hoped that he and Poppy would have managed a marriage and a love like theirs one day. However, despite what he'd always felt for Poppy, Cap and Caroline's relationship had seemed too impossible to replicate.

"Cap," Alex groaned, looking at him. "I'm so sorry."

Cap smiled thinly and nodded. "Thank you. It came as quite a shock, and the children… Well, it was a painful time for all of us."

Alex nodded in understanding, thinking of Cap's children and what it must have been like to lose their mother, particularly when their father was gone so often.

"But," Cap continued, smiling more broadly, "just this year, I married again."

"You did?" Alex was stunned and didn't bother hiding it. "I'd have thought…"

Cap chuckled, sitting back against his chair. "Trust me, so did I. But Beth…" He laughed again, grinning outright, which was a bewildering sight. "Beth changed everything."

Impossibly, Cap truly seemed happy. Beyond happy, but it had to have gutted him to lose Caroline.

Clearly, Alex had missed a great deal.

"That's wonderful," Alex told him. "Congratulations, Cap."

He inclined his head, then looked down the line of the others, and back at Alex. "Mine wasn't the only wedding while you were away. Gent went first."

Alex barked a laugh and looked at Gent. "Did you, indeed? One of your damsels in distress, was it?"

Rook and Gabe hooted in laughter, while Gent only grinned. "Yes and no. She wasn't when I met her, and then she was, all of a sudden. But she loves me somehow, and we have a daughter, with another child on the way, and I thank God my daughter looks like her mother and not me."

"We are all very grateful for that, I believe," Rook acknowledged, crossing himself.

Gent glowered at him and kicked at the chair. "You could be kinder, you know, now that you are in the family."

Alex looked between them, smiling in spite of his confusion. "Excuse me?"

Rook rolled his eyes and sighed dramatically. "I married his wife's favorite cousin very recently, and he seems to think that particular family tie means I should change my nature to suit him."

"One can hope," Gabe muttered, shaking his head. "Poor Helen."

"You don't like Helen," Rook and Gent said together, making

Cap and Weaver laugh.

"I don't *dislike* Helen," Gabe protested moodily.

"I hope you're more convincing with your wife than you are with us," Rook told him with a sniff.

Alex looked at his cousin with wide eyes. "I beg your pardon?"

"Thanks for that," Gabe muttered, shooting a dark look at his colleague, who was as delighted as a child at this change of events.

"Gabe." Alex was already smiling, wondering if it was possible that his cousin... His *cousin*, who was, by all accounts, the most difficult man on the planet, had a wife?

Gabe growled and gave him a reluctant smile. "I got married, Alex."

"I think that part he got," Rook whispered.

"So help me, Rook, I will blacken the other eye," Gabe snapped, though there was no venom in his tone.

Alex laughed and put a hand to his head. "Gabe! Did you fall in love? Did you compromise someone? Who in the world is she?"

Rook and Gent snickered uncontrollably, both clamping down on their lips hard, while Weaver and Cap only shook their heads and grinned.

Gabe sighed, smiling himself. "She may or may not be the long-lost daughter of Eagle."

"No," Alex moaned, laughing helplessly and covering his face with his hands. "No, you didn't."

"Oh, I can assure you, I did," his cousin replied, finally laughing with the rest of them. "My life will be all the more complicated from here on out."

Alex dropped his hands and looked at his cousin, grinning. "Gabe! You're married!"

"And a father, actually," Gabe pointed out, wrinkling his nose in embarrassment.

The floor could have fallen away, and Alex wouldn't have been more shocked. "What?" he said, though the word had no volume.

Gabe's typical cynicism and scowling vanished, and he smiled at Alex with surprising warmth. "I have a son. Just recently, as it happens. And we've named him Alex."

A croak of sorts escaped Alex's throat, and he swallowed

repeatedly.

"Under the circumstances," Gent mused out loud, watching the cousins fondly, "I think I'd better remove myself from the tentative position of godfather when you christen the lad, and offer the position to Trace here, would you agree?"

Gabe grinned, still staring at Alex. "It's all right with me. Alex?"

"I can't," he managed. "I can't take that from you, Gent."

"Oh, I have no doubt that Amelia will give Rogue plenty more children," Gent assured him, shrugging easily. "I'll be in for one of them, I'm sure."

Rook made a face. "I'm not sure Amelia would appreciate that turn of phrase, Gent. Giving Rogue something, let alone children. She might take offense for that, and you know what that means." He shivered and made a face.

Alex forced his emotions aside and looked at the rest of them, his delight feeling strange and foreign to him.

"Tell me everything, lads. I want to hear it all. But please, for the love of God, tell me all about this Amelia, the daughter of Eagle, and how Gabe was still alive when it came time to marry her."

Chapter Eight

Dawn did not feel any better than dusk had, but there was nothing for it. Poppy had work to see to, and no emotional upheaval could prevent that.

Perhaps they had all disappeared in the night and she could get back to her quiet life. Somehow, she doubted things would be that simple.

Steeling herself, brushing off her skirt, and patting her hair carefully, she strode out of her bedroom, fixing a polite smile on her face.

Except the kitchen was completely empty.

She frowned, propping her hands on her hips, looking around. They had certainly cleaned up well, everything neat and tidy, possibly even more so than it had been before, which was more than she could say for the times when she'd had her hired help in the kitchen. At least her house was still in one piece, and they hadn't created additional work for her.

Still, she hadn't forgiven Alex, or any of them, for the revelations of last night. She would need a great deal of time, and some more information and understanding, which would prove difficult if everyone were gone.

She looked in Alex's bedroom, but that, too, was empty.

A faint whistle met her ears, and she looked out the window where Stanton was leading two horses from the barn.

Well, at least one of them was here.

Poppy shook her head and marched out of the cottage, walking quickly out to the farm.

"Stanton!" she called, forcing her tone to be calm and unaffected.

He turned back to her, smiling as she approached. "Miss Edgewood."

"Where's Alex?" she asked without preamble. "He's not in his bed, and we didn't change his dressings."

"I changed them this morning," Stanton assured her. "Everything is healing very well."

Poppy huffed and shook her head. "Where is he, Stanton?"

His mouth curved, and he pointed towards the field. "Out there with the rest of them, working on the harvest."

He was *what?*

"He can't be harvesting!" Poppy protested. "He'll tear the skin right open with all of the motion, and out here in the fields with dust and grass and who knows what else… And he'll be sweating… Stanton, what were you thinking?" She shook her head at him and picked up her skirt, practically running for the lower fields.

She might be furious with him, but that didn't mean she wanted him to spend whatever reserves he'd built up in her fields and then drop dead in them. She'd have to take care of him all over again, and she didn't know if she could manage that with the same fierceness as before.

Or with the same patience.

She paused at the head of the field, her brow furrowing at the sight that met her eyes.

The men they had hired to help with the harvest were there, working steadily, but so were Alex and each of the men that had come last night. They all looked the same in their dark trousers and plain linen shirts, and they worked in an almost perfect synchrony. Scythes moved fluidly in the fields, slicing easily through the crops, and the arms that wielded them were sure and steadfast. At this rate, they would be finished with the harvest far sooner than she'd ever expected, or than she'd ever managed before.

There was no way she could pay all of them for the work they were doing, but she'd have to find some way to make this worth their efforts.

She watched them all for a very long moment, unable to move

for the longest time.

Each of the men worked hard, and none of them complained about the tasks they were engaged in. However, none of the others worked as hard as Alex.

He moved twice as fast as the others, his strokes swifter, his efforts more aggressive. His shirt rapidly dampened despite the chill of the morning, and the material seemed to strain over his slender frame, despite the discrepancy in size. His features were just as strained, something hard and almost frantic in them. It worried Poppy to see him like this, to see some unseen force driving him into this sort of madness.

Or, in his case, some horror.

She shook her head slowly and started forward, only to have her arm caught gently.

Poppy turned to see Weaver there, a knowing look in his eye.

"Leave him be, Miss Edgewood," Weaver said, tilting his head towards Alex. "He needs this."

She scowled at the man. "He's not strong enough to be working like this."

His hold on her arm remained. "I think Trace will surprise you, ma'am."

"I don't know Trace," she said pointedly, pulling her arm out of his hold. "Apparently, I don't even know Alex, but I do know that man over there is badly injured, and not just physically, and it concerns me that no one else sees it."

"Oh, we see it, Miss Edgewood," Weaver told her, not at all concerned by her coolness toward him. "More than that, I think we understand it."

"Maybe so," she conceded, "but you're not the one who will have to tend him if he's worse after this."

Weaver folded his arms and gave her a thorough look, smiling slightly. "If he *is* worse, I will personally sit by his bedside all night and tend him like he is an ailing grandmother."

Poppy returned the look, finally softening, sensing this man cared for Alex in a way beyond simply professional. "I may take you up on that, Weaver."

He grinned briefly at that. "Do me a favor, Miss Edgewood. Call me Fritz. You're not a spy, you don't need to call me by the codename."

"Are you sure?" Poppy asked with a raised brow. "I'm not well versed in the spy etiquette, but your identity seems to be an important thing to protect."

Fritz leaned forward slightly. "Are you planning on telling anyone that I'm a spy called Weaver, but my real name is Fritz?"

That made Poppy giggle in spite of herself. "No, of course not."

He nodded once. "Then, I am sure you may call me Fritz." He looked over at Alex, and so did she.

Alex had been working hard without speaking to anyone, not even his cousin, who toiled just as silently beside him.

"I'm worried about him, Fritz," Poppy murmured as they watched. "I can't even say why. Yes, he's injured, but it's more than that. He's so changed…"

"Honestly, I'm worried, too," Fritz admitted with a frown. "Trace was one of our best. I'd never seen anything like him, and I've been doing this a long time. He always had a potent vitality about him, something that made him seem invincible. Larger than life."

"Yes," Poppy whispered, tears filling her eyes, surprising her. "It was one of the reasons I couldn't believe Alex was dead for the longest time. He just couldn't die. He couldn't."

Fritz nodded and patted Poppy's arm softly. "Exactly. I never stopped trying to find the truth, couldn't believe in my heart that he was gone… Turns out we were both right, but…"

"But how much of him is left?" Poppy finished absently.

"I thought we'd get some more information last night," Fritz sighed, sliding his hands into his pockets, "but he's more damaged than I thought, and he needs time to heal, so we spent the evening trying to brighten things up, if reminding him of what he missed can brighten things."

Poppy nodded to herself. "I did the same thing yesterday, in a way. We talked about friends and acquaintances we had in our youth, and for a few hours, it was as if my Alex was back with me. And yet…" She trailed off and looked up at Fritz for help. "How long until he is his old self?"

Fritz made an amused sound, though she sensed there was no

humor in it. "I don't believe he is going to be his old self again, Miss Edgewood. At any time. In the kindest sense, I think you need to stop looking for that."

She had been afraid of that, but she'd also known somehow that it would be the case. Alex was too changed, had endured too much, had lost too much of himself to be the man she knew.

She knew it, but she felt something crack in her heart now as she accepted it.

"Then when will he be healed?" she asked Fritz, a hitch in her voice as she asked.

Fritz shook his head and tsked. "That, I'm afraid, is a much more complicated question to answer."

"Which means?" she prodded.

He grinned. "I haven't the faintest idea." He sobered and exhaled slowly. "It will take a long time, Miss Edgewood. A very, very long time, I'm afraid."

Poppy had suspected that, too, and she looked up at him with a scowl. "Are all spies as filled with doom and gloom as you are, Fritz? Or as maddening?"

"Usually, as it happens," he quipped with another nod. "I'm actually one of the more pleasant and optimistic ones."

"Oh, good," she muttered, brushing her hands on her skirts again. "Then it will be delightful to have you all around for a bit."

"At least for the harvest, Miss Edgewood," he assured her. "We've given you more trouble than we meant, and the least we can do is help get the harvest in. And I think we're repairing your barn, mending the fence, and anything else you need."

Poppy gaped up at him. "You don't need to do that, Fritz! I have Stanton, and there are others…"

Fritz silenced her with a look. "You seem to think that you have a say in this, Miss Edgewood. And don't think for a moment that Stanton isn't putting us all through our paces."

"I was under the impression that you were the superior to all these men," Poppy said, smiling suspiciously.

"I try to tell them all that," Fritz told her, his eyes wide with exasperation, "but they seem to forget at every waking moment."

"Weaver!" Rook barked from further along the line. "Stop

conversing with Miss Edgewood! You won't get out of working the field that easily! I'll make John Barry here come show you how it's done in very great detail."

Fritz rolled his eyes and gave Poppy a look. "Exhibit A, Miss Edgewood."

Poppy giggled and stepped back. "I'll leave you to it, then. I'll go get water for everyone and see what I can do to help."

"A rag in Rook's mouth would help us all a great deal," Fritz told her with a wink, turning back to his work.

Poppy laughed again and turned away, wondering at the men that were now helping her harvest, and apparently were planning to help with other things, though they truly didn't owe her anything at all.

What were the ties that bound them all together? Spies for the Crown, and yet they were more like family than anything she'd seen, even in her own family. One of their brothers had come back from the dead, had been wounded beyond belief, and was in need, and they had come to be with him. He wanted to work in the fields, and they worked with him. He needed to heal, and they were giving him time.

But they were here.

Alex had all the support and strength in the world from them.

Would it be enough?

"Trace, come on, take a rest."

"There's more to be done."

"There will always be more to be done. You need to rest."

"I'm not used to rest. Rest makes you weak. Rest makes you slow. Rest means…"

"Alex, stop."

Alex stilled at the soft command from Cap, knowing better than to do otherwise. He hadn't been a spy in years, but it appeared that some instincts were more deeply engrained than he thought.

"I can't, Cap," Alex rasped, glancing over at his superior and friend. "I can't. *Pas de repose jusqu'à la mort.*"

"No rest until death?" Cap repeated in English. "Is that what you've been trained to say?"

"Trained to believe," Alex grunted as he went back to harvesting. "Trained to repeat. Trained to obey."

All the time. Every time. Or it was lash after lash upon his back while he worked, as if that could make him work faster, harder, or better. He hadn't rested during work for as long as he could remember.

He couldn't stop.

Couldn't.

Cap exhaled sharply. "Alex, it's over. That's all over. You have a choice now. You can choose to stop."

"I can't," Alex insisted. "I can't."

A heavy hand fell on his shoulder and gripped hard. "Then obey me now. Stop."

Alex's lungs constricted on a faint gasp, and the scythe fell from his hands, rustling the wheat beneath it. He hunched over, bracing his elbows on his knees as he panted hard, finally feeling the weakness and pain the day's activities were bringing him. Every single rib ached, his left arm seemed heavier than his right, his legs shook, and his head swam.

If he hadn't stopped, he wouldn't have known.

That was how this had always worked for him.

Cap's hand gripped harder. "Come on, Trace. We need a drink and a rest."

"Don't call me Trace," Alex begged as he straightened. "I'm not Trace. Not anymore. I'm not anything."

"Alex," Cap corrected, keeping his hand on Alex's shoulder. "Come on."

He pulled Alex away from his work, keeping his hand on his shoulder and pressing firmly against him.

That pressure was the only thing steadying Alex at the moment.

"Why are you all here?" Alex asked hoarsely, swallowing. "Why come?"

Cap gave him a bewildered look. "Are you serious? The moment we discovered you were alive, none of us could rest until we had figured out how to save you."

"No one saved me," Alex replied bitterly. "Not even…" He trailed off, shaking his head.

"We didn't know, Alex," Cap murmured. "We couldn't know."

"I know that, Cap," he hissed, his eyes burning. "I don't blame you. You thought I was dead. I should have been dead. I knew it every day I was in that hold, every time I was lashed or flayed, every time they questioned me… I knew I was dead; I just couldn't seem to die."

Cap took a deep breath and released it shakily. "Saints above, Alex…"

"There are no saints above or below," Alex muttered. "I know. I prayed to each and every one I knew."

"Alex…"

"I am grateful to have you all here," he went on. "I am. But I'll also be grateful to see the backs of you as you leave me in peace."

Cap stopped by the bucket of drinking water, taking a ladleful and drinking deeply, then offered it to Alex. "Understood."

Alex took the ladle, giving his friend a curious look. "Really? Just like that?"

"Absolutely," came the calm reply. "You've been through hell, and our being here must be a sharp reminder of how we failed you."

"You didn't fail me," Alex scoffed as he drank from the ladle. "None of you did."

Cap slowly shook his head. "You will never, ever convince a single one of us of that. That is why we are here, Alex. Not because we missed you or we needed to see you, though all of that is true. Not even because we need answers that only you can give, though that is certainly true. We are here because we failed you before. We could have saved you if we had only done more digging, tried harder, been better…"

"Stop," Alex managed, setting the ladle back into the bucket.

"So, when we got Stanton's message," Cap went on, "it was providential. We rode up at once, no question. We could not fail you again."

Alex closed his eyes and turned away. "Cap…"

"I don't know what you went through, Alex, but you're not getting rid of us forever. We're always going to be your brothers, here or in London."

"I know." Alex exhaled very slowly, then opened his eyes and turned back to face him. "What do you need to know?"

Cap's brows shot up. "At the moment? How your ribs are."

"I'm being serious, Cap," Alex said with a scowl, moving to sit on a stool against the barn wall.

"So am I. How are the ribs?" Cap asked, coming over to lean beside him.

Alex looked up at Cap wryly. "They hurt."

His mentor nodded once. "And the lash marks?"

Alex stiffened, one hand forming a fist on his knee. "How did you know about that?"

Cap glanced down at Alex, expression sardonic. "You mentioned lashing. And it's typical punishment onboard a ship. Besides, that shirt is fairly thin, so as you worked, the moisture from the sweat made the fabric nearly transparent. I saw them. Did you take off the bandages Stanton placed there this morning? I'm fairly certain he placed some, you walked much more awkwardly first thing this morning."

No one should have known that Alex removed the bandages. He'd taken great care to avoid being seen when he'd taken them off, mostly out of fear that it would be reported to Poppy. Or that Stanton would be upset and wrap him tighter, making working the fields impossible.

"You notice too much, you know that?" Alex grumbled, looking away.

"I'm a spy, remember?" Cap chuckled at his own quip, and patted Alex on the shoulder. "I'm not going to press you on details yet. There's time."

Alex snorted softly. "There's never time with things like this. You're probably strapped for information and losing footing, if not operatives, and I probably hold the key to getting a leg up on the whole Faction, right?"

"Something like that."

Leave it to Cap to not soften the blow.

Alex dropped his head with a groan. "Didn't you all find my notes and ledgers?"

"Yes," Cap said simply. "A few weeks ago."

That wasn't the answer that he'd expected, and Alex looked up at the senior operative of one of the most secret organizations devised by the Shopkeepers and heads of state in England.

"What do you mean a few weeks ago?"

"Just that," Cap replied, folding his arms. "Weaver had Rook looking into you and your investigations without telling the rest of us, thinking we were all too biased and too close to the situation to see it for what it was."

"Which was probably true," Alex interjected.

Cap smirked. "Which was absolutely true." He sobered, leaning his head back against the barn. "Rook came up here and somehow found the bench everyone else, including all of us, missed."

Alex scoffed loudly. "You didn't think I'd hide my stash in Parkerton, did you?"

Silence met his question, and Alex sat back, thumping his head against the wall. "You did, didn't you?"

"We didn't realize you'd had a particular spot," Cap admitted apologetically. "None of us could see it."

"Rook did, though." Alex shook his head slowly. "A man who didn't know me at all could find the bench." He looked up at Cap in disbelief. "What did you think I meant when I said to tend the flowers?"

Cap's high brow furrowed. "To look after Poppy Edgewood, of course."

Alex groaned and pressed the heels of his hands into his eyes. "Why the hell would I need you lot to tend Poppy? I've had measures put into place for that from the beginning. You gave her Stanton, but did you know I put John Barry here? And Thomas Burton, Amos Clayton, and Peter Melville."

"Good heavens, Alex."

"I had Poppy taken care of," Alex said firmly. "But that bench that I built myself, with the secret compartment, that has a very particular carving of a flower on it…"

Cap swore softly, cutting Alex off at once.

"Quite," Alex answered, laughing once. "That was instruction to find the information you needed."

"You know the irony here?" Cap told him, releasing a reluctant chuckle. "The only reason Rook said he found it was because he was so distracted in thinking of Helen that he thought of your feelings for

95

Poppy. Analyzing what those might have been and how they would have affected you, thinking you must have wanted to make the most of your time with her…"

"All true," Alex murmured, looking off towards the cottage with sudden pangs of longing.

"And that is how he found the bench," Cap finished with a nod. "It was less about being a spy, and more about being a man in love."

Alex sighed, nodding himself. "I've always been the latter, Cap. The former came into my life long after."

"And now?"

There was no easy way to answer that question, especially as Alex had no idea what he was or how he felt, what he should do… Nothing from his past was the same, and there was nothing he could hold on to now but the day itself.

"Now," Alex sighed, rising slowly, "I'm a poor imitation of both, and not much good for anything."

Cap gripped his shoulder again. "Not true, but I won't waste breath arguing." He eyed Alex up and down. "Are you fit enough to work the rest of the afternoon? You look done for."

Alex gave him a very thin smile. "I always look done for these days. My face doesn't know any other way to look."

Cap wasn't amused by that response. "I'm serious. I will put you back into the cottage and have Stanton stand guard. Or have Miss Edgewood do so."

"You can't order me about here, Cap," Alex told him with a scowl. "I'm not in the League now."

"I was your commanding officer before I was senior operative," Cap reminded him with all the superiority and firmness he'd ever managed. "I know you haven't forgotten that."

"I can work just fine," Alex snapped. "I've worked in a far worse condition and lived to tell the tale. Nothing makes me feel worse than being idle now."

Cap nodded and gestured for him to return to the field. "Tonight, we should talk, Alex. About everything, if you can manage."

Alex nodded once, swallowing. "Bring rum, and I'll sing like a canary. I don't need secrets anymore. Not that many remain."

Chapter Nine

$\mathcal{B}$ranbury Hall was dark and gloomy, though the year-round staff kept it up admirably. Alex hadn't ever been in it before, but it looked much the same as any other fine house a man of status would inhabit.

And Tailor had purchased it, had he? To keep an eye on Poppy? The interference of everyone into Poppy's life was astonishing. It was no wonder she was upset with the discovery. Alex couldn't manage the same effrontery, but he could at least acknowledge the truth of the matter as it stood. Poppy's life was not her own in any sense of the word.

And that was his fault.

"When did Tailor purchase the house?" Alex asked as the others pulled chairs around the large fireplace in the great room.

"Roughly four and a half years ago," Weaver said with a glance and a grin at him over a wingback chair he'd commandeered from somewhere.

Alex didn't smile back at the line. "Why?"

"Why?" Gent repeated with a laugh as he settled himself in his own chair. "Because you were dead, and we didn't know if you had been compromised and sensitive information would be seized, or if your Miss Edgewood would be in danger, or…"

"All right, all right," Alex interrupted waving him off. "It just seems excessive for one operative."

"You weren't just any operative, Alex," Gabe told him, taking the seat beside him. "And once it became clear that Poppy would need assistance and to be watched over…"

Alex shook his head slowly. "We've all gone to excesses over her, and she's as poor as a church mouse, as it is."

"Not exactly," Weaver admitted, a peculiar smile on his face.

Everyone in the room turned to look at him, only the sound of the fire meeting his odd interjection.

Sensing he had the attention of all, Weaver shrugged and rubbed at the back of his head. "Tailor's fixed it all rather nicely. Poppy has everything she needs for her lands and farm every year, but she has no idea that, despite her earnings from the farm itself, the tax she pays to her rather absent landlord only goes into a growing account for her future. Tailor has settled some amount on her, though how much I am not aware, and should anything happen to Tailor, Poppy would still be perfectly comfortable for the rest of her days."

"In a cottage," Alex pointed out, too numb to feel any sort of gratitude. "On a farm."

Weaver's dark eyes held his gaze steadily. "He could hardly bring her into his household, could he? She's made the decision to stay, she bought the cottage and farm on her own, and unless you wanted her to know all of this far earlier than yesterday, there really wasn't much else to be done."

Alex looked away, heat scalding his cheeks and the back of his neck.

Poppy could leave now, whatever her reasons for staying had been. She might wish to leave, considering the state of things. The cottage had been their imagined future, should all things fall away, a laugh they had shared knowing how her parents had felt about him before his inheritance had been assured. Now it was hers, as all things had fallen away in truth, and nothing was as it seemed. Would her pride be wounded by all that had been unearthed?

There was no telling.

The Poppy he had known in his youth had not been hard or particularly stubborn, unless her mother were involved, and had been vibrant and alive with an energy that kept her from truly belonging in the height of proper Society. The woman she was now had a tough exterior and a deep determination, no hint of airs or delicacy, and barely resembled the girl she had once been.

He needed to make up for the hardship her ties to him had

brought her and do what he could to alleviate the strain on her current financial situation, despite Tailor's intervention. He would see this harvest done, complete the repairs on the barn, the house, the lands, and anything he could do with his efforts to reduce her suffering.

He owed her no less.

What he would do after that was far less certain.

"Alex."

He looked up at Cap's surprisingly gentle tone, and found the entire group staring at him in a sort of worried expectation.

Alex nodded once, even as a frigid chill seeped into his bones. "I'll only be able to do this once, and some things I'm not discussing. It won't serve anything to go into it. Understood?"

A general murmur came up from the rest, and a glass of amber liquid was placed in his hand.

Odd that that seemed to ground him more than anything else had yet.

He'd always done his best talking when alcohol had been involved on the *Amelie Claire*. It seemed only right that now he had some.

To drink at his will, not to be forced down his throat. Or poured down when he'd given up fighting it. Or guzzling desperately while he could, knowing it would deaden the pain that would come.

This… This he could sip at leisure, warm his insides when the coldness became too much.

Or he could go numb, if it all became too much.

How long he'd wished for numbness and never found it.

"They knew who I was," Alex began, already feeling his hands shake despite the glass he held. "I didn't know it at the time, I thought my cover was intact. I'd never had a whiff of trouble before, but that night on the docks, when I led you all into the mess, I didn't know…"

"You couldn't have known, Alex," Cap insisted. "None of us did, and none of our contacts did."

Alex shook his head slowly. "I should have. I knew the Cardieu brothers had too much interest in the Faction, too many sympathies, and their professional interests were spotty at best, though business had been improving for them. There was a foreman that I had been in the process of investigating, Mainsley…"

Rook cleared his throat and sat forward. "He is the key player there, I'm sure of it. He had men come after me, and no one who had ties to you ought to have known me."

Alex groaned and rubbed his free hand over his face. "Lord, Rook…"

"If an apology is about to come out of your mouth, you'd best swallow that," Rook said at once with a harsh tone. "I need none, and you've got better things to fill your mind with. Move on."

It occurred to Alex to thank him for that, but the fleeting gratitude died where it grew, and he only nodded.

"I was stabbed in the stomach that night," Alex continued, hardly recognizing his own voice. "Thought I would die on the deck of that bloody ship, the *Jemima*. Turns out, that was the best time on a ship I'd have in four and a half years." His words caught in his throat, and he shook his head. "I was moved to a sister ship, the *Georgina*, for safekeeping. I'd lost so much blood from the wound, I was unconscious for a full day, at least. But they meticulously tended and nursed me back to health, and the *Jemima* was burned from keel to stern and sunk to avoid suspicion. When I was fit to be transported, I was transferred to the *Amelie Claire* and Captain Laurent Battier, the one they call *La Belette*. Smuggler. No loyalty to anyone except the one who paid the most. And the Faction paid him a great deal at regular intervals."

"That would explain why the *Jemima* seemed to vanish," Gent murmured, nodding in thought. "We searched for it for months."

"Never came across the name Battier though," Gabe grunted in irritation. "Odd that such a smuggler would be unknown to us."

Alex shook his head slowly. "You're forgetting the Cardieus. They protected Battier because he was of use to their business and interests. Considering he is funded by the Faction on one side and them on the other, he is powerful enough to be relatively undetected by official means. Ask any smuggler about *La Belette*, however…"

"I've heard that name," Gabe broke in, sounding hopeful.

"As have I," Rook added with a nod. "No one could tell me anything about *La Belette*, other than he was cunning, but never any details."

Alex swallowed and lifted his glass to his mouth, sipping slowly, finding the equally slow burn against his throat comforting.

"You said they knew who you were," Weaver said, looking at Alex intently. "Did Battier?"

A slow ripple of distaste washed over him, and he nodded once. "He did. He and Acosta and Janssen, and a handful of others at most. They called me Trace in interrogation, or *Le Trace* if they were feeling particularly mocking."

No one said anything for a moment, the logs in the fireplace crackling ominously.

"Interrogated," Gabe repeated in a low tone.

Alex nodded once. "Often. Regularly. And at times brutally. Their knowledge was very accurate, and the questions they asked were very particular. At first, it was easy to resist, we've been trained for that, and they didn't stray into extremes. Then suddenly, they did. The sessions became more and more difficult to withstand, the tactics more and more agonizing. I had no idea a body could endure so much, and the effect it has on the mind…" He raised his glass again, though it shook tremulously. "I could barely recall one day from the next, let alone who I was. But somehow I knew enough to avoid telling them what they wanted to know."

Rook whistled low and drew Alex's attention, Rook's eyes were wide in the light of the fire. "You didn't tell them anything? At all?"

"Impossible," Cap breathed. "Surely they'd have killed you if you'd resisted entirely."

"They would have, undoubtedly," Alex told them, "but they found me useful. When I inevitably reached my wit's end, I'd give them something, and they would leave me alone until they'd passed it on and seen it through."

The others looked at each other, then back to him, each of them with furrowed brow. "What do you mean by 'give them something,' Alex?" Cap asked slowly.

Alex smiled grimly. "I gave them information. Old information, already completed missions, retired operatives, and the like. Combined details of past tasks into a grander-sounding scheme… It became a game for me, though I doubt they found it amusing when everything I gave them proved outdated."

Gabe swore softly beside him. "It's astonishing that they didn't kill you after your first betrayal there."

He shrugged in response. "It took months to get that sort of information validated, and it was true enough to ensure that I was useful, and how could I be blamed for a mission already completed if I was on their ship? I gave them just enough to ensure I would be kept alive, but not enough to have me be labeled a traitor." He looked over at Weaver with a faint smile. "You may want to inform the old Hawks company that they shouldn't regroup for another round."

Weaver chuckled and gave him a casual salute. "I shall pass that along, thank you."

"Where were you kept, Alex?" Rook murmured, ignoring the faint humor. "I've been on board many ships of late, and I don't see…"

"The hold," Alex overrode darkly. "Basically, in a box created for me. Either bound in the corner or hanging from chains. I was tended carefully by the ship's surgeon, and my every injury was seen to as though I were a valued officer on board. When he approved, which was far sooner than any other physician would have, I was fit to return to my duties."

Gent sat back slowly, making a soft sound of acknowledgement. "As a crew member."

Alex nodded, shrugging one shoulder. "Less than any other, apart from the other prisoners that occasionally came and went. No one else knew me as Trace, but they all gleefully took up the new name I had been given. *Torchon*."

"Dishcloth?" Cap translated with a raised brow. "Lovely."

"Rather apt, too." Alex swallowed and shuddered in memory. "They knew how to wring me out, scrub me raw, and put me to use however they saw fit." He cleared his throat and looked up at each of them in turn. "I never betrayed the League in any way. I gave them no names. Not one."

Gabe grunted, leaning forward. "We never suspected you would."

"And wouldn't have blamed you if you had," Gent murmured softly.

Heads bobbed all about the room.

They could say grand and noble things such as that, but if Alex had given any of them up, if he had betrayed this brotherhood or any of the other offices with covert operatives, their stories would have changed a great deal.

What ate away at him now was the fact that he didn't know why he hadn't given in at the end. Why he hadn't given them a real name that might have allowed Battier and the Faction some real progress. Why had he stayed resolutely silent on the subject of his colleagues and their tasks, their missions, their history? It hadn't been out of loyalty, he was sure, for he'd forgotten anything so honorable had ever existed in him.

Habit was all he could claim. Habit and training.

And neither of those were a particularly noble reason.

"I was bound," Alex rushed on, clearing his throat, "every time we came into port. Acosta would string me up, so I was suspended in the hold if he was the one confining me. Janssen was more lenient and would only bind me to the wall. Battier would lash me for good measure before he left, but he didn't care how I was confined, so long as I was. Before last week, I hadn't touched land since that night on the docks."

He trailed off, lost in the memories of his time on the ship, of the other day when he'd realized he was on land once more… Such a simple pleasure, being on land, but the joy it had sent through his system had been potent indeed.

He still felt as though he didn't quite have his footing, but the joy had receded into only the very furthest corners of his mind. Other emotions had pressed their way into the forefront and were currently reigning supreme.

Guilt, for one, and uncertainty for another.

"Alex," Cap said suddenly, turning slightly in his chair to face Alex clearly, "you never said a word to us about your investigations, and we never questioned because your information was impeccable. But after all of this… Who was your contact in the smuggling world? And why couldn't they do something for you, or give us an indication you were alive?"

"Jackal," Alex told him, sipping his beverage.

Cap swore softly under his breath, as did a few others. "Really?"

Alex nodded as he swallowed. "Yes."

"I had no idea he was still in the game," Weaver murmured, wide-eyed.

Somehow, that was more amusing than anything else. Weaver, who was one of the Shopkeepers and thus one of the most powerful men in England, did not know everything relating to the covert world.

"Oh, he is," Alex assured them all. "Very much so. And as for doing something for me... How would he know where I was? It wasn't as though Battier spread the word that he had me. I was only another slave on board the ship. Besides, I only saw Jackal once while aboard the *Amelie Claire*, and it was only recently. He was examining crewmembers and slaves for the taking, and when he saw me... Well, I knew he knew me, but he kept his cover perfectly, and was just as derogatory as anyone else. It wouldn't surprise me if he were the one to confirm that I was alive."

"Or maybe to get you off the boat?" Rook pressed.

Alex smirked just a little. "When I consider the timing, gentlemen, I think, perhaps, he did."

Poppy woke with a jolt, her heart racing in her chest, a startled cry on her lips. It never reached her ears, which had to be a small mercy of sorts.

She looked around the darkened room, only the light of the moon streaming through her partially closed curtains. Grateful, she saw that whatever had woken her was not in the room with her. Still trembling, she pressed her hands to her face, then slid them back to grip her plaited hair. It wasn't often that her sleep was disrupted anymore, despite having trouble enough in her finer days, but everything had changed now.

Everything.

A low, harsh groan met her ears, and she slowly turned towards the sound.

The wall held no answers, but beyond that wall...

Another growling sound came from it, followed by a series of short, unintelligible cries as though pain were being inflicted.

Poppy was out of her bed in an instant, grabbing a thick shawl and wrapping it around her as she opened the door to her room and headed towards the spare room. She gripped the handle tightly in her hand, closing her eyes just as tightly, but still she hesitated.

Alex practically roared within, and she imagined his body arching off the bed as it had in his illness, every muscle straining against some imagined or unseen bonds.

It was utter agony to hear him, but it had to be sheer anguish to feel. She had no comfort to give for demons she did not understand. But to hear him like this…

She moaned faintly as another cry reached her, and she laid her brow against the door, exhaling softly. It would not do him any good for her to stand here and listen, and she could not go in to help him. He would hate to know that she had heard his cries, that she had witnessed his distress, that she might have some inkling of what he suffered, and she could not let his time here be more wretched than it already would be.

Poppy pushed off the door and turned towards the kitchen, then thought better of sitting at the table and waiting for Alex's nightmare to end.

She unlatched the front door, heading out into the cool night air. She inhaled deeply, the faintest hint of the glorious scent of harvest still lingering on the air. There was nothing so refreshing as that smell, she had discovered, though her mother and sisters would have disagreed emphatically. It spoke of sun and hard work and health, of a natural goodness, and a fresh earthiness that satisfied the soul.

They'd cleared the entire lower field, and most of the upper as well, so they would easily finish by week's end. It would be the fastest she had ever harvested, and the crop this year was destined to be one of her best.

But then what? A good harvest quickly done, a fair price for it, and help that she hadn't asked for… And then she would occupy herself with the rest of the village concerns? Stocking up enough for winter, praying the repairs were enough to hold, and keeping herself away from the gossip yet again?

Her life had become a series of monotonous tasks, a sequence of motions to give the impression that all was well in hand. It wasn't well in hand. It was careening out of control, a maddening cycle that was rapidly spiraling beyond the careful constraints she'd grown accustomed to.

All because Alex wasn't dead and had come back into her life. She hadn't even taken the time to properly comprehend that fact.

Alex, who had been her everything.

Alex, whose smile had brightened every corner of her heart.

Alex, who had promised her so much. Had given so much.

He was alive, and he was *here*.

An unexpected sob escaped her, and she covered her mouth quickly, her eyes filling with tears. Alex was alive, and all the pain she had felt being parted from him all this time suddenly filled her soul again. She'd grown so used to mourning him, missing him, that there hadn't been room for much else, and now…

Now…

Her hand fell to her chest, and she looked up at the stars, endless in their majesty and vast in number. She had cried so many nights under such skies, remembering the more romantic times she and Alex had spent under the stars, making wishes and dreams, plotting their own constellations…

She missed Alex fiercely with only such stars for company.

Looking up at them now, she found herself missing him again, only for entirely different reasons. She was so changed. *He* was so changed, and she missed who they had once been. But perhaps the changes were enough that…

Well, she couldn't think about that now. It was too soon, the wounds were too fresh, and she was too confused to consider much beyond the day at hand.

She inhaled and exhaled slowly, until she had control and was calm once more, then she shivered and turned back into the house, taking great care to latch the door again as silently as possible.

Turning to return to her room, Poppy stopped in her tracks.

Alex stood before the fire, his back to her, hands balled into fists at his sides. He wore no nightshirt and his feet were bare, and the trousers he wore were the ones from his arrival, the fabric of each leg nearly shredded as they hung against his calves.

The limited light from the fire cast his back into stark shadows, each mark somehow seeming worse than they had been before. There was no pattern to them, each line crossing several others, some deeper marks no longer defined, creating ridges and valleys along his lean yet defined musculature that ought not to be there. His arms bore scars as well, much fainter and less easily traced, and along several ribs there seemed to be an odd line as if to trace the bone itself.

Strange how she should notice so much about a back she had so recently tended. She'd only seen the fresh marks then. A lump rose in her throat, and she took two steps forward, knowing he would have heard the door.

"I didn't hear you come in tonight," she murmured.

He glanced back at her slightly, though did not turn towards her. "I didn't know you still slept poorly."

Poppy smiled very faintly. "I do occasionally. Working on a farm doesn't lend itself to sleeping poorly. Most of the time, I have no trouble. Some nights, though, the old habit returns, and…."

"That I remember." He returned his attention to the flames once more. "I don't mean to disturb you. Or to keep you."

"You aren't," Poppy replied. "I'm still not as fatigued as I ought to be."

"Nor I."

She took another step. "Are you sure? You worked so hard today, and you're not used to…"

"I'm used to it," he interrupted, his voice more of a growl. "Believe me, I'm used to far worse."

Poppy swallowed hard and folded her shawl across her tightly. "I was afraid of that."

He stiffened, his hands clenching harder, trembling slightly in their aggression.

"The marks look like they are healing well," she told him, coming closer still. "I'm surprised none of them opened with your exertions today."

Alex nodded once. "No doubt due to your capable ministrations."

She chuckled a little. "That, or your impeccable ability to heal. Everything looks clean and seems to be healing perfectly. It's extraordinary, really."

He said nothing to that, his hands still clenched.

"Alex," she murmured as gently as she could, "what happened?"

A sharp intake of breath made her wince, but she remained where she was, just as she was.

"I can see the marks, Alex," she went on. "And I know there are more I haven't seen. I see how lean you are compared to what you were. If you weren't clearly so very strong, the look of you would terrify me to the core."

"Poppy…"

The strain in his voice was clear, and she ached at its tone. "Alex, please."

His head lowered, and she watched as a shudder rippled down his sinewy spine. "I can't."

"Alex."

His head shook slowly from side to side. "I can't, Poppy."

Poppy ground her teeth together. "Can't?" she snapped. "Or won't?"

Alex inhaled slowly, then exhaled the same. "Good night, Poppy."

The old Poppy would have stayed firm, would have battered him into confessing, would have teased and pressed and situated herself at the kitchen table until he relented and gave her what she wanted.

This Poppy did not want to put forth the effort. She wasn't sure it would be worth it.

"Good night, Alex," she muttered, marching past him and returning to her bedchamber, though sleep did not come again for quite some time.

Chapter Ten

"*I* can't do it. I just cannot do it."

"Oh, come now, Rook. You've been through worse."

"I'm not entirely certain I have."

"I doubt that very much."

"No, it's true. I cannot eat one more bite of this abysmal excuse for a meal."

Poppy raised a brow at the handsome, smiling man whose dramatic remarks had been going on for some time now.

"If you don't like it, Rook, I invite you to do something productive for the first time since you've been here. You cook instead of me. I'll take your place mending the fence, and get it done in half the time you would."

The men around her laughed uproariously, while Rook looked delighted, inclining his head in deference.

Even Alex laughed, eyeing them both with amusement. He loved that she was bantering with his friends, that she was not intimidated by them or ashamed of her situation, and that she could give as good as she got. The men would never have been so free with provocation or cynicism had they not had encouragement from her, but now that they had it, there was no restraint at all.

He'd smiled so much in the past two days that it was startling. There was no hint of the man plagued by nightmares she'd seen standing in front of the fireplace, and only this lighter, almost robust version remained. Yet every night, she heard his nightmares rage, and every night, she listened without entering, letting his demons work upon him in private.

There were only traces of them by morning light, but he never spoke of it, and once he was with these friends again, the traces were nearly invisible.

Nearly.

"I'd rather not eat anything Rook makes, Poppy," Alex's cousin Gabe said with a wince. "It would be all too inedible."

Poppy shrugged, smiling a little at the supposedly acerbic man. "He finds my cooking inedible, so it seems there would be no change there."

"Do you see anyone else complaining?" Gabe asked, giving her a dubious look.

"No, but neither do I see you eating," she pointed out, bringing more laughter from the group. She sighed heavily and wrapped her arms around her knees, shaking her head. "I suppose I shall have to take the money I was planning to pay my workers and take on Mrs. Burgh for a cook whilst you all are here."

"That's not necessary," Alex said at once, sobering.

"No, really," Fritz added, his face contorted with worry. "Please don't…"

Stanton coughed loudly. "Please do. You'll all leave, I remain, and you don't know what I've suffered."

Poppy screeched in mock outrage, picked up an apple, and chucked it at him hard. He caught it easily and smirked, taking a large bite out of it.

"I thought I'd perish all the sooner for enduring my recent meals," Alex offered, wrinkling up his nose.

"You, sir, are barely beyond broth," Poppy pointed out.

"Indeed," he replied, giving her a derisive look, "which makes one wonder…"

Fritz hooted a laugh. "Tread carefully, Alex. I would put money on Poppy here."

Alex didn't even glance at Fritz, but kept his gaze on Poppy. "It would be a draw."

"Doubtful," Gabe offered, making a face.

"We've fought before," Poppy informed the rest, "and it was a draw."

"Oh, you took pity on him?" Gent made a sympathetic noise.

"Very kind of you."

Poppy inclined her head, smiling a little. "I'll bring in Mrs. Burgh, if only to save myself the pain of your noise, sirs."

"I'd happily test out her cooking for the group," Rook offered with a raise of his hand. "We couldn't possibly let everyone be subjected to the food prepared by unknown hands. Surely, one must sacrifice himself for the good of the others."

"Very noble," Poppy told him with a snort. She looked around at the others. "Is he always like this?"

They all answered as one in the affirmative, and Rook only shrugged in response, giving her a sheepish smile.

Poppy shook her head slowly. "It's a wonder your wife tolerates you at all."

"He's not had her long enough to know what she tolerates," Gabe muttered, finally showing the sardonic nature everyone said he had.

"I tried to talk her out of marrying him," Gent pointed out, taking a bite of bread. "She's unfortunately quite taken with him."

"Poor girl," at least three of them said at the same time.

Rook squawked in protest, but Poppy laughed along with the rest, tossing her head back, and breathing deeply.

It had been so long since she had associated with other people like this. People who laughed freely without fear of judgment, who sat and enjoyed a luncheon on the grass without having critical work to return to.

She could have been wrong, it had been so long, but this felt a bit like friendship.

Or something like it.

"I happen to rather like Miss Edgewood's meal," Cap offered as he reached into the basket for another bit of cheese.

Poppy beamed at him. "And for that, Cap, you will have two baked apples tonight, if you will all deign to come to the cottage."

Fritz chuckled and tipped his cap back a bit. "We were going to invite you to Branbury tonight, Poppy."

"Well, I don't see why we can't do both," Stanton suggested with a wry grin. "Branbury for the meal, then the cottage for apples and mead?"

"Mead?" Poppy laughed as she looked at him. "Who said anything about mead?"

"I'd be in favor of mead," Rook announced.

Poppy sighed heavily and looked over at Alex. "And when are they leaving again?"

"Not soon enough," he replied as he looked up at the clouds, smiling despite his serious tone.

"Well, if you'd make up your mind about coming back to London," Gent teased with a crooked grin, "we'd all get out of Miss Edgewood's hair that much sooner."

"Gent," Cap said sharply just as Alex's face turned a shade of grey.

Silence reigned over the group for an awkwardly long moment, Alex unable to meet the gaze of any, though most of the men stared at him.

It was then that realization dawned on Poppy. They expected, or had requested, that he take up his position amongst them in London. Return to the life of a spy. Alex, it seemed, had given no answer.

With all that he had suffered and endured, they expected him to return to the life that had brought him to it? They could not know how he screamed in the night, or the depths of his wounds, the scars that he bore, or the shadows he lived with. If he ever returned to that life, and she freely admitted that she knew nothing of it, they could not expect that he would do so any time soon.

Alex suddenly looked small, frail, and weak under such a burden, and no one was doing anything to relieve him of it.

Poppy got to her feet, wiping off her hands, and then held one out to him. "Alex, come walk with me."

He looked up at her slowly, almost fearfully, nearly childlike in his manner.

Smiling as gently as she could, she extended her hand out further still, adding a firm, "Walk with me."

He took her hand and let her help him up, averting his eyes from her and the others as they moved away, passing the barn and the cottage, and letting his hand fall from hers once they found the nearly invisible footpath.

Poppy plucked a small blossom from a flowering bush and

fiddled with it absently, content to wait for Alex to speak, if he chose to talk at all.

Walking a country lane with him would be just as comforting without conversation, especially if doing so could save him the torment of expectation from his closest friends.

"They want me to come back," Alex said after a long moment.

Poppy glanced up at him. "To spying?"

He nodded once.

"Surely not so soon," Poppy protested, her brow furrowing.

"No, not yet," he assured her, his eyes fixed on the horizon. "When I'm well and… whole." He snorted softly. "But they want an answer soon. They want me to take that life back."

There was a hard edge to his voice that Poppy wasn't sure she cared for and didn't think she understood. "I see."

He exhaled roughly. "Back to secrets and danger and adventure. Back to subversion and subtlety and subterfuge. Back to recklessness and risking everything and…"

Poppy smiled sadly as he trailed off. "What do *you* want, Alex?"

He stopped short and looked confused.

"What do I want?" he repeated. "What do I want?"

"Yes." She took his arm and steered him off the path towards a small hill just above a creek. "What do you want?"

Alex's brow wrinkled in thought as he stood on top of the hill. "Quiet. Peace. Freedom."

She smiled and sat down, patting the grass beside her.

"And being a spy doesn't allow that?"

He sank down on the ground beside her, his posture as burdened as his manner.

"I don't know. Once, I found freedom in it. Exhilaration. Purpose. But now…"

"All is changed?" Poppy finished his sentence as she reached out and covered his hand with hers.

He nodded, swallowing repeatedly. "All is changed. Four and a half years trapped in the hold of a ship is what my life as a spy brought me, no matter the good I did before. No matter how many lives I may have saved or plots I may have prevented, no matter how it thrilled me once before…"

"Alex…"

"I don't know," he whispered, closing his eyes and tilting his head back in the noonday sun. "It's as if I can't remember that life. I can't remember who I was or how I managed it all. Every time I think of Trace, all I can remember is that hold, and knowing that there would never be anything else as long as I lived."

Suddenly, Alex shuddered and lowered his head, blinking hard as if to erase something from his sight, then pressed his hands against his eyes and leaned forward.

Poppy shook her head and gripped his arm, pulling him towards her with a tug.

He surprised her by almost falling towards her, and she cradled him against her. His body shook faintly, the tremors vibrating into her frame with more effect than it seemed to have on him. There was nothing to do but hold him, rub his arms gently, and murmur the vague sorts of nothings that the one in need never truly hears.

"Tell me, Alex," she whispered. "You can tell me."

But he only shuddered and closed his eyes tightly in her hold.

"I take back everything I ever said about your ability to cook, bake, mix, blend, or roast anything at all, Poppy. On my honor."

Alex smirked as Poppy raised a brow at Rook and chuckled at the snort he heard from her.

"The only reason you'd do that, Rook, is to get a second baked apple," Poppy scolded, folding her arms over the apron she'd donned over what she'd called her best calico.

She looked like a farmer's wife thus, all warmth and friendliness, and generous despite having nothing to share. Her color was high, and her hair sensibly pulled back, though slightly disarrayed now, her apron stained with the general mess a kitchen brings. He'd never have thought it before with how long he'd known her, and all the times he'd seen her in her finery, but this look suited her rather well.

She tossed a grin at Gent after he'd made some comment about Rook that Alex had missed, and he was struck by the brilliance of that smile.

It might not have dazzled anyone the way it could have in a ballroom under the glittering influence of candles and jewels, but there was something enchanting about such a smile in such a setting. Something amazing, and there was raw delight in being so surprised.

Dinner at Branbury had been an evening to remember, though he could not honestly say that he recalled any particular topic of conversation. He and Stanton had escorted Poppy up to the house, and she'd seemed somehow delighted by an opportunity to wear something fresh and to feel more a fine lady than she had in some time, though there had been nothing fine or fancy about her. Nor had her company been anything of significance, though if she knew the station of some of their companions, she might have had some reservations.

On the other hand, she might have only been emboldened more by it.

After all, he himself was a lord, and she had never bitten her tongue in his presence.

He did recall that she'd wanted to explore as much of Branbury as she could, seeing as she was a tenant of the estate, and she was completely unashamed to ask questions about Lord Cartwright, now she knew that he had ties to the rest of them.

The life of a covert operative was one of half-truths and diversionary tactics, and they had employed both equally on that subject. Lord Cartwright had ties to the government, everybody knew that, though he was wildly considered a boring old man whose time of influence had passed. The greatest scheme of all time had to be the fact that he was, in fact, the most important man in England, apart from the King and prime minister, and at times, even they were not so crucial to the security of England as he.

But no, the truth about Tailor would remain a secret each of them would take to their graves.

If Poppy were put off by their clear reticence to discuss him in earnest, she hid it well. She'd praised the décor, admired the scope of the house, and approved of the sensible furnishings, which she claimed spoke well of the man who owned it. Or, she added with a knowing look, of his wife.

None of them would argue that point.

The meal itself had been decent enough, though hardly a fine one, not that any of them had cared overly much. It was a refreshing change to be properly dressed, he in clothing he'd borrowed from his cousin, and to be reminded, even faintly, of how they all had once lived.

And yet there had been relief in returning to the cottage and sitting easily around Poppy's well-worn table while they feasted on baked apples.

Relief, comfort, and the strangest sense of home. How had he come so far?

"Well, I think we'd best return to Branbury before we are all dozing contentedly around Poppy's table," Fritz said as he rose with a groan. "You all know how Rook gets when he's had too much to drink."

"Hard to tell," Gent said with a tilt of his head. "Most of the time I suspect he's inebriated, so when he truly is, there's not much change."

Stanton chortled and rapped his knuckles on the table. "Surely with this rather soft brewed mead, he'll not be too overcome."

"Alex can't hold his liquor," Gabe pointed out, "so we had best check with his status presently to know Rook's."

Alex rolled his eyes and waved his cousin off. "I've always been able to out-drink you, cousin, and under the table at that."

Gent made a face and rose swiftly. "And Rogue drinks that horrid stuff from Prussia that takes one's breath away. Strong boast, Alex…"

"Alex has always only boasted what he is able," Poppy pointed out with a sly smile, her eyes on him. "Apart from racing with me."

The others made loud cries of approval, while Alex coughed in mock effrontery.

"What?" he demanded, laying his hand flat against the table. "Have you forgotten how many times I trounced you solidly in a footrace?"

"You trounced a young lady of quality?" Gabe shook his head in disapproval, moaning softly. "Alex, that is most unseemly, and downright rude."

Rook nudged Gabe hard. "Those mean the same thing," he

whispered loudly.

Gabe nodded at that. "It bears repeating in multiple ways for emphasis where Poppy is concerned."

Alex looked at his cousin with suspicion, as did everyone else. "That's not like you. Why are you being polite?"

"Because I have great sympathy for Miss Edgewood," Gabe informed him, and the others, who scoffed loudly.

"Really?" Poppy giggled.

Gabe inclined his head with great respect. "Really, Miss Edgewood. You were attached to my cousin at one time. You have my sympathies."

Laughter filled the room, and Alex threw a soft chunk of apple at his cousin, who caught it easily with his mouth, bringing a round of applause from all.

"Now I know it's time to depart," Fritz muttered, smiling wryly. "Up, boys, and make your farewells to our esteemed hostess."

"Oh, lord," Poppy laughed as she removed her apron and folded it. "That makes me sound rather grand for a woman who does her own hemming."

Rook stepped forward and bowed deeply. "And a very fine hem it is, too, Poppy."

Cap surprised them all by cuffing Rook on the back of the head once he straightened, and Poppy covered her mouth as she snorted a laugh.

They all bid her goodnight, and obediently traipsed out of the cottage, nodding at Alex and smiling their amusement.

Well, if he'd ever been hoping for approval from his colleagues and friends on the woman he'd loved, he had it now. She'd won them over so handily and completely that he felt that he was the outsider instead of she.

But that was Poppy's way, and always had been. She held power over everyone that came into her sphere.

She'd always had power over him.

Once they heard the door latch, Poppy exhaled loudly and dropped herself onto her stool by the fire. "I am very fond of them, Alex, but I am so tired, I'm strangely glad to see the backs of them."

He shrugged, propping his legs up on a chair. "Not so strange,

I'm glad to see the backs of them, too. It's a common enough emotion where they are concerned."

She grinned at him, giggling softly, then craned her neck from side to side. "It was good to dine somewhere other than here, though. And I never imagined Branbury to be so reserved a place. From the outside, it looks like any other grand house, but within…"

"You'll find Lord Cartwright enjoys defying expectation," Alex told her when she trailed off. "Even if it's not in the direction one thinks it will be."

Poppy looked at the fire, her smile turning soft. "I've met Lord Cartwright, as it happens. I didn't think I would, knowing he is a man of government in London, but he comes every spring and sees all of his tenants personally. He seems a very trusting, capable man, and one with sense and taste. I like him immensely, not the least because he isn't at all domineering and leaves me alone here."

Alex smiled to himself. "Yes, he tends to do that."

"He certainly does," Stanton added, snorting softly and shaking his head.

Poppy turned to look at each of them, scowling playfully.

"I refuse to be included in conversation that I alone do not fully comprehend, you two. You both apparently know him better than I, but I'm asking no questions. Speak of Lord Cartwright the man, not the spy, or find a new topic."

Stanton stared at her, then turned to Alex. "She's very direct."

"Always was," Alex told him. "It's one of the greatest and most maddening things about her."

"And I refuse to be excluded from conversation when I am sitting within earshot of it!" Poppy laughed, clasping her hands before her.

"Then I'd best be about settling the animals for the night and myself as well, or I'll say something that may injure me permanently," Stanton said, heaving himself up and out of the chair. He nodded at Poppy, smiling fondly, then nodded at Alex with a smirk before leaving the cottage, the latch echoing almost ominously.

The sounds of the fire crackled a warm, familiar sound, and Alex smiled at the comfort he found in it.

"You worked hard today," Poppy murmured from her place by

the fire. "Are you exhausted?"

"As a matter of fact, yes," Alex told her, laughing a little. "But not from any injury. More from weakness, I think. And the laughter of the day did me good."

Poppy smiled fondly, rubbing her hands together a little. "I hoped it would. You need to laugh more, Alex. You need to smile and feel warmth. I think that might help you heal."

His smile faded slightly, but he nodded in thought. "It just might."

"Alex..." she began hesitantly, and he knew where her query was headed.

"No, Poppy," he said with a hint of bite to his tone. "No."

She sighed heavily, her brow wrinkling in distress. "How can I help you if I don't know?"

"You don't need to know," he grunted, averting his eyes. "And you don't need to help. I'll manage."

She said nothing in response, but he could feel the tension from her more than the warmth of the fire. There wasn't anything he could do about that. He could not discuss the darkness with her. He could not bring her into it.

He would not.

Alex cleared his throat and shifted in his seat. "You're going to lose most of your workmen tomorrow."

"Am I?" she asked, sounding only mildly concerned. "Why?"

"They return to London," he said simply. "We've made good progress on the harvest, finished most of the repairs, and they have things to see to in London that are relatively urgent."

Poppy's lips pursed slightly. "And you?"

One side of his mouth lifted in a smile. "I remain. I told Cap no."

Her brows shot up. "You did? You're not going back to being a spy?"

Alex slowly shook his head, feeling the ease with which he breathed since giving Cap his answer.

"Alex!" Poppy sat forward with some urgency. "What did he say?"

"He asked me to reconsider," Alex reflected, his eyes unfocusing momentarily. "Said he understood, would give me some time, but asked me to reconsider."

"And will you?"

He shrugged one shoulder. "I don't know. I imagine I'll toss it over and over in my mind for the next few days, see if my mind and heart will change, and perhaps find myself longing for that life once more. But for now..." He looked up at her and smiled, his heart suddenly warming within him. "For now, I'll just stay here and take a little more time to heal. With you."

Poppy's lips parted in surprise, and then relaxed into a gentle, delighted smile.

Chapter Eleven

Alex was staying.

Why that was important confused and bewildered her. There was no way he could possibly return to the life he had once had in the spy world. He needed to heal a great deal still, and everybody knew that. Apparently, even Cap had known that, insisting that Alex not commence with their work until he was well and whole, but the expectation had still been there.

But they were gone now, and Alex remained.

Indefinitely.

Poppy's cheeks suddenly flushed, and she had to press a cool hand to them, scolding herself for being absolutely ridiculous and rather silly.

There was no reason for her to be so delighted or to get so excited about the idea. Alex was her responsibility until he was strong enough and well enough to fend for himself, and they were old friends. He was slowly returning to life and activity by working her farm, apparently in exchange for the room and board, which made him a hired hand of sorts.

Nothing remotely resembling their former attachment had been mentioned or experienced, and she was not about to bring it up.

"Miss Edgewood!"

Poppy groaned to herself, then turned with a polite smile to see the approaching figure of Mrs. Blaine, the most doddering busybody in Moulton or anywhere else. If the determined expression on the scrawny woman's face was anything to go by, Poppy would be in for it now.

"Miss Edgewood," Mrs. Blaine said again, smiling tersely as she reached her.

"Good morning, Mrs. Blaine," Poppy greeted, looping her basket over one arm. "It's lovely to see you."

Mrs. Blaine waved her spindly fingers dismissively. "Enough with the pleasantries. Miss Edgewood, Mrs. Kennard's maid, Sara, told my maid, Jessie, that Eddie Hall saw men in your fields two days past. Far more than your usual two or three."

Poppy kept her expression as mild and unaffected as she could, though a laugh threatened to well up. "Indeed, Mrs. Blaine? And what were these men doing?"

Mrs. Blaine's eyes widened meaningfully. "Harvesting, Miss Edgewood."

"Well, it is that time of the year," Poppy allowed, feigning ignorance. "Perhaps Stanton hired more than usual this time."

"But Miss Edgewood," Mrs. Blaine continued, leaning forward, "can you afford so many workers? With your limited finances, it will be quite a strain, I fear. And you, not having a fresh dress in so long, dear…"

Poppy forced a bare imitation of a polite smile at the busybody's remarks.

"We will make do, Mrs. Blaine, as we have always done. We must have a good harvest to improve matters, and the additional men we had will aid in that."

"I hope so, Miss Edgewood, for your sake." Mrs. Blaine tutted and reached out to pat Poppy's arm, though it felt more like slapping. Her eyes suddenly narrowed on Poppy's cheeks. "You look flushed, Miss Edgewood. Are you quite well?"

"Indeed," Poppy replied quickly, "just the exertion of the day. So much to do and not much time, you know. I must return to the farm and take care of matters, and in my haste, I tend to flush."

That did not seem to appease Mrs. Blaine, and she hummed absently.

"Not healthy, my dear. What is so urgent about…?" She paused to peer into the basket. "Bread, produce, linen, and something wrapped from the butcher? And quite a bit more of it than you are used to procuring, is it not?"

What wanted desperately to be a shriek became a low hum of would-be amusement, and Poppy's smile became more strained than ever.

"I thought I might cook for the workers today, Mrs. Blaine. A show of appreciation and gratitude."

"Rather generous for a woman who cannot afford to feed herself most of the time," Mrs. Blaine responded with a sniff, looking suspicious, "but I'll not naysay your Christian tendencies towards your fellow man."

"Thank you," Poppy muttered dryly. "If you'll excuse me, Mrs. Blaine, I'll go indulge in those tendencies in the hopes that I might improve myself in the meantime."

Mrs. Blaine hummed, but turned away and hurried back down the lane, no doubt anxiously seeking someone else to investigate.

A rough exhale escaped Poppy, and she sputtered noisily like a horse, turning on her heel to stride out of Moulton as quickly as possible. The village had never truly suited her with its meddlesome inhabitants and attempts at bustling, though it was too small to be anything except cluttered. The high and mighty were aplenty here, even though their influence extended only so far as the town boundaries.

For some reason, they'd always had a keen interest in this fallen daughter of a respectable family.

She'd always treated them well regardless of their interest, hiding her spite so well it could never be detected in her replies, but she raged about them once safely away and able to walk, skip, or run her way home.

There wasn't anything to be done about it, but it felt good to rage privately.

Poppy inhaled and exhaled calming breaths through her nose, glancing at Mrs. Brown's cottage as she passed. The friendly woman was nowhere to be seen, which was a pity. She'd always taken care of Poppy despite what others had said, and a good cup of tea in her kitchen could soothe a world of pain.

She wouldn't have stopped today, but it might have helped to see a smiling face and wave.

Beyond Mrs. Brown's, she was safer to express her irritation appropriately, and she did so, gritting her teeth and screeching up at the sky. She exhaled a rough pant of air and removed her bonnet, shaking her head moodily.

It hadn't been pleasant living in Moulton all this time, but sometimes she really felt the pains of it more than others. Couldn't anybody see that she was doing the best she could? Wouldn't anyone praise her for adjusting from the daughter of a respectable family to a capable and mildly successful farmer?

Would they always see only her downfall when they saw her?

"Damn this place," Poppy hissed, swiping her bonnet across the side of her leg.

"That bad?"

She jumped with a small yelp, eyes wide, and turned to see Alex there. Somehow, he'd managed to sneak up to walk beside her without her noticing.

She frowned. "Where did you come from?"

He jerked his thumb behind him, smiling at her.

"Mr. Taylor. Stanton asked me to take some tools to him for repair, and I needed the walk."

Poppy looked at him, looked behind her, then back to him.

"How did you come up here without me noticing?"

"I'm a spy," he replied with a wide, mischievous grin.

Poppy blinked at him, then scowled. "How long have you been wanting to use that line on me for anything you could?"

"Ages," he groaned, sweeping his hands behind his back and clasping them. "Ages and ages."

"I thought you might," she muttered, continuing to walk towards home. "I'm going to have to go over every moment of our entire lives to find the places where that little fact makes sense."

Alex made a soft noise of amusement as he fell into place beside her. "Well, you can avoid the years before I was eighteen."

Poppy glanced up at him, an odd hitch in her lungs rendering her speechless for a moment. "That young?"

"No," he said quickly, "I didn't begin until much later. But that's when I started showing the proper aptitude, I've been told."

Eighteen. When he'd gone off to the army, and she'd begun to fear for his life. How long had she needed to fear for it and hadn't?

When he'd left her the final time and his death had been reported to her, she hadn't known there was any danger to see to. He hadn't given her any indication, and he never had, that what he was doing was in any way dangerous.

All he'd said was that he needed to see to some interests in London, and she'd accepted that. He was always dashing off to this place or that, and the one time she'd enjoyed a Season in London, she'd never seen him. They'd exchanged letters, but she'd had no idea where they were coming from. Supposedly, he'd been off with the Army and unable to get away.

Now that she knew the truth, she wondered.

When had his army time ended, and his spy life begun? Or had they been simultaneous?

"You're not a spy now," she murmured softly, a bitter pang burning her throat. "Unless you've lied about that, as well."

A faint hiss met her ears, but she couldn't look at him. Couldn't see the pain that she still heard every night as he slept. Couldn't see the guilt he seemed to struggle with.

"I didn't," Alex told her. "I'm not a spy now. I may never be again. There's too much... too much I remember, and too much to forget."

"You can tell me, Alex," Poppy insisted. "You can tell me anything."

"Not this," he rasped, shaking his head. "Not this."

Poppy bit the inside of her lip and walked in silence, wondering how long she could be patient in this. Or why it was so important to her to know.

He didn't have to tell her, in truth. It wasn't her place to know, didn't concern her at all, and would serve no purpose.

Except she was now caught up in his life again, and she had been left without answers four and a half years ago. She was growing ever more concerned that she did not know the man beside her at all.

If she'd not seen the proof of his suffering, and heard it as well, she might have been more forceful, more demanding, more insistent that answers were due. As it was, she would say nothing more on the subject.

For now.

"Stanton told me that Fritz and Gabe didn't go back with the others," Poppy said with a slight clearing of the throat, "and that they intend to help finish the harvest."

Alex stared at her for a long moment, then nodded once. "Yes, Gabe decided to remain with me, and Fritz said he needed to help with some situation at Branbury."

"That's a lie," Poppy retorted bluntly. "He's staying to keep you in his line of sight."

A warm chuckle beside her sent an unexpected ripple of delight down her spine. "He is, yes, and Gabe, being my cousin, needs no excuse."

Poppy glanced up at him, finally smiling. "You're very fond of him, aren't you?"

"I am," he confirmed. "We've always been more like brothers. I'm glad he stayed; we can use the time together."

"Good," Poppy murmured, surprised that she meant it so fervently.

Alex was apparently surprised, as well. "Why aren't you mad at me anymore?"

Poppy sighed and squinted up at the sky. "I figured seeing the evidence of what you suffered negated my right to indignation."

"I don't think so."

She snorted once. "You want me to be mad at you?"

Alex seemed to shrug without really shrugging. "I think I would feel better about things if you were."

"Well," she responded with a smirk, "I won't claim to be perfectly content with the situation, now that I know what it is…"

"That's a promising beginning."

Poppy exhaled softly. "But I don't know that I'll rage at you after all."

She didn't miss the way Alex's breath caught at her words. "No?"

She shook her head. "No. At least… not now."

Alex said nothing to that, but tentatively, he slid his hand into her free one, his fingers curving around hers.

She let them, giving his hand a brief squeeze in return.

"Torchon! Torchon! Tu n'es rien! Et ils vous appellent Trace? Le Trace! Nous vous voyons…"

Crack!

Alex bolted upright with a choked cry, heart racing, his skin tingling in anticipation of the lash that had been forthcoming with the taunting of his captors. He looked around, panting frantically, but the darkened room was silent and empty. No boat, no captors, no lash, and no danger whatsoever. Only the taunting words echoing in his head. "Dishcloth! Dishcloth! You are nothing! And they call you Trace? Trace. We see you!"

Exhaling shakily and swallowing hard, he ran his hands over his hair, gripping the back of his neck almost painfully tight. His skin was damp with perspiration, and tremors coursed through him in waves, deeply rooted fear coming to light in the confines of his nightmares.

He couldn't even remember most of what he'd been dreaming, but the content didn't matter. It was all the same.

Memories… and the imagined scenarios if he hadn't escaped, none of which were beyond the realm of possibility. The voices that had mocked him were well known, the taunts they had used were old ones, and still each one ate away at whatever remained of his soul. Would he ever be rid of any of it?

His throat clenched in distress, and he gasped at the sensation.

Alex swung his legs over the edge of the bed and moved to the window, wiping at his brow with the sleeve of his nightshirt. He gripped the windowsill tightly, staring out at the moonlit lands without truly seeing any of it.

This had to stop. The nightmares were incessant, each one as violent and harrowing as the last, and despite his exhaustion each day, there was no reprieve from the terror he woke with.

If it continued much longer, he would be asking Stanton to drug him with laudanum every night just to sleep completely. He had no desire to become addicted to the stuff, but the idea of truly resting and not dreading what may come in his most vulnerable moments was a temptation he was not above succumbing to.

He turned to the bowl of water nearby and splashed his face, patted the skin with a nearby towel, then reached for his trousers and slid them on. He needed the night air and a drink if he wanted any hope of returning to sleep. Not that he expected he would, given the new depths of disturbance his nightmares had taken him to, but the attempt would be important.

And they wanted him to go back to the League? He was barely managing from day to day, there was no possible way he could take on covert operations and the responsibility of other lives as he was.

His own life was questionable enough.

The kitchen fire was built up, which seemed odd for the middle of the night, and Alex stopped, staring at it.

"Couldn't sleep?" a soft, sleepy voice asked.

Alex turned to see Poppy sitting at the large table, wrapped in a thick, grey shawl, her hair loosely plaited, the copper color muted by the light of the fire. Her eyes were soft on him, but also held a knowing light he wasn't sure he cared for.

She shouldn't know anything. She shouldn't be awake. She shouldn't be here.

"No," Alex mumbled, scratching the back of his neck absently. "You?"

She shook her head and gestured for him to sit. "Please, join me."

His first instinct was to refuse her, to avoid staring at her when she looked this rumpled, to keep himself from the power of her eyes and save himself… but he only stood there.

Staring anyway.

"I was going to take a walk," he told her distractedly, eyes fixed on her. "Night air and all that."

Poppy nodded slowly, smiling a little. "I understand. You don't have to join me if you'd rather walk."

There was nothing petulant in her tone in any way, but suddenly there was a sense of guilt rising within him about leaving her for the solitude of the night. He didn't want to hurt her, and certainly didn't want her to think that he was avoiding her or didn't wish to be in her presence.

But…

He pulled out the chair closest and sat roughly, rubbing his hands over his face. Then he looked over at Poppy and smiled a little.

"We really need to stop meeting like this."

"Yes." She chuckled and leaned back in her chair. "The middle of the night does seem to be our most frequent time of passing, doesn't it?" Her fingers started absently pulling at the ends of her plait, her smile warm. "Do you remember the time we snuck out of our houses and went to our tree to see the falling stars?"

Alex grinned and drew up a knee, lacing his fingers over it. "And we never saw a single one?"

"But we laughed all night," Poppy reminded him.

That they had, and it was one of his favorite memories of Poppy and himself. He'd kissed her for the first time that night.

But he wouldn't bring that up.

"How old were we?" he asked, though he knew full well.

"I was fifteen," Poppy said, laughing to herself. "Though I thought I was so much older than that."

Alex watched her, seeing that fifteen-year-old girl with energy and vitality, who laughed with her soul and smiled with the light of the sun. He'd adored Poppy at every age, and though she was altered now, every one of the girls she had ever been was still there.

"You were," he murmured, shaking his head. "You were so much older than your age at any given time. Why else would someone of my considerable years spend time with someone so young?"

Poppy's brow creased as she laughed in disbelief. "You are three years older, if that. You are not so ancient."

Alex sighed and looked back at the fire. "I feel ancient."

"Now?" she asked gently. "Or then?"

"Both." He stared at the flames as they rose and fell, devouring the logs within them with ease. "That's the problem with overexposure to the evils of the world. It makes you old before your time and suspicious of everyone. You see things you have no wish or need to see, notice everything that should be hidden, and can't forget anything. Ever. It's… exhausting."

"Are you happy to be rid of it, then?" Poppy asked as the fire crackled loudly.

He hesitated a long moment, considering what he could admit and must keep back, wondering what she already knew or suspected.

"I don't know," he admitted. "I'm not sure who I am without it."

"I'm sorry," she whispered in response.

He smiled very faintly at that. "You are the last person on earth who needs to be sorry where I am concerned."

She shifted in her chair, drawing his gaze back to her. "I'm sorry that you're hurting," she clarified, sitting forward. "I'm sorry that you're torn about this, and I am sorry that I don't understand."

"That's not your fault, either," he insisted.

Poppy tilted her head in a way he knew all too well.

She'd caught him somehow, and he was left scrambling, thinking back quickly on where his fault had been.

"I know that," she finally said. "It's not my fault, but it doesn't follow that it's yours either."

Alex frowned as her fingers resumed their toying of the ends of her hair, which was strangely distracting for him. He suddenly wanted to feel her hair between his fingers, as he'd done so often before. But that was years ago, and now he had no grounds to do so, yet the inclination was still there.

Strange that it hadn't faded with time.

"Alex…" Poppy said slowly.

"What?" he breathed, his chest tightening in an oddly pleasant way.

She exhaled slowly. "I haven't been completely forthcoming with you."

His stomach plunged awkwardly.

"No?" he asked with a rough swallow, fearing the admission to come.

Her eyes turned serious and sober.

"I know why you're up tonight. I know why you're up every night."

No…

"I know you're having nightmares," she went on. "The walls of this cottage are thin, and your room is next to mine. They wake me up, Alex, so I cannot imagine what they do to you."

He stared at her in horror. He felt angry, miserable, and raging with guilt, hating the sight of her for what it truly meant.

Her smile grew sad. "I never went in to you because I didn't know how you would react to me. I didn't know what you faced in the nightmares, so how could I know if my presence would help or hinder them? Then, I see you after the fact, the way you go throughout the day, the shadows you try to hide... Did you forget how well I know you, Alex?"

He had forgotten. He wished he'd considered all of that, any of that, so he could have slept in the barn, on the fields, or even in the remnants of the lodge. Anywhere but here. He would have acted more convincingly, taken less strenuous tasks to avoid the appearance of his weakness...

"I don't want to make you tell me things that will pain you," Poppy said, sighing quietly. "I don't mean to plague you about this. But you see, I know enough to be afraid of what I don't. I've seen your wounds and your scars. I've heard your screams." Her voice broke and she swallowed hard. "I need you to fill the gaps."

Lord above, his guilt would know no bounds where she was concerned. He should never have come here, but once he had, he should have left the moment he was out of danger. This was no place for him, not with someone as innocent as to the true nature of the world as Poppy was. She didn't need to know the cruel ugliness he had endured, nor that it still plagued him.

Alex rose slowly, keeping his gaze on her. "I can't, Poppy. Not because I don't trust you, or because you don't deserve it, but... I can't." He cleared his throat. "I think I'll go walk outside after all, Poppy. Go back to bed. I'm sorry I disturbed you."

He could see her wilt before his eyes, and he wrenched his gaze away to avoid apologizing for many more things. He didn't wait for her response; he pushed open the door and walked as quickly as he could out of doors, barefoot and without a coat. He didn't care. He needed fresh air and a deep breath or seven.

He needed to leave the cottage soon, and for good.

For all their sakes.

Chapter Twelve

It was raining the next morning, which wasn't much of a surprise. Being England, it tended to rain quite a bit, but it had been some time since they'd experienced a proper downpour which created the puddles and sludge that everyone seemed to dread.

But the rain this time was a blessing in disguise.

The cottage had a leak during the particularly heavy rains, no doubt due to its age and thatched roof. Stanton hadn't managed to fix it since the last time, so Alex was taking it upon himself to fix it today. Why he was fixing it while the rain was currently going on was a mystery Poppy was too afraid to ask on, but if he wanted to behave so foolishly, she was more than delighted to let him.

He'd only spoken a handful of words to her since their conversation the night before, and he never met her gaze, so it seemed perfectly natural for him to exclude himself from the potential of any further conversation for a while by removing himself to the roof.

If he fell from the precarious surface and injured himself again or took ill from being in the rain too long, he would never hear the end of it from her.

Stanton was on strict duty to watch over him and make sure Alex didn't kill himself.

Poppy had other things to do.

She'd had a devil of a time going back to sleep last night after what Alex said. She'd considered her words long and hard before saying them, truly thinking Alex would finally open up once he understood her perspective on the situation. But his refusal, his statement that he could not, had stumped her.

She could not force him to say what he could not, but she was still without answers, and she needed them. It became the chief subject of her thoughts, and she would not be able to rest until she understood in some way what his life had been, if she could not know what he had endured.

Luckily for her, there were other alternatives to Alex himself, and the rain would not keep her from pursuing them.

Nor would he know what she was about to do.

The doors to Branbury were large and old, and in desperate need of upkeep or replacement, but they had the effect of being an imposing entrance to an already intimidating edifice. If she hadn't known the men within, or felt so strongly about her purpose, the image of such a place on a stormy day would have sent her running back home.

Luckily, she was made of sterner stuff than that today.

She knocked a handful of times, flinging back the hood of her plain but sturdy cloak, choosing to venture without a bonnet despite the rain. She only had the one, and in weather like today, it would hardly help her. She turned with a sigh, looking out over the grounds, currently being pummeled by the rain, and felt grateful to have had the harvest in already. Everything would have been ruined if they'd still had work to do.

An almost bellowing creak from the door turned her back around, and Gabe stood there, surprise evident in his features.

"Miss Edgewood," he greeted, thick brows near his hairline. "Did you come by foot?"

Poppy nodded once, looking down at her skirts and laughing at herself. "Clearly, yes."

"In this weather?" he pressed with a step forward to get a better look at the skies.

"Well, it was gorgeously sunny and bright up until I arrived..." she told him dryly, shaking out her skirt with a bit of an obvious motion.

Gabe shook himself and smiled sheepishly. "Please come in, forgive me for my rudeness." He stepped back and gestured for her to enter.

She returned his smile and crossed the threshold, untying her cloak deftly. "I've been led to believe that's to be expected from you, Gabe. Everybody says you're irascible and the like."

"I am," he grunted and took her cloak, shaking it and hanging it over a rack near the door. "I'm quite rude on regular occasions, but in this case, I really didn't mean to be. Besides, you seemed to handle it well enough."

Poppy wiped at the wet tendrils of hair near her temples, chuckling to herself. "I've been used to the freedom of speaking my mind no matter who the recipient is. One of the benefits of being given independence, I expect."

Gabe grinned at that. "I expect you're right. I think Fritz has a fire going in the drawing room, would you like to sit before it? Might dry you out a little and warm you up."

"Please," Poppy replied, rubbing her hands together.

He led the way and took her down the surprisingly open corridor, then into the comfortably situated drawing room where Fritz was already seated with a book.

"Fritz, we have a guest," Gabe informed him, a wry note in his tone.

Fritz's dark head lifted, and he grinned warmly when he saw Poppy, rising quickly. "Poppy! Lovely, I was just thinking I could use some fine company."

Poppy snorted and curtseyed quickly. "I'm not sure I qualify."

"His other option is me," Gabe reminded her. "You do qualify, trust me."

She dimpled a smile at him, then moved over to the fire, holding her hands out to warm them.

"Sit here, Poppy," Fritz said, gesturing to the chair he'd just vacated. "I insist."

Well, she wasn't about to argue with such an offer when she was wet and cold, particularly given what she was about to ask them.

"Only if you both sit, as well," she told them with severe looks, then smiled to offset it.

They did so, glancing at each other in what was undoubtedly supposed to be a surreptitious way.

Poppy had to smile at that. They didn't have to be spies of any kind to figure out that Poppy had a purpose for being here. Why else would she call on them when the person who tied them all together was back at the cottage?

Pretenses are sometimes incredibly unnecessary.

"What brings you to see us this cold, rainy, and rather unpleasant day?" Fritz asked, giving her a would-be innocent smile.

Poppy sat up and clasped her hands before her. "Alex."

"Ah ha," Fritz murmured, sitting back against the settee. "I thought it might be something like that."

Gabe nodded slowly, his eyes fixed on Poppy with unnerving steadiness. "I assumed you'd have questions eventually. It's only natural."

"I wouldn't have come to you," Poppy said quickly, the impropriety of the situation suddenly occurring to her. "Only Alex isn't talking about anything. I know there are things that cannot be discussed, and I don't want to invade the privacy and security of what you lot do…"

"We wouldn't let you," Gabe overrode with a quick grin. "We're quite accustomed to keeping the secret things secret."

Poppy nodded, smiling in return, then letting the smile recede.

Fritz raised a brow at her. "We might be spies, Poppy, but we're not mind readers. What is troubling you specifically?"

She exhaled shortly and wrung her hands a little. "His scars. His wounds. Who he is."

"He's not telling you any of that?" Fritz asked sympathetically.

Poppy shook her head. "I'm probably plaguing him with asking, but… He's having nightmares. Brutal, terrifying nightmares, and I can hear every cry he makes. I'm worried, and he won't talk about it."

Gabe and Fritz made the same sort of knowing, noncommittal sound, but said nothing.

"What?" Poppy queried, looking at them both. "What is it?"

"Well," Gabe sighed, rubbing his hands together, "we're not particularly accustomed to talking about ourselves or our work, let alone what we endure in the line of it, and Alex has more secrets than the rest of us." He smiled very faintly. "Yet another example of our family similarities."

Fritz snorted to himself. "That and your bad tempers."

"I feel as though I don't truly know him," Poppy whispered, ignoring their light banter, "that perhaps I never did."

"No," Fritz said at once, sobering and leaning towards her. "No, that's not it at all."

Poppy looked at him with no small measure of derision. "How would you know?"

"Because we are never so completely different in our personal lives," Gabe told her firmly. "That's who we have been all along. The fact that we have secrets and cannot always say where we are going or what we are doing does not take away from who we are. If you doubt me, there are quite a few wives I could have you speak with who would confirm it."

Fritz was nodding at the response and Poppy looked back at him. "So, Alex is…?"

"The same as he always was to you," Fritz assured her, "only with more secrets and abilities, none of which alter that fact."

"But I don't know that part of him," Poppy insisted, almost pleading for them to understand now. "I always thought I knew him so well, and now I find there is another part of him. One that he refuses to talk about. I want to help him through whatever he is suffering, but…" She sighed and sat back in her chair. "Will you tell me what he will not?"

Gabe snorted softly. "There is nothing I'd love better than to talk about the sort of man Alex is, particularly when he's not here to refute it. But you must understand, Poppy… I don't know, and nor does Fritz, what Alex endured on that ship. Not really."

She nodded slowly, letting that admission sink in. Then she smiled slightly, almost apologetically. "Tell me whatever you can."

Both men returned her smile, and Gabe rubbed his hands together eagerly. "Excellent. I have been wanting to talk about him for years."

"Far be it from me to prevent you," Poppy muttered, still smiling.

"Alex," Gabe began with a sigh, "was the best of us, and I don't say that lightly. He was brilliant in his strategy and methods, made connections that no one else would comprehend, and his instincts were always right on point. He could find clues where everyone else saw dust, could think five steps ahead of anyone else, and never once showed hesitation in his actions. He was absolutely fearless in every respect. You could ask him to take on a roomful of armed mercenaries, and he would grin and ask you when."

Poppy's smile became less forced and more genuine. "That sounds like him. He's always been reckless."

Fritz grunted an odd laugh. "Reckless. Yes, he is, but never needlessly so. Everything he did was careful and precise, exactly what was required for his task or investigation. I'd never seen anything quite like him in all the years I'd been working covert operations. It was as though he was designed for strategy and built for intrigue. It would have been a crime against humanity to have him go into any other profession." He smiled faintly. "And he was never close to compromise, ever. He could get in and out of a place of danger without any trace of it. That was why we dubbed him Trace, as it were."

Gabe's brow furrowed as he looked at Fritz. "How many plots did he foil? Or did we because of his information?"

"Let's see," Fritz mused. "There was Bonaparte's circle, and saving Prinny… Then the Italian ambassador and his family…"

"And the uprising in '18," Gabe pointed out.

"What uprising?" Poppy interjected, completely caught up in their tales now.

"Exactly," they said together in the same satisfied tone.

She laughed and put a hand to her brow. "So many?"

Gabe chuckled at her antics. "We're not done yet, but you get the idea."

She did get the idea, and that was the most bewildering part. Alex had been gifted in this realm, somehow more than a man and less than an immortal. Confident, proud, and determined, just as he had always been with her, and she could see the Alex she had known in the world they had described.

"So, what happened?" she asked, looking between them.

Gabe winced and looked away while Fritz exhaled slowly. "Alex had been investigating a particularly dangerous group," Fritz told her, his expression somber. "This wasn't unusual for him, and he told nobody either the details or the key players. Again, this was his way.

He reported regularly with appropriate information, but unless he required help or approval or insight, he kept the specifics to himself."

"I used to mock him for it," Gabe broke in bitterly. "Teased him for not trusting any of us, but it turned out he was right all along." He swallowed and looked up at Poppy, pale eyes glinting in the firelight. "He asked for our help one night, said he was in over his head and hadn't known it. We all went down to the East London docks with the all the information he could provide us, which was limited, given the urgency of the situation." He shook his head slowly, lost in the memories of that night.

"We were ambushed. Somehow, we had failed to make the necessary connections on our ends to ensure that this problematic situation within Alex's investigation could be contained. So, like a powder keg, it exploded. We fought with everything we had, but more and more of them continued to come from a ship, each one of them like the pirates of old, everything you would think of when you imagine pirates. I'd been stabbed in the leg and shoulder and was losing blood fast, Gent had a pair of black eyes and a dislocated shoulder, Cap was mostly unscratched but had broken ribs, and Eagle had broken a wrist and was bleeding from a cut on his face. We were outnumbered and going to die there."

The scene he described unfolded before Poppy as though illustrated, and her heart raced with the danger and adventure, the thrill of the action, and then her stomach clenched in apprehension.

"And Alex?" she asked, her stomach dropping.

Gabe cleared his throat, shaking his head. "Alex was cut in several places and wheezing badly, but he saw the situation and made a decision. A stupid, reckless, foolhardy decision. He bolted down the dock with many of our attackers following him. He boarded the ship the smugglers had been on, wrenching the gangplank away, and dumping one or two smugglers there. Then he cut the ropes of the ship in the dock and surrendered himself to them."

"No," Poppy breathed.

"I arrived about this time," Fritz told her, his voice slightly clogged with emotion. "The ship had drifted just far enough away from the dock that we had no hope of getting to her in our condition. We fired weapons, but no one returned fire. Then we heard the unmistakable sound of someone being stabbed, a strident, harsh noise that gives the listener a pained sensation as though they are the one injured, and a cry of agony from its victim. The roar of the crew aboard told us what we already knew."

Poppy hiccupped softly on a wash of tears. "It was Alex."

They both nodded.

"We searched for years," Fritz went on. "Desperate to find out if he truly was dead, and to honor him if he were, or to save him if he was not. We found nothing. Not a thing to indicate he had ever existed, and no trace of those that had killed him. We wanted justice for him, vengeance for our friend, and we couldn't get it. We set men to watch over you in his honor, knowing he would have done so were he able. We didn't know what else to do."

"And then you had word," she murmured, "when he came to Cheshire and was found at my door…"

"We had to come," Gabe said firmly. "We *had* to."

Poppy nodded repeatedly now, understanding in some small portion their loyalty and desperation, their drive for answers.

She'd felt the same thing, only she hadn't the resources to pursue it.

"He sacrificed himself for us," Gabe continued. "That's the sort of man he is, and the sort of spy he was. And he may never be able to tell us the full extent of what he suffered at the hands of his captors, but I can tell you that he was tortured and interrogated and forced to work and live in demeaning circumstances. He knew the sort of men he was giving himself up to, and still he did so, though I doubt any of this is what he anticipated."

"So, if he isn't talking about any of this…" Poppy prodded gingerly.

Fritz heaved a sad sigh but smiled at her. "There can be only two explanations. Either he is protecting you, or he cannot bear the recollection of the horrors he endured."

Poppy swallowed with difficulty, her fingers feeling numb as they sat entangled together. "Which do you think it is?"

Gabe grunted softly, sitting back in his seat, and looked at Poppy with a gentle fondness she would not have expected from him.

"Knowing Alex? Both."

Poppy had been in and out of the cottage all day, and Alex was grateful to have her gone for a bit. Everything got so muddled when she was around, and he needed to think clearly. He needed to be parted from the warmth of her presence in order to process appropriately.

He'd spent the early part of the day fixing her abysmal excuse for a roof, and the rain had added to the pitiful picture he had undoubtedly presented. But it had given him ample motivation to complete the task and avoid conversing with anyone, which is all he had wanted.

He couldn't say that he'd actually mended a roof in his life, but that wasn't about to stop him from spending as long as he needed to work away at it. Finally, it had stopped leaking, so he supposed he had done his job well.

Or well enough, at any rate.

He saw Poppy return from her errand, and it hadn't taken much to understand that she'd gone to Branbury, for whatever reason. He'd taken care to force his curiosity far, far away, determined to distance himself from her and from the situation. There was far too much for him to do, and she couldn't have anything to do with any of it.

After the cottage roof, he'd moved on to the barn, shoveling it out, even though Stanton had informed him it was unnecessary. He'd long been trained to work when he needed an escape, or whenever he was able, and sometimes even when he wasn't able. There was comfort in the monotony of hard labor, of letting his mind wander where it would without much by way of direction. He became less burdened, less congested by emotions and thought.

Work was what he needed. Work. Purpose. Drive.

Reason.

As he sat before the fire attempting to dry out now, Alex smirked to himself. He needed reason, and he wasn't sure where he was going to find it. Nothing he had done since his escape had been reasonable or been anything close to resembling it. All he had done was survive.

For years.

"You're shaking, Alex."

Alex looked up at Gabe, sitting near the fire with him, watching him with amusement.

"That's because it's cold," Alex told him, barely able to keep his teeth from chattering.

Gabe chuckled. "It's not, actually, but we'll go with that. I'd say something about the wisdom of working out in the rain all day, but when you're miserable tomorrow, you'll understand it all too well."

"I had to be outside," Alex told him with a scowl. "There wasn't anything to do inside."

"You're going mad with all this, aren't you?" Gabe asked, sobering just a little. "Adjusting to life outside of the ship, not having tasks to complete or expectations…"

Alex began nodding before Gabe trailed off. "I found out Poppy has been hearing my nightmares."

"Ah…"

He glanced up at his cousin warily, hearing a knowing tone in the one word. Sure enough, Gabe's smirk was smug, and his eyes twinkled.

"What?" Alex snapped irritably. "There is nothing to smile about in that."

"No, of course not," Gabe assured him with the barest hint of sincerity. "But it certainly lends some depth to your current state of mind and being."

Alex huffed and waved a hand. "Explain yourself."

Gabe sat back, folding his arms, and chuckling to himself.

"Anyone in your situation would have nightmares. Hell, we've all had nightmares at some point because of what we faced, and nothing was close to your situation. You're right, it's not amusing at all." He grinned, despite his words. "But Poppy hearing your nightmares is your biggest concern? It was bound to happen, Alex, and nothing is keeping you in this cottage."

"I know." He shook his head slowly. "I could leave at any time. I *should* leave. I'm not sick or weak anymore…"

"Debatable."

"…And it's really not proper for me to be here now," Alex went on, ignoring his cousin's outburst. "But where would I go? Parkerton is in shambles."

Gabe shrugged. "Come to Branbury. We can restore Parkerton easily enough, and it gives you a place to stay in the meantime."

Alex shook his head immediately. "I can't live off the charity of others anymore. I need to become someone again, whoever I need to be now."

"Charity?" Gabe snorted, his boot skidding on the stone floor. "It's not charity, it's a house, and I'm staying in that house, I'll remind you, not because I am a vagrant, but because someone I know offered."

"Also, because you enjoy taking advantage," Alex pointed out.

Gabe tilted his head in thought. "Well, yes, there is that. But still, not charity."

Alex finally smiled, dropping his head back against the chair. "Why are you here, Gabe? There has got to be so much to do back in London, I doubt there is time for you to take a holiday up here with me."

His cousin shrugged evasively and looked at the fire. "There's plenty of help."

That may have been true, but none of those people would be Gabe, and it was well known that Gabe as the Rogue had a mass of contacts that would not associate with anyone else. Valuable information could be gained from them, and his presence here would prevent that.

"But not you," Alex said, raising his brow.

Gabe shrugged again, and Alex waited.

The fire crackled loudly, and then Gabe groaned and shifted in his seat.

"Oh, all right, I might as well tell you."

"Probably best," Alex told him with a sage nod.

Gabe exhaled roughly, making a face. "I may or may not have been compromised earlier this year."

Any amusement Alex was feeling at his cousin's expense evaporated, and he straightened in his seat.

"Are you serious?"

"We're not sure how much," Gabe admitted with a brisk nod of acknowledgement. "And we're not sure by whom, or how, but I was, and so I've needed to keep to a lower profile than even before any of this."

"Damn," Alex swore, leaning forward and putting his head into his hands.

"Yes, but there is no way that can be twisted to be your fault. So, stop that."

Alex drew his hands down and looked at his cousin and colleague, feeling pained. "Isn't it my fault? I had answers, Gabe."

Gabe's brow furrowed with derision. "We all had answers. Circumstances changed multiple times, so there's no guaranteeing anything at all."

"Fair enough." Alex dropped his hands completely and cleared his throat. "So why not go to your wife and son?"

"Amelia wants me here," Gabe assured him. "I saw her and the baby shortly before we found out where you were, and she told me to find you and do what I had to reunite us properly. She has no siblings; I have no siblings; and neither of us have much by way of family." He wrinkled his nose up slightly. "That, and not knowing how compromised I am means it's harder to go home for risk of endangering Amelia and little Alex. Eagle is with them, so they're quite safe."

"You've got to resolve this, Gabe," Alex said, shaking his head slowly. "The League's got to end it."

"We're trying, believe me," Gabe said, looking back into the fire. "They almost got Cap's wife and children a few months ago. Managed to get that one written off as folly, so no one truly believes Cap is one of us, but it was close. Surely, it will all come to a head soon. It has to."

They both fell silent again, darker thoughts and pressures occupying their minds.

The door to the cottage opened then, and Poppy appeared, shaking her damp cloak and wringing out her dripping hair. She looked at the two men by the fire, then smiled.

"I've made a decision, Alex."

Distracted by her fresh countenance and highlighted figure due to her sodden dress, Alex jerked at hearing his name and looked up.

"Yes?"

"You need to stop hiding out on this farm," Poppy said briskly, though her smile warmed at his look. "It's time for you to escape from everything that is bothering you and get beyond it. You need to have fun and laugh and forget all you've suffered. You need to smile and mean it, and I mean to see that you do."

He swallowed and cocked his head. "What do you have in mind?"

Poppy's smile grew, and with it, Alex's wariness.

"A ball at the village assembly rooms. It's in two days, and you can't refuse me because I've already confirmed the carriage with Mr. Ryland, and we're sharing with the Monroe girls. You know how they would gossip if I went alone after all this time."

"I can't go as myself," he said frantically, his stomach clenching and his neck heating. "I'll need a new name."

"I think we can agree on that." She grinned briefly. "We wouldn't want Lord Parkerton to get ambushed, would we?" She moved past them both to the bedchambers.

Only when they heard the door to her room close did the cousins look at each other, and Alex groaned weakly.

"A ball? Really? Did she think my feelings on those things changed while I was away?"

Gabe shrugged, laughing to himself. "She didn't invite me, and I am so grateful."

"I hate you," Alex muttered.

"I know." Gabe paused, then added, "She is right, though. You do need to laugh and smile again."

Alex nodded once. "I know."

Chapter Thirteen

"*D*o not embarrass me."

"When have I ever embarrassed you?"

"Oh, if only we had time to elaborate on that."

"I have never embarrassed you in any public setting."

Poppy rolled her eyes and gave Alex a look that made him chuckle.

"Well, only to your family, then," Alex amended with a grin.

"Yes, because that is so much better." Poppy exhaled roughly and sat back hard against the seat of the coach. "Don't say anything untoward before the Monroe sisters. It'll be all over town if you do."

Alex looked at her sharply, raising a brow. "Remind me who I am and why I'm going to a ball, then. I'll never manage to behave properly without the proper information."

Poppy turned her head towards him, keeping it against the seat. "I don't care what your name is, but you ought to be my cousin or some such. You are visiting me from somewhere and you've convinced me to give up my existence as a hermit for one night for the simple pleasures of dancing."

He stared at her for a long minute. "Well," he finally said, "as long as we're truly thinking this out..."

She waved her hand dismissively and turned to look out the window. "The details are not important."

"Trust me," he told her with a sharp laugh, "the details can be *very* important."

Again, she waved her hand. "You're the spy, you come up with something."

"Former spy."

"Not officially."

Alex grumbled and turned to look out of his own window at the passing scenery, barely visible in the fading light. "Right. Well, let's just remember the reason you stated for doing this. To make me smile and laugh and have fun." He snorted very softly. "Huzzah."

His leg was awkwardly kicked then, and he glanced over at Poppy with a frown, though she wasn't looking at him.

"At least you managed to appear the part," Poppy grumbled. "You still look scrawny in clothes that don't belong to you."

"Well, you look lovely, if I'm permitted to pay compliments to my cousin," Alex informed her stiffly. "I didn't think you still had anything from your old life, let alone that dress."

Poppy jerked to look at him, eyes wide, brow furrowed. "You remember this one?"

"Not sure I could forget it." Alex smiled as he eyed what he could of her with her dark cloak obscuring much of it. "You were wearing that dress when you told me you loved me."

Even in the dark of the coach, he could see Poppy's cheeks flush, and her throat moved as she swallowed. Then she cleared her throat and averted her eyes. "I also threw punch in your face in this dress without getting a drop on myself. I've had it for quite some time."

"Still," Alex grunted, shifting in his seat. "It's nice to know not everything has changed."

Truth be told, he'd been transported by the sight of her when she'd come out of her room, somehow more elegant and finer than she'd ever been in his memories. The gown itself wasn't anything spectacular except for the sentiment he'd placed on it for years. Its simple, soft green highlighted everything that was naturally Poppy without taking anything away from her. He was fully aware of the very slight fraying at the neckline, hemline, and sleeves, and of the faded lace dotting each surface, but her rosy color distracted from all that.

How she managed to make her own hair look so splendidly elegant was beyond him, but he supposed she was used to it by now. It wouldn't match the styles of the other girls this evening who had maids to do the work for them, but it suited Poppy well, and that was all that it needed to do. Alex was only grateful to have found a proper set of evening clothes lying around at Branbury, and a set that fit, no less.

Even if he had his own clothing, it would have looked ridiculous on him now. He didn't have proof, but he suspected he was roughly half the size he was before, and a scarecrow of a man wasn't much of a match for Poppy when she looked as she did.

Not that they were a match.

They weren't.

The carriage pulled to a stop in front of a house on the edge of the village, and Alex peered up at the overly lit building.

"Why is it that we have to share a coach with the Monroe girls when they could easily walk to the assembly rooms?"

"Because they are determined to be fine young ladies," Poppy told him, smiling to herself, "and fine young ladies always travel by coach."

Alex made a face. "Well, then."

He sighed and opened the door to the coach, descending to do his proper duty to the forthcoming girls. Renting a coach from Mr. Ryland did not provide a footman to accompany the group, so Alex, as a gentleman, would have to do the honors.

Although he didn't really think he would be considered a real gentleman tonight. His eveningwear was fine, but not that of a gentleman. It was perfect for a merchant on the rise, which would be an excellent story to pose for himself, he supposed.

If anyone asked.

If Moulton were as full of gossiping busybodies as he recalled, at least a few would ask. Not directly, mind, but they would ask each other.

Faintly, he wondered if it was too late to find himself ill.

"Oh look, Bess! That's a strapping man, isn't it?"

"Indeed, Di. I'll ride in a coach with that, no question."

Alex muttered incoherently under his breath as the two overly trimmed girls bounced their way down to the coach, their matching dark eyes taking in every inch of him as he stood there. He bowed, smiling as politely as he could and offered them a hand into the coach.

Each of them held his hand for longer than was necessary, and in grips that would have made lesser men wince.

He looked up at the night sky, casting up a fervent prayer for release, then entered the coach himself, grateful that the sisters had sat together instead of one taking the seat beside Poppy.

"La, Poppy Edgewood," Diana Monroe said with a salacious smile at Alex. "Where did you find this divine piece of meat?"

Alex saw Poppy's jaw clench, but she smiled very tightly. "He's my cousin, Miss Diana."

"And does this cousin have a name?" her sister asked, looking all the more interested.

"George Turner, Miss Monroe," Alex murmured, tapping the brim of his hat as he nodded.

"It is indeed a pleasure," Bess said, nodding herself, followed quickly by Diana. "We don't normally get such fine fish at our little assemblies."

"Not since Anne Hansen's husband showed up, anyway," Diana added, looking at her sister. "He was very handsome."

Bess sighed and made a show of fanning herself. "Oh yes. He was lovely." She exhaled a fluttery sigh and looked at Poppy again, tsking sadly. "Oh, Miss Edgewood, is that the same old dress you wore last time we saw you? It's at least five years out of fashion, dear. You should have asked to borrow one."

"Yes, it is rather tatty, isn't it?" Diana winced and shuddered. "It reminds me of Viola Hardy's gown last year, remember, Bess?"

"Oh, Lord, that was an eyesore," Bess groaned, her fingers stretching to their fullest extent as though she would be ill. "She looked far worse than you, Miss Edgewood, and she is a full five years younger, and ought to know better."

Poppy pretended to look either impressed or interested or both, but she said nothing, which was perfect, as the sisters continued to ramble on and on about gowns and men and silly girls. They needed no input from either of them.

Poppy leaned closer to Alex, and he leaned towards her to listen as she hissed, "This is why they couldn't walk. They'd never get there with all the distractions."

Alex choked on a laugh, but nodded sagely, straightening, and waiting for the coach to arrive at the assembly rooms.

Soon enough, it did, and the Monroe sisters paid little attention to Alex or his hand this time as they descended the coach and rushed into the rooms. Poppy took her time exiting, huffing a little as she took his hand to get down neatly. She shook her skirts, and tossed her hair, exhaling slowly, still holding his hand.

Alex looked down at her, waiting for her to release it, but sensing she wasn't actually aware of touching him. Her eyes were fixed on the lit assembly rooms, and her jaw was tight as she stared at it.

"Poppy?" he finally prodded, keeping his tone soft and unassuming.

She shook her head very slightly. "Give me a minute, Alex. I don't… I don't socialize much, and I have to prepare myself to do so."

Alex frowned at that. "Why? Because of your circumstances?"

There was a pained flash across her features, and a tremor ran down her spine and arms.

"Something like that," she replied absently. Then she exhaled again, nodded once, and released his hand. "Right. We are here to have fun. Let's do so." She strode ahead, leaving Alex behind.

He shook his head slowly as he followed. "Then why does it feel more like going into battle? I know all too well what *that* feels like."

There was no answer, only the path ahead of him, and he took it, knowing that the dangers inside wouldn't be nearly as treacherous as the ones he had already faced in his life. It would still force him to watch his footing, but the dangers were different. He didn't know these dangers, but he never had.

Perhaps he ought to have prepared, as well.

"Too late now, old boy," he muttered to himself as footmen took his hat and her cloak, then indicated the way.

"What was that?" Poppy whispered, glancing up at him.

"Nothing important," he assured her, shaking his head. "Just preparing myself."

She scoffed and forced a bright smile on her face. "You do remember how to dance, don't you?"

"Of course," he grunted, nodding at an inquisitive guest. "Left foot, right foot, turn, turn, swivel…"

Poppy snorted a laugh and brought her gloved hand to her

mouth, her body shaking with more laughter.

"I'm sure it will all come back to me," Alex said confidently. "How difficult could it be?"

Very difficult, as it happened, and Poppy was sure to remind Alex of it repeatedly.

He didn't seem to mind. He'd simply laughed it off or shrugged, and that reminded her so much of the Alex she had known that she couldn't even mind that half of the time he danced, he did it wrong.

They'd danced twice already, and Alex was at this moment dancing with the Fletcher girl, who was far too young to really be a candidate for anyone of Alex's age. Still, her youth and energy were boundless, and she was a pretty thing. Not particularly sensible, but not nearly as silly as the Monroe girls. She would undoubtedly fall in love with the handsome, albeit clumsy, Mr. Turner and use him as the standard by which all future suitors would be judged.

Poor men would never stand a chance.

There was no one like Alex, and it wasn't worth the effort to try to find otherwise. Better for the poor girl to forget Alex and move on before she found herself too far down the cavernous hole Alex was capable of creating within one's heart.

"That's a serious expression, Miss Edgewood," Mrs. Blaine commented as she somehow appeared at Poppy's side. "Are you well?"

Poppy smiled at the woman, making it as genuine as possible. "Quite well, Mrs. Blaine, thank you for asking."

Mrs. Blaine's expression was suspicious and not at all convinced. "You were frowning quite fixedly."

"It's only…" Poppy trailed off with a sigh.

"Yes?"

Poppy looked at the older woman forlornly. "I wish there were a more equal number of men to women at this assembly. One does feel so self-conscious standing during a dance."

Mrs. Blaine nodded sympathetically, the large feathers in her hair bobbing. "I understand completely, dear. But you have danced tonight, haven't you?"

"I have, yes," she replied, taking a glass of punch from a footman passing. "Twice with my cousin, once each with Mr. Hartley, Mr. Simmons, and Mr. Beech."

"Oh, a fine number for a spinster such as yourself!" Mrs. Blaine praised, clapping her hands. "You must be so pleased."

Poppy bit back a snarl and smiled further. "Yes, quite. I'd forgotten how much I adore dancing."

Mrs. Blaine turned more fully to her, fanning herself with an old ebony and ivory fan, though the room was cool.

"I tell you what, Miss Edgewood," she began conspiratorially. "If you spent less time on that farm of yours and more time out and about, you might yet get a husband for yourself."

"Indeed?" Poppy inquired as politely as possible. "At my advanced age?"

She received a firm nod in return. "Despite that unruly and vile-colored hair of yours. You have a pretty face still, though not as fair now as it once was. There are men who would yet take you, if you'd be amenable. It really would be best for you."

Poppy stared at Mrs. Blaine, wondering what in the world possessed the woman to insult Poppy while trying to be encouraging, as she instructed her on finding a husband as though she truly knew best. Or cared about what was best for Poppy.

"And what of my farm, Mrs. Blaine?" Poppy asked, somehow still smiling. "What will become of my farm if I venture out to be more social?"

"Why, your workers would see to it," Mrs. Blaine said with a flick of her fan. "You hire a foreman to mind it, or whatever the proper position is, and you don't even have to think about the blasted business. All you would need to do would be to reap the benefits and make your prospects even more appealing to potential suitors."

Poppy's smile turned to more of a snarl, though Mrs. Blaine didn't seem to notice. "I work my farm as well as the workers I hire, Mrs. Blaine."

Mrs. Blaine's eyes widened. "That won't do at all, Miss Edgewood. It's bad enough you have your cousin to stay with you without a chaperone, but to be laborious yourself?"

The mention of Alex made Poppy stiffen, and her snarling smile faded as she prepared to say something she may have cause to regret tomorrow or the next day once she thought on it properly.

"Come, cousin, I reserved this dance, as you recall," Alex's voice said jauntily near her right ear, and her arm was suddenly tugged before she could say anything.

Poppy glared up at him.

"I have a drink in my hand, *cousin*, and I wasn't done with her."

Alex returned her glare playfully.

"Drink up then, or Mrs. Blaine will find something else to say about you, and I really don't think you ought to go after her in such a public place."

Poppy ground her teeth, then downed the remaining punch quickly, making a face as she did so.

"Oh, that's really not that good."

"Doesn't surprise you, does it?" he quipped, plucking the cup from her and handing it off to someone else. "Now, forget what the biddy said and look as though you're enjoying yourself. Make a good show of it."

Poppy quirked a brow at him as she curtseyed with the ladies a little dramatically.

"Only if you do, Mr. Turner."

"I plan to," he informed her with a deep bow.

The musicians struck up a jaunty tune, and Poppy moved with the other ladies in a lively skip around and through the line of gentlemen, looking very graceful and light on her feet, returning to her spot with a smirk and raise of a brow.

Alex mirrored it as the gentlemen did the same around and through the line of ladies, keeping his steps just as light.

"How spritely you dance, Miss Edgewood," he complimented as he passed her.

"And you, Mr. Turner," she replied as they both turned in place.

He inclined his head in acknowledgement, stepping forward with extended hand, which she took as they proceeded up the row of couples.

"I'm only trying to match you, cousin."

"Just don't surpass me," she said airily as they moved backwards.

"Never," he affirmed as they circled each other.

They parted as the gentlemen linked arms with each other and danced down the line, the ladies doing the same on their side, turning in place again once they reached their new position.

"You are so graceful, Miss Edgewood," Alex praised as he skipped forward to Mrs. Jones beside her, who was watching them both with a delighted interest, and linked her arm with his as they circled. "As are you, madam," Alex told his current partner. "So many graceful ladies."

Poppy snickered as she proceeded forward to Mr. Jones on Alex's right, and he to her.

"Mr. Turner is determined to be complimentary, Mr. Jones, but I think he just flatters."

"Well placed flattery is not a crime, Miss Edgewood," Mr. Jones said with a friendly wink as he circled her.

"Too true, sir," Alex agreed as they all clapped their hands three times. "I find flattery gets a poor name from those who use it ill."

"You would," Poppy told him simply, making Mrs. Jones laugh as they all curtseyed and bowed again.

Alex's eyes danced as much as his feet did, and he kept up a constant stream of entertainment, to which Poppy could only reply, and hopefully match his wit. The couples beside them seemed to enjoy whatever they were saying, but few of them joined in.

Poppy made no attempt to keep her voice down and neither did Alex. The general volume of the room was such that only those nearest would hear them, and none of those currently dancing were stuffy enough to mind whatever they said. The stuffy ones couldn't endure the country dances and so had to watch them from the outer circles of the room.

They would have much to see as it was.

Alex grinned most of the time, and the brilliance of the sun was in that grin. He was a handsome man no matter what he did, but his smile was a thing to behold, and those unfamiliar with it would find it quite striking indeed. Because Alex was smiling, and laughing, so too was Poppy, and it had to be a well-known fact that Poppy Edgewood did not smile often.

And she laughed, to boot!

The dance ended, and each of them gave dramatic bows and curtseys, then laughed as they applauded with the others.

Alex suddenly grabbed Poppy's hand, his smile and now slightly disheveled hair reminding her of the boy he'd once been. "Come on, Poppy!"

Feeling roughly fifteen years old herself, she returned his grin and nodded, letting him tug her along. He pulled her off the dance floor and in between various guests, his hold on her secure, and his steps nearly as quick as they had been in the dance.

"Do you know where you're going?" she laughed as she was slightly jostled between people.

"Of course, I do. I've been here before, you know," he retorted, glancing back at her briefly.

Poppy chortled at that. "Not for ages, and you avoided dances here like the plague."

"Did not."

"Did too."

"Dances *were* the plague in those days," he admitted as they found a free area in the corner of the room.

Alex pushed open the door there and led them down a corridor, then through another door that found them out on a balcony overlooking the mews.

Poppy laughed as she looked down at them, hearing the horses whinnying to each other, and feeling the cool night air wash over her after.

"How did you know about this?"

"A wise man knows all of the best exits in an uncomfortable situation," he replied as he stood next to her, leaning against the rail of the balcony. "It's not much by way of a view, but…" He broke off and started to laugh.

"What?" Poppy asked, nudging him and giggling at his laughter. "Why are you laughing?"

Alex looked at her, laughter rampant on his face. "I made such a fuss about coming, and I find that I haven't enjoyed myself this much in ages."

"Really?" Poppy cried, positively beaming now. "You're not just saying that?"

He shook his head, his smile crinkling his eyes. "I'm not just saying that. This has been fun, much to my eternal surprise."

Poppy giggled again, tossing her hair slightly as she turned back to face the mews.

"I knew it! I knew it would be."

"You did not," he protested.

"Did too."

"Do you always have to be right?"

She nodded once. "Always. And if I'm wrong, somehow, I'm actually right."

Alex hooted a laugh and looked at her. "Now that sounds like your mother."

Poppy gasped and whirled to face him.

"You take that back!" she giggled, unable to keep up the pretense of offense.

"Never," he replied, shaking his head insistently.

A puff of wind passed through the balcony, dislodging a lock of Poppy's hair at her brow and sending it across her eyes.

"Curse this hair," she muttered, lifting her hand to push it back.

Alex beat her to it, his fingers gently tucking her hair back into place, then running his thumb down her cheek, his laughter and amusement fading though his color was still high.

The feeling of his touch on her skin awakened something in Poppy, caught her breath and forced a long dormant flower within her to suddenly bloom. She would have trembled had she any sensation at all, but his thumb was making its way down to her jaw, and all she could feel was him.

"Never," Alex said again, this time very softly. "Never curse that hair. It's… it's one of the most beautiful things I've ever seen."

A strangled pant escaped Poppy's lips, and it occurred to her to thank him for the compliment, only she didn't have words.

She couldn't say anything.

Her eyes darted to his lips involuntarily and she wrenched them away as Alex's hand fell from her face. He turned to face the mews, exhaling slowly, and so did she, though she doubted for the same reason.

For her part, she felt bewildered, confused, and unsettled, and in desperate need of a long walk or a drink or a patch of grass to watch the stars from.

Because the moment Alex had touched her face, she'd discovered something. She had some significant feelings towards the man beside her. Not the man he had once been, but this one, damaged, baffling, and maddening as he was.

And that was terrifying.

Chapter Fourteen

"Ah! What are you doing?"

"Making you breakfast, what does it look like?"

"Alex, step away from my pan."

"Can't do that. There are eggs in it, and they'll burn."

"They'll burn anyway, if you're the one doing the cooking!" Poppy laughed, sitting herself down at the table, despite her protestations.

Alex turned to frown at her over his shoulder. "I am not so inept as all that. I'll have you know I was one of very few soldiers who didn't need to have his food cooked for him. I did just fine on my own."

Poppy grinned and held up her hands in surrender. "Apologies for not seeing your strength in culinary realms, Lord Parkerton. I await the masterpiece of your creation."

"Too right," he said with a grin, returning to his work.

She wasn't sure what had gotten into Alex, but ever since the ball two days ago, he'd been teasing and warm and so much like his old self that it made her heart ache, though in a way that thrilled her rather than pained her. They'd laughed their way through grooming the horses yesterday before riding them across the lands, just as they'd done in their younger days. Whatever injuries Alex had suffered, they seemed to not pain him nearly so much these days. He still had nightmares, she could tell, but those would be much more difficult to resolve, no matter how he smiled throughout the day.

And how he smiled!

She could barely keep up with his good humor and wit, his

boundless energy and delight. They'd even danced again as they finished the harvest with the others and celebrated with a feast at Branbury in Lord Cartwright's honor, as he was the landowner and she his lowly tenant farmer. Fritz insisted he would have approved, so they might as well do the thing properly.

Poppy had danced with Fritz, Gabe, Alex, John Barry, and all the rest of the workers who had been helping, and it had been such a rousing good time that she actually found herself wishing the harvest wasn't completed.

Which was, of course, nonsense.

It was not as though there wasn't a great deal to do. The actual harvest was only a very small portion of the process. Now they could focus on the rest of it, and the sheep, and the cattle, and everything else she and the other tenant farmers under Lord Cartwright's care dealt with.

But not at this moment.

For now, she would let Stanton see to the details while she enjoyed having breakfast made for her.

"Do you know how I like my eggs?" Poppy inquired mildly.

"Edible, I presume."

Poppy snorted and put her head into her hands. This could be a terrible breakfast, but the attempt was adorable.

And odd. Why would Alex decide to make breakfast for her? There was no reason for him to do so, not when they'd been having only a basic meal when they could between harvesting and other tasks the farm needed completed.

She frowned at him suspiciously. "Why are you doing this? What are you up to?"

"Nothing," he refuted adamantly. "Why can't I just cook breakfast for you after all you've done for me?"

"Because you never do anything without a reason," Poppy retorted with a smile. "And you've already repaid me by seeing to the harvest and repairs."

Alex glanced at her over his shoulder again. "No, that was paying room and board." He moved over to the table and scooped almost perfectly done eggs onto her plate. "Sausages would have accompanied this, but you don't have any." He gave her a scolding look, then turned to grab the bread and jam.

"Wait a moment," Poppy said, holding up a finger. "You drop dead on my doorstep with multiple injuries and fatigue, I nurse you to health through sleepless nights and fevers and allow you to remain in my home, and according to you, all I get in return is a breakfast?" She scoffed loudly and stuck her fork into the eggs pointedly. "These had better be eggs fit for a queen."

He put the bread and jam down on the table and set his hands on his hips, brow furrowed.

"You go right ahead and take a bite, Miss Indignant Greedykins, and see if they aren't."

With a dramatic bit of flourish with her fork, Poppy did so, and if she were to be completely honest, she would have said that the eggs weren't among the best she had ever had, nor were they among the worst. But as she had expected them to be vile, she would have to admit to being pleasantly surprised. She swallowed and gave him a smile.

"Perfect."

Alex grinned at that. "Liar. I barely did anything to them, and I am quite out of practice, but I'll accept the compliment of your lie and bring you tea as a reward."

She giggled at his playful bow and reached for a large piece of bread, forgoing the jam in favor of butter. "Oh, well, if that's all it takes…"

Her cup was promptly filled with tea, and Alex surprised her by adding just the right amount of cream and sugar to it.

She stared up at him, her buttered bread halfway to her mouth. "You remembered how I like my tea?"

"Of course," he replied without any of the tension she was currently experiencing. "You're quite particular about it, or did you forget the time you broke one of your mother's teapots over my head when you were twelve?"

Poppy gasped and dropped her bread to the table. "I did not!"

Alex barked a laugh and dropped himself into chair. "I can assure you that you did. Sometimes I can still feel it running down my neck and back."

She hadn't done that. She couldn't have. She'd always been the controlled sibling in her family, in control of her temper, her manners, her behavior...

The lie made her wince, and she shook her head.

"I don't remember," she admitted as she shrugged and picked up her bread once more, taking a pointed bite.

"So many lies," Alex sighed, rocking his chair back on its back legs. "Perhaps I'll change my plans for the day."

"Plans?" Poppy perked up. "What plans? Aren't we working in the barn?"

A slow, sly, perfectly Alex grin spread across his face as he gave her a painfully deliberate shake of the head. "No, Miss Edgewood, we are not."

"Well?" She asked, her spine suddenly tingling in anticipation. "What are we doing, then?"

Alex drummed his fingers on the table, still grinning. "We're taking a holiday."

Poppy's eyes widened, and she swallowed hard. "We... we can't take a holiday. There's far too much to do, and you're still recovering. We cannot possibly go anywhere, Alex. And..." She trailed off, blushing. "And we can't go alone."

"How you jump to conclusions," he teased, his fingers tapping against the wood again. "We're not going anywhere, and nothing scandalous or untoward is going to take place."

"Really?" she asked with a dubious look. "You're too giddy for this to not be some fiasco waiting to happen."

He coughed in mock offense and put a hand to his chest. "I beg your pardon. I am not giddy." He sniffed and wrinkled up his nose in an almost grin. "But I am rather excited, I'll grant you that."

Poppy shook her head and took a bite of eggs, chewing quickly. "So, what are we doing, then? If we're not going anywhere?"

Alex tilted his head, smiling fondly. "I told you. I'm repaying you for your kindness to me."

Unperturbed, Poppy took another bite of her breakfast. "That tells me nothing," she informed him after a quick swallow.

"According to several sources," Alex intoned, folding his arms, "you've been working as hard and as much as any of the laborers you hire, despite being mistress of the house."

"Yes," Poppy muttered with a snort, "and such a grand estate is mine to be mistress of."

Alex ignored her and brought his chair back to all fours. "A lady such as yourself should not have to work her delicate fingers to the bone without any respite."

Poppy laughed at that. "Who has time for respite?"

She received a scolding look for that, so she held up a hand in apology as she continued to eat her food. Clearly, Alex was going to say whatever he liked, and she was supposed to sit here and let him go on in this ridiculous way.

So be it.

At least she had breakfast.

"So, I thought we would spend the day reminding you of what goodness can come from a relief of your duties and occupation," Alex went on. "You're not needed here today, not when Stanton and your hardy workers can take care of everything." He offered her another mischievous grin. "When was the last time *you* had fun, Poppy? And don't say the dance, that doesn't count."

She opened her mouth to object, but she caught herself at the question.

When had she?

It wasn't that she did not enjoy her life, because at times, she truly did. She enjoyed the solitude and freedom, the satisfaction of hard work, and the independence of being her own woman without reference to anybody else. She had often gone out into the meadow and sighed with the fresh air, feeling content with her situation. The village had its moments of loveliness, when it didn't plague her, though she had rarely taken the time to go in unless for necessities.

But fun?

No, she hadn't had fun in ages. But how had he known that?

She glanced up at him, unaware that she had looked away, and saw him watching her with an understanding smile.

"I know you, Poppy Edgewood," Alex said in a surprisingly gentle voice. "Once you have a cause or occupation, you devote yourself to it completely and almost never come up for breath."

It was an astonishingly adept description, which both startled and pleased her, and startled her how much it pleased her, that Alex should know her so well.

"I suppose I don't," Poppy murmured, her breakfast almost entirely forgotten. She smiled helplessly and felt an odd tickling sensation in her stomach at the warmth in his eyes.

She'd not been so unsettled by it before, had she?

Surely not. But then, that had been practically a boy's look, and nothing at all like that of the man he now was.

"Let me give you a day, Poppy," Alex begged softly. "You deserve it."

Oh, there went her heart in the face of his smile and sweetness, and it was all she could do to not crumple against her chair from the recurring effects.

"All right, then," she whispered, giggling a little. "What do you have in mind?"

Alex chuckled and folded his arms more tightly. "You'll see. Finish your breakfast, and we'll get on with it."

Poppy speared some egg and made a show of putting it in her mouth, making sure to moan with dramatic pleasure.

"Good girl."

There was nothing in the world like the sound of Poppy's laugh. Alex had heard it over and over in his head for four and a half years, but the reality of it was somehow above and beyond anything he recalled.

He'd had the chance to hear her laugh so much over the course of the day, each giggle seeming to surprise her, as though she hadn't quite remembered how.

That alone would have convinced him to do more of this stealing her away from her duties and entertaining her, but the shadows that flittered across her features in her moments of solitude were what had done it for him.

So, he'd started with breakfast for her, and then he'd taken her out of the house. They'd gone into the village, in full disguise, and wandered the shops and markets, darting between them like the children of the village did. They found all of their old alleys from days gone by, talked the baker into giving his freshest loaf to them rather than put it out for others to purchase, and had a footrace down the only empty lane they could find, which Poppy easily won. Alex would vow until he died that he had let her do so, but the truth of the matter was that he could barely manage to keep pace with her, and he would not have won in any case.

After the exertion of the footrace, Alex had taken Poppy to the pond on the grounds of Whitesdown, and, after far too much persuasion, convinced her that they should go for a swim. She'd given her fair protestations of having nothing else to wear, which he'd countered by reminding her that they could see her cottage from the pond itself and she would only need to return there for a change.

Poppy had surprised him by jumping into the pond fully clothed, despite having no bathing dress, though her gown was dark enough to mimic one. He'd removed his cravat and jumped in after her. They splashed and swam around, playing childish games and racing, yet again, from one side of the pond to the other. Alex would have won had Poppy not leapt on his back and attempted to drown him. Never one to back down from a challenge, Alex had done the same, though not quite so dramatically.

When Poppy began to shiver, Alex turned his back while she ran back to the cottage, only sneaking a peek once or twice for good measure. When she was safely away, Alex got out and changed into the fresh clothing he had brought for himself, then ventured back to the cottage for the next bit of his surprise.

A picnic luncheon, prepared by the friendly and discreet Mrs. Brown, followed by a hayride, which Stanton was only too pleased to provide, and with a delightful commentary that had them all roaring with laughter.

Then there had been the in-depth tour of the library at Branbury, with Fritz attempting to impress them both with his wisdom and insight, of which he had none. Poppy seemed to enjoy the library very much, which Alex had suspected.

She had once had a decent enough library when living at Whitesdown, but at the cottage she did not. He'd only spotted a handful of books. While Poppy had never been a bluestocking, she had enjoyed books enough. And these days, she took no leisure time to do anything at all, let alone read.

In the library at Branbury, she'd read for a solid two hours, apart from the moments where she had laughed and then read the bits out loud to Alex for his enjoyment. True to expectation, he had enjoyed every one of them. More because it had amused Poppy than because it ought to have amused him, but the result was the same, so it made little difference.

Alex had his own book to read but had no interest in it.

Poppy's face bore an exquisite variety of expressions when she read, and they captivated him beyond measure. Had he ever seen such a gentle, subtle shift from amusement to curiosity to anticipation in a face? Or ever noticed the many forms her smile could take? Her lips altered their shape with such fluid grace that it was impossible to look anywhere else. He could have memorized every single one of them, if he only knew how many existed.

He'd thought himself bound to Poppy before he'd been taken away, but what he felt for her now bordered on the extreme. A madness was overtaking him, a delirium of sorts that made him giddy with its shifts and sensations. He delighted in everything she did, and everything she was, and what pains he had felt in his life seemed but a distant memory when he was with her. He needed nothing in this world but her, and he would prove himself worthy in time.

Worthy of what, he couldn't quite admit yet, but the thought remained.

A fine dinner at Branbury had rounded off their visit there, and now they were walking back towards the cottage hand in hand, which seemed to be continuously sending sparks up his arm.

He didn't mind that one bit.

Poppy sighed a deep, contented sigh that seemed to give him some relief, as well. "Thank you so much for making me do this today, Alex," she said, squeezing his hand. "I had no idea how much I needed a day just like this."

He smiled at her easily, loving the way her barely contained hair seemed as wild as they had been today, and it suited her so perfectly.

"It really was my pleasure, and you are very welcome. But you know… we're not finished yet."

She turned to look at him with such force they nearly stumbled, and he laughed at it.

"We're not?"

Alex shook his head, grinning now.

"No, ma'am, we are not."

Poppy moved in front of him, walking backwards to face him, shifting her hold on his hand to accommodate the new position.

"Tell me! What else is there?"

He shrugged and looked up at the darkening sky, a few stars beginning to make themselves known.

"Oh, one or two things. At this time of day, there really aren't many options…"

"Alex!" Poppy demanded, squeezing his hand hard. "Tell me! Now!"

"Patience, my dear Miss Edgewood." He chuckled and wagged a finger at her. "All will be revealed in time."

She groaned, rolled her eyes, and resumed her place beside him.

"Fine," she muttered reluctantly.

"We're almost there, anyway," he assured her, rubbing her hand with his thumb. "Promise."

She gave him a harsh look. "We're almost *home*, Alex."

"Just wait." He cocked his head a moment, then looked back at her. "Does your cottage have a name? An official one?"

"No, not that I'm aware of," she replied, shaking her head. "We always called it 'the Cottage,' and not much has changed since then."

He made a face. "Not particularly specific, that. It deserves a proper name."

"Proper houses get proper names," Poppy retorted, tossing that magnificent hair. "Crumbling cottages like this get names such as Lilac Cottage or Whitewash or Old Cottage."

Alex grunted, smiling slightly at her suggestions. "Well, I don't like any of those."

"Not your house," she reminded him.

"Still," he said as they approached the spot he'd intended, where Stanton had seen to his other task admirably. "I think that… What have we here?"

Poppy stopped and looked just ahead of them, a faint gasp escaping. "No… You didn't!"

"I did," Alex claimed with a nod. "Well, technically, Stanton did, but it was my idea."

"I don't care who actually set out the blankets," Poppy protested with a sharp shake of her head, releasing Alex's hand to go sit on the two stacked blankets. "Only that they're here!" She sat without any grace or delicacy and looked up at the sky, grinning brilliantly, her eyes shifting to Alex. "We're looking at stars, aren't we?"

That smile… There was a massive list of extraordinary things he would do for that smile, and a list of quite ordinary things he couldn't seem to do because of it.

Like breathe. Or speak.

Or think.

But he could nod, and he did so twice, waiting for something else to happen.

Poppy saved him by squealing and leaning back on her elbows, her eyes back on the heavens. "I should have guessed that. It should have been obvious."

"Not *that* obvious, I trust," Alex finally replied, his voice deciding to recover itself. He dropped himself down to the blankets, matching Poppy's pose. "I only knew how much you love the stars."

She turned to smile at him, making his heart skip in his chest. "We loved the stars together. How many times did we sneak out to see them?"

He laughed and looked up at the sky, more stars appearing now.

"I lost count. All of our best talks happened under the stars, didn't they?"

Poppy sighed beside him, her hand suddenly overlapping his. "Yes, they did."

They both fell silent for a long moment, content with that slight contact while the night sky began its artistic display, the sounds of the wind in the grass and trees meeting their ears and adding a refreshing symphony of sounds.

Alex had looked at the stars as best as he could from the deck of the ship, when he was able, and once in a while he would find a constellation he recognized from home, but there was something about looking at the stars that brought him back from being *Torchon*. Something magical that steadied him on the worst days. Even when the layout of the sky was so different from his usual one that it disoriented him, he still felt secure in it.

At the time, he hadn't identified it properly, but now he knew. The stars were Poppy, and Poppy was home.

This was home.

"I know I've put you out a great deal since coming here," Alex murmured, keeping his attention on the skies, "but I am eternally grateful. And there was no place else I wanted to be but here."

A soft stroking of his hand made him swallow, and he turned to look at Poppy, who was watching him now, her expression open. Somehow, the stars had managed to find their way into her eyes, and he couldn't look away.

"Alex," she whispered, smiling tenderly.

His free hand reached for her face, and her lashes fluttered at the contact, his fingers brushing her skin gently. They fit against her perfectly, just as they always had, but somehow it was more significant now.

After all this time, it was still perfect.

His body shuddered once as that truth sank into him, and before he could lose the heady sensation sweeping over him, he leaned in, his eyes closing.

"Poppy," he breathed, his lips brushing very faintly against hers with her name.

She sighed, and somehow that sound and the touch of her lips shocked him, and he pulled back at once, resuming his position, attention directly on the skies and nowhere else. He knew Poppy was staring at him, but he refused to see her expression, afraid of disappointment, confusion, pain, or anything else to make him feel worse about retreating so frantically from so sweet a moment.

It had been perfect, and it *was* perfect, he still felt it. Perfect, but not right.

He wasn't right, and until he was, they couldn't be right.

But for now, they had the stars, and he would enjoy them with her while he could.

Chapter Fifteen

$\mathscr{P}$oppy hadn't felt this wistful in years, if ever, and there was nothing she could do about the smile on her face. She'd tried everything, and it was not going anywhere.

There would be no explaining *that* to Stanton when she saw him, but she didn't mind so very much, which was also unusual.

She smiled to herself now as she mixed porridge, of all things, and wondering why she hadn't heard Alex's nightmares last night. She hadn't thought that she'd slept particularly soundly, nor did she think Alex had enjoyed pleasant dreams, but perhaps they were lessening in their intensity. Or perhaps having such a lovely and perfect day had distracted him sufficiently from those thoughts.

She hoped that was the case.

Yesterday had been heaven on earth, and her soul felt rejuvenated from it. Today seemed brighter, her cottage cheerier, and her future... well, she hadn't really thought much of her future, considering her circumstances, but she suddenly wanted to think of it. Possibly even make plans for it. What plans, she couldn't have said, but surely, she could plan something.

Anything, really.

After last night, she wondered if Alex might yet be a part of them. She bit her lip on an embarrassed giggle, then laughed loudly as she realized she was nearly burning the porridge because of her absentminded musings. She quickly pulled it from the heat, stirring quickly. She blew on it, laughing still, waving her hand over the pot in a vain attempt to cool it, knowing it would be fruitless.

"Oh, good. It's been ages since we've had porridge well done,"

Stanton commented dryly as he entered the cottage, his clothing already dampened from the work of the morning.

"It's not that bad," Poppy replied, scowling playfully as she continued to stir the pot. "A bit of honey will set it all to rights."

He grunted at that. "You always say honey will set it to rights, and all it does is make a sweeter burned porridge."

"Would you like some?" she asked as she pulled down a few bowls. "I know how you love a good porridge well done."

Stanton coughed a laugh and shook his head, holding up a hand.

"No, I've eaten, as has Trace. We're already hard at work, and don't need our stomachs soiled for the remainder of the day."

"Then how did you ever know to come in at just this precise time?" Poppy demanded, scooping out porridge for herself. She moved to the table and raised a brow at him. "If you didn't know there was a fine meal to be had, what brought you in?"

"Smoke," Stanton informed her brusquely. "I thought you might be in distress."

Poppy burst out laughing as she sank into a chair.

"And you just walked in as though it were any usual morning stroll? No haste?"

He shrugged his broad shoulders and leaned against the door. "I figured you would be able to save yourself, for the most part."

"Oh, Stanton," Poppy laughed, putting a hand to her brow.

"Was I wrong?"

She smiled up at him cheekily. "No, you were not." She took a bite of porridge, which was rather more burnt-tasting than she would have liked, but she wasn't about to show that to Stanton. She swallowed and cleared her throat.

"What did you want, then? Tell me now, I'm off to market in a bit."

"I've come to tell you not to go to market," he replied, his lips curving in an ironic smile.

"Why?" Poppy asked around a mouthful of porridge.

Stanton hesitated, which was unlike him, and it drew Poppy's attention with more interest.

"Stanton?"

He made a face but met her look frankly. "Rumors, Miss

Edgewood."

Poppy's brows shot up. "Rumors? About what?"

"About whom, you mean."

Her body stilled, and she swallowed the bite of porridge she'd taken. "About whom, then."

"You, naturally," he said with a nod. "And your Mr. Turner."

"My who?" Poppy asked, her head feeling as though it were in a fog and everything seemed to tingle within and without. Then it cleared just enough for her mind to process the words properly and understanding dawned. "Oh... Alex."

Stanton nodded again. "I've just seen Mrs. Brown, who came to fetch the basket she packed for you and Trace yesterday, and she told me it's all over the village. Mrs. Blaine, no doubt, had something to do with the information, as her spies have had far too much interest in our fields and workers of late."

"What are they saying?" Poppy whispered, glancing out of the window as though she could see a village spy there.

Stanton growled a sigh, which was never a good sign, and tugged at his collar, though there was no cravat there to irritate him.

"That he is not your cousin, but your lover. That he is living here with you out of wedlock and engaging in all manner of sin, while he continues to work the farm at his leisure. That the men who had been here helping with the harvest that have now departed might also have been..." He trailed off, hesitating.

"Have been what?" Poppy demanded, gripping her spoon so tightly it cut into her skin. "More lovers?"

"Possibly," Stanton admitted. "Though that seems to be rather farfetched for everyone to take in. But these rumors are bringing on more rumors and more rumors... Mrs. Brown says it's rather reminding her of what things were like nearly five years ago for you, and most of that speculation is being brought up again."

Poppy gasped in disbelief, letting her eyes fall closed.

These were people who knew her, worked with her, worked for her, and saw her regularly. They smiled at her, greeted her, gave her reduced prices on their wares, asked her about her farm and her day... They danced with her only days ago at the assembly rooms, praising her with warmth and goodness, making her smile and laugh.

And to be brought back to this.

To be reminded that none of them knew her, liked her, or cared about her. That she was still a fixture for gossip and would always be the fallen daughter of one of their most respected men, though he had chosen to remove himself from them. Because of her.

An outcast.

A subject more than a person, and hardly one worth investigating properly. Why bother with anything beyond speculation? The truth would either be less exciting or more scandalous, and neither of those options could be borne.

"Did they see anything yesterday?" she whispered weakly. "Did she say?"

"She didn't say specifically," Stanton told her, shaking his head slowly. "But you know Mrs. Brown. She isn't likely to say much that's unfavorable of anybody."

Poppy turned in her chair to stare at Stanton for a moment. "But?" she prodded gently.

His expression didn't change. "But what?"

"I sensed a 'but'." She waved a hand for him to go on, though he was clearly reluctant to do so.

Stanton frowned a little, then exhaled heavily.

"She did mention that a person claimed to have seen you swimming with someone in the pond at one time, though it was not specified as to when."

Poppy cursed and dropped her head to the table, covering her head with her arms.

"No," she moaned, gripping at her hair. "Must they take everything from me?"

"It will pass, madam," Stanton assured her. "It will."

She lifted her head to look at him in disbelief.

"It will pass? Like it has passed already? Like the manner in which my reputation has passed into memory? It will pass, just as everything else has passed, and they will move on to someone else, or something else?"

"I…"

"There *is* nothing else!" she cried, her hands fisting. "There has never been anything else. They will always talk about me in some way or another." She exhaled slowly, looked down at her porridge, and straightened in her chair, extending her fingers to their fullest ability. "Right. That's enough getting excited over it."

Stanton made a noncommittal sound, but she didn't look at him.

"We'll weather this." Poppy nodded slowly to herself, her mind whirling. "It might not pass, but there is no saying that we can't bear it. We'll just move on from it and keep our heads high. And be a little more discreet in things, knowing now that the entire neighborhood is apparently watching everything that goes on here."

"Apparently, Miss Edgewood."

Now she looked at him, eyes narrowed.

"Don't they have farms? Or livelihoods? Anything else that requires their attention besides my farm and my life?"

"You would think so, and yet…"

"Right." Poppy pushed aside her porridge and rose, clearing her throat. "We are not telling Alex any of this."

"Absolutely not."

"It would destroy him," Poppy said firmly, eyeing her large friend with utter severity.

He frowned. "Why are you looking at me like that? I know Trace perfectly well enough to know not to tell him something like this when he is in this state."

"Yes, but I don't know how deep that vein of loyalty lies within you lot." Poppy pushed away from the table and started pacing. "What if he asks you about it? What if he wants to know what we were talking about for so long in here? Surely, he knows you've come in, as you are not out there with him."

"I'd lie to him," Stanton said simply. "Easily and freely."

Poppy snorted once. "Lies? Really?"

He shrugged without concern. "I am a spy, as is he."

"Then your loyalty cannot be so very great."

Stanton tilted his head, eyes suddenly hard.

"Were you a man, I would call you out for that."

Poppy folded her arms and stared at Stanton.

"I meant no offense, and you know it. But how can you be loyal to someone you lie to?"

"Some lies protect us, or others," he replied, returning more to his natural self. "In this case, it would be in his best interest to have a lie rather than truth. He's a protective man, and there is no telling what he might do in the state he is in if he knew the truth. So, I will lie, because I am loyal to him, and to you."

The fierceness in his words made her smile, and softened her heart, though she hadn't known it to be particularly hard.

"I'll accept that, thank you."

Stanton nodded and pushed away from the door, moved to the fire, and turned a log within it.

"We'll have to come up with something to tell him, of course, and inform Rogue and Weaver, should they hear of it."

"Perhaps he should sleep in the barn for a time, as you do," Poppy suggested, picking at the skirt of her faded calico. "It would not be such a scandal if he did."

"True, but what would we tell him?"

Poppy ground her teeth together and groaned, hating convention, her situation, and the fact that she no more wanted Alex to go to the barn than she wanted him to go anywhere else.

She wanted him here.

With her.

Suddenly, the door of the cottage burst open, and Alex himself stormed in, looking furious and somehow panicked.

"Alex?" Poppy asked, worried by the expression he bore.

He gave her a dark look. "What is this I hear about rumors?"

How could he have been so blind and so foolish? He should have known that he couldn't behave as he had been and have things go unnoticed. He should never have let himself open up and revert back to the habits of his former years when he and Poppy had been free.

When he'd had something to offer.

When there were no shadows.

Now, he'd ruined everything by staying as long as he had. He should have gone on, taken up residence in the boarding house or at Branbury, or even the barn. Any of those places would have done while he recovered, and he still could have helped Poppy with the harvest and repairs and all else as he had been doing.

He couldn't stay anymore, and he couldn't help anymore. He needed to leave and keep his distance for her sake, and undoubtedly for his, as well. He'd begun to hope again, and he'd learned long ago that he could not afford to hope.

Stanton had attempted to lie to him about the rumors, but even if he'd managed to do so convincingly, Alex had heard everything he needed to from John Barry just now. Poppy had said nothing during the exchange while Stanton tried to explain the rumors in more detail, but the slight creases in her brow told him she was not unmoved by them either.

That alone would have convinced him to leave, but his honor and his guilt were also in the mix, and they reigned supreme. There was nothing to pack but the sparse items he'd come in, which would have been better served as kindling for a fire than clothing for a man.

Rather like him.

He looked around the small room he'd come to know as his own, and the only one he'd known in four and a half years. He grunted as a bit of emotion began to rise within him.

That was quite enough of that. This wasn't his home, and it never would be. He turned on his heel and strode for the door, heading into the kitchen.

Where Poppy waited.

He barely looked at her as he moved into the room, noticeably dimmer than before, thanks to the cloud cover of the day. It would rain later, but for now it was only gloomy and sullen, as it ought to have been at the moment.

Cheshire's beauties were somehow enhanced on such days.

He'd forgotten that.

Alex glanced at Poppy briefly where she sat at the table, watching him, but there was nothing more to be said. After Stanton had related the truth of the rumors, Alex had said he had to leave, and left the room.

Poppy had said nothing then, and she said nothing now.

All the better.

He nodded in her direction and moved to the door, his hand gripping the handle tightly.

"Why?" Poppy said softly.

Her voice caught him somewhere in the middle of his chest, even as it made his stomach drop.

"You know why," he murmured.

"I need to hear you say it," she ground out, the words catching in a way that pained him as much as it must have her.

Alex sighed and slowly released the handle, keeping his face to the door.

"Because you are a young woman living alone."

She scoffed loudly. "Not that young."

He ignored the outburst.

"And I am a wreck of a man who refuses to ruin your reputation," he continued in the same tone. "By staying here a moment longer, I risk that."

"My reputation?" Poppy repeated, her tone suddenly shrill, her chair scraping against the floor. "My *reputation*, Alex?"

He turned in surprise, wishing he didn't have to look at her. It would only make leaving all the more painful.

Poppy stood by the table, her frame shaking, her eyes red rimmed, but strangely absent of tears.

"Shall I tell you what has become of my reputation?"

As if to completely contrast Poppy's visible tremor, Alex stilled so completely he wondered if he was breathing at all. He couldn't move, couldn't speak, and couldn't do more than blink as dread began to fill every inch of him.

"Do you think," Poppy began in a tight voice, "that I live in this cottage and on this farm because I desired it? That I decided to give up Society and all I was brought up to love and appreciate on a whim? All of this, my financial difficulty, my having to work the land, my complete lack of family and servants and friends is due to one thing and one thing only. You."

A faint pant of air rushed past his lips, and he felt as though he ought to lean against the door for balance, though he didn't dare move one inch. How was he to blame? It wasn't possible, it couldn't be possible. He'd been gone for so long, and there wasn't anything that could have...

"When I was told that you were dead," Poppy went on, her eyes cold on him, "my world came crumbling down around my ears. I was inconsolable for days, and perfectly numb afterwards. My parents gave me the solitude I required, as they knew about our attachment, but they never fully grasped the severity of it. My sisters told me I was being silly and ridiculous, and begged me to think of how it would look, but I didn't care how it looked. I cared about how it felt."

Her jaw trembled, and she clenched down hard, her face tensing, and the faintest sheen of tears began to form.

"I wore black," she whispered shakily. "I insisted upon properly mourning you. I couldn't believe that you were dead, and I refused to believe it, but I had to mourn you all the same."

Oh Lord, but that would have brought comment… Her parents would have hated the attention it would have drawn, and it would have given them cause to hate him more.

Poppy smirked then, though he doubted it was at him.

"My parents were furious, and my siblings appalled. I put myself into mourning with all the restrictions and sacrifices that brought. I refused social engagements and callers, ate in my room whenever I was permitted, and spent my time going for long walks, often to Parkerton or our bench."

It was all Alex could do not to stiffen at the mention of her doing such things. The League and other offices had sent men to tear the house apart and find whatever they could to aid in their investigations and in avenging him. She could have seen them at any time, and who knows what might have occurred if that had happened. Their bench had held all of the answers that those very men had been searching for, not that Poppy should have known any of it. He'd made that blasted thing on a whim, as a desperate attempt to combine his need for seeing Poppy as often as possible with the need to have a place of safety for his notes and reports that he could visit without suspicion.

The flower he'd carved on it had been the only sentimental thing about the bench at all, really.

Practicality, not sentimentality.

"I even slept on the bench one night," Poppy murmured. "Thinking of you, wondering if I really was being as foolish as everybody said."

Alex swallowed hard, wishing he had some strength to speak.

She cleared her throat and tossed her hair a little.

"The village, as you might imagine, began to talk, as did my friends. Why was I going to such extremes for a man to whom I was not bound? It was clear to them that I had somehow behaved shamefully, and the rumors began to swirl and take root. Some said we had gone off to Gretna, and I was actually your wife. Some thought I might have forgotten myself and was carrying your child."

With a faint hiss, Alex closed his eyes and looked away, revulsion becoming a roaring tide within him. Not at the thought of marrying her, or the thought of a child between them, but at the damage such rumors could inflict on a girl and her family. At the injustice of such behavior towards a woman who was only disappointed by the loss of someone she cared for.

"Everybody had been expecting an engagement between us," Poppy said faintly. "Everyone. It didn't come, and they talked. Then, they saw me mourning, and they talked. All they have ever done is talk and talk and talk. My reputation, as you called it, has been nothing but ruins and tatters since that day the men came to tell me you were dead. My family began to wonder at the rumors themselves. My sisters watched my stomach, waiting for my waistline to expand, giving me sidelong looks of disapproval they didn't bother to hide."

Alex tried to say her name, tried to comfort her in some way for the pains she had suffered at his expense, but there was no sound.

She sighed and moved to the window, which was closer to him than she had been, and he felt the change in distance with a sweet agony.

"They told me I had to give you up and stop the nonsense. I refused." She smiled a small, tight smile. "Henceforth, I was no longer a member of the family. The rumors had become too much, and they refused to be dragged down with me. My father kindly loaned me enough upfront to purchase the cottage and farm, and I have repaid him already, but there was to be nothing else. I'm not even sure I will inherit anything on his death."

It was worse than he could have imagined, and he had imagined a good deal since being back around her. Her situation had worried him, haunted him in a way, and there had been no opportunity for him to properly inquire about it. And there had been some consolation in not knowing. He had his secrets, she had hers.

Now she had no secrets, and he had too many, though whose had been more painful was unclear.

Poppy turned to look at Alex again, tears now evident.

"I have no reputation to speak of, Alex. None. Our night at the dance was the first night I have been out socially in months because it's too painful and embarrassing to do so. My reputation has been ruined for almost five years because I refused to pretend that I felt nothing for you. That you meant nothing to me. Everything I knew is gone because of you. And I hated you for it."

Tears began to roll down her cheeks, and Alex reached out to gently wipe them away, cupping her cheek as his heart seemed to shatter within him. He knew better than to believe she hated him now with the intensity she once did, but even that could not have matched the hatred he felt for himself, especially at this moment.

"I'm so sorry," he whispered.

She didn't bother hiding her tears or fighting them now. She let them fall onto his hand, covering it with her own.

"Don't go," she whispered. "I don't blame you for any of this."

"How can you not?" he asked. "I ruined your life, and then came back into it and ruined it again."

"I never minded having you here," Poppy insisted, pressing her hand against his. She swallowed hard and shook her head. "Because having you back made everything else worth it."

Alex couldn't breathe and could barely see, desperate to kiss her and desperate to flee.

He couldn't kiss her. He stroked her cheek once them stepped back, averting his eyes.

"I should go."

"I loved you, Alex," Poppy whispered, as if the words alone were agony.

He closed his eyes briefly, then turned back to her, letting her see the pain in them.

"I know, and I never would have left you if I'd had any choice." He blinked and felt himself straighten, turning from her and forcing himself to inhabit a role he already hated. "I shouldn't have indulged in a world that no longer exists. It was foolish to pretend we were the same people as before, and it's not fair to you to continue on like this."

Her pained gasp lanced him in both lungs, but he forced himself to keep moving, gripping the door handle and wrenching the door open.

"Alex…" Poppy pleaded, her tears now clear in her words. "Please."

"I can't," he insisted, pausing at the door. Slowly, he shook his head. "I'm sorry." He lifted his chin and strode out the door, heading straight for Branbury, giving Stanton a brisk nod as he passed, but not waiting to see how the servant and operative responded.

It wouldn't matter, anyway.

"Alex!" Poppy called, crying in earnest now.

He barely glanced behind him, his step slowing, but he didn't stop.

Couldn't stop.

Wouldn't.

He returned his attention to Branbury, praying his cousin and Fritz would have a better opinion of him than he did of himself.

Then, he would turn his attention to Parkerton, the title, and the house, and get on with his life.

It was the only thing left for him now.

Chapter Sixteen

"*And then* I find out that she'd been there before me, not only asking the same questions I had, but with the same punishments I usually engage in for preliminary interrogation! And she did it well!"

"And you loved her right then and there, did you?"

"Well, probably, but I didn't admit it."

Alex grunted and picked up yet another broken chair, tossing it out of the open window. Or what had once been a window. They'd kicked out the few panes of glass remaining, all of which had been broken in some way, and removed the frame as well, leaving a gaping hole in the shape of a perfect square in the wall, which was ideal for sending broken pieces of furniture through to crash to the ground below.

As of this moment, five chairs, one table, one chest, and half of a settee had embarked on a journey through that hole. How there had only been one half of a settee to be had was still a mystery.

Three days they'd been at work setting Parkerton to rights, if such a thing were possible in its current state of disaster. They hadn't even begun actual repairs of anything yet, as there was still far more to clear and clean first. What wasn't riddled with dust, moth holes, and some creature's teeth marks, was broken, breaking, or damaged beyond mending. It had occurred to Alex at least seven times that it might go better if he burned the entire place to the ground and started fresh.

He hadn't told Gabe that, as his cousin had volunteered to work beside him until it was done, but he was quite sure his cousin would have agreed with him. Alex hadn't said much as they'd worked, nor had he taken the time to explain to Gabe why he was no longer staying at the cottage or working the farm. He'd only stayed at Branbury the one night, and since then had opted to find a moderately clean patch of floor somewhere at Parkerton for his rest. Not that he was resting much, or at all, but he made a show of it at times.

When he did sleep, the nightmares raged at him as furiously as they ever had, more memory than imagination. Every now and then, Poppy made an appearance in them, which terrified him more than the usual ones did. Only last night, his cousin had shaken him awake from one such, though Gabe swore Alex had been incoherently screaming, so he had no idea what the subject of his nightmares had been.

There was a small mercy in that.

It would have been better for Gabe to remain at Branbury, and Alex had told him so multiple times, but Gabe was adamant that he would remain with Alex as long as necessary. Alex wasn't sure if it was fear of losing him again or protective instincts, but he was secretly quite grateful.

He'd had enough of being alone in his life.

Today, for some bizarre reason, Gabe felt the need to talk incessantly, which was quite unlike him, and it was beginning to grate on Alex's nerves. Not that he didn't wish to hear about his cousin's wife, who by all accounts was a remarkable woman and rather perfect for him, but he didn't particularly wish to hear about anything at all. His ears were still too full of the screaming of his nightmares for anything else to be particularly pleasing.

Wherever his reticent and surly cousin had gone, he wanted him back.

"And what did Eagle say about your marriage proposal to his long-lost daughter?" Alex asked as he picked up a tarnished mirror, cracked to an extreme degree, and tossed it out of the window, the crash on the ground oddly satisfying.

Gabe paused in his dismantling of the bannister of the stairs and frowned slightly.

"Do you know, I don't think we asked him… I'm fairly certain I never even asked Amelia; we just decided to do it, and he showed up at the appropriate time and gave her away."

Alex rolled his eyes and turned to the windows, where the drapes hung askew, their tattered and torn fabric looking as rough, worn, and useless as he felt. He grabbed the fabric and pulled hard, the rod and drapes tumbling to the ground with bits of plaster.

"It astounds me that he didn't murder you." Alex coughed as he spoke, waving away the plaster dust that enshrouded him.

"Oh, he might have done if she'd been in his life," Gabe informed him as he swung his large mallet at the bannister again. "But as I was the one who found her and discovered the connection, and reunited them, he was rather keen to give me whatever I wanted."

Alex choked as he pulled the other set of drapes and rod down, showering himself yet again with dust and debris.

"Knowing you as he did, I'm surprised he didn't just pay you for your efforts and bar you from her presence," he said when his choking subsided.

Gabe chuckled even as he grunted with the effort of another swing of his mallet into the railing, the wood splintering in every direction.

"Amelia wouldn't have allowed that. She's a terror when she doesn't get her way."

"God help your children."

The dust finally clearing, Alex balled up the fabric and tossed it down to the growing mass of furniture and furnishings no longer fit for the purpose they had been intended. It was an impressive heap, and they hadn't even gone through the bedrooms yet. He paused, leaning against the wall, wiping the perspiration from his brow and sighing heavily.

"Why are we doing this again?"

His cousin tossed a few of the stair spindles at him with a grin.

"Because you're Lord Parkerton, and you're supposed to live at Parkerton Lodge, which is a bloody mess."

"So," Alex grunted, "our only option is to clear and repair it?"

"And improve it," Gabe agreed with a firm nod. "Maybe by demolishing the entire east wing."

"What?" Alex cried. "Why?"

His cousin raised a thick brow of derision. "Don't you remember the east wing? Ugly, drafty, and smelled of Aunt Ethel."

Alex frowned, jabbing a finger at his cousin. "You visited me once when we were ten. Uncle Parkerton wouldn't let you come after that."

"Because I tried to demolish the east wing…"

That drew a snort of reluctant laughter from Alex, and he shook his head as Gabe set the mallet aside and came towards him.

"Come on, cousin," Gabe said, tilting his head towards the back stairs, which were in far better shape than the front ones. "We need a reprieve and a beverage, and luckily for you, I know where we can get both."

Alex followed without much enthusiasm.

"Did I leave brandy in the study before I died or something?"

"You know us better than that," Gabe responded with a dark look, though there was amusement in his countenance. "We consumed it in your honor when we searched the place."

"Destroyed it, more like," Alex muttered as they ventured outside, wincing at the bright sky.

"The brandy or the house?" Gabe laughed at his own jest, but Alex didn't feel the need to.

Besides, it wasn't that amusing.

"So where are we going?" Alex asked, exhaling roughly. "I'm not dressed for much."

"Don't have to be," Gabe told him, shrugging without much concern. "We're headed into the village and down to the Red Goblet, where we should be able to down several of them."

Alex glanced at him curiously. "Red goblets?"

"It's their signature drink," Gabe said with a nod. He clasped his hands behind his back and strolled like a dandy. "I don't know what they put in it, but it's a new favorite."

"Oh lord," Alex groaned. "You're talking about signature drinks. You, who would drink the drippings from a pan if there were enough alcohol in it." He shook his head in disgust. "Signature drink, indeed. I'm ashamed of you."

"Keep that up, and you'll be a shade of your former self," Gabe grunted with a slap to the back of Alex's head.

Alex jerked away with a scowl, though he quickly smirked.

"Oh, there's my cousin after all. Pleased to have you here."

"Shove off."

Once, Gabe's demonstration of sour behavior would have made Alex smile in appreciation. Now, he just grunted at it. Whether the change was significant or not, he couldn't have said. He simply found nothing to smile about in it anymore.

Soon enough, they were in the village with all the locals bustling about, busy with the market and the arrival of the postal cart from Northwich. No one paid them any mind, which Alex was especially appreciative of. Eventually, he would be known as Lord Parkerton and never be permitted to wander the streets of Moulton without drawing the attention of those with scheming ideals and the desire to climb the societal ladder, as it were.

Never mind that Lord Parkerton wasn't even on said ladder, the effort would be made.

At the moment, however, he would be vaguely familiar to anyone that had been at the dance or the blacksmith's, but they would undoubtedly forget his name, as Turner was an unremarkable surname of no significance.

The sounds of the village filled his ears, drowning out his thoughts, which was a blessed relief after the storm they had been of late. His eyes cast about the streets without much effort, glancing over faces and details with a dismissive air. It was a relief to notice nothing, to allow his mind to wander as it would, and to hardly exist but for faint thoughts. He'd been thinking, feeling, and experiencing far too much of late.

"That was an excellent nab," Gabe muttered, nudging Alex hard.

Alex jerked and looked at his cousin. "What?"

"That boy just nicked something from the grocer." Gabe nodded towards a lad of perhaps twelve who was making his way down the streets without any sort of haste.

Alex looked closer at the lad, his brow furrowing. He was dirty and threadbare, but there was nothing waifish about him. He skipped a step and matched the pace of the lady in front of him.

"Nicely done again," Gabe praised under his breath.

What? Alex blinked at the lad, not seeing anything that had changed, then glanced at his cousin. "Again?"

Gabe chuckled and clapped Alex on the back. "Keep up, cousin.

There's a lot going on in Moulton today."

Was there? Didn't seem to be anything of interest, apart from the usual activity of a village in the middle of the day. Bartering over prices, crying children, horses whinnying... Nothing but the everyday sounds of Moulton, and its everyday characters behaving normally.

"Oh, ho ho, his wife isn't going to be happy," Gabe scoffed darkly. "For shame, Master Grocer... A bit on the side, eh?"

Truly bewildered now, Alex looked at the grocer, expecting some blatant sign of infidelity, but only seeing the grocer smiling at an older woman inquiring about the apples, her utterly bored daughter standing nearby looking longingly towards the dressmakers.

Alex turned to Gabe in exasperation. "What are you doing?"

"Didn't you see it?" His cousin frowned at him.

"See what?" Alex demanded, truly lost now.

"Did you see the secret letters?" Gabe prodded, his brows knitting together. "The criminal hiding by the mews? The man pretending that he hadn't been up all night drowning in ale?"

"Gabe!" Alex stopped and shook his head wildly. "I'm not seeing what you're seeing! I'm not catching any of this."

Gabe had stopped just a pace or two in front of him and now turned to face him, expression unreadable.

"You ought to be seeing this. Noticing it, at least. It's second nature for people like us. We were doing this even before we were spies."

"It's not in my nature anymore," Alex told him, embarrassment and irritation rising in equal measure, "and I'm no longer a spy."

Before Gabe could say anything more, Alex turned on his heel and strode away, heading out of the village as fast as his feet could carry him without drawing attention to his haste.

It was, perhaps, juvenile to storm off in this situation, but there was nothing for it. He did not want to see the disappointment on his cousin's face, or sense just how far he had fallen from where he had been. He was unable to make it through the night without almost screaming himself awake, and he was supposed to spot a pickpocket in the middle of a snatch?

How could no one see how far he had come since his escape and leave it at that? Why did everyone want him to go beyond that and be exactly the man he was before? This was the man he was now. This broken shell of a man who saw only what was on the surface and could barely look at himself in the mirror. The one who shook during thunder and feared being alone as much as he craved it. The one who flinched at an accent and only felt comfortable when he was working himself to the bone.

This was Alex Sommerville. There was no Trace anymore.

Parkerton Lodge loomed before him suddenly, a crumbling façade of a once fine structure. It was imposing in its deterioration and needed no other way to ward others off but to exist.

Rather like him.

"I have good news!" Fritz called when he saw Alex approaching the house. "I came by to tell you, but you were gone."

Alex glared and moved to the pile of debris from their clearing, reaching for what might have been salvageable and what was not, tossing each into a respective pile.

"Well, I'm here now."

Fritz was undeterred and cheerfully joined in the task.

"Indeed. I'm pleased to inform you that you are now officially back from the dead."

"Huzzah," Alex muttered as he tossed a piece of carved wood into a pile.

"There are great advantages to being alive, you know," Fritz told him, reaching for a demolished painting. "For one, it will allow you to obtain the funds to fix this place up."

"That would help." Alex pulled the fabric of the draperies from the pile, shaking them out.

"Correction," Gabe announced as he strolled up. "That would change everything." He snorted loudly and looked the house up and down. "It's going to take a fortune to repair this eyesore."

That was true, but for some reason, the comment felt more like an insult directed at him. He knew Gabe hadn't meant that, but the sting remained.

"And for two," Fritz went on as though Gabe hadn't said anything, which was fairly typical where Gabe was concerned, "it allows you to come back and work for the League without any trouble whatsoever."

Alex paused as he reached for another length of drapery. He heard Gabe wince aloud. He had a good reason to.

Slowly, Alex drew himself up to give a cool look at one of the most powerful men in England, and his former mentor in many ways.

"Come back?" he repeated in a carefully stiff voice.

For a spy, Fritz was hopelessly dimwitted at times.

"Yes, to come back to work."

"Fritz," Gabe warned softly, all amusement gone from his tone.

Alex kept his eyes on the taller man. "I've told Cap I'm not coming back."

Fritz nodded, not at all surprised, and his expression showed understanding. "Not until you're ready, naturally."

"Perhaps not ever, Fritz," Alex told him, his hands clenching into fists.

His friend saw the motion, and his eyes flicked back up to Alex's.

"You can go into training, Alex. We'll give you all the time that you need, all the training and help you need, and before you know it…"

Alex's expression darkened, and Fritz trailed off when he saw it, his brow furrowing despite his hesitation.

"Alex?" Gabe prodded warily.

Tremors had begun to course through Alex, legs and arms quivering, spine tingling, and it was all he could do to keep still where he stood.

"Do you think I am in any state to return to my old life, Weaver?" he spat. "With my diminished stability and rusted instincts? With my inability to sleep without nightmares and my weakened mental capabilities? You want me to go back into training as if I were merely inexperienced and in need of education?"

"Alex," Gabe barked.

Fritz and Alex ignored him completely, locked in a glaring match with each other, a test of wills Alex refused to lose.

"I only ask that you consider Cap's suggestion, Trace."

"Don't call me that," Alex spat.

Fritz's dark gaze never wavered.

"Give yourself some time. You have all the resources we can offer at your disposal, and we are more than willing. You are one of us, Trace, and we would love to have you back."

Alex stared at him, the tremors subsiding only slightly.

"I'll never be back, Weaver," he said in a low voice. "Not to who I was, and not to who Trace was."

"Just consider it."

Consider it. Did he think that Alex hadn't considered it from every angle when he'd refused Cap before?

"Maybe when I stop feeling straps of braided rope with bits of metal in it slashing across my chest and back, I'll consider it," Alex said slowly, lifting his chin as a chilling calm settled on him. "Maybe when I can close my eyes without anticipating a glowing fire iron searing the soles of my feet, I'll consider it."

Fritz blinked unsteadily, and Alex heard Gabe shift behind him, though neither said a word.

"Maybe," Alex went on, his voice rising, "just maybe, when waking up with my arms above my head doesn't terrify me with the thought of someone trying to carve out a rib or two, I'll consider it."

With a brisk nod, Alex brushed past Fritz and moved to the garden remnants, long destroyed by the intruders of the house and the neglect of years. He could hack away at any of the dying plants with a spade or an axe and feel himself more to rights without having to converse with a single soul. Well, provided Gabe and Fritz took the hint from his tirade and left him to himself.

The crack of a twig brought Alex's head up, but he looked ahead instead of behind him. His heart sank when he saw Poppy standing there, a basket on her arm, her eyes wide as she stared at him. He cursed under his breath. Clearly, she had heard his outburst, and if anyone else had been wandering by the grounds, they'd have heard him, too.

Perfect.

"Well?" he demanded as he glared at her. "Do you have something else to add? Some other area in which I lack now but once excelled in? Would you like to voice a complaint about my current state and choices in the hopes that it might motivate me to become something else?"

He saw Poppy's throat move in a swift swallow, and she took two steps forward. "Stanton said you were working on Parkerton, and

I assumed that the kitchens were in no state to provide anything. So, I brought some things."

Oh.

Alex swallowed and tried to glower less aggressively, but it appeared he had reached his limit.

"Did you make them or did someone capable?"

"Mrs. Brown did, thank you very much," Poppy responded, her forehead knitted in irritation, "and if you are going to be such a troll about it, I'll take it back home and enjoy it myself. Lord knows, it's been some time since I've enjoyed a meal I did not have to prepare."

"I'd say it's been a long time since you've enjoyed a meal at all, since you prepare them."

She huffed loudly and set the basket down, folding her arms.

"Did you toss your manners out of the window with all this mess, or are you just feeling especially cantankerous because now you have to put in some effort to get what you want?"

Alex opened his mouth to respond when Poppy looked behind him and beamed a delighted smile.

"Good day, Fritz. Good day, Gabe."

They responded in kind, but Alex couldn't spare them a look.

How could she look at him that way, speak to him that way, and have such joy for the others? Why was he to blame for everything? What did it matter anyway?

"I've left some food from Mrs. Brown for you gentlemen," Poppy told the others, refusing to look at Alex. "I'm not sure what she did, but it smells wonderful."

"Don't bother with charity," Alex snarled, gripping a bush nearby just for the sake of having something to clench. "We don't need it."

Poppy slid her suddenly cold eyes to him, her mouth tightening.

"Charity requires that I feel something generous within me," she informed him in a low voice. "That isn't what this is."

"Then what is it?"

"Pity. Pathetic, condescending, pride-offending pity, and may you choke on it, Alex Sommerville." She turned on her heel and marched away, her coppery curls dancing in agitation as she moved.

Alex watched her go, hating himself to a new depth for spurning her kindness, for provoking her, for sending her retreating in such a way. Once he was better than that.

Now…

"Damn, Alex," Gabe hissed suddenly close to him.

Alex exhaled irritably. "I know, but if you understood what went on between us…"

"Not that," Gabe interrupted sharply. "You're a damned fool, and we can berate you later for that. Let go of the thorns before you bleed to death."

That made Alex scowl with an accompanying growl as he looked over his shoulder. "Metaphors, cousin?"

"No, although that would be a good one." Gabe's wide eyes gave Alex pause. "I mean you need to actually let go of the thorny bush you are clenching in your right hand before your physical body bleeds to death."

"What?" Alex looked down at his hand, where, sure enough, he was clutching a bush of thorns, and ruby red blood was pouring from him. "Oh…"

"How did you not know?" Gabe murmured, staring at Alex's hand, just as Alex was.

There were no answers for that. Nothing to say. Nothing he could explain.

Slowly, one finger at a time, Alex forced his hand open, looking at the fresh wounds as though they could give him answers.

"Perhaps I'm immune to pain now," Alex murmured, "or I'm accustomed to it."

But there was something quite chilling about the way he could watch drops of his blood fall from his hand to the ground beneath them, all without feeling any pain from the injuries themselves.

"I can't go back, Gabe," Alex rasped, transfixed by his blood. "I can't."

"Then don't go back," Gabe replied, removing his cravat and wrapping it around Alex's hand swiftly, applying a sharp pressure that Alex did feel.

His cousin met his eyes, and Alex found a steadying influence within them.

"Don't go back," Gabe said again. "Go forward."

Forward. The word struck Alex and reverberated in his mind long after Gabe tied off the cravat and went back to work.

He could go forward.

But where would forward go?

Chapter Seventeen

There wasn't anything more maddening than a matter left unsettled, and when the matter was one of the heart, it was infinitely more maddening. For the last few days, Poppy had been teetering on the very edge of such madness. It wasn't her fault she was going mad, and she refused to pretend that it was.

The blame could lie fairly and squarely on the broadening shoulders of Alex Sommerville. Somehow, his brooding and his surliness had increased with his departure from her cottage, which was surely the exact opposite of what he had intended, and after their most recent interaction, she seemed to be the recipient of a particularly bitter aspect of his darkness.

Why, she could not say. What had she done but treat his injuries with all her energy and give him the space and peace he needed after his ordeal and try to bring him back to the light? How dare she do such a thing?

She hadn't dared venture to Parkerton after he'd snapped at her, having no desire to see him like that, if she could help it. What he'd said hadn't bothered her as much as the tone he had said it in. They had mocked her cooking ability time and time again, but always with a hint of mischief. There had been no mischief in that last exchange. There had been nothing light or warm or friendly in it, and nothing she could have smiled about. Somehow, it had almost seemed as though he had been intentionally trying to wound her.

That wasn't her Alex, and it would never be her Alex. He would never have hurt her, or anyone, with intention, nor spoken with the sort of spite that she had heard.

Therein lay the crux of her madness.

Was the Alex she had known and loved gone forever? Had the brief interlude they had shared since his return been something imagined and fleeting? What had been real and what had been imagined?

While Alex had lived under her roof, her sleep had been disturbed because of his nightmares. After he'd gone, her sleep had grown disturbed because of her own thoughts and dreams. She wasn't sure there were words for her dreams. Nightmares would have been too harsh a title, and yet there was something haunting and lingering about them. Something that kept her awake for most of the night, sent her to examine the night sky, whether star filled, or cloud covered, and occupied her thoughts for days on end.

Memories filled those dreams, moments she had shared with Alex in her past and treasured, only now those memories were altered. There was a strange light in Alex's eyes now, and a darker tint to everything. Something suspicious and twisted that brought with it doubts that assailed her in her waking hours. Doubts, questions, uncertainty, all rose within her at regular intervals, and suddenly nothing she had known seemed real anymore. Nothing any of them had told her seemed real.

Unfortunately, this meant she couldn't face any of them for fear of saying something she would regret, asking questions she ought not, and raising old fears that would be better left in the past.

Even Stanton had avoided her of late, though he was still working the farm and harvest just as he always had. But their conversations were strictly related to farm matters and without any additional warmth or extraneous topics.

He left her alone. They all did.

Especially Alex.

Against all her natural proclivities, Poppy had decided that the only way she could work out her emotions and aggression was to make bread, which she had never done successfully. But as she kneaded the dough now, she felt aggression and anger building.

"After all this time," she ground out as she pummeled the dough. "All this time, and *now* you decide to give me reason to hate you? Now you become the villain they all said you were?"

She grunted as she reached for more flour, her fingers covered in the clingy, sticky mass. She sprinkled the flour on the table, picked up the dough, and set it down on the floured surface, muttering to herself.

"Do I have anything to add?" she grunted under her breath. "Do I have anything to add, Alex? Oh, where do I begin? Which year should I start with, hmm? I have several things to add, if you truly wish to start with that."

She worked the dough hard, pushing and grinding her knuckles into it, snarling under her breath.

"He doesn't need charity?" She laughed once to herself. "He needs absolutely everything. A house, funds, an occupation... Manners... Not to mention health and strength, which is still sadly lacking, as anyone with eyes can see."

The dough made a faint sputtering noise as she pressed into it again, and she stared at it in disgust.

"Don't need charity from me?" she snapped, reaching for more flour. "And then to insult my cooking? I'd like to see him do better. The kitchens at Parkerton would be perfectly empty after this long, so what, pray tell, is he eating? Is he so high and mighty that he cannot accept something from a neighbor, though it was not prepared by his own chef?"

There was no sound from the dough, but her knuckles pounding against the wood of the table seemed to emphasize things nicely.

"As if I have had nothing better to do with the last five years than wait for him to show up and justify my state." She huffed loudly as her fingers worked in the mixture, still not finding the traction she needed to make this bread dough actually resemble such. "And now he's got me making bread to work out my agitation. Bread, of all things. Not a walk, not beating something, as he would undoubtedly do, and not even hard labor on my own farm. No, I am making bread."

"Yes, and you seem to be struggling with that."

Poppy whirled with a gasp, fingers taking far too many remnants of the dough with them.

Gabe stood in the doorway, looking rather polite and apologetic, smiling a little at her. "Do you mind, Poppy? The door wasn't latched."

Poppy swallowed as she stared at the man, his dark, curly hair not fitting with his usually irritable persona, though his shockingly pale eyes more than made up for it. She was tempted to tell him to leave off, to go back to Parkerton and his infuriating cousin, and to take his secrets with him.

But she couldn't.

"I don't mind," Poppy muttered, her fingers absently moving, sticking together with the dough upon them, "I suppose."

Gabe had begun to nod, and then stopped at her added words. One corner of his mouth drew up. "We deserve that, but thank you."

Well, as long as he could admit it…

Poppy nodded once and turned back to her bread. "What can I do for you, Gabe?"

"At the moment, I'm more concerned about your bread than my task here," he said, sounding almost pained as he neared her.

She slapped her hands on the wood and glared at him.

"I've already received enough criticism of my efforts for a lifetime, in case you didn't hear them for yourself."

Gabe winced and came closer still.

"I don't mean to insult you, my dear. Only… you are beating that poor bread so that it may become an inedible slab rather than rise appropriately." He smiled weakly with a small shrug. "And you seem to be wearing more of it than you are working. You could butter your fingers or use more flour on the surface."

Poppy returned her attention to the dough in front of her, grinding her teeth.

"You are a bread expert now, Gabe? Not just a spy?"

"I spent months working at a bakery on one of my assignments," he replied with an easy chuckle, a surprising amount of warmth in the sound for one who was supposed to be so cantankerous. "I'm no expert by any stretch, but I do know my way around a loaf."

"Of course, you do," she muttered, peeling the dough from her fingers and tossing it back with the rest. "Perfect."

"Hardly perfect, Poppy," Gabe teased, coming to stand beside her. "I can teach you, though, if you wish."

"Go right ahead." She gestured faintly to the bread, making a face.

He reached across her for more flour, dusting it over the surface of the bread before pressing his hands into it almost gently, seeming to caress the dough over and over, turning the now smooth round over in his hands and on the table. He lengthened it as he did so, making it longer and thinner in size.

"Aren't you supposed to make it a loaf?" Poppy asked, not bothering to remove the bite from her tone.

"Usually, yes," Gabe replied with a nod, still smiling crookedly, "but with what you've put this poor matter through, an alternative method must be employed."

Poppy watched as his hands worked the dough expertly, despite his claiming he was otherwise. It seemed odd to her, almost bewildering, that hands so prone to fighting and hard labor should be equally attentive to something as soft and pliable as baking bread.

Curious, indeed, for a spy.

And a lord, if she had her facts correct.

"You seemed to be rather intent on beating this dough rather than kneading it," Gabe said in an almost offhand way as he now pressed the dough nearly to its extremes. "Care to share? It might not be as cathartic or satisfying as beating something, which I am usually in favor of myself, but it may save your hands and your dinner."

Poppy folded her arms across her chest, a disgruntled hum escaping. "We're having stew for dinner, if you can't smell it."

"Can't smell it." Gabe shook his head once as he peeled the edges of the dough from the table along one long stretch. "You must not be using enough spices, but bread and stew are the perfect combination, so you will want this to accompany it."

She scowled as she moved to the pot of stew she'd only just put on and reached for pepper and salt as well as some herbs, tossing them all blindly in. Perhaps he would be able to smell it now, and perhaps Stanton wouldn't complain about his meal if she added more into it.

Perhaps.

"Now, what are you doing with the bread?" she asked, turning back to Gabe, who still worked the dough carefully into a long roll.

"You'll see," he told her as he rolled the dough completely. Then, he buttered his hands and pressed the side of one hand directly into the middle, splitting the roll in two, pinching the edges and separating them. "Work the ends of the roll until they are completely tucked under and no trace of the layers can be seen. Nice and smooth, like this. You see?" He showed her the end of his that he'd worked into a smooth, round edge.

Poppy nodded, buttering her hands and trying to mimic his actions with her inexperience, failing almost at once.

He pretended not to notice as he finished his other side, then set his created loaf, seam side down, into the pan. "Seam side down so that it doesn't open but will spread. You do the same with yours, and you'll have two perfect loaves ready to bake in an hour or two."

Poppy placed her sloppy loaf into a pan, frowning slightly at the sight of it.

"That's not ever how I've done it."

"Well, it's only one way to do it," Gabe laughed, shrugging a shoulder, "but I promise it will do the trick admirably."

"You underestimate my inabilities," she assured him as she dropped herself into a chair, wiping her hands on her apron. "I could still burn them until they resemble bacon."

He picked up a towel and wiped his hands, grinning at her. "If your bread turns to bacon, you had best run, for your house is on fire."

Poppy snorted and covered her face with her hands, groaning softly. She heard the chair beside her scrape against the floor, then groan when it became occupied. Sighing, she dropped her hands into her lap, looking over at the man beside her without any emotion but resignation.

"Why are you here, Gabe? What can I help you with?"

"What can you help me with?" He cocked his head, a slight furrow appearing between his brows. "I rather thought it was I who could help you, for once."

"With my bread?" Poppy smirked in amusement. "Consider it done."

Gabe shook his head. "Not with the bread, though it was nice to work dough again. It's been some time."

"I can imagine," she murmured, smiling more fully at the

thought of this man enjoying baking bread, of all things.

He quirked a thick brow at her. "Can you, indeed?"

That made Poppy sit back in thought, recalling with too-perfect clarity just what the man before her was.

"No," she replied, her voice sounding far away. "I suppose not."

His smile was one of understanding, and he nodded slowly.

"That's what I thought. Which is why I thought that I might come see you this afternoon. Especially given your last meeting with my cousin."

"I don't want to talk about Alex. That's over." Poppy wrenched her gaze away and looked out the window.

"That's almost exactly what he said today." Gabe grunted to himself. "The similarity in tone and expression, let alone words, is really quite disconcerting."

Reluctantly, she glanced over at him once more.

"Did he? So there really is nothing to discuss then."

"On the contrary," Gabe replied with a very determined shake of his head. "I believe there is a great deal to discuss."

Poppy frowned at him fully now, pressing her tongue hard against her teeth for a moment.

"You aren't going to listen if I refuse, are you?"

He ginned very briefly. "Not even a little bit."

Of course not. She waved a dismissive hand at him, rolling her eyes.

"Go ahead, then. Get it over with."

"Thank you," Gabe replied sagely. "This won't take long. I'm not a meddler."

"And yet..."

He ignored that, folding his arms over his broad chest, smiling a little. "I think you know that Alex's lashing out the other day was a defense mechanism. He doesn't really feel that way, nor is he that hard of a man. He leaves that sort of thing to me."

Poppy nodded once but said nothing. She did know that about Alex, but it didn't take away the sting of experiencing it. Of being abandoned by him yet again. Of losing him in a more acutely painful way than before.

"I won't pretend to know what you have been through in the last five years," Gabe said bluntly, surprising her. "Nor will I pretend to know what Alex has been through, though I probably have a fairer idea of his suffering than yours."

"They are hardly comparable," Poppy protested in a low voice, shame heating her cheeks.

Hadn't she been telling herself the same sort thing? That Alex had no idea what she'd suffered and had forgotten her in all of this? Yet to hear it said aloud was nearly unbearable, and she felt the need to defend Alex, even to his own cousin.

"Not all scars are visible ones, my dear," Gabe chided, giving her a hard look. "You should know that by now."

She swallowed and looked down at her worn fingernails tracing absent patterns on the wood surface.

"Yes, you may have a faint inkling of what Alex suffered physically," he went on, leaning back in his chair. "I'll be blunt and tell you it's likely a hundred times worse than anything you can imagine."

Impossibly, furious at Alex though she was, her eyes burned at his claim and her throat tried to close. Gabe cleared his throat harshly as if he, too, had the same sensations.

"But possibly even worse than all of that is what he endured in other ways that are less visible. Wounds that are much more difficult to heal. While the damage inflicted may be very different, this is the sort of wound that you, too, have experienced."

"I'm not wounded," Poppy whispered, intent now on her fingernails.

"Oh, please," Gabe scoffed quietly. "Tell that to someone a bit less intuitive or observant."

She looked over at him again, startled to find him smiling with the utmost gentleness. Fondly, even. As though she were a sister of sorts. Someone he truly cared for.

But he couldn't, could he?

"You do not have to have the exact same stripes laid upon you to understand," Gabe told her, his smile lopsided. "You have both suffered greatly by what has happened. In different ways, certainly, but suffering still, and in ways that linger for years. The difference is that Alex never thought his would end but by his death. Yours would at least be something you could eventually learn to live with or grow accustomed to, if I'm not mistaken."

Poppy nodded yet again.

"I did learn," she murmured. "It didn't hurt any less from day to day, but I learned to live with the pain. It didn't feel as sharp, nor did I dwell on it as much. I adapted to my surroundings and to my life. I had to."

"Alex needs to learn the same," Gabe insisted kindly, reaching forward to cover her hand with his. "We all want him to be the same man he was before all of this, but the truth is, he won't be. Parts of him will be the same, will always be the same, but parts of him will be forever changed. He needs to learn how to live with those changes, how to adapt to his new life of freedom, and to accept his past as part of who he is now." He squeezed her hand gently. "And he needs patience while he figures that out. It is something he has to do on his own until he is ready to let anyone else in."

Patience. She wasn't sure she had enough patience, not after all these years. It was selfish and cruel, but she wanted answers. She wanted proof.

She wanted Alex.

Poppy shook her head as the painful truth rose within her. "It won't be me that is let in, Gabe. It will be you, his family. He left me again," she whispered with complete honesty. "I don't mean anything to him now."

"Oh, my dear girl," Gabe said with a small chuckle. "Do you forget that it was you he came to see when he escaped?"

"Only because it was closer," she insisted firmly.

She earned a reproving look from him with that. "Believe me, he could have come to me if he wished it, or had word sent to me. But he didn't. He went to you." He grinned yet again, his eyes crinkling at the corners. "It's you, Poppy. You, above all others."

She couldn't bear that. Couldn't believe that. After all this time, she just couldn't.

Gabe sighed softly and rose, tugging her up with him.

"Come with me, Poppy. Come see him. Ask him."

"I can't ask him that," she told him as she grudgingly rose. "Not now, he would say something I couldn't bear to hear."

"Then, ask him one of the twenty-seven other questions in your head," Gabe responded, taking her shoulders in hand. "Don't mind how he barks. Just listen beyond the words."

Poppy exhaled heavily, but let Gabe take her out of the cottage and walk with her down to Parkerton.

"And you say you're not a meddler."

"Not habitually, certainly," He said, shrugging one shoulder, "but being a spy, there does tend to be some meddling involved. And with Alex, I do tend to meddle. It does so annoy him when I do."

She laughed at that, tossing her head back and letting herself do so freely, the fresh country air filling her lungs.

"Do you think he'll go back to being a spy?"

"Not sure, to be perfectly honest," Gabe answered easily, not seeming particularly concerned about it. "I'd rather he go back to being a human, if nothing else."

There was a dark truth to that, and it sobered Poppy considerably. She hadn't been fair to Alex, demanding so much and expecting so much. He was alive, and that should have been enough for her.

"I've been selfish," Poppy whispered, shaking her head.

"So has he," Gabe said at once. "That's to be expected when you both have only had yourselves to think about all this time. Don't waste a moment on guilt for that."

He could say that all he liked, but guilt was Poppy's constant companion of late. Guilt, doubt, and fear.

They made for a depressing trio of companions.

Parkerton Lodge was before them soon enough, and out in the garden, Alex worked tirelessly on clearing the rubble and the dead plants. The house didn't look much better from the exterior, but she suspected the place had been almost entirely gutted from within. It would take ages to restore it, but it seemed Alex was willing to accomplish it, no matter what.

"I'll go stand out of earshot," Gabe murmured, squeezing Poppy's arm. "I don't need to meddle that much."

She nodded as he left, and approached Alex as calmly as she could, several questions swirling in her mind. She couldn't ask him much, wasn't sure she wanted to ask him anything, but seeing him brought her a measure of comfort she hadn't expected.

He paused his work when he saw her, leaning heavily on his spade.

"Poppy…"

The hesitation in his voice, the warmth in his eyes, settled her considerably. Gabe was right. It wasn't over.

"I have a question for you," Poppy said, folding her hands before her, keeping her expression calm.

Alex's dark eyes remained on her, and he stood perfectly still.

She exhaled shortly, then asked, "Were you planning on marrying me, Alex? Before all of this? Was that ever part of your plans?"

His face tightened briefly. "I'm not sure that matters now."

"I don't care if it does," Poppy replied, hearing the despondent note in his voice and taking courage from it. "But if I am to have no answers about anything else, you owe me that."

She watched those words sink in and held her breath.

"Yes," Alex told her in a very low voice, nodding once. "I was planning that."

"Thank you." She managed to smile only faintly, though her heart seemed to skip with sudden delight. She turned away, walking very quickly back towards the cottage.

Alex didn't call after her, but she hardly expected him to. She hoped he saw her smile, and hoped it made him wonder. Made him hope. Made him smile.

But there would be time for that later. There would be time for everything later.

Poppy laughed to herself as she practically skipped home, now determined to give Alex everything he needed, even if it were time, space, and patience. He might hate it, might rage at her, and she might rage right back, but until he was a much better version of himself, until he was whole, and could tell her it was over, she would not believe it. After all, she had refused to believe he was truly dead for so long, how much more difficult could this possibly be?

The cottage was quiet when she returned, though it did smell a good deal better with the spices in the stew, and the bread rising nicely. Still too soon to bake, but it seemed that Gabe's method would certainly work well. She made a mental note to take him at least half of a loaf for his care and instruction.

And meddling.

That made her smile further still, and she couldn't wait to tease him about it when things became clearer and more settled for them all.

Whistling an absent tune, Poppy turned to sample the stew, knowing it wouldn't be quite ready, but well on its way.

A band of fabric was suddenly forced into her mouth and pulled tightly, completely muffling her scream. Then, something hit her soundly on the back of her head.

And everything went black.

Chapter Eighteen

*A*lex wasn't sure what Poppy had been about when she'd asked him that question today, but after three days of not seeing her, wondering if she finally hated him the way she ought to, the sight of her had struck him with an intensity he was entirely unprepared for.

And she'd smiled at his answer.

Why had she smiled?

It was too confusing, and too much to bear. How was he to manage his affairs and the renovation of his estate, taking up his lands and title once more, if his mind were too fixed on Poppy? His mind needed to be clear and open, and he needed to be above reproof in all things. At this moment, he could reprove himself for many things. His behavior towards her, for example. There was enough reproof there to feel guilty for a lifetime.

Distance ought to have helped him, but in order for that to work, there would need to actually be distance. Despite being removed from the cottage, removed from her, he felt anything but distant. He could see the cottage from the windows of his bedroom, and it tended to draw his attention quite fixedly when he retired. Not that there was much within the room to consider it his bedchamber in truth, but it had at least become a place of refuge for him.

And it was not as though he slept in the room much. He rarely slept at all anymore. The nightmares were growing too dark, too twisted, too haunting to risk enduring, and he had little enough to distract him during the day from the memories of them. But staring at the light in the cottage until it faded into the night seemed to give him a moment of reprieve.

He'd come to crave that reprieve nightly. If he could not converse with Poppy during the day with sanity and control, or even be near her, at least he could have this.

It might not be much, and certainly couldn't last forever, but for now…

"Where is your head at, Alex?" Gabe asked, tossing a clump of dirt at his back.

Alex grunted and brushed at his back quickly, frowning at his cousin.

"You don't want to know."

"Probably true," Gabe said easily as he worked away at the roots of a long dead bush. "But I'd wager I can guess."

Impossibly, that made Alex chuckle, and he went back to work on the pile of rubbish they'd tossed from the house, which was now diminishing by the day, thanks to his efforts and the pilfering of locals.

"There's only two guesses worth making, so there's no wager in it at all."

"I'd wager I can be very specific with my guess."

"No," Alex laughed, picking up a chunk of wood and tossing it in Gabe's direction, not caring if it hit him or fell far short. The satisfaction was in the effort, and in the lightness he felt in it.

His nightmares may be worse, but his days were certainly growing easier. He was beginning to feel more himself than he had in years, and it was freeing. There was still a long way to go before he would truly be free, but he was beginning to hope, and that was just as foreign and freeing as anything else.

Gabe hadn't said anything about returning to London or to his life as a spy, and Fritz had also been perfectly silent on the subject. They seemed content to respect his wishes and allow him the time he needed to heal and discover for himself what would lie in store for his life. If there were any doubts about his abilities given what he had endured, they hadn't said anything, though they had exchanged looks enough when Alex had missed something or reacted poorly to assure him that they spoke about it privately.

That was to be as expected, he supposed.

"Trace! Rogue!"

Alex looked at Gabe in confusion, then turned to see Stanton dashing towards them, his horse nearby, and the large man was absolutely frantic.

"Stanton," Alex greeted, wiping his hands off. "What's the trouble?"

"It's Poppy," Stanton panted, bending over with his hands on his knees. "I can't find her anywhere."

Gabe tossed aside his spade and hurried over.

"I was just there hours ago. Everything seemed fine."

Stanton shook his head, chest heaving.

"I've been settling the details of the harvest all day. Returned to the farm an hour ago. She's not there, not on the land, not in the village... The lock on the cottage door was broken. Something isn't right..."

Alex stared at the older man, his heart seeming to beat outside his chest, the day suddenly frigid.

"Are you sure?" he murmured.

"Positive," Stanton said with a swift nod. "The stew she was making had completely spilled over into the fire, and the bread was never set to bake... Nothing was missing from the cottage, not even out of place. I've ridden all over the place. She's gone."

Gone. Poppy was gone.

Taken.

Various tumblers in Alex's mind spun and shifted, clicking together and catching on one another, forcing away a fog he hadn't known resided within him. Everything continued to spin and whirl, racing in forty-two directions with energy and ease, as though the path were familiar and the way clear.

Clarity. Suddenly, everything was clear as crystal, and a long-forgotten twinge of warmth began to burn within him and spread into his limbs. His brows snapped down and he nodded once.

"Go to all of the local contacts. Every single one of them. We need everything they have, information, rumors, speculation, conjecture. I don't care if we can rely on it or not, I want to know."

"Yes, sir." Stanton nodded, straightening. "Report back here?"

"Yes," Alex told him, moving for the stables. "Alert Thomkins in the village. He was my man before, and he'll report here and take in whatever reports come if I'm not here."

"Where would you be?" Stanton inquired as he walked with him.

Alex tipped his head towards Poppy's home. "Cottage. I'll investigate every inch of it for clues, any sign that you may have missed in your search for her."

Stanton grunted once. "I didn't miss anything."

"There's not time to worry about offended airs or wounded pride, Stanton," Alex barked. "Go!"

The large man flashed a quick grin and mounted his horse, riding away quickly.

"I'll go to Weaver," Gabe told Alex as he came up behind him, "then meet you at the cottage. Two sets of eyes never hurt."

"Good." Alex turned, thinking quickly. "Have him send word to the League but leave out the Shopkeepers or the Convent until we know more. No sense in bringing up the entirety of British covert operations until we have need. But Stanton's instincts shouldn't be doubted, so preliminary warnings should be prepared."

Gabe was already on his horse and nodding. "I'll be at the cottage shortly. Tread carefully."

Alex snorted at his cousin as he moved to the horse they'd brought over from Branbury for him.

"I'm always careful," he responded.

"There's a laugh." Gabe shook his head and took off at a hard gallop for Branbury.

That was true, but Alex didn't think it bore stating at this moment.

He mounted the horse and dug his heels in, heading across the lands wildly, somehow barely hearing the pounding of horse hooves over the sound of his own heartbeat.

It was steady, to his surprise, and not frantic but for a faint edge that pained him at times. He ought to have been utterly terrified for Poppy, panicked to a worrying degree and filled with guilt. Yet there was a calm that had settled on him, an intense focus that he wouldn't pretend to understand at this moment, but he greeted it as he would an old friend.

Excitement filled him with every beat of his heart, though it was hardly something he was pleased with. He was livid beyond belief, and his lungs burned with fear, only he was not paralyzed by either of them. Rather, he felt driven. Shoved forward into the fray before him, oddly confident and determined about his course. What exactly the course was seemed to be less certain, but it would come to him, he was sure. At the moment, he only needed answers. Answers provided direction, and direction was all he needed.

He slid off the horse once the cottage was before him, racing towards the building only to stop himself, and slowly pace backwards, eyes on the ground.

There was only one way to the cottage from the main road unless one crossed the lands as he had just done, but it wasn't a structure of any significance. It would not stand out to anyone unfamiliar with its position in the countryside. From the wrong side of things, it could easily be missed.

But someone coming from the village with the intent of taking her would have brought something to transport her with, even if it were a cart or a horse. There ought to be evidence of whatever method they had chosen, but whether they would be able to discern that from the marks of their own carts and horses would be more difficult to predict.

He scanned the ground back and forth, his eyes grazing over the details that only days before had been invisible and insignificant. Poppy usually went on foot back and forth to the village, and Stanton's horse doubled as the farm horse, which wasn't necessarily designed for travel or excursions, even if Stanton had been inclined. No recent signs of a cart or wagon, not much to indicate horses or excessive foot traffic.

Had it been a single man, then? It would have been easy to take Poppy unawares in this small cottage, particularly after her trip down to his lands at Parkerton. She was untrained and unsuspecting, so there would be absolutely no wariness in her manner about anything, let alone entering her own house, but she would have noticed a cart or wagon, an unfamiliar horse, surely.

Alex hummed to himself, then glanced over at the barn in thought.

To truly be hidden, there would need to be a place to hide. What better than a shelter already provided? Alex had hidden in a barn or two himself on his escape, so why should they not do the same?

He strode over to the barn, eyes moving swiftly across the shelter and the entrance, looking for the slightest sign of disruption or bit of evidence. The interior looked as neat and tidy as it ever had, hardly a piece of straw out of place on the barn floor. Their harvest remained untouched in the corner, the cart was in its usual place, and the horses' stalls seemed to be nearly pristine.

Except…

Alex paused at the spare stall, cocking his head as he examined it more carefully. Something was odd in this space. Something prodded at the edges of his mind, and his eyes raked the area with thoroughness and focus to find the problem.

"Ah ha," Alex murmured to himself with a smile as he found it. He stooped to the ground and ran his fingers over the surface, skimming over the straw, brushing some aside to reveal what lay beneath.

Oats.

Stanton kept the barn almost spotless, and he took great care not to waste any of the feed, let alone to let it remain on the floor.

Oats in the spare stall? Not bloody likely.

"Someone's horse got hungry while he waited," Alex grunted, kicking the straw back over the mess as the intruder must have done. It hid everything quite well and might have worked for an untrained eye.

Alex had no such eye.

But how would the man have hauled an unconscious Poppy on a horse in the middle of the day without raising suspicion? Riding away from Moulton would have been easy enough, but there were others about on the road at any given time. She would have had to be unconscious if there were to be any true escape. Poppy would have screamed herself to high heaven before being carried off, if she could have done.

Echoes of the screams he'd heard in his dreams resounded in his ears, and he swallowed hard, his newfound composure cracking for the first time. Those screams he had heard without cause, borne of his deepest fears and darkest memories, and now…

He shook his head swiftly, turning from the barn to return to the cottage. There was nothing to be gained by dwelling on the emotional and personal ramifications of this right now. There was far too much at stake and too much to do to waste time there.

He needed all his mental faculties now, rusty and dull though they might have been. Yet now, they seemed to be fully functioning, which was a blessed relief. Poppy deserved everything he could give her. Knowing now that there was far more to offer in these circumstances made all the difference.

Gabe rode up just as he reached the cottage, and Alex nodded at him in greeting.

"Weaver's sent off word, and he's riding over to Chester to meet up with a contact of his own. He'll meet us at Parkerton tonight, unless we've already got things figured and settled." Gabe dismounted and patted his horse, who began grazing beside Alex's. "What do you know?"

"Not much." Alex shook his head. "Haven't gone inside yet. Thought I ought to see the barn first."

"And?"

He grinned at his cousin. "Someone used the spare stall. The horse stole some oats."

Gabe smirked at that, his eyes glinting.

"Nothing taken? Cart, blankets…?"

"Not a thing," Alex told him. "Everything else is perfect."

"Hmm," Gabe mused, folding his arms in thought. "One man, one horse, middle of the day? That's odd."

"Atypical, certainly," Alex allowed, nodding and looking up towards the main road. "Cart waiting, you think?"

"Undoubtedly," Gabe replied, nodding slowly, "though I suspect it would be a bit of a distance out. A waiting cart by the head of the lane on the main road would give rise to comment from the doting neighbors."

Alex gave Gabe a sidelong look.

"We may have to question those doting neighbors eventually, if our contacts don't give us enough to go on."

"And alert them all to her disappearance?" Gabe scoffed a loud laugh. "Poppy would never forgive us for that, even if it did aid in her recovery." He inclined his head towards the cottage, giving Alex a meaningful look.

That was true, at least. It was difficult enough for Poppy to live in this place with all that had passed, but if word got out of her kidnapping and disappearance? It would make things even worse than before. But that, too, would do better to wait until they knew more.

Alex moved to the door and opened it, looking at the locking mechanism. It wasn't obviously broken or disturbed, and the wood around it was still perfectly intact. He'd rather expected that, or Poppy would have noticed.

He and Gabe entered, then turned to face the door as one, watching the mechanism at work. It seemed perfectly in place, but completely failed to latch.

"Why go to the trouble of dismantling the entire thing?" Alex wondered aloud. "Why not just pick the lock? It isn't complicated."

"No skills, perhaps?" Gabe proposed, eyeing the mechanism carefully. "It would only have been the work of a minute, anyone trained could have done it. Even trained on the streets."

Alex nodded in thought, his eyes shifting to the corner of the room, perfectly hidden by the door when it opened.

"So, this hired hand, untrained as he was, dismantles the lock that he cannot pick, then tucks himself in that corner, and waits."

Gabe stepped forward, putting himself into the corner, looking at the floor. "Fresh marks, no doubt from the muck of the barn or just outside." He turned, glancing out of the window beside him. "They'd have had to watch the house. To know when Poppy was gone and when would be safe to sneak in. I doubt they knew much of the layout of the house coming in, I can see the hesitation marks on the floor."

Alex saw them as well, and he nodded, looking around the kitchen.

"Poppy would have come in and gone straight for the fire…" He moved there himself, imagining every step she took and taking it himself. "She'd have wanted to take the stew off, or check it, at least."

He eyed the pot, now safely free of the fire, but dried streams of the liquid had hardened and crusted on the outside. "Stanton said it was boiling over, yes?"

"He did."

Alex moved the pot back into position in the fire, stepping back. "So, she either checked it and set it back, or did not check it. And the bread…" He glanced over at the table where the two loaves sat unbaked beneath a light cloth.

"Just as we left it," Gabe reported from his spot. "I think we can safely say that she was not here long after seeing us. So, back to the door with you and come in…"

Alex complied, and Gabe silently moved up behind him.

"Easy enough," Alex murmured. "But how to take her…" He glanced around the kitchen quickly. "No signs of distress, the table and chairs in their place, nothing…"

"Alex."

He paused at Gabe's tone and glanced over his shoulder at his cousin.

Gabe was looking down at the floor, brow furrowed.

Alex looked, then crouched at once.

"Blood," he grunted unnecessarily.

"Not much, though," Gabe added. "A few drops. So, did she hit him, or did he hit her?"

It was impossible to tell, impossible to know, and truly it couldn't have been especially important to the situation. A large amount of blood, yes, but a few drops? That told them absolutely nothing.

"No one heard anything," Alex murmured, staring at the blood as though it were crucial. "They gagged her, no doubt. Or she was unconscious first."

"Just another sign of ignorance," Gabe grunted. "No need to gag if they are unconscious."

Alex rose and glared at his cousin. "Thank you for that, Gabe."

Gabe looked surprised and held up his hands in surrender.

"I'm only trying to give scope to our villain. I'm as ready to cut off the man's head as anyone for taking Poppy, surely you know that."

That was true, and he knew it well. They all loved Poppy and would go to extraordinary lengths to save her, though they knew nothing about the situation at present. It wasn't that Alex doubted Gabe's love for her. It was only that he loved her better.

"Right," Alex said at once, striding for the door. "Back to Parkerton. Hopefully our contacts and assets can give us more to go on."

Gabe nodded and followed him out, and silently, they rode on to Parkerton, the severity of the situation seeming to weigh down on them both.

Who would want Poppy? She owed nothing to anyone, and she had been quite proud of the fact. She had no enemies and worked studiously to be a friend to all. She had no fortune from her family, or herself, and there was nothing to be gained by taking her.

Had her family decided to take a more drastic approach by removing her from her situation? It hardly seemed likely, and certainly never in a way to draw blood.

Then again, her mother might have been that desperate. She'd hated Alex beyond anything. It was entirely possible that…

No, now he was being ridiculous and impractical. The most likely case was that it was not about Poppy at all. Chances were, in fact, that Alex himself was entirely to blame.

How, where, and why were less clear, but when one engaged in such dangerous work as he had done, it was really the most probable conclusion. Poppy had never done a sinful deed in her life and had no cause to be caught up in this.

What had Alex done? How had they known about Poppy? How determined were they about any of this?

"Stop."

Alex looked over at his cousin, sensing he was not instructing him in the procession of their return to Parkerton.

"Stop what?"

"We don't know what's going on here," Gabe said, keeping his expression clear as he rode. "We don't know it's your fault, her fault, my fault, or Stanton's fault. We don't know anything but that she is gone, and until we have information, there's no point in pretending blame or reason can be set."

Alex stared at Gabe for a long moment, then growled an exhale as he returned his attention to the ride before him.

"It's very unnerving when you do that."

"Don't be so easy to read, and it wouldn't be."

"Apologies," Alex muttered. "Out of practice."

Gabe chuckled and pushed his horse harder.

"We'll have information soon, and then we can act. Be patient."

"Patient," Alex repeated. "No, I don't think I know that one."

Gabe rolled his eyes and lifted his chin.

"Looks like we have one already."

Up ahead, one of the older contacts from Alex's early days in the League stood outside of Parkerton, hat in hand.

Alex pushed on ahead, scrambling off the horse when he arrived.

"Abel, pleased to see you again."

Abel nodded in greeting, no hint of nerves but for the way his fingers fidgeted against his cap.

"Trace. Is that Rogue coming up behind you? I ain't seen him since Lord knows when."

"Abel," Alex growled, "you can greet Rogue and swap tales in a moment, but I need you to tell me what you have first."

" 'Course, Trace," Abel replied eagerly. "Pleased to have ye alive again, sir. And I ain't got much, but there was a man in Moulton recently. Asking about a man at the dance at the assembly rooms. Asking very keenly, he was, and not politely. I wouldn't have thought of it, but the name he wanted was Turner, sir. And tha's one of yours, I recall."

Mr. Turner. That was one of his, and it was the most dangerous one he'd had. Why the *hell* had he used it again?

Alex swallowed with difficulty and looked at Gabe, who had heard the last and looked horrified.

"Well, Rogue, can we blame me now?"

Chapter Nineteen

There wasn't much that was more satisfying than riding a horse as it pounded furiously against the ground in pursuit of something, particularly when one was to be the victor in the matter. Even if danger, death, and destruction lay ahead, the ride into it all was exhilarating. The fact that this ride was going all the way to Liverpool didn't lessen that fact, but it was rather hard to maintain it for such an extensive amount of time.

The last twenty-four hours had been filled with answers and questions, questions and answers, and now they were riding like mad for Liverpool, where their best chance of finding Poppy lay, by all accounts.

The night had been filled with reports from assets and contacts, some useful and some not, but every one of them had reiterated what Abel had said initially. Mr. Turner was the key to everything, it seemed, and the cottage had been under watch for weeks, as had the entire village. There was money to be given to those that would report anything they knew about Mr. Turner, and any of the neighbors could have done so at any time.

There was no way to tell who might have told what, or if anyone had said anything at all, but the idea of such a request being made…

Well, Alex had felt guilty before, but it was far worse now.

He hadn't allowed himself to dwell on it while they were still receiving new information from their contacts, what with Gabe analyzing everything as it came and keeping Alex's focus on the investigation. It was undoubtedly for the best that he focused while he could, and while there was so much to take in.

Now that they had a destination, however, he could feel the guilt all he liked. In a few short hours, he would have to return his mind to the facts of the case, to securing Poppy's release, and to seeing this wretched thing through to the end, whatever end that happened to be. He would, no doubt, face the evils that had been his entire existence for four and a half years, and possibly even the faces it bore.

He wasn't entirely prepared for that, but there was no way to prepare for such a thing. Yet for Poppy, he would face it. He would do whatever needed to be done at the risk of his own life, sanity, health, and anything else to see her freed from the men he knew had her. Or would have her, at any rate.

He doubted the men themselves had come for her or done any of the work to get her. They never did any of the baser work, finding it too menial for their status, which was an irony in itself, as there was no status in their title or lives to speak of.

They were, however, capable of quite a deal of evil, as he himself was proof. If Poppy fell into their hands, there was no telling what might happen.

The contacts had been surprisingly filled with insight about what had gone on, each of them adding where the others lacked, until a fairly reliable picture had presented itself. Someone had been watching the cottage and the farm carefully, and for some time, and then today, a man was seen riding away from the village on horseback, a woman in his grasp, though it was hard to say the condition she had been in. At the edge of town, the man and horse had met a cart, deposited the woman into it, and they'd continued out of Moulton towards Northwich.

And according to the contacts of his contacts, that cart was headed for Liverpool.

It made perfect sense to Alex, considering that had been where he himself had been bound when he was still *Torchon*, and the Cardieus, the esteemed employers of his smuggling associates, had recently moved their headquarters to Liverpool to remove the suspicion of London from their business.

The only question was if the Cardieus had Poppy on behalf of Battier, or of their foreman, Mainsley, who, as a proud member of the French Faction, was allowed to do as he pleased within their employment for that particular cause.

Battier would be ruthless, but at least it was something they could work with. He was fairly loyal to the cause, but as a smuggler, and shrewd businessman, he also greatly valued funds and power.

The Faction would care little for Poppy and would see her as expendable once they got what they wanted.

Neither choice was particularly pleasant, but he could work with Battier.

The Faction could require greater sacrifice.

He wasn't sure which he preferred.

The Faction had never specifically beaten, thrashed, or tormented him. Battier had. At their direction and discretion, it was true, but his was the face that Alex saw in his nightmares.

Whoever had Poppy, whatever the risk or the cost, he would pay it, do it, fulfill it. It could be the end of him so long as it was not the end of her. In that respect, he supposed he was still Trace. He'd always been Trace, and now he knew he always would be Trace. There was an odd comfort in that, though it seemed a poor moment for comfort. Yet Alex Sommerville couldn't have saved Poppy from this danger.

Trace, on the other hand…

This was his specialty.

Well, not saving women in particular, though he had done that before, but the dangerous unknown of England's darkest aspects? That was more familiar to him than any ballroom ever had been, and he could manage.

Odd how the habits of years past hadn't fully left him, despite his certainty of that.

Alex looked up as he rode on, another horseman joining them in their ride. They'd picked up a handful on the way, and Fritz seemed to know them all.

Fritz seemed to know everyone.

He'd come back from Chester in the early morning hours just before dawn, though what it was he'd actually done was far less clear. He'd only told Alex that they would have the assistance required no matter what the task was and that his contacts were working hard to arrange matters for them when they arrived in Liverpool.

How Fritz had known their destination would be Liverpool without being present for that discussion was a mystery, but Alex wasn't prepared to get into that discussion.

Now, they all rode on together with contacts and operatives, of whom Alex only knew a few, and all were armed appropriately. It seemed that the weapons cache at Parkerton, though discovered, had not been emptied or disrupted like the rest of the house, which had proven quite useful. Once armed, they'd ridden off and were now almost to the city limits of Liverpool, which meant they would need to proceed with more caution.

Liverpool was an expansive place, and there was no telling where Poppy might be kept. This ought to be where Fritz's contacts would be of use. Gabe and Alex could have done extraordinary things in London, but Liverpool was completely different. Other offices had operatives there, and they'd need to rely on them to accomplish the mission.

Alex had never been comfortable relying on others, preferring to take care of matters himself, but he would hardly argue the point now. Poppy's life and safety were at stake, and he would do everything to secure her. Accept any help, submit to any torment, and go to any lengths.

Fritz suddenly rode up fast beside him, moving to the front of the pack, and gesturing down a lane skirting the edge of the town. They all followed with the fluid grace of skilled horsemen, reining in only a few moments later at a boarding house which seemed less than appealing from the exterior. Cracked windows, warped wood, and no sign of life evident from within, aside from a faint light.

"Weaver…" Alex murmured uncertainly as they dismounted.

Fritz gave him a quick look. "Trust me. Go on in, ask for Harper."

Alex glanced at Gabe, who shrugged, but gestured for them to do as instructed. He followed as the others saw to the horses, brow furrowing.

"What's that look for?" Gabe asked as they entered.

"I don't want to stop," Alex grunted, nodding at the burly doorman who let them in. "Harper?"

The large man tilted his head towards the back of the inn without saying a word, glancing out the window as though anticipating someone or something else.

Gabe snorted and rounded a table as they moved on through the taproom.

"It's not as though we're taking a rest in the rooms upstairs, Trace. We need a location to gather, collect, and plot our move from. We're the London League, not the Liverpool League, and we need their resources. Unless we do, we'd be scouring the city all night for any sign of Poppy."

"I know that," Alex scoffed, sliding a chair out of his path. "I know all of that, but it doesn't help in the least, because at this moment, I would prefer scouring the street for her."

"Believe me," his cousin replied, clapping him on the back as they proceeded to the kitchen at the back of the inn. "I entirely comprehend that sentiment myself."

In the kitchen, leaning over a worn table covered with maps, documents, and even a few disguises on one corner, was a large man smoking a cigar, his long, dark hair pulled back with a dark ribbon. His clothing was faded and washed out in a way that Alex was all too familiar with.

Life on board a ship tended to affect all clothing similarly.

He was glad to see such a thing at this moment. If they had a contact who understood the ways of the docks and the shipyards, smugglers and privateers, he would be all the more use to them now.

And when the man looked up at them, darker eyes glinting in the candlelight, Alex gaped outright. "Jackal?"

He grinned back at Alex. "You look much better now than when last I saw you, Trace. Glad they got you off."

Alex swallowed, suddenly finding his throat dry and raw. "You got me off, didn't you?"

Jackal shrugged one broad shoulder, his smile fading. "Might have been me, or it might have been a sound decision by the captain. You were a pathetic waif by my eyes, and that couldn't serve any captain well."

Alex grinned unabashedly and came further into the room, rounding the table. "In case it happens to be the first, let me shake your hand."

Gabe was hard on his heels. "And then me as well, sir. The name's Rogue. London League."

Jackal snorted and shook both hands firmly, the hard callouses scratching against their palms. "Charmed, chuffed, and all that. Can we move on?" He gestured to the maps and documents on the table. "I've only got a few hours before my crew comes off leave, and I can't be anywhere near here when they do."

Immediately, Alex and Gabe snapped back into character and took up position on either side of him. "How well do you know Liverpool?" Alex asked as he eyed the maps of the docks.

"Better than most," Jackal replied without looking over. "Better than London, not as well as Lisbon."

Gabe glanced up at Jackal with furrowed brows. "How is it that you are here, Jackal?"

"I do occasionally come into port, Rogue," Jackal sighed heavily, glancing up at him.

"I mean *here*," Gabe insisted, not put off in the least. "You're too valuable, aren't you?"

"He is, undoubtedly," Fritz announced as he entered. "We're not risking him, but when he heard Trace's lady had been taken, he offered his services while he could."

Alex looked at Jackal in bewilderment. "You what?"

A slight, lopsided smile crossed Jackal's face as he returned the look. "It's not often I get to participate with brothers in arms anymore, and we've been contacts for ages, Trace. I may not be able to ride out with you, but I'll give you everything I can to succeed." A mischievous glint entered his eye. "If I can actually get anywhere with all of this. May we get on?"

They all laughed and turned their attention to the table, drawing up battle plans and waiting for the scouts to return with intelligence they could act upon. Still, Jackal's information was enough to give them a fair idea of the area they would be going into, what to expect, and the best way to remove themselves from the scene of the action before it drew too much attention.

"So, your opinion is that this is bigger than Battier," Alex surmised after Jackal had given him all that he could.

Jackal nodded once, taking a long draw of his cigar. "Absolutely.

I'd doubt the Cardieus are directly involved, but Mainsley will likely have a part. Battier isn't bright enough or conniving enough to form a plot on his own, though he does a fine enough job of pretending otherwise. I can't imagine he's pleased about losing you, but even *Torchon* isn't worth all this trouble. Trace, however…"

Alex swore under his breath and punched the table, then folded his arms and looked at the papers again, grinding his teeth.

"Mainsley doesn't know me from Adam. He only met Mr. Turner once, and Mr. Turner doesn't look anything like me."

"You hope," Gabe muttered under his breath, wiping his brow.

He glanced at his cousin severely, though he knew the point was all too true. They may never know just how his identity had been compromised with the smuggler's ring, and if there was too much resemblance…

Still, Poppy was worth the risk.

"The point is," Alex went on, "that if it is down at Cardieus and Mainsley is there, there is no reason for him to think it's me."

Fritz nodded slowly. "True, very true, and he won't know Rogue or myself."

"But there's no saying that Mainsley is the one who has her," Gabe pointed out.

Alex shook his head. "Mainsley was always just the enforcer, he never gave his own commands. The occasional judgment call, but he takes orders with the rest of them. He may have her, but someone else will be pulling the strings." He looked over the maps in thought, then drew an imaginary circle around three warehouses in a seemingly forgotten corner of the docks. "If I were up to something less than savory, even by smuggling standards, I'd go here. Not necessarily convenient for the shipping interests of Cardieus, but this isn't in their interest, particularly, and it's close enough for their resources if need be. Once scouts come back to us, I'd say we start there. Small groups, two to three at most, and we keep an eye on the water at all times."

Fritz raised his brows in surprise. "At this time of night?"

"Best time for smugglers, Weaver," Jackal told him, Alex nodding beside him. "Less foot traffic, less patrol, more inclined to look the other way for a price…"

"And," Alex broke in, "less inclined to pay any attention at all, particularly if we've purloined a stock of liquor from an unsuspecting warehouse store and bestowed it upon them."

There was an appreciative round of chuckles from the group, and Alex grinned at them, feeling the thrill of impending action rising within him.

Gabe looked over at Alex, grinning without reserve. "I know this is a terrible time to say this, but... it is very good to have the real you back."

Alex gave him a wry look, snorting softly. "You're right. This is a terrible time to say that."

How could it be possible for opening one's eyes to be painful?

Poppy had been well awake for bursts of the trip, jostling about in a wagon and on horseback on what must have been yesterday, if not the day before. The knock to the back of the head had been compounded by opium, whenever her consciousness was noticed by her captors, and there was so much confusion with being asleep and awake that she'd quite lost all sense of it. Everything hurt all the time, her head pounded so fiercely she was nearly incapable of thought, and for the present, she could only presume she was upright because she couldn't feel her head touching anything at all.

Upright was the first new position she'd been in in ages.

What a thought.

She swallowed with some difficulty, her throat raw and parched, resisting the thought of moisture of any kind. With her captors being reluctant to have her awake and alert, they'd forgone any semblance of food or drink but for the very faintest amount of water at times.

The only sense she'd ever made of that came when one of them had muttered, "Can't 'ave Trace comin' to find a corpse. 'Eads would roll."

It took her quite a long time to process that, given her state, and given that she couldn't quite remember who or what Trace was. Once she did, she felt worse than when the opium had left her.

Alex.

Oh, Alex...

After all they had been through, she was now going to be the cause of his troubles. No matter who he had been before or what he had done, what dangers he had faced, she had never been part of it. Now, she was bait for him, and his pursuit of her, should he have done so, would lead to his ruin.

She would never be able to forgive herself for that.

The men were quiet now, and the room was dim, which was better for her at the moment. A bright room would have made her squint, and they would have known she was conscious once more.

She couldn't bear another dose of opium, and she needed to somehow find a way out of here. Or, at the very least, she needed to find something that might be useful to Alex when he came for her.

If he came for her.

Poppy kept her eyelids lowered, though open, and scanned the room. It wasn't especially large, but it was filled with crates and boxes, large barrels, and a few wagons sparsely filled. A large desk sat in a corner of the room, its wood grey with age. A large man sat behind it, his filthy boots propped atop. Another sat on the floor against the desk, whittling at a piece of wood, sniffing frequently as though his nose dripped. Both looked as though they had seen their share of fights and may have even won a few of them.

A deep creaking sound seemed to come from beneath the floorboards, and the smaller man on the floor paused his whittling, eyes wide.

"Wha's that, Ernie?" he half yelped.

"Don't pay it no mind, Fleet," Ernie grunted, cap over his eyes. "It's a dock, the water below makes it creak."

Fleet scowled and moodily resumed his whittling.

"I don't see why we has to sit here and play nanny to a bound and unconscious woman. This ain't what that Mainsley bloke promised when he hired me."

"You'd better forget your complaint before tha' Sir Vincent comes tonight. 'E is the one paying us, and you'll not get any clink wif your whining so much."

Fleet snorted softly, his eyes widening with derision. "Sir Vincent. What sort of grand sir is he to come all the way up here from London to see to the docks? Stupidest thing I've ever heard. As if

Mainsley ain't puffed up enough to make one sick, now we've got a sir to contend wif? Not worth the coin, Ern. Not worth it."

Ernie thumbed his cap back and looked down where Fleet sat.

"Want me to tell the captain tha' later? He's comin' in, too, you know. Got a load to take back wif 'im, an' I 'ave no doubt he'll see us and Mainsley afore he goes."

For the first time, Fleet looked apprehensive.

"No' the cap'n. I've no complaints against him. I jus' don't see the point in tending the miss when she's not made a peep."

Ernie sighed heavily and leaned back in his chair again. "Me neither, but it's better than being on patrol on all the docks."

"I'd rather be on the docks," Fleet insisted with a firm shake of his head.

"Then tell Mick when he comes in, and you can trade," Ernie told him, clearly exasperated. "It'll save my ears the trouble of hearing you! Now, go check the girl."

Poppy snapped her eyes completely shut, forcing her body to go limp as Fleet got to his feet and made his way over.

He reeked of alcohol and fish and sawdust with a hint of cigar smoke, and the stench of him was enough to nearly choke her, but somehow, she managed to contain her reaction.

Fleet tugged at the ropes at her ankles, still painfully tight and tied to the legs of the chair. He moved up to test the ropes around her stomach, which were also quite secure, and then moved around to the back of the chair and tightened the ropes around her wrists. Those were also fastened to the back legs of the chair, and tightening them forced her arms further down and her back to arch.

It couldn't be painful for her were she unconscious, so she couldn't show the strain of it now, though the urge to screech in distress rose.

Fleet chuckled darkly as he tightened the ropes further. "Look at this, Ern. Look what I can make her do."

Poppy waited with bated breath, praying he wouldn't do anything despicable while she was in such a vulnerable position. She couldn't fight as she was, and she couldn't let them know she was alert, or they would have drugged her yet again, or subjected her to something far worse.

She was utterly and completely helpless.

Fleet suddenly lifted her head, which she had been hanging off to the right, up to a natural position. His fingers tickled the underside of her chin as he moved to stand in front of her, and then his thumb moved to pull her bottom lip down a little.

Please, no, Poppy silently begged, her fingers tensing against the ropes at her wrist.

"Wha' if Trace doesn't come, Ern?" Fleet asked in a dark tone. "Fink they'll let us have a taste o' her?"

"Leave her be, Fleet. Poor lass has been through enough without you touching her."

Fleet's hand dropped, and she heard him turn. "Poor lass? This here is Trace's tart, an' you feel sorry for her?"

"Don't pretend you know Trace enough to 'ave 'ard feelings about him," Ernie barked, "and aye, I do feel sorry for her."

"Don't. Look at this."

Suddenly, Fleet lashed out and struck Poppy across her face, her head snapping back, then lolling to her left side.

"I can hit her, and she don't wake. Don't even stir. Not a whisper."

The sound of a gun cocking rang through the warehouse.

"Don't hit her," Ernie growled. "Step away."

"Ernie," Fleet stammered, his voice growing distant from her. "Ernie, put the gun down."

Poppy strained to hear Ernie's response, wondering why he'd stopped Fleet's mischief.

"I may be a mangy cur," Ernie growled, "but I draw the line at hitting a woman. Don't touch her."

"All right, Ern, as you say. No harm done. She won't even know."

"She'd better not, Fleet, and next time she wakes, she gets your dinner while you find something else."

Fleet whined in protest, but Poppy fought a smile, which seemed impossible, given her situation. Still, she hadn't expected chivalry in her captors, and it was a pleasant surprise.

Her amusement faded as the reality of her situation sank in. Ernie might oppose her being beaten, but that hardly made him a gentleman. There was no telling what would lie ahead, how long she would be here, or if another man tasked with minding her would be so accommodating where violence was concerned.

Poppy swallowed and forced herself to remain as limp as possible.

Oh, Alex... Please hurry...

Chapter Twenty

"Your best bet is in the last building, men. Scouts tell me the other two are dark and filled to the brim with stock."

Alex nodded once, smirking at Jackal as they headed out of the inn. "And have your scouts removed the excess stock from these sadly filled warehouses?"

Jackal smiled just a little. "I've no idea what the scouts have done on their own time and without my express knowledge. They're Tailor's men, not mine."

Fritz snorted once, then turned it to a cough, clearing his throat with a frown.

"All right, there, Weaver?" Jackal asked, thumping him on the back.

"Perfect," Fritz fake coughed.

Two of the men brought their horses forward, as well as their own, while a third brought a great black stallion out, stopping before Jackal.

Gabe scoffed loudly.

"How's a man who spends his entire life at sea in possession of such a fine animal as that? Not exactly feasible."

Jackal mounted his horse smoothly, then raised a brow at Gabe.

"When you've grown as rich as I have, Rogue, you'll find you can be in possession of anything you like, feasible or not."

That earned him a round of appreciative laughter from the group, and Jackal was the first to sober.

"Good luck, men. Trace, get your woman back and slit a few throats for her."

Alex nodded almost obediently. "Thank you, Jackal. For everything."

Jackal dipped his chin in return. "A pleasure for a brother in arms. Just remember, I was never here." He nodded once more, then kicked his heels in, sending the horse bolting away from the inn.

Alex watched him go for a moment, feeling a faint sense of disappointment and abandonment that the best of them were riding from them, though he understood the need for it. Jackal couldn't be involved and couldn't be seen, for his safety and for the good of the kingdom. There was no telling how many operations may hinge on him at any given time, so Alex could not possibly expect him to remain to go after the woman he loved out of loyalty.

Still, the pang was there.

He exhaled slowly, willing the feeling away and reminding himself who he was, and who he had with him.

"Right," he murmured to no one in particular. "Let's mount up."

As one, the six men present mounted their horses, with Alex just moments behind. The others that had joined them on the ride had dispersed across the city to collect whatever information they could and see to any trouble they might have faced from the opposition, either in their attempts to rescue Poppy or in their exiting Liverpool. The scouts Jackal had sent out had given them a general idea and reported the sight of Poppy being brought in hours ago, but as far as the specifics of what they were facing, there was less certainty.

He was used to less certainty. He could work with that.

Gabe, Fritz, and the others looked at him expectantly, and he looked back at them for a long moment, steeling himself for what lay ahead.

"Ready?" he asked his friends, smiling just a little.

His cousin returned the smile. "Are you? This is your operation, Trace. We ride on your order."

Fritz nodded in agreement and raised a brow in question.

Alex grinned and thought of the woman he loved being held in a warehouse on the Liverpool docks by men looking for him. His grin turned almost savage, and his heart began to race in anticipation.

"Let's go get Poppy," he growled, nudging his horse on and galloping away, hearing the others take off behind him.

The map of Liverpool they had studied unfolded in his mind; the shortcuts Jackal's scouts had given them almost illuminated for him as clearly as they might have been in daylight. He knew each path to take, each curve of the road, how far they had to go, and where they would stash the horses until the task was done. He remembered everything they had talked about, and in far greater detail than he expected.

Had he always been able to do this? It felt more like a habit than an aberration, but he was so out of practice, he couldn't be sure. Was this how Trace had always acted? Or was this due to Poppy being the focus of this mission? It might have been impossible to separate the two. He wasn't sure he minded that so much.

It was oddly apt.

It wasn't far to the docks from where they had been, especially with the shortcuts that Jackal's maps had given them. A group of their size would certainly attract attention with the night wardens, so Alex signaled for half of the men to split off. They'd make their way to the warehouse separately, no doubt taking care of some of the lingering criminals loitering about.

Alex was pleased enough to have Gabe and Fritz with him. Gabe was a fiend with fists and staffs, and Fritz was unmatched with any blade. Alex wasn't sure if he would go with his knives, newly sharpened and fitting perfectly at his side, as was his inclination, or if he would thrash whoever it was with his fists alone. Either way, he was looking forward to engaging in whatever violence was before him to get Poppy back.

There was nothing quite like extremes in situation to test his limits.

Apparently, he had very few where Poppy was concerned.

He held up his fist and they all slowed, dismounting in complete silence. Fritz snapped his fingers at a boy watching them nearby, holding up two coins. Immediately, the boy came over to them, eyes alight.

Alex paid little attention to what Fritz was saying to the lad, trusting him to take care of the arrangements. He started down the road towards the docks, tucking the cap of his disguise down low. His chest burned already, and he forced his breathing to calm, to steady him, to give him clarity. He always had clarity before a big mission, which was what made them successful. Despite his best attempts, there was no clarity here.

This wasn't a regular mission. This was personal.

"Horses will be waiting two blocks from here," Fritz said in a near whisper as he caught up with Alex and Gabe. "I promised him double."

Alex nodded once, his teeth grinding of their own accord.

The three of them silently made their way down the road, the docks coming into view.

It was strange how the smell of the sea could suddenly make Alex both excited and wary, apprehensive and alert, and how the scars on his back all seemed to itch at the same time. His mind suddenly seemed confined to the dark corners of his hold aboard the *Amelie Claire*, and his throat went dry as though he had done something in defiance of his superiors and would soon receive his punishment. He forced himself to swallow hard, his brow furrowing darkly as the warehouses came into sight.

A man standing nearby swept a finger across his cap, and Alex went to him, nodding once.

"Last warehouse," the man whispered, tapping the ash from the end of his cigar. "Water side, to the right."

"How many?" Alex replied in the same tone.

"Seven." The man drew in a long puff of his cigar, then held it, tilting his head back to slowly blow it out. "Two of them have been in there all day. Drunk now. Back door lock doesn't work."

Alex tapped a finger to his cap and moved on, the others following silently.

"Sentry," Gabe hissed, inclining his head towards a slowly meandering figure on the dockside.

"Damned weak one," Fritz scoffed under his breath.

Alex didn't respond to either of them. He'd seen the sentry and judged his level of inebriation from the manner of his walking. He would be no trouble and wasn't worth considering. So long as they weren't obvious, they had nothing to worry about. Considering they were rarely obvious; he wouldn't give it a second thought.

The back door of the warehouse was suddenly before them, and

Alex tried the handle, wincing in anticipation of the squeak. No squeak came as it opened.

"Oil on the hinges," Gabe breathed, reaching out to touch them, then sniffing his fingers. "Genius."

Alex nodded, exhaling his relief. He nodded for Fritz to enter first, and then he followed, Gabe trailing him.

There wasn't much space for them to maneuver, but that had never stopped them before. The crates were pressed up nearly to the wall with only enough room to get by, no doubt for the foreman to count. Hardly enough space for anyone to suspect an attack from invaders.

All the more perfect.

Alex directed Fritz and Gabe in opposite directions, while he would go over the crates. They were of varying heights and size, unevenly stacked, but sturdy enough. Over was generally not his preference, but the crates seemed to span the entire back wall of the building, and there was no guarantee that the paths on either side would actually exist. Gabe and Fritz may have wound up needing to go along the same route, or over as he was.

Unlikely, but possible.

Alex scaled the crates, suddenly grateful for all the times he had spent scaling the ladders aboard the *Amelie Claire* for his tasks even in the most treacherous conditions. It enabled him to reach the top quickly, making hardly a sound in his attempts.

There was plenty of space atop the crates and Alex could see the entire room easily, his half of the building more in shadow than anything else.

Five men were out in the open, though it wasn't much of an open space there, either. The other two sat against the door, nearly asleep. A stocky one sat behind a desk with his legs propped up, a scrawny one was sprawled out on the floor, and three others of varying size between those two extremes lounged against various crates. Two telltale dark bottles sat atop the desk, and two more were on the floor, clearly empty now.

Facing the desk, away from Alex's eyes, was a lone chair and a single woman with copper hair tied to it. Her head was bowed, and his heart stopped as he took in the sight of her.

Breathe, he ordered in his mind as he stared at her. *Breathe, darling.*

On cue, Poppy's shoulders moved on an inhale, and Alex could have fallen over with the relief he felt.

Good. Had she neglected to do so, Alex would have given up any and all ideas of stealth and secrecy and lashed out at all five men present with the sort of rabid enthusiasm one usually expected of wolves or tigers. As it was, he would continue on.

Slowly, steadily, he made his way across the tops of the crates, praising whoever had stacked them so sturdily for doing so, as it made his path far less treacherous than it would have been otherwise. He crept closer and closer, breathing in silent bursts as he moved, eyeing the distance to Poppy's chair and the shadows created by it.

He moved himself more in line with her, then began the more dangerous prospect of making his way down. There was no easy way to do it, and the risk of crates toppling over increased at least tenfold.

Had he been the same weight and stature he had been at the time of his capture, this would not have been possible. Now that he was far more slender, though certainly not so thin as he had been when he dropped on Poppy's doorstep, he could maneuver with ease, almost light of foot.

Almost.

He was convinced that if he had been closer to the men than he was, they would have heard his tread. Provided, of course, they were not too inebriated to pay attention.

Alex paused for a moment, eyeing all seven curiously. Why so many guards if they were not actually standing on guard? Why seven of them for one woman, if they were not properly armed?

None of them seemed to be anticipating anything, nor were they even looking in Poppy's direction.

Hired hands, just as before, and likely they had no idea, or very few, about what was commencing in the wider world. So long as they could line their pockets, they were satisfied. But did they have ties to Battier? Mainsley? One of the Cardieus?

There was no way to tell until everything went down, and if they were mercenary enough to talk for the right negotiation. Loyal soldiers had to be broken. Hired thugs only needed bribes.

Alex was perfectly willing and able to do one or the other. Or both.

He carefully continued on his way down, keeping to the shadows cast by the crates, and thus mostly out of sight. The men were talking amongst themselves, but it was an idle sort of conversation that did not require any of them to look remotely interested or raise their tone in the least. They appeared to be just as bored with themselves as they were with the situation as a whole.

It wasn't often that he got to participate in an assignment that had no complications or trouble, but this might have been one. He wouldn't mind having a simple time of it. It would be a fine way to ease back into this life.

He paused as he reflected on that. Ease back in…

He wanted back in.

He blinked at his realization, then shook his head quickly. He could dwell on that thought another time, when the woman he loved was free of her restraints and not in danger of dying or being used as bait for him.

Alex clambered silently down to the last few crates, then frowned as he saw very little by way of footing to the ground. He could jump it, but he doubted that would be silent. He didn't dare move forward, for that would put him more in the light.

Thinking quickly, he gripped the side of the crate he was on, setting his feet against the wood of the crate below, and let his feet slide down the boards, wincing as the wood at his fingertips dug itself into his skin. He dropped to the ground without a sound, then pulled the splinter out with his teeth, tossing it aside quickly.

Now, he would have to tread more carefully than before, as the shadows could no longer protect him. Still, an indolent audience was quite helpful, and there was no cause for them to look this direction unless he made a significant misstep.

Which he never did.

Exhaling slowly, settling his pounding heart, Alex moved forward, crouched low to the ground and moving in a direct line to Poppy, praying her skirts and position would hide him from the view of others.

He reached her in moments, and he knew in an instant that she was not unconscious. She stiffened as he drew close, no doubt sensing him there, but keeping her head down.

"Good evening, love," he whispered, smiling a little as he took her bound hand in his. "Don't react."

Her fingers instantly curved around his tightly, shaking just a little.

"I'll loosen these, but I can't release you fully until we take care of your friends over there."

Her fingers tensed against his briefly.

Alex reached for one of his knives and cut the ropes attaching her wrists to the chair legs, almost snarling at that. It put her in such a painful, vulnerable position, as though she were served up on a platter for these men.

"Oh, love…" he breathed as his blade cut through the ropes. "Are you all right?"

Again, her fingers tensed against his.

He exhaled and cupped his hands around hers. "I need to thrash some annoying thugs in the room, but I'll be right back. And I brought friends, so no worries. You're safe now. I promise."

He rose up just enough to kiss the back of her neck, then glanced to the left just ahead of him, where Gabe waited in the shadows, eyes on him. Alex couldn't see much to his right with all of the crates, but Gabe indicated that Fritz was there.

They were ready.

Alex gripped his knife tightly in one hand, exhaled, then nodded at Gabe as he rose from the ground quickly, striding forward to the blearily unsuspecting men.

They saw him almost at once and attempted to scramble to their feet, but Gabe reached one first, punching him square across the jaw. Fritz came up from Alex's right, swinging a club of sorts that he had found, and the one on the floor eyed it in terror before it swung up into his face.

Two of them came at Alex, and he whirled to stab one in the thigh and jab one in the nose with his free fist. He pulled the knife out of its victim, then slammed the man in the back of the head with the hilt, sending him crashing to the floor.

Gabe kicked the man he'd knocked to the floor, then swiped the legs out from under the one Alex had hit. Fritz upended the desk into the lap of the burly one, who couldn't get out of the way fast enough. He went crashing to the floor, the chair breaking beneath him as the heavy desk descended. He struggled against it, pressing the flat surface away from him.

Alex growled and picked up the one he'd stabbed and knocked out, heaving him over to land atop of the overturned desk, and the pained whimper from the trapped man brought him some satisfaction.

Fritz's club whirled again as the two by the door came barreling towards him, and it collided with one's chest while the other dodged it, only to have Alex send him sprawling with a quick succession of punches to the head.

The door burst open, and three more men came in, looking far less inebriated than the ones before.

"Lovely," Alex grunted, fingering his knives as Gabe had the last of the original five by the throat, the man looking rather pale indeed at the moment.

The three men charged at them, but all activity stopped with the sound of a gunshot.

Alex jerked, fearing the worst, when the man in the center suddenly fell to his knees as his shirt turned red, his comrades staring in shock.

A dark and blinding whirl of movement appeared from the door, taking another by surprise, and Alex took advantage of the moment by darting over to the third, bashing his own head into his, then driving his fists into his ribs and stomach, and taking a hard punch himself into his face.

Alex tasted blood, but it only fueled him on, and he grabbed the man by the shirt and threw him hard as he roared his fury.

Gabe was there to catch him, pummeling him and dodging the clumsy blows he received in return.

The dark, whirling figure had made short work of the remaining man, with slight aid from Fritz, and then suddenly pulled out a gun and pointed it at the man under the desk, whose hand had somehow managed to wriggle down towards his own pistol.

"I wouldn't do that if I were you," a woman's cultured voice rang out clearly. "Move those pudgy fingers up above your head. There's a good lad."

Alex smiled at the sound of her, glancing over at Gabe, whose opponent was now as unconscious as his fellows. Gabe wiped at his bleeding lip and came over, panting a little.

"Well, that was fun. Weaver?"

Fritz propped his club on his shoulder, grinning like a much younger man. "I haven't had that much fun in years."

"You forgot the sentry, who wasn't nearly as inebriated as he appeared. I took care of him for you." The woman looked at all of them, smirking with surprisingly full lips. "You couldn't wait for me?"

Alex shrugged. "Didn't know you were coming. And you are?"

"Ivy." She held out a hand to him like a man would have. "I take it you're Trace?"

He shook her hand, trying not to show how impressed he was. Ivy was one of the Garden, an elite foursome of female spies that no one really knew much about, except that they were commanded by Milliner.

"I am, yes. That's Rogue, and Weaver I presume you know."

Ivy grinned at Fritz. "I do, but it's been years."

"It has, my dear," Fritz replied, nodding and smiling rather fondly. "I'm grateful for your assistance. Milliner sent you?"

"She did, yes. Word reached her of the situation, and she knew I was in the area, so I thought I'd offer what help I could." Ivy tilted her chin towards Poppy. "Now, I think you'd better do right by her, Trace. She looks done for."

Alex turned at once and ran back to Poppy, whose eyes were wide and terrified, her lips parted in shock. Her cheeks were stained with tears, the tracks of them shining through the dirt that covered her face.

"Oh sweetheart," Alex murmured as he sliced through the ropes at her ankles. "I'm so sorry. I'm so sorry you had to see that."

"You're h-here," Poppy whispered, her voice breaking on the word. "You came for me."

"Too bloody right, I did," Alex choked out. He cut the ropes at her middle, then lifted her out of the chair, arms bound behind her as they were.

He didn't care.

He hauled her into his arms, holding her impossibly close, as though he could have taken her into himself.

"Oh, Poppy, I'm so sorry. Are you hurt?"

"No," she insisted, pulling back. "No, I'm fine."

Alex brushed some of her hair out of her face, shaking his head.

"Fine isn't even on the list of things you are right now." He leaned down and kissed her hard, stunned to find her lips eager and engaging against his own.

Lord, how he'd wanted to kiss her like this for weeks now… Just like this, with passion and relief and enthusiasm.

But she'd been through hell and had just seen him at his most violent. There was no telling how that would affect her when it all settled.

He pulled back and laughed, shaking his head again.

"I haven't even finished freeing you. Turn around."

Poppy did so, smiling a little.

"I don't even feel the ropes anymore, honestly."

"That is a sad statement, indeed," Alex replied with a sigh, as he removed the last of her bonds. A wave of guilt rode through him painfully.

She turned back, her expression hesitant and shy, though she didn't seem to tremble now. "Alex… Hold me? I can't… can't seem to feel my feet, and I'm afraid this isn't real…"

"Oh, darling," he moaned, pulling her gently back into his arms. "I'll hold you as long as I can. As long as you need."

Her slender arms wrapped around his waist and she buried her face into his chest, her frame shaking on a weak exhale. He kissed her hair and rested his chin on top of her head, sighing himself.

Then, Alex heard horses outside the building, and he tensed, looking at Fritz and Gabe. Ivy strode to the door, her tall boots hardly making a sound on the floor. She looked out, then snorted and poked her head back in.

"Your cavalry is here," she told them drily.

"What?" Alex asked, smiling at her tone.

"Oh, come on," a loud voice complained outside. "I see a sentry down already, and Ivy's smiling, which means we missed all the good parts. I did not ride through the night on too many horses to count to not thrash someone!"

"Dammit," Gabe groaned and rubbed his eyes. "Who invited Rook?"

On cue, Rook, Gent, and Cap entered the warehouse, considering the room with interest, and looking positively haggard themselves.

"Evening, all," Gent greeted, placing his hands on his hips. "I see the culprits are down, and the damsel recovered. So, shall we go? I'm really very tired and could use a drink."

"Yes, by all means," Alex chuckled and nodded, heading towards him, his arm around Poppy. "Let's remove ourselves from this place."

Cap raised a brow. "Is it over, then?" He looked at Poppy for confirmation. "Did they say anything about who hired them or what was going on?"

Poppy shook her head, then stopped, frowning. "Well…"

Alex looked down at her with interest. "Poppy?"

She glanced up at him. "I didn't think it was significant at the time, but they mentioned a captain that would be coming in tonight, and a man called Mainsley, and a Sir Vincent? I don't know if it means anything, but it's all I heard."

Alex stared at her as horror sunk his stomach down to his toes, then forced his eyes up and away into the equally stunned faces of his comrades. "Battier. Mainsley. Castleton."

Cap swore softly, which was unheard of for him.

"It's not a kidnapping at all," he murmured.

Alex swallowed and shook his head very slowly. "It's a trap."

Chapter Twenty-One

They moved quickly from the warehouse, praying that the lethargic guards they had encountered spoke of good timing on their part rather than the plot against them. The horses were removed back to the rest, and they regrouped with the other contacts and operatives in the area at an office Gabe picked the lock of.

Alex held Poppy's hand, though he couldn't feel it, and his mind raced frantically, skimming over details at its most rapid pace yet. He'd known all along that this situation was more about him than it was about her. Hell, it had been his alias that had gotten them all into this mess. But he'd been operating under the assumption that it was one group or the other, the smugglers or the Faction.

Not both.

Never both.

Sir Vincent Castleton he didn't know at all, but Gabe had brought him up to speed back at Parkerton about what had gone on in his absence, so he knew very well who he was and what he was capable off. The man had been foiled in his attempts to fund the Faction with Margaret Easton's fortune, thanks to Gent's actions and subsequent marriage of the woman in question, and according to everyone else, Castleton had been remarkably quiet since that time.

Alex couldn't blame him; if he'd failed in an attempt to bring great things into his organization after so much trust had been placed in him, he'd have turned hermit, too.

And he would have been desperate to prove himself again.

No doubt Castleton was feeling that pressure now, and somehow had earned himself a measure of trust despite his failing that now permitted him to oversee this operation. He would be more determined, more dangerous, and more unpredictable.

Mainsley was an opportunistic mongrel who had only been placed within Cardieus because of their alliance with the Faction. He was ruthless in his treatment of others, whether associated with the Faction or not, and he'd been given free reign by his employers, which was all the man needed to create his own dictatorship within the ranks.

He could hire whatever power he wanted no matter the cost, given he was funded by both the Faction and the Cardieus, and he was clearly one of the most useful assets the Faction had on English soil.

And Battier...

Alex's skin prickled all over as the captain's face swam into his mind's eye. The too fair and unmarked complexion that belied cold, calculating eyes and a vindictive nature. The almost permanent sneer he saved for those he despised. The slow, mocking laughter that never reached his eyes.

He shivered.

"Alex?" she asked, looking at him in concern.

He shook his head once. "We need to get Poppy out of here. Now."

"What?" she cried. "No!"

"Yes," at least three of them said at the same time.

She looked around at them all, clearly betrayed.

Weaver took pity on her, though his expression was hard. "My dear, there is no telling what danger lies ahead of us, and it could be far worse than what you just escaped. We cannot possibly have you anywhere near here."

"But..."

"Stanton is nearby, and he will see you safely back home," Weaver overrode with his usual charming authority. "Best to do so now before the danger starts, and we can no longer protect you."

Poppy's brow furrowed in disgruntlement, and Alex looked away.

"Surely, I can..." she tried again.

Weaver took her hand and tugged her up, and she did not resist.

He pulled her a bit away and whispered in a low voice they all could still hear.

"Do you think Trace would be able to accomplish what needs to be done tonight if you are nearby? If there is the slightest chance of danger for you, do you think he'll be able to function the way we need him to?"

Alex swallowed, not caring that he could hear what was being said. After all, it was true. He, of all people, knew what could be coming, and if Poppy were anywhere in the vicinity, he would be distracted and worried.

Spies could not be distracted and worried. That would complicate things and prevent confidence and skill from being at the forefront, which would endanger their lives and the lives of their comrades.

Poppy needed to go. For all their sakes.

She was silent for a long moment, then finally, she spoke in a small voice.

"I understand. Of course. Thank you all so very much for coming to my rescue."

They all bobbed their heads in a series of nods, too focused on the task before them to bother with politeness or words.

There was a long pause, and Alex sensed she was looking at him, but at that moment, the door opened, and he heard Weaver giving instructions to the contact outside to take her to Stanton at the boarding house.

He waited for the sound of the horses to fade completely, and then sighed to himself. Right. That was done, now it was time for the rest of this mess to get sorted, and for all of this to end once and for all.

Alex looked up at Gabe and Ivy, feeling his body settle into a controlled intensity, his mind steeled and engaged.

"Anything from the men we left back at the warehouse?"

"The beefy one under the desk is singing like a canary," Gabe reported with a brief grin. "He grew quite protective of your Poppy, and he told Benson everything. Sir Vincent is on his way here from London; Mainsley is to wait for him; and Battier's ship is off the coast and due ashore once he has the signal."

Alex nodded slowly, processing it all as Weaver reentered the room.

"We need the signal to be given," Alex said at last. "Whatever it is, whenever it was supposed to happen, it needs to. Will this man do so?"

"I think we can make him do so," Rook pointed out, shrugging once. "He's been very accommodating so far. Surely, the Crown can protect him for services rendered."

Weaver grunted and scratched the back of his neck. "Possibly. If it works, at any rate."

"What are you thinking, Trace?" Gent asked, looking intrigued.

Alex's mind spun on the information he had, on the most likely scenarios and outcomes, and the sort of power they had in their possession.

"Mainsley is stocky and has henchmen. He'll be a fighter, but Sir Vincent, from the sound of it…"

"Leave that one to me," Gent muttered in a surprisingly dark tone. "He's mine."

Alex wasn't about to argue with that and nodded once.

"Battier will be a different sort altogether. He'll fight on his own, and he has several crew members that are loyal and sinister. They'll be with him, no doubt, but whether they come ashore is another matter entirely."

"Did they usually go with him?" Cap asked, folding his arms and leaning against the desk. "What do your instincts say?"

Instincts. Alex hadn't thought much of his instincts where the smugglers had been concerned since leaving them, but he could not deny that there had been a pattern to the madness that had gone on aboard the ship. Certain men always went ashore, others only when required, so the question that remained was if this was an excursion that Battier felt required more men or fewer.

"Twelve men," Alex settled on, "besides Battier himself. If there is trouble, the rest would follow under the command of Janssen or Acosta for reinforcements, as he will certainly bring one of them with him."

"We can handle twelve," Gabe said with a snort.

Alex gave his cousin a hard look. "Twelve of the most vicious and skilled sailors to ever board a vessel, who fight for sport and pleasure and take no care for its violence or extremes, and take pride in the damage they can do? More animal than man, and answer only to their captain? You think we can handle that without much difficulty? Not to mention the number Mainsley could bring?"

Gabe met his eyes and nodded. "Without much difficulty, yes. Some difficulty, no. We've come through worse unscathed, Trace. There are more of us here now than we've had in the past, and we are stronger. Let Battier come at us with his crew and his fighters. They have no idea we are aware of their plan or ahead of their schedule. We may not have much time, but we will not be caught as unaware as they expect. Jackal showed us the layout, and I know you remember every detail. Let's see what sort of hell we can raise, eh?"

"Please," Rook added in an almost plaintive tone. "I am in desperate need of some hell-raising."

Alex snorted, but his fingers began to drum on the arm of the chair he sat in, a simple, steady pattern that echoed the steady whirling of his mind, the idea not quite formed, but close.

If he anticipated all of this correctly, he and his comrades were supposed to find Poppy some hours from now, if not days, and no one would be sure how many men Alex would be able to drum up to help him. Reinforcements could be coming with Sir Vincent, and he highly doubted that the end goal was for him to be placed back on the ship as *Torchon*.

They would want far more from him now that they knew he hadn't been broken by their treatment of him. He and his friends would be captured and taken to France to endure worse torments at the hands of the Faction to further their cause and heighten their position, increasing the threat against the French monarchy, and the English one, to boot.

"Well, how do we surround a ship?" Ivy asked the group.

"I left my armada at home," Rook quipped with an audible wince, "or I would absolutely offer it up to this cause."

"Really, it's just a matter of predicting what they think is happening," Gent informed them, ignoring Rook entirely. "Where do they think we'll be? Where will they meet? What do they know?"

"Yes, but there is still the matter of the ship," Ivy insisted. "A very large ship. Filled with smugglers, as you recall."

Gabe scoffed and waved his hand. "Oh, they won't care what's happening on shore unless they get some reward. They'll be content with a good drink."

"Rather like your husband, Ivy, dear," Weaver suggested with a wink.

Ivy rolled her eyes but smiled. "Weaver, you really should be nicer about my husband, considering he's friends with over half of your more polite associates, at least half of your less polite ones, and they all like him better than you. Besides, he is quite partial to my wishes, so if word were to reach him that you'd upset me..."

Alex listened carefully, then smiled as the knots in his mind began to unravel and form into a structured, calculated plan that just might enable them to make the most of the situation before them.

"Why's he smiling?" Rook asked warily, eyes wide.

"I haven't the faintest idea," Weaver replied, starting to smile himself, "but I think we're going to like it."

Two by two they came to the docks, not in the structured form of soldiers, but in a leisurely, almost ambling manner. There was no haste in their actions, and nothing particularly cautious about their approach.

Nothing was amiss, then. All the better.

Alex watched and waited, only Gabe in his sight as the others had scattered about in strategic positions along with various contacts and associates recruited for their plan.

His plan.

Any moment now, the rest should follow, if their new informant was to be believed. A carriage would roll up, and the pompous, rotund, and greying man wielding all the power would disembark. Then, the rough and determined man bearing all the force would appear to meet him, followed by the malicious and seafaring man holding all the funds.

All would arrive in a moment, and the attack would commence.

On cue, he heard carriage wheels on the nearby cobblestone, and

Alex felt a smile curve his lips as a satisfied sigh escaped. The anticipation of action was quite an addictive feeling. He'd forgotten that, but its return now was as welcome as a long lost friend.

The carriage appeared, and the driver hopped down, moving to open the door with precision. Only then did a too-finely dressed man exit the vehicle, hat in place, fashionable cane extended. He looked around the dockyards, his nose wrinkled up in distaste, and then a shudder rippled across his expansive girth. He strode forward two steps, then paused, waiting.

Alex shifted in his hiding place, eyeing the offices across the yard, where, only minutes before, a few candles had been lit. A shadow crossed in front of a window, and then the candles were extinguished.

Oars splashed into water behind him, but he couldn't turn to see. Gabe would have a better view of the water, as would Gent, and they could keep watch there. Still, Alex's ears were trained enough now to know what he was hearing.

A small rowboat bearing three or four sets of rowing arms, no doubt with Battier riding in the front like Napoleon himself, propped up as though for a painting. Behind them was another more heavily laden boat with nearly double the oars, though it did not have the same crisp sounds as the first.

Rowing the captain ashore always ensured precision for fear of punishment.

Alex turned to look at Gabe, and his cousin met his eyes, nodding once. Alex returned the nod, touching the brim of his cap with one finger. He watched as Gabe gave a similar signal to the contact nearest him, and sensed, rather than saw, that the message was being relayed down the line.

Just a few moments more.

The warehouse where Poppy had been held was ready, still alight as it had been before. A sentry was even walking the dock near it, giving the appearance that all was well. For anyone who had an interest in the goings on of this evening, there was nothing untoward at all. They would never suspect.

Alex watched as Mainsley met Sir Vincent, shaking hands with grim smiles, both eyeing the docks, then moving in that direction. Mainsley's three men followed, briefly looking about them in a cursory examination of the area, which was laughable.

A cursory examination would not show them anything.

Alex had intentionally not given himself a clear view of the docks or of the warehouse, waiting instead for the signal, as the rest would do. Despite what the others had said, this was not his operation. He was not the leader, and he did not have charge over any of them.

He had always been just one cog in the wheel of their team, their operations, sometimes spinning and working alone, but never at the head of the rest. He had no aspirations for leadership or status, much preferring to be part of something than guiding it. He could not do this alone, none of them could. But when they called upon the strengths and abilities of each man they had, miraculous things could occur, and had occurred.

This was not about Trace or Gent or Rogue or Weaver; it wasn't about any of the Shopkeepers, the Garden, or any other group of operatives.

This was about England and her interests. Her protection. Her security.

England, who had always had his heart, and to whom he would still devote his life and his energies. She, who was greater than them all, and worth every one of them. She, whom he had vowed to serve and honor at all costs, and who had never let him down. England and her people were at the heart of his work, had all his loyalty, and whose soil his blood could only be so fortunate as to water. For her, he would do what had to be done, and had done, at the expense of his life.

England and Poppy Edgewood.

His heart soared momentarily, the nobility of his life's calling reaching the corners of his being that had yet remained dark from his ordeal. Now, he was illuminated by purpose and renewal, restored to his former abilities, and magnified by his suffering and growth.

Trace was once more at large, and England would have no more valiant a servant.

And Poppy Edgewood would see him clearly for the very first time. No more secrets, no more shadows.

Whatever happened.

A lantern across the street was suddenly raised into view, then dropped down once more.

Alex smiled and slipped from his position behind the crates, sticking to the shadows of the buildings. His knives seemed to tingle at his side, reminding him of their presence, and his fingers itched in response. He clenched his hands, the tension oddly comforting, and he exhaled silently, pressing his back against the wall, now facing the docks.

Gabe was soon beside him, a makeshift quarterstaff in hand, followed by another contact, burly enough to be a skilled hand-to-hand fighter, and Alex nodded at them both.

"I counted fourteen on the dock," Gabe breathed. "Not twelve."

"Shut up," Alex hissed, smiling.

"I'll take the spare two," the contact offered, grinning himself. "I need the extra work."

Alex nodded.

"Help yourself, Checks." He drew in a slow breath, then exhaled it, nodding to himself.

It was time.

The calm of battle filled him, and he strode out from the shadows, Gabe and Checks flanking him. His knives remained in their sheaths, and his fingers unclenched in anticipation of the fight ahead. He heard Gabe twirling the quarterstaff in his hands, could feel the energy from it, the eagerness of Checks and Gent and Weaver and everyone else involved in this plot of theirs.

The men on the docks saw them coming and shouted, but their words were lost on Alex. The sentry sprang into action, boarding up the door to the warehouse while three other contacts appeared and began clearing the men nearby.

Alex only spared them a passing look, eager and anxious to get his hands dirty with the men up ahead. Despite having fought only a few hours ago, it might as well have been a lifetime, and he craved more.

He met them with fists already swinging, roaring with a mixture of delight and fury. He connected with skin and cloth at once, slamming his elbow into the face of one while his fist collided with the jaw of another. He barely felt the blows he received, though he knew some of them would do damage or draw blood, but they were slow and clumsy to him as he moved and attacked, seeming to dole out two blows for every one thrown at him.

Gabe bellowed a laugh as his quarterstaff whirled and twirled with the skill of a performer in the streets as it whacked and pummeled and jabbed. They worked in tandem, nearly back to back, as they once had done, while Checks nearly bowled men over in his efforts. They would not come out from the melee unscathed, any of them, but they seemed to have the advantage over the rest, despite the number.

The cries and grunts and groans rent the air, mixing with the sound of fighting, and the occasional body splashing into the water. The dock creaked beneath them, and men in the distance called out in protest, racing towards them, only to be attacked themselves as the others flew from their hiding spots. The dockyards were filled with men now, fourteen of Battier's and a few of Mainsley's, while spies and contacts mingled among them, fighting with energy and gusto. They would overrun all of them soon, but Battier's reinforcements were not far away, and all of this needed to be over before then.

One of the men landed a punch in Alex's ribs, and he felt the bones crack within him, bringing him up slightly with the sharp pains. He whirled towards the man and kicked out hard, a satisfying crack resounding from the impact. The man crumpled, crying out, then rolled directly into Gabe's whirling quarterstaff, and went still.

Shots rang out, and Alex glanced at the warehouse in fear, only to find one of Mainsley's men falling to the wood of the docks.

"God save the King!" Rook bellowed from a nearby rooftop, whooping from his position.

"Saints above," Gabe muttered darkly. "I hate him so much." He turned and broke the staff over the head of a particularly large man, then slammed the broken halves across his face. "Trace!" he barked over his shoulder. "Get to the warehouse. Checks and I have this."

"Not bloody likely," Alex replied as he removed his knives from their sheaths, spinning them in his hands before slamming both into the sides of the man before him.

"Trace!" Checks shouted. "Look, we have help!"

Alex glanced over to find two burly men coming towards them, both whistling God Save The King loudly.

Well, that was one way to show allegiance.

Wiping off the knives against his worn jacket, Alex dashed from the dock and headed towards the warehouse, where his men had cleared the way, and now held the door against those within.

Weaver, Gent, and Cap had taken on more of Battier's men, and were still engaged with them, all bloodied in some way, as he was. Gent saw him and whistled, then slammed his fists into the side of his attacker's head, tumbling him easily. He grabbed the gun from the man, then jogged over to Alex, one eye swelling already. But he grinned, a few of his teeth stained with blood.

"Having fun?" Alex asked, raising a brow.

"Of course," Gent replied, craning his neck, releasing at least three cracks there. They both jumped as Rook released another shot from the room, whooping yet again when another man fell.

"I worry about him," Alex muttered, shaking his head.

"Speak for yourself," Gent returned, with a salute up to Rook. "I'm related to the hellion now."

"Could be worse," Ivy added, appearing on Alex's other side.

Alex looked down at her, bemused. "Where have you been, and why are you spotless?"

Ivy shook her head, a pitying smile on her lips.

"Son, just because I am without blood or tarnishing does not mean that I haven't done my fair share of roughhousing. I'm quick on my feet and know how to dodge, which, it appears, the pair of you could learn to do better." She eyed them up and down, wincing. "Perhaps you'd both better come to the Convent and have Fists give you some lessons."

Gent grumbled incoherently under his breath while Alex just grunted once and twirled his knives again. "I could teach Fists a thing or two, if given a chance."

"I'll be sure to tell him next time I'm at the Convent," Ivy quipped, now grinning outright. "And Milliner, too. Perhaps we'll get you a position there, Trace."

"A bit busy, Ivy," he replied, eyes fixed on the warehouse. "Sorry."

She barked a laugh and shrugged as she walked on beside him, her smile fading into a satisfied smirk.

"How are we going in, Trace?"

"Through the front door," he told her, a snarl welling up.

"And if one of them has a loaded pistol and shoots at you?" she returned.

He didn't answer, knowing it was a real possibility, and that he wouldn't have much of a chance if that happened. He couldn't think about that now.

Nodding at the two men securing the door, and taking in the bullet holes on it, Alex waited as they removed the boards, both cocking pistols and taking up position behind them.

Alex exhaled slowly, then reached for the door, pulling it open.

"What's going on out there?" Sir Vincent demanded when he caught sight of them, Mainsley and Battier coming to face them as well. "What's happening?"

"What's happening, Sir Vincent," Gent growled, "is your plan going to hell, along with the rest of you, momentarily."

Mainsley clenched his fists and started forward, but Battier put a hand to his chest, stopping him as he now stared at Alex with wide eyes. He smiled, nodding slowly.

"*Torchon.*"

The voice that had haunted his dreams sent a cold shiver down his spine, and his old name made him inclined to answer with obedient responses.

He bit down on his tongue to keep himself from doing any such thing.

"Very good, *Torchon,*" Battier praised, stepping forward, clasping his hands behind his back. "Luring us into our own trap, lying in wait for us, and taking out our forces while we were trapped here." He nodded as if in approval. "But surely, you did not suppose we would be unarmed, did you?" He brushed at his long frock coat where his pistol sat against his hip, and instantly Gent and the two other men pointed their weapons at him.

Mainsley's eyes widened, and Sir Vincent seemed to whimper and cower.

Slowly, Battier removed his hand, and showed both to the group. "*Pardon*, gentlemen. No gun. No weapons."

None of them moved their weapons an inch.

Battier chuckled in his high-pitched way. "Ah, *Torchon*, I have missed seeing this energy in you. It's been absent for years. You are back from the dead, as it were. Better than ever before. You remind me of my favorite words: *J'ai vécu*. I have lived."

Alex stared at him hard, still biting his tongue, though not against obedience any longer. Those words bristled, the meaning irrelevant, given the significance of them.

Battier wasn't just an asset for the Faction; he was a believer in them.

There was so much Alex wanted to say, could have said, things he'd spent years imagining he'd say, and yet his ability to speak was absent. He couldn't say a single word; he could only grip his knives tightly and feel the hilt slide against his moistening skin.

Battier clearly took his silence for hesitation, and a new light entered his eyes. "Why don't you have the guns step outside, *Torchon*? Leave the angry one for your protection, but you don't need them. Let us fight this out, eh? You and me. *Le Capitaine et le Torchon*. Only fists. These two will not participate, he and she will not participate. We fight, *Torchon*, and you avenge your woman yourself." He grinned, his teeth flashing in the faint light of the warehouse. "Like a real man."

Alex blinked, then looked away, pretending to think it over. In reality, he was close to laughing. Battier had no power over him now, and his words fell perfectly flat. They rankled when he dared to mention Poppy, but Alex had training enough to be collected at this moment. His eyes raised enough to see the back door open, and he felt another satisfied wave crash over him.

Reinforcements, though they weren't particularly needed.

Perfect.

Battier loved nothing more than to talk about himself, so if he could continue on...

More shots rang out from outside, and Alex looked at Battier, who was staring at the door, his jaw working, teeth grinding. His eyes ' flicked to Alex, and he struggled to regain his cool captain act, failing to reach the same levels as before.

"Come, *Torchon*," Battier taunted, his mouth curving. "Are you going to be the great *espion* you are reputed to be? Or are you nothing but a *le faible?*"

Ivy snarled beside him and started to move, but Alex grabbed her arm.

Battier chuckled, looking at her now. "Oh, let her come, *Torchon.* I'd like nothing more."

Rook, Cap, and Weaver were now visible to Alex, and he lifted his chin, fixing his gaze on the captain who had taken the last four and a half years from him, broken him, and ruined his life, along with several others. This worm of a man who was less than nothing, and yet held such power in the world.

No more.

"I don't need to prove anything to you, Battier," Alex said calmly, letting his knives hang by his sides. "I don't need to avenge anything. Because despite what you think, you did not break me. You did not kill me. You have no power anymore, not over me and not in the world. It's over, Battier, and that's enough for me. I am free of you, and that is all I ever wanted." He smiled, nodding in satisfaction. "And my name, Battier, is Trace. Not *Torchon.* There is no *Torchon.*" He nodded once more, then turned for the door, clapping Gent on the shoulder.

For a moment, there was no sound as he moved.

Then, Battier snarled a filthy French curse. "Don't you turn your back on me, *Torchon!*" A rustle rent the otherwise silent air, accompanied by a sound that Alex knew only too well.

Alex whirled, sending his knives flying.

Battier stood there, dagger in hand, staring with wide eyes, both knives in his chest. His shirt began to dampen with blood as everyone in the room watched silently.

"I told you, *La Capitaine,*" Alex hissed with the darkness he'd hidden well. "There is no *Torchon.* My name is Trace, and I am a covert operative in the service of His Majesty, the King of England. I serve England, I honor England, and I *am* England. That is who I am." He lowered his chin to glower more darkly. "Now, rot in hell, *La Bellette,* and I will sleep peacefully at last, knowing I sent you there."

Battier dropped to the ground, hands fumbling for the knives, his face pale.

Alex snorted in derision, exhaling again, then turning away. "When he's done making a meal of his death and finally turning cold, bring my knives back to me, will you, Gent? I rather like those."

"Of course, Trace," Gent replied easily. "I'll even clean them for you."

"No matter," Alex told him. "His blood staining my blades would be a fitting improvement of them, don't you think?"

"I quite agree," Ivy said with pride. "Very patriotic."

"How did you know?" Gent asked as Alex passed him. "I didn't even get a warning out."

Alex flicked his eyes to his friend's, a humorless smile crossing his lips. "He keeps his prized dagger at his chest, easily accessible. It was his favorite toy when he wanted information. I could hear that blade in my sleep and know exactly what it was."

Gent's eyes widened, and he swallowed hard, nodding only once.

And with that, Alex moved to the door and opened it, breathing in the night air deeply.

Though there were loose ends still to be tied up with Mainsley, Castleton, and the other men, not to mention the smugglers onboard the ship, it was over.

Finally, at long last, it was over.

Chapter Twenty-Two

$\mathcal{I}$t had been a long time since he had enjoyed England in the rain. He had experienced it since finding his freedom, of course, but never with the peace and joy he currently felt. Had he ever stood out in the falling rain and breathed it in, tipping his head back to catch more of the drops, feel more of the rich goodness, tune himself to the nature around him? He couldn't have. This was England, after all, and rain was commonplace. Then again, nothing could be commonplace to him anymore.

He'd missed England in the rain.

Still, there was work to be done, and he couldn't very well avoid it. He'd spent the last two days seeing to the interiors of Parkerton, now that the debris had been cleared, and having mended the roof, replaced the broken windows, and repaired the occasional holes in the wall, there was no need to fear that anything would leak and ruin his work. He didn't need to rummage through the remaining furnishings and place them, he didn't need to think about finishing rooms or refilling the gaps in the gallery.

What he did need, however, was firewood.

Parkerton Lodge had an inordinate number of fireplaces and chimneys, and he and the chimney sweeps had spent the better part of yesterday clearing them all.

Tomorrow, the beginnings of his new staff, and a few of his old, would come to the lodge, and the kitchens, at least, needed a working fire.

Wet wood would help no one, but they'd make do.

So here he was, out in his garden, chopping the wood and brush from what he'd removed and broken down into log-sized pieces they could work with. It was healthy, satisfying work, chopping wood, and although Tailor had clearly told him that he could take whatever he wanted from Branbury, Alex had no desire to do anything of the sort.

Except, perhaps, for stocking the kitchens.

And perhaps his lordship's finest bed.

But he could certainly chop his own firewood, especially when there was wood enough to spare. He'd quite enjoy sitting by a fire fueled from shards of his uncle's favorite furniture. He chuckled as he swung the axe down, splitting the wood cleanly. Poor uncle Parkerton would turn in his grave, but it would be worth it.

Alex sighed and tilted his head back yet again, loving the feeling of being back on his lands, at his home, and being well-rested.

And at rest.

Since that night on the docks, he'd slept through the night without trouble. No nightmares plagued him, no fear seized his heart, and his shirt was no longer damp from a cold sweat. He could breathe freely and clearly, could smile and laugh, and had managed a full and detailed debrief with the Shopkeepers and several other operatives without the slightest trouble. Not that it had been comfortable, but it now felt as though it had been a lifetime ago. Ages of time, and almost as if it occurred to another person entirely.

There was a cool distance between what had happened and what now was. He wasn't naïve enough to think that he would be free of the shadows and the memories forever; he knew full well they would revisit him from time to time. But if they were no longer his constant companions, he would be content. He had reclaimed himself from the ashes of who he had been and what he had become, and now...

Now...

Well, now it was time to move forward. Tailor and Weaver had made that clear to him when he'd given his full debrief, and his solicitor, much relieved that he no longer had to hold interests in trust for a suspected dead man, had assured Alex of the complete security of his finances and estate, despite losing some tenants and his staff. Cap and his brothers in the League had been delighted by his decision to return to them, and they'd rearranged the offices accordingly. All would change soon enough, with Eagle having made the decision to retire and Cap being unanimously nominated to fill his position as their leader and commander, but for now, they would be fully staffed and ready for whatever fallout occurred from their disruption of the Faction's plans.

Castleton had been arrested and would soon be found guilty of treason, Mainsley would suffer the same fate, and with the death of Battier, all of the crew of *La Belette* would now fall under a new commander, one who happened to be on the docks that night.

Janssen had showed absolutely no remorse or regret over the death of his captain and had assumed the command of the *Amelie Claire* with satisfaction. Loyalties were now turned, as Janssen had assured Alex that he, "as a Dutchman, had no fondness for French politics, nor French coin". He fell short of forging an alliance with the League, but he had surprised Alex by offering his apologies for the treatment he had endured.

Remembering Janssen as the most humane of the officers, and the only one to avoid the outright torturing and taunting of him, Alex had no reservations in accepting the apology.

La Belette might have been gone from the seas, but soon enough, Janssen, now dubbed *De Havik,* would take his place in legend and in fear.

Well, perhaps not that soon. The crew had reportedly been exceptionally drunk that night, compliments of the casks Jackal had informed them of, and the contacts who had delivered the drink had been only too delighted to repeat the stories they'd been told.

London had been an experience for Alex. Nearly five years since he had been there, and yet it was nearly unchanged from his memories. The Shopkeepers had been delighted to see him, and some of the old operatives he had known had found their way to League headquarters to pay their respects. He felt more and more a spectacle than an operative, but it was good to see former comrades all the same. Wisely, none of them had asked about his time away from them. Whether that had been due to orders against doing so or simply knowing better, he couldn't say, but he didn't care.

He was moving on, and everyone else needed to, as well.

There was still uncertainty as to how Trace had been compromised as Mr. Turner in the first place, but that investigation would likely be ongoing for ages. Presently, there was more concern for the missing clerk, whom they had all dubbed One, rather than what had caused the compromise four and a half years ago. The clerk known as Two had been absolutely no help in that regard. He was too busy being upset over having twice the work now that his colleague had vanished without a word to care about reasons or circumstance.

Alex hadn't stayed to look into the matter with the rest, and they'd all waved him off to set his life and affairs back to rights. He'd take some time to be Alex Sommerville and nothing more, then officially reenter training for however long it took for the powers that be to consider him fit for fieldwork once more, which shouldn't take long, he was assured. Then, he'd be back into the world and life he had known before, older and wiser, and with a few more scars for his trouble.

Now, here he was, back in his house and on his lands, a far cry from anything being fully restored, but well on his way. The list of details was undoubtedly longer than the list of repairs, and he was quite certain that when his butler, Bridges, was restored to him, he would let him know just how long that list was.

Alex was, strangely enough, looking forward to it. Any sense of normalcy would be welcome, no matter how trivial.

He swung the axe down again, severing the remains of what was once a chair, and paused to collect the chopped wood into a pile, scooping it all into his arms and carrying it over to the stables. His horse greeted him with a snuffle, coming to the edge of his stall in anticipation. At the moment, he only had the one horse, though there was space for a good many more in the expansive stables. He chuckled at the anxious nickering of the creature.

He stacked the wood neatly in the dry stall beside the horse, then moved over to rub the animal's nose.

"You don't want to go out in this, do you?" he teased. "It's a cold rain, and we've only been back from London a few days. I took you for a long ride yesterday, so what are you complaining about, hmm?"

The horse nudged against his hand insistently.

Alex laughed and scratched between the horse's ears. "I don't have any treats for you, my friend. I don't even have treats for me. We'll have to ride over to Branbury tonight, and let you enjoy their stables and stores, eh?

The horse nickered in approval, and Alex rubbed it's nose again, grinning.

"Good boy." He patted his neck and stepped away. "I'll be back later, all right? We may even go for a ride, if you stop fussing."

The horse made no response, eliciting a loud laugh from Alex as he strode from the stables. Returning to the woodpile, he glanced up and saw the cottage in the distance. His stomach clenched, and he wrenched his gaze away, his heart protesting with wild pattering. He shook his head and began splitting the logs again, determined to focus all his attention and energies there.

Whatever contentment he'd felt in returning to Parkerton, it could not smother the feelings with regards to that cottage, and the woman within.

He hadn't seen Poppy since he'd returned, and he wasn't sure he had plans to. Oh, he wanted to see her, and desperately, but after what she'd seen and endured, he wasn't sure he could bear it. The dreams, once full of torment and torture, were now full of Poppy; having grand and histrionic reunions with her, running his hands over her to ensure her injuries were minimal at most. Yet, he woke with empty arms, no such reassurance, and overwhelming guilt.

He'd had word of her from Stanton and knew full well that she was fine. But fine was not good enough.

It would never be good enough.

Staying holed up at Parkerton wasn't good enough, either. She deserved more from him. She deserved answers and apologies, and some assurance of his regard. Something relating to the future, no doubt, and anything else he could think of to offer her. She had endured far too much for his sake before this, and now with what she'd endured in Liverpool…

A more valiant man would have retreated heroically from her life, falling upon his own sword to give her the protection she deserved.

Alex wasn't that valiant. He would never be able to be parted from her forever, yet he was unable to move any closer. He was trapped in this world of in-between, not one thing or the other, and the undefined state of them was enough to restrain his actions.

What if she turned away? What if, upon reflection, she no longer cared for him in any way? He didn't know for certain what she felt for him now, and their distance before Liverpool had been strained.

Now…

He swung the axe down on a new log, grunting with the unnecessary force of his blow. He kicked aside the smaller shard, and then reset what remained, swinging again and splitting it nearly even.

The rain poured down on him, and he wiped his hand across his sweat and rain dampened brow. He wondered if a man who was brave in the world could truly be so cowardly in his heart.

He swung the axe blade down on the now empty block, leaning against the handle, then looked up towards the cottage again.

Except Poppy was standing there now.

Not at the cottage, but there. Before him.

Watching him.

Poppy swallowed harshly as Alex finally stared back at her, his shirt and his hair damp from the rain, his eyes dark and unreadable. Her loose bonnet dripped rain in an odd cadence with her heart, but she ignored it. She could scarcely breathe now that they saw each other, and she'd had a hard-enough time with watching him work. There was a deep vitality to him now that had been so absent since he'd been back. An intensity that was intoxicating and captivating, thrilling and wild. While it certainly reminded her of the man she had known before, it was so much more in this man he'd become.

She'd wondered for days when he would come back, though Stanton had repeatedly assured her that he was very well, that they all were, but that operations such as the one that had gone on in Liverpool required many meetings, lots of paperwork, and a good deal of resolution that could take quite some time. She could easily believe that, but she also refused to believe that they would keep Alex for so long to see to the details when he had endured so much already.

She had been going absolutely mad up at the cottage, unable to think or to sit still, completely and perfectly useless to anyone and anything. Her worries and fears had grown exponentially since they'd returned, particularly with Stanton refusing to give her any real understanding of what might have gone on. Her imagination had run rampant, destroying her dreams and any hope of optimism.

Then, last night, she'd seen light within the windows of Parkerton, and it had taken all of her self-control to keep from riding over that moment.

Or first thing this morning.

But she was here now, and so was he. Her bruises were almost gone, while his injuries would take longer. Yet, they were clearly healing, and he was not in any way limited by them.

Seeing him healthy and vibrant and strong before her, it was as though he had come back to her all over again.

She was fairly certain she wouldn't strike him this time.

Alex watched her steadily, his chest rising and falling without the slightest hint of distress, and his calm unnerved her. She'd practiced several things to say as she'd crossed the miles to come face him, but now they all vanished into thin air.

He was here. She was here.

That was all she knew.

She opened her mouth to say something, to say anything, but all that came out was a sob she hadn't known was welling.

Alex moved the moment he heard it, and she watched him come, more sobs surging up and begging for release.

They never got the chance.

His mouth crashed down on hers, his arms sliding around her and pulling her closer than she thought was humanly possible. She latched her fingers into his hair and kissed him back with everything she had, frantically trying to keep up with the fervor and passion he was bestowing on her suddenly trembling frame. They kissed deeply, eagerly, and then with tenderness and feeling that brought more tears to her eyes.

He groaned as his hold tightened, their lips parting only for his to dance across her face and brow. Breathlessly, Poppy cradled his head against her, arching up to meet him, sighing with every touch of his lips against her suddenly feverish skin. His mouth found hers once more, one hand cupping her face as the other fixed itself around her waist, keeping her in place.

"Alex," Poppy gasped as he broke off again, his brow and nose touching hers as their frantic pants mingled between them. She touched his jaw, curled her fingers into his hair, nuzzled softly as her senses continued to reel in ecstasy.

"I love you, Poppy," he rasped, grazing his lips across her. "Still love you. Have always loved you. Every minute of every day of every one of those years that I was in that hole, my only thought was you."

Poppy shook in his arms at the confession and gripped his shirt with one hand, desperate for the anchor of him to keep her steady.

"You are my everything," he went on. "I exist for you. I'd have died a thousand times over in that place to be by your side for just a moment. And when you were taken…" He broke off with a pained growl and shook his head. "I'd have endured it all again just to get you back."

Poppy exhaled a dry sob and pulled back, wetting her lips as she met his eyes, her knees quivering. "I lied, Alex, when I told you that I loved you."

Alex stiffened in her hold, and he began to pull away, averting his eyes.

She seized his face with her free hand and tightened her hold in his soaking shirt, forcing his gaze to remain on her. "I made you think I'd stopped loving you," she said. "But I couldn't. I didn't. I can't."

Alex moaned softly and brought her back to him, pressing his lips to her brow.

"I never stopped loving you, Alex," Poppy whispered. "Not for a moment. I still love you."

He kissed her into silence, cradling her against him as though she would break with too much force.

"Oh, my love," he murmured against her lips, sealing his over hers again and again. "I'm so sorry. So very sorry."

"Shh." She pressed her fingers to his lips and shook her head. "I don't want an apology. I don't need one."

"But you deserve one," he insisted. He sighed and held her against his shoulder, burying his face into her hair, her bonnet now long gone. "You deserve so much, and I can't give you half of it."

Poppy wrapped her arms around him, holding him now as much as he was her. "I don't care," she told him. "I don't care about any of that. I just want you, Alex. You're all I have ever wanted."

He shuddered at her words, his mouth at her ear. "I am a broken man, Poppy. I may never be whole again."

She smiled and pulled back, running her fingers through his hair. "A treasured thing once broken becomes more favored, does it not? More precious for the fear of losing it forever? We are more careful with it, more mindful, and more aware. The damage wakes us to the true, irreplaceable value of it, and we love it all the more."

Alex smiled back, took one of her hands and pressed a warm kiss to the palm, then laid it against his heart. "And being apart from what we love most only makes the love and longing greater, the reunion sweeter, and the dreams more precious." He touched his brow to hers again, sighing heavily. "Tell me I may finally live those dreams with you now, Poppy Edgewood. Tell me I may have you as my wife, as my lady, as my love… That when my shadows find me in the night you will be there to bring me back to the light. That you will always be beside me." He suddenly grinned and nudged his nose with hers. "And that you will fill this ramshackle house with as many children as you can tolerate without killing me."

Poppy laughed and kissed Alex with all the joy in her heart, still laughing against his lips. "Yes, Alex," she finally said when his kiss turned hot. "Yes to all that and everything more."

His eyes crinkled with his smile and he pulled her in for a warm embrace, each of them laughing breathlessly. "Good," he eventually said, relief washing over them both. Then he paused. "Does your being cut off prevent me from having to ask your father for your hand?" Alex asked hopefully. "He's never liked me, you know, and I don't think…"

He broke off when Poppy cuffed him along the back of the head, pulling back to give him a warning look. "Really, Alex?"

He shrugged, still outright grinning. "I'll write to him today, but I don't care what he says, you know. I'm marrying you no matter what. Nothing's going to stop me."

"Really?" Poppy said again, unable to keep from smiling back.

Alex's eyes darkened. "Not a damned thing, my love. I'm a spy for the Crown, after all. Back from the dead, even." He nodded slowly, smiling in a way that made her toes curl. "And when all is said and done, you are the only thing I really need."

Four weeks later, knees shaking, stomach filled with butterflies, arms filled with flowers, Poppy Edgewood made her way down the aisle of the church at Parkerton, Fritz leading her proudly in place of her father, who sent his regrets, as did most of her family.

Violet was here, though, and they had spent the entire night before laughing and becoming reacquainted as sisters and friends.

She didn't mind. After all, she had Alex, and his family was just as small as hers.

Well, he had Gabe, anyway, and Gabe had Amelia and little Alex, and for some reason, they had gained Gabe's aunt Geraldine as their own. It was an utter mess, but it still felt more a family to her than hers had ever truly been.

She was content with this, and now she would be Lady Parkerton.

What a thought.

Faintly, her mind whirled back over the last few weeks as they had prepared for this moment, as she and Alex had worked tirelessly on restoring Parkerton into some sort of livable home, filled it with staff, with furniture, with all the trimmings a great house needed, yet still there was more to do. But now it would be her home, and she could take the time to do things however she liked.

Alex wouldn't care. Alex didn't care. He just wanted her to live there with him and said he could endure anything else.

She doubted that, but he *had* said so…

She looked up towards the front of the church now, and Alex defied tradition by turning to watch her come, making her heart seize up in her chest.

The last few weeks had been wonderful for them both, but it had certainly brought a significant change in Alex. Gone was the gaunt man from her doorstep, gone was the slender man with shadows. In his place was a robust, healthy, magnificently built man who had learned once more how to smile in the way that had always made her forget her thoughts.

She saw his broad chest catch, saw his eyes dart over every inch of her in the lace covered gown she had refused to let him see, saw the way those eyes darkened when they returned to hers.

And that smile...

That was the man she remembered. Only now she knew him on a much deeper level, knew his secrets and his shadows, and he knew hers, and they loved each other all the better for it.

She knew he wasn't the same man. He was better. He was more.

And damn it all, he was hers.

*E*pilogue

"*T*here was no hope. They were entirely surrounded, outnumbered, outgunned, and outmaneuvered. The enemy was advancing. All of them were injured, and any number of them could have died at any moment. There was no help at hand, no reinforcements to save them, no more moves to make. It was the end of the line for all of them. Every single one. Except..."

Wide eyes stared back at the storyteller with bated breath and riveted attention.

"There was something else to do. Something none of them had thought of, and no one would dream of. But Trace knew what he had to do. He ran down the dock, abandoning his friends and comrades, leapt aboard the enemy's ship, and severed the lines tying her in port. Away she sailed, catching the tide, and leaving the injured members of the League behind. Valiantly, Trace fought, even more outnumbered than before, until finally, the dastardly captain stabbed him, the sounds of his death ringing in the silent night of London's east docks."

A whimper broke the story, and Alexander Sommerville, Lord Parkerton, hushed his infant son, rocking him a little and smiling gently.

"No, no, it's all right, son," he insisted, running a finger along the plump cheek. "He wasn't really dead. He was presumed dead, and who could blame them for thinking so? Trace was very much alive."

The sounds of distress faded and young Anthony Gabriel Sommerville nestled up against his father's chest, eyelids drooping with the swaying.

"He was alive," Alex went on in a much softer voice. "But at the mercy of his captors. They tried to break him, tortured him and forced him into slave labor, made him forget who he was and what he had been. But Trace wouldn't break, wouldn't even bend. He was too strong for them, and when they least suspected it, he escaped…"

Memories and feelings rose up in Alex and he faded off, shaking his head as he rocked his son.

It had been over a year since his escape and the docks at Liverpool, and still, they were sweeping up the pieces from it. The Faction was still in operation and more conniving than ever. He'd only returned a few hours ago from his latest mission, one of the more dangerous ones he'd engaged in since returning, but a successful one. Rook had been his partner for the operation, which had proved essential to its success, and the pair of them were becoming quite the powerful team. Rogue and Gent were quite jealous of it and strove to match them, when situations allowed for pairs.

Rook and Alex were convinced they never would come close, and they had considered putting certain measures in place to ensure that.

Cap didn't need to know those things, though.

Alex looked around the room, smiling to himself. The nursery had barely been completed in time for Anthony's arrival, but that was the way things had turned out in Parkerton Lodge. There was always something to update and see to, even though they had done a fine job of restoring it. Finally, they were reaching the point where Poppy could start redoing rooms for pleasure and not out of necessity. She insisted that she had no intention of doing so, but he'd seen her eyeing the ballroom with speculation after their last ball, and he knew it wouldn't be long in coming. Despite their years away from finery, they had both adjusted to its return quite handily, and while they still owned the farm on the Branbury estate and occasionally went to work it, they were quite content to leave it to the tenants to see to.

Tailor had kept Branbury and visited when London became too oppressive, but he seemed to enjoy being the anomaly of Moulton society and kept his distance.

Having an operative for a solicitor seemed to work quite well for Tailor, though he refused to tell Alex who it was.

He was close to discovering the truth for himself, though.

He could hardly believe that his life was his own, as it was. Life with Poppy had been a heaven beyond his wildest dreams, and she was the perfect wife and companion for him. She kept him grounded and steady, brought him back from the abyss when he went too far, and made him the man he had always wanted to be for her. He hadn't thought he could love her any more than he had the day they married, but when she had borne their son a few months ago, he found his heart expanded and magnified, filled to the brim with her and for her, and somehow, still had the whole of it to bestow on his new son.

His son, who was already brilliant and destined to be the greatest of all the League male offspring including Cap's sons, Gent's boy, and Alex's own godson and namesake.

There was nothing to humble and terrify a man like becoming a father, but it was the greatest, grandest adventure Alex could have asked for, and nighttime stories such as these would only get better as his son grew old enough to properly appreciate it.

Though, granted, the details would have to grow more muddled as time went on.

No matter.

"He escaped," Alex finally went on, taking his son's sleepily flailing hand in his own, "and though he was badly injured and very weak, he ran. Faster than lightning, quiet as the night, he ran across two counties. He borrowed food and horses and fresh clothing, slept during the day, and rode or ran like the devil in the night, until he came to his fair damsel's house. She took care of him, tended him, loved him, until he was nearly whole. And then the enemy took her, evil villains that they were."

Anthony made a soft cooing sound, and Alex smiled, kissing his hand quickly.

"Yes," he told his son as though he had made a sound of distress at his tale. "They took her, and Trace refused to let the fair damsel be subjected to their evil designs. So, he mustered up men to ride after her, some of his old comrades joining in the pursuit, and they followed the enemy. Without fear or hesitation, they gave chase, knowing they had to be quick and sure. The plan was clear from the beginning, and they devised a cunning, exceptional plan to fool the enemy, save the damsel, and protect England from the underhanded schemes of the enemy. They charged the docks of Liverpool, swept aside forty of the most evil, dastardly pirates the world has ever known, and Trace freed the damsel, and then they all rode off into the sunset in grand, victorious style. England was saved, and they were all given great honors for their deeds, though none so great as Trace, whose damsel was so grateful, so delighted, so overcome with his actions in saving her that she…"

He trailed off at a sound behind him, then smiled as he glanced over his shoulder.

"That she agreed to take such an idiot to be her husband and has endured his antics with grace and patience ever since," he finished sheepishly.

Soft, warm laughter met his ears, and a familiar pair of slender arms slid around his waist. "That's my favorite part of the story," Poppy murmured, resting her chin against his back. "The poor damsel must be a woman of great strength and courage to endure so much."

"She is," Alex told her, and his son. "The most remarkable woman in the world, and the most beautiful, compassionate, intelligent, understanding…"

Her hold around him tightened, and she laughed against him. "Now I know you're making her up. No woman is that perfect."

"I can assure you, Lady Parkerton," he protested gently, "that Trace's wife certainly is."

She hummed another laugh, and laid her cheek against his bare back, sighing. "You didn't stay in bed long. We haven't even talked."

Alex chuckled, still rocking his son a little. "You were more than half asleep when I came in. I did kiss you."

"I think I remember that…" She made a soft sound of appreciation as she hugged herself closer. "How did it go? Did you find One?"

Alex shook his head, now staring out of the window. "No, we didn't. Not a trace, ironically enough. Rook and I got into quite a bit of trouble, but nothing we couldn't manage." He exhaled roughly, his brow furrowing. "I don't know where he is, or what's happened, Poppy. None of us do. He's just vanished into thin air."

Poppy shifted against him, raising her chin again. "Does it remind you of your troubles?"

"No," he told her softly. "Rook asked me the same thing, and so did Gabe. But no, it doesn't, and everyone else feels the same way. This isn't the same thing at all. They're bringing in one of the girls from the Convent to look into it, but I don't know what she'll find."

"Trust Cap and Milliner to take care of it," Poppy insisted softly. "They'll come to you if they need you, but One wasn't just working with the League, was he?"

Again, Alex shook his head. "No, he came from Foreign Office, I think. We have resources to help, but no leads." He sighed and leaned his head back against her. "You're right, though."

"Of course, I am," she quipped, making him laugh. "But about what?"

"Cap and Milliner," he retorted, snorting softly. "They clearly know more than we do, and I'm sure whoever they bring in will be able to build on what we've found and give it scope. I have to meet up with Janssen soon anyway and can't possibly look for a missing clerk with all that going on."

Poppy was silent for a long moment, then asked wryly, "Did you tell Anthony you took care of forty evil pirates?"

Alex lifted his head, shaking it firmly. "Absolutely not. I told him it was twenty-five, just as it was."

"I thought it was fourteen and a handful."

"You thought wrong."

"And what honors were you given? I'm not aware of any."

"Secret honors that the world can't know about."

"Naturally, and no doubt given in a secret ceremony with gracious thanks of a monarch."

Alex smiled, trying not to laugh. "Two monarchs, actually. And a great many horns for a proper fanfare."

"Must have been quite the sight."

"It really was."

Poppy hugged him close for a long moment. "I missed you, Alex," she whispered. "So much."

Alex bit back a groan. "I missed you, too, love. Always do."

Her lips suddenly pressed into the center of his back, lingering.

He did groan now. "Don't do that when I can't hold you," he begged her.

He could feel her smile against his skin, and then she did it again, her lips slowly leaving kisses along his spine.

His skin rippled in response. "Poppy…"

"Put the baby down and do something about it," she told him in a coy tone.

Alex smiled slowly, loving his wife's teasing, playful nature. "You want me to put down our son just to satisfy you?"

Poppy nuzzled his skin and kissed it again. "Who said anything about me? Besides, he's asleep again."

Alex looked down at the infant in his arms. "That's my boy." He stepped out of Poppy's inviting embrace to put his son back in his bassinet, then stepped back towards her, waiting.

Poppy stifled a laugh, slowly wrapped her arms around him once more, then kissed his back again very tenderly.

This time, Alex turned and took her chin in hand, pressing a hot kiss to her full lips that drew a ragged gasp from her.

He grinned against her mouth, kissed her again, then picked her up in his arms and carried back to their bed, where he proceeded to do some very naughty things indeed.

And really, one could not expect much else from a spy.

Coming Soon

To Sketch a Sphinx

The London League
Book Six

"The end was just the beginning..."

by

Rebecca Connolly